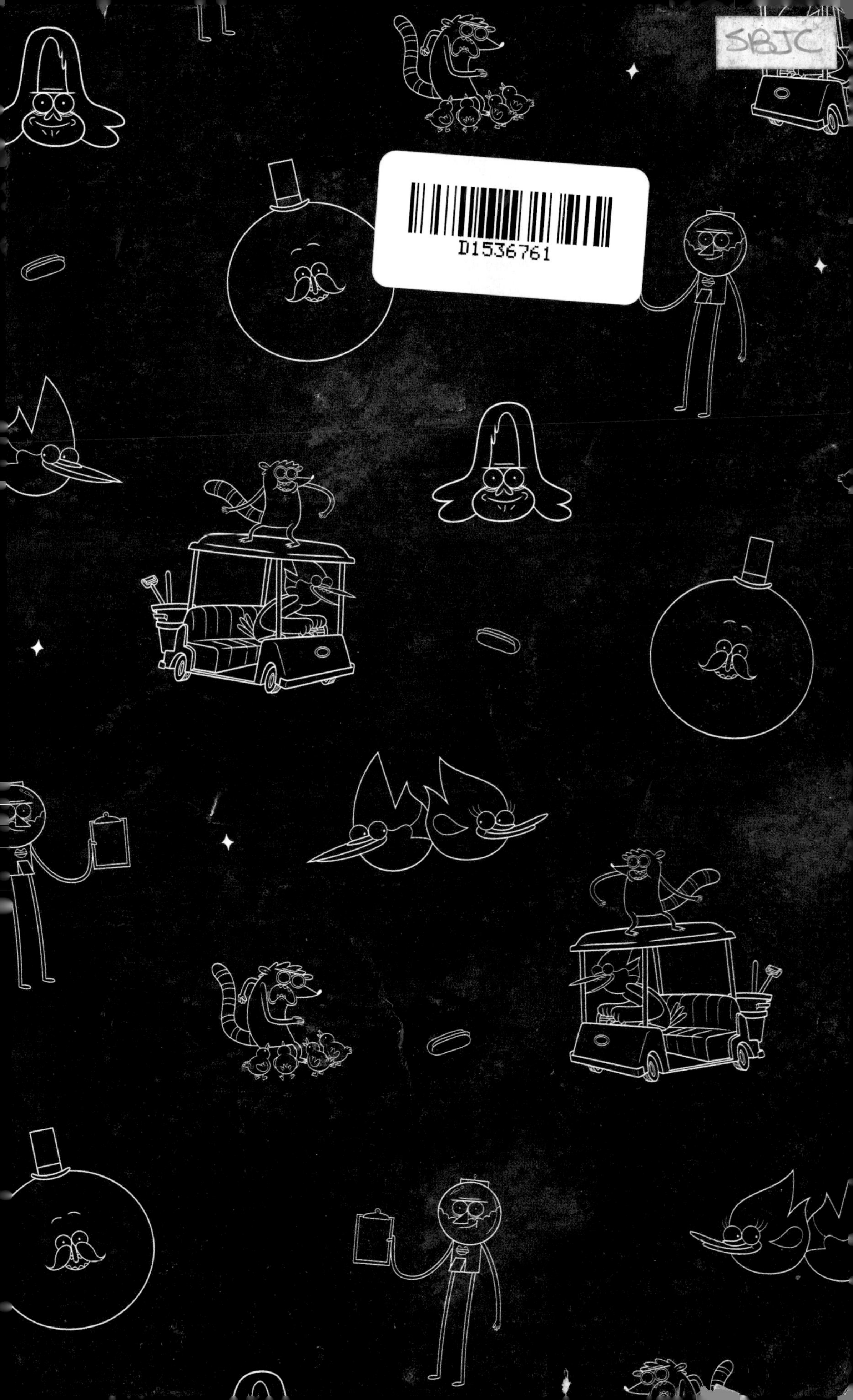

REGULAR SHOW Volume Six, June 2016. Published by KaBOOM!, a division of Boom Entertainment, Inc. REGULAR SHOW, CARTOON NETWORK, the logos, and all related characters and elements are trademarks of and © Cartoon Network. (S16) Originally published in single magazine form as REGULAR SHOW No. 21-24. © Cartoon Network. (S15) All rights reserved. KaBOOM!™ and the KaBOOM! logo are trademarks of Boom Entertainment, Inc., registered in various countries and categories. All characters, events, and institutions depicted herein are fictional. Any similarity between any of the names, characters, persons, events, and/or institutions in this publication to actual names, characters, and persons, whether living or dead, events, and/or institutions is unintended and purely coincidental. KaBOOM! does not read or accept unsolicited submissions of ideas, stories, or artwork.

A catalog record of this book is available from OCLC and from the KaBOOM! website, www.kaboom-studios.com, on the Librarians Page.

BOOM! Studios, 5670 Wilshire Boulevard, Suite 450, Los Angeles, CA 90036-5679. Printed in China. First Printing.

ISBN: 978-1-60886-841-4, eISBN: 978-1-61398-512-0

REGULAR SHOW™

VOLUME SIX

REGULAR

CREATED BY JG QUINTEL

SCRIPT BY MAD RUPERT

ART BY ALLISON STREJLAU

COLORS BY LISA MOORE

LETTERS BY STEVE WANDS

COVER BY
ANDY HIRSCH

DESIGNER
SCOTT NEWMAN

ASSISTANT EDITOR
MARY GUMPORT

ORIGINAL SERIES EDITOR
SHANNON WATTERS

COLLECTION EDITOR
SIERRA HAHN

SHOW™

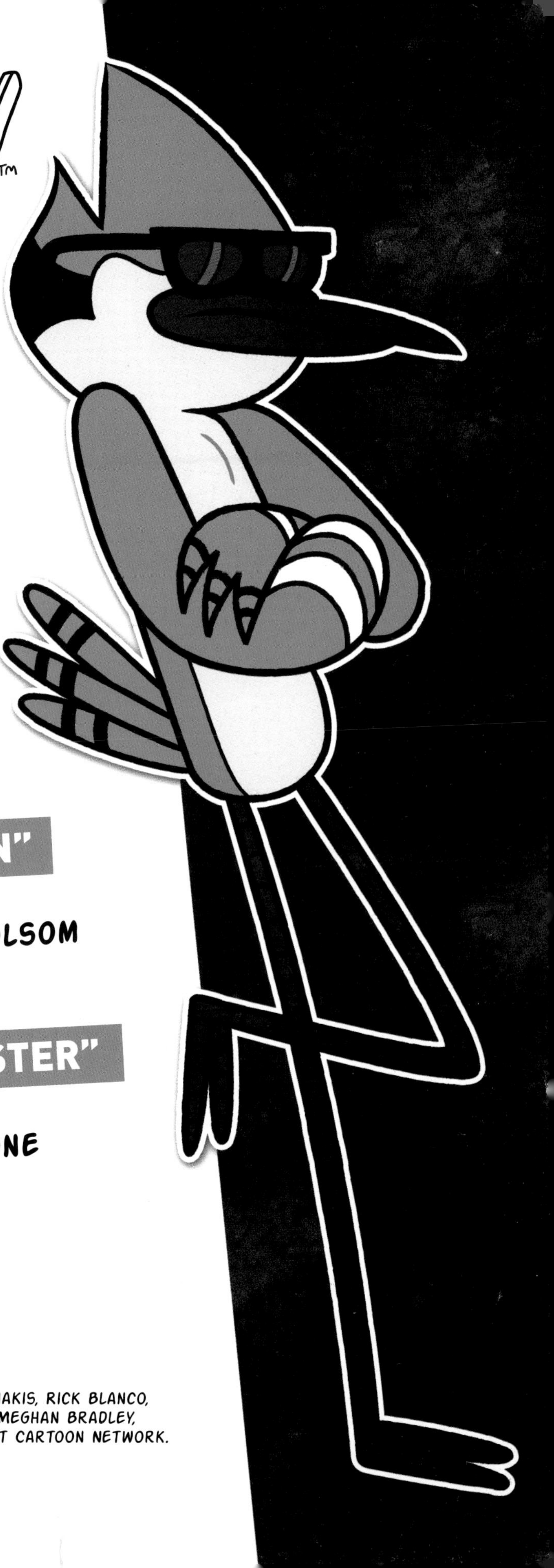

"GREY GOO"

SCRIPT BY **KEVIN CHURCH**
ART BY **MAD RUPERT**
COLORS BY **LISA MOORE**
LETTERS BY **STEVE WANDS**

"SAD MALL"

SCRIPT & ART BY
KEVIN BURKHALTER

"BEING BENSON"

SCRIPT & ART BY
LIZ PRINCE & KYLE FOLSOM

"RECIPE FOR DISASTER"

SCRIPT & ART BY
ANDREW GREENSTONE

WITH SPECIAL THANKS TO MARISA MARIONAKIS, RICK BLANCO, CURTIS LELASH, CONRAD MONTGOMERY, MEGHAN BRADLEY, RYAN SLATER, AND THE WONDERFUL FOLKS AT CARTOON NETWORK.

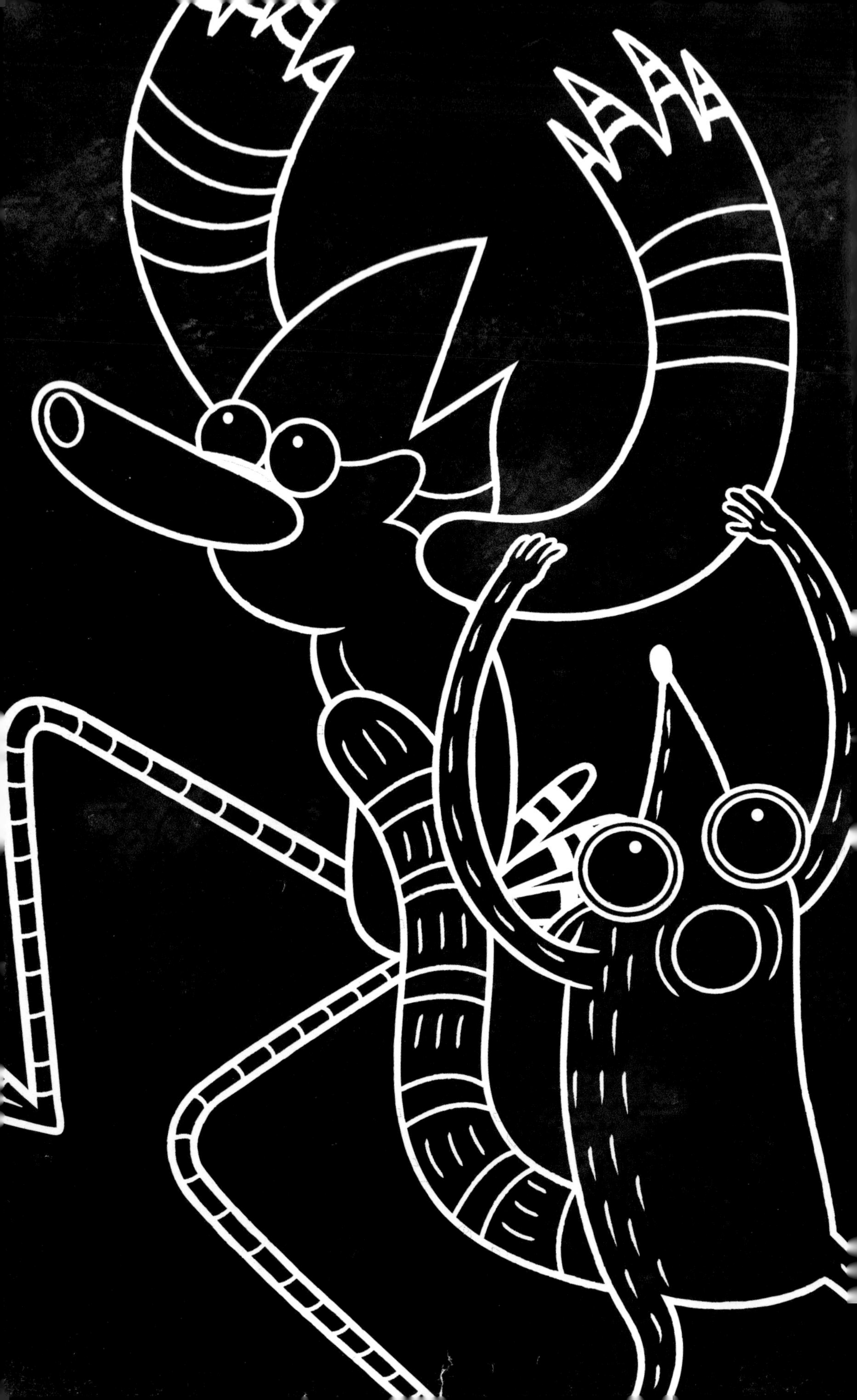

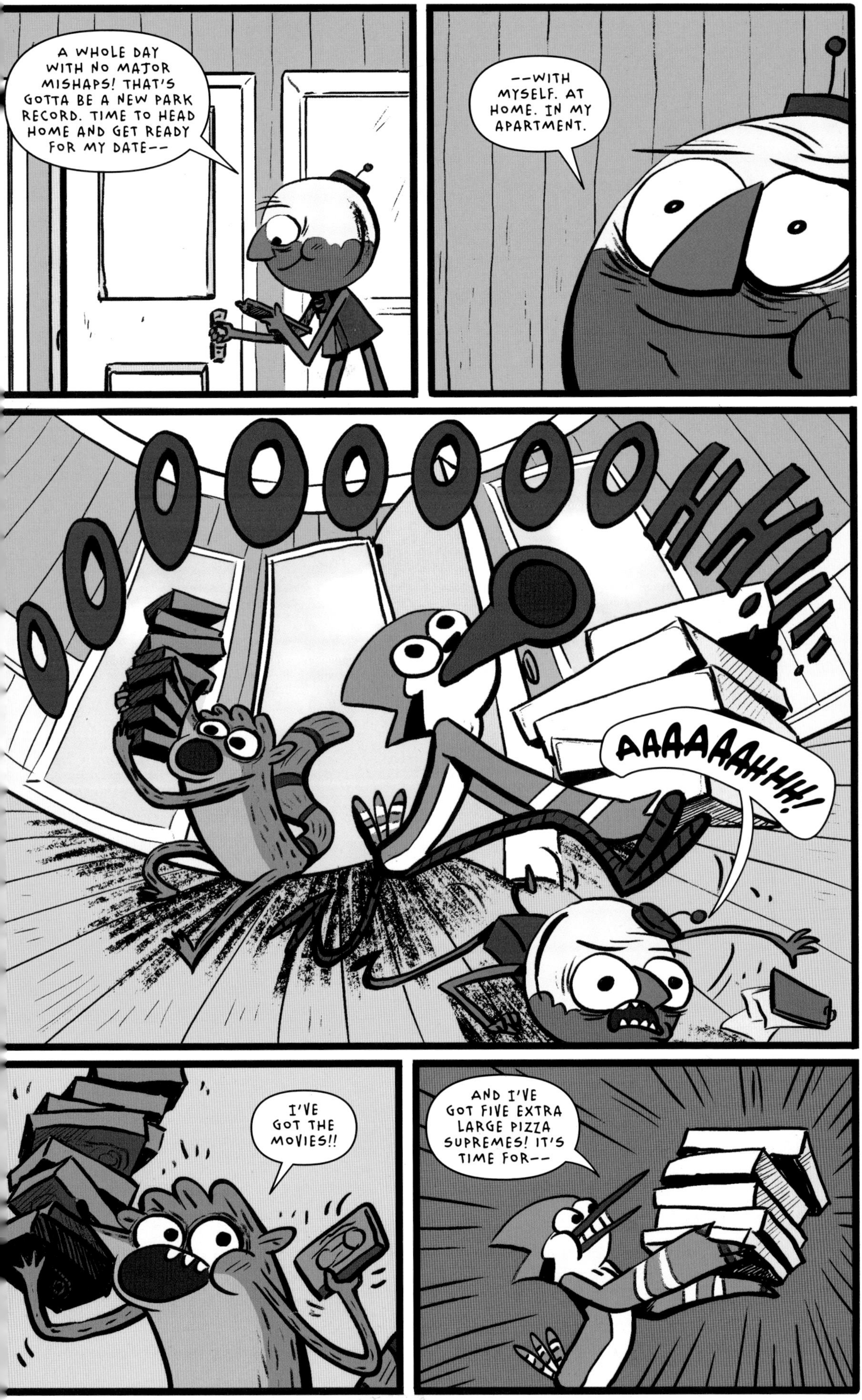
A WHOLE DAY WITH NO MAJOR MISHAPS! THAT'S GOTTA BE A NEW PARK RECORD. TIME TO HEAD HOME AND GET READY FOR MY DATE--
--WITH MYSELF. AT HOME. IN MY APARTMENT.
OOOOOOOOOHHH!!!
AAAAAAHHH!
I'VE GOT THE MOVIES!!
AND I'VE GOT FIVE EXTRA LARGE PIZZA SUPREMES! IT'S TIME FOR--

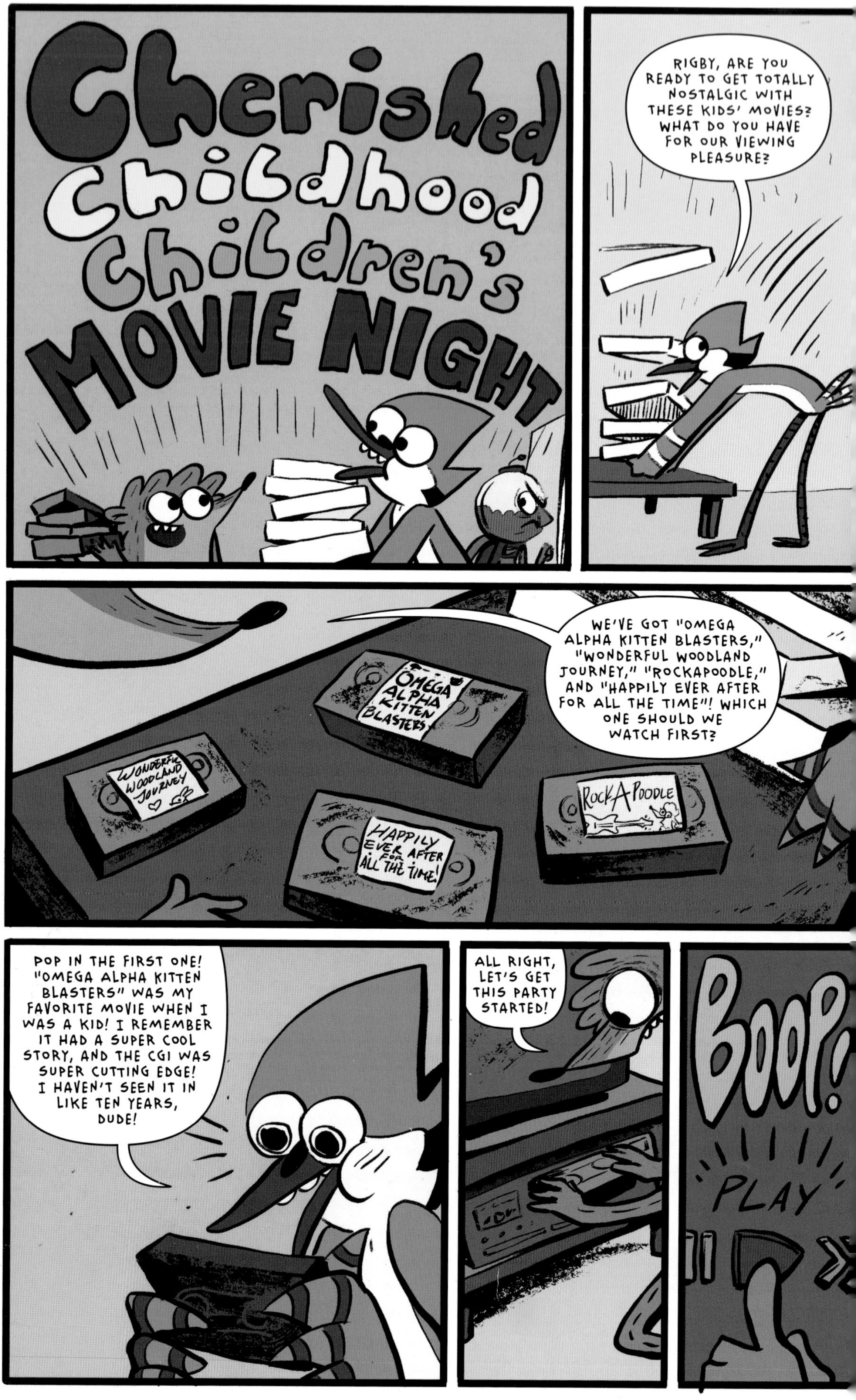

Cherished Childhood Children's MOVIE NIGHT
RIGBY, ARE YOU READY TO GET TOTALLY NOSTALGIC WITH THESE KIDS' MOVIES? WHAT DO YOU HAVE FOR OUR VIEWING PLEASURE?
WE'VE GOT "OMEGA ALPHA KITTEN BLASTERS," "WONDERFUL WOODLAND JOURNEY," "ROCKAPOODLE," AND "HAPPILY EVER AFTER FOR ALL THE TIME"! WHICH ONE SHOULD WE WATCH FIRST?
OMEGA ALPHA KITTEN BLASTERS
WONDERFUL WOODLAND JOURNEY
ROCKAPOODLE
HAPPILY EVER AFTER FOR ALL THE TIME!
POP IN THE FIRST ONE! "OMEGA ALPHA KITTEN BLASTERS" WAS MY FAVORITE MOVIE WHEN I WAS A KID! I REMEMBER IT HAD A SUPER COOL STORY, AND THE CGI WAS SUPER CUTTING EDGE! I HAVEN'T SEEN IT IN LIKE TEN YEARS, DUDE!
ALL RIGHT, LET'S GET THIS PARTY STARTED!
BOOP!
PLAY

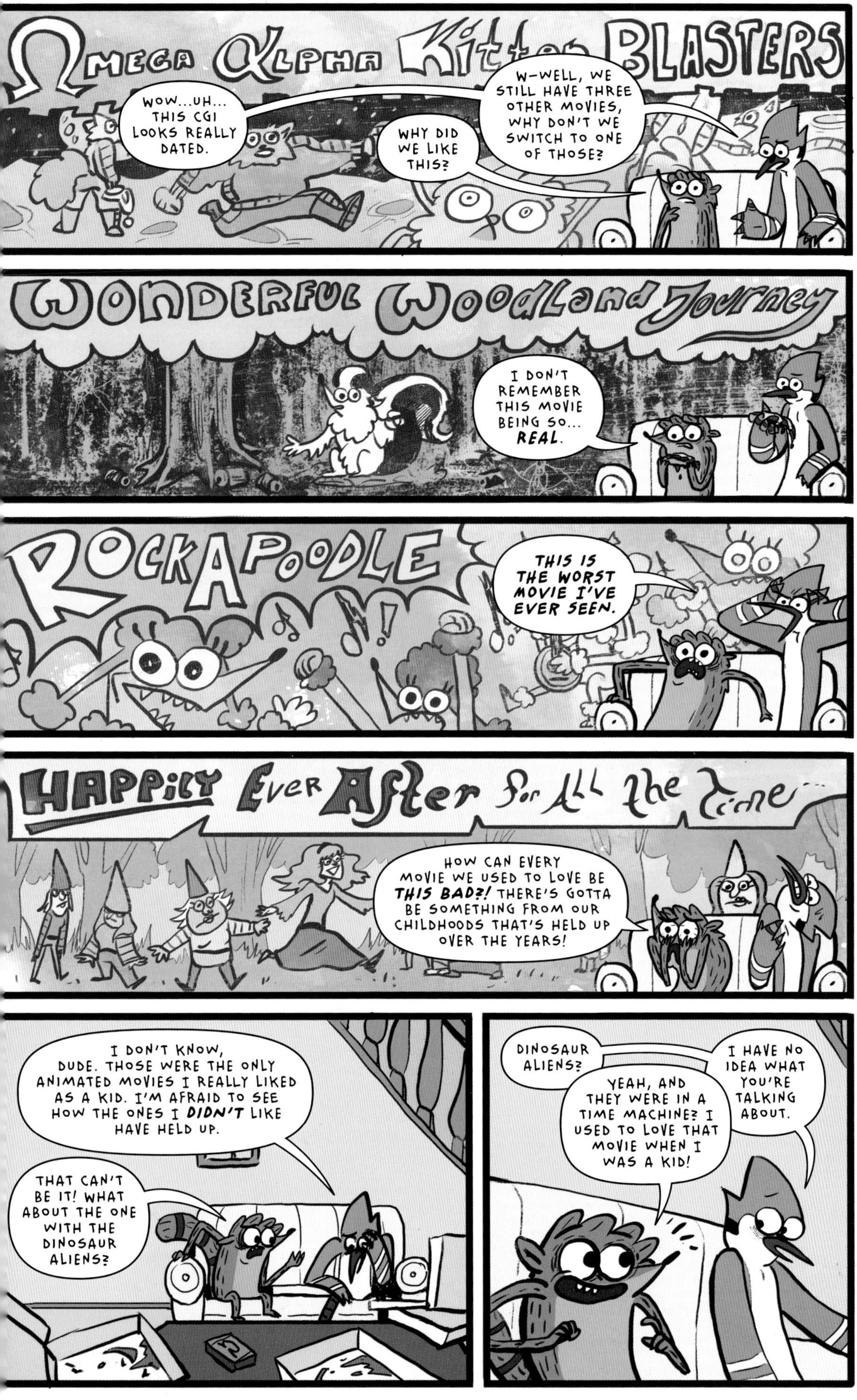
Omega Alpha Kitten BLASTERS
WOW...UH... THIS CGI LOOKS REALLY DATED.
WHY DID WE LIKE THIS?
W-WELL, WE STILL HAVE THREE OTHER MOVIES, WHY DON'T WE SWITCH TO ONE OF THOSE?
WONDERFUL Woodland Journey
I DON'T REMEMBER THIS MOVIE BEING SO... REAL.
ROCKAPOODLE
THIS IS THE WORST MOVIE I'VE EVER SEEN.
HAPPILY Ever After for All the Time...
HOW CAN EVERY MOVIE WE USED TO LOVE BE THIS BAD?! THERE'S GOTTA BE SOMETHING FROM OUR CHILDHOODS THAT'S HELD UP OVER THE YEARS!
I DON'T KNOW, DUDE. THOSE WERE THE ONLY ANIMATED MOVIES I REALLY LIKED AS A KID. I'M AFRAID TO SEE HOW THE ONES I DIDN'T LIKE HAVE HELD UP.
THAT CAN'T BE IT! WHAT ABOUT THE ONE WITH THE DINOSAUR ALIENS?
DINOSAUR ALIENS?
YEAH, AND THEY WERE IN A TIME MACHINE? I USED TO LOVE THAT MOVIE WHEN I WAS A KID!
I HAVE NO IDEA WHAT YOU'RE TALKING ABOUT.

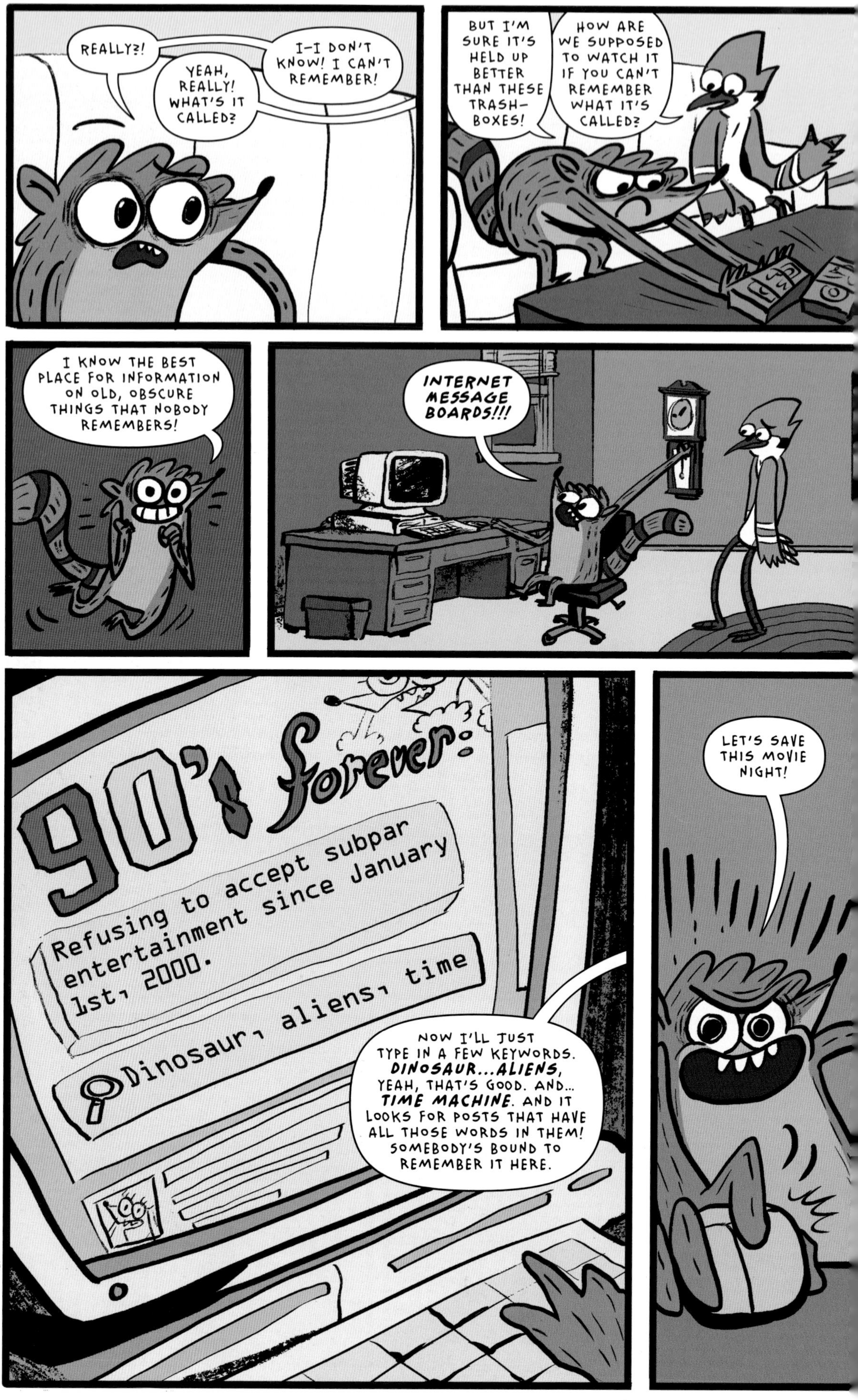
REALLY?!
YEAH, REALLY! WHAT'S IT CALLED?
I-I DON'T KNOW! I CAN'T REMEMBER!
BUT I'M SURE IT'S HELD UP BETTER THAN THESE TRASH-BOXES!
HOW ARE WE SUPPOSED TO WATCH IT IF YOU CAN'T REMEMBER WHAT IT'S CALLED?
I KNOW THE BEST PLACE FOR INFORMATION ON OLD, OBSCURE THINGS THAT NOBODY REMEMBERS!
INTERNET MESSAGE BOARDS!!!
90's forever:
Refusing to accept subpar entertainment since January 1st, 2000.
Dinosaur, aliens, time
NOW I'LL JUST TYPE IN A FEW KEYWORDS. DINOSAUR...ALIENS, YEAH, THAT'S GOOD. AND... TIME MACHINE. AND IT LOOKS FOR POSTS THAT HAVE ALL THOSE WORDS IN THEM! SOMEBODY'S BOUND TO REMEMBER IT HERE.
LET'S SAVE THIS MOVIE NIGHT!

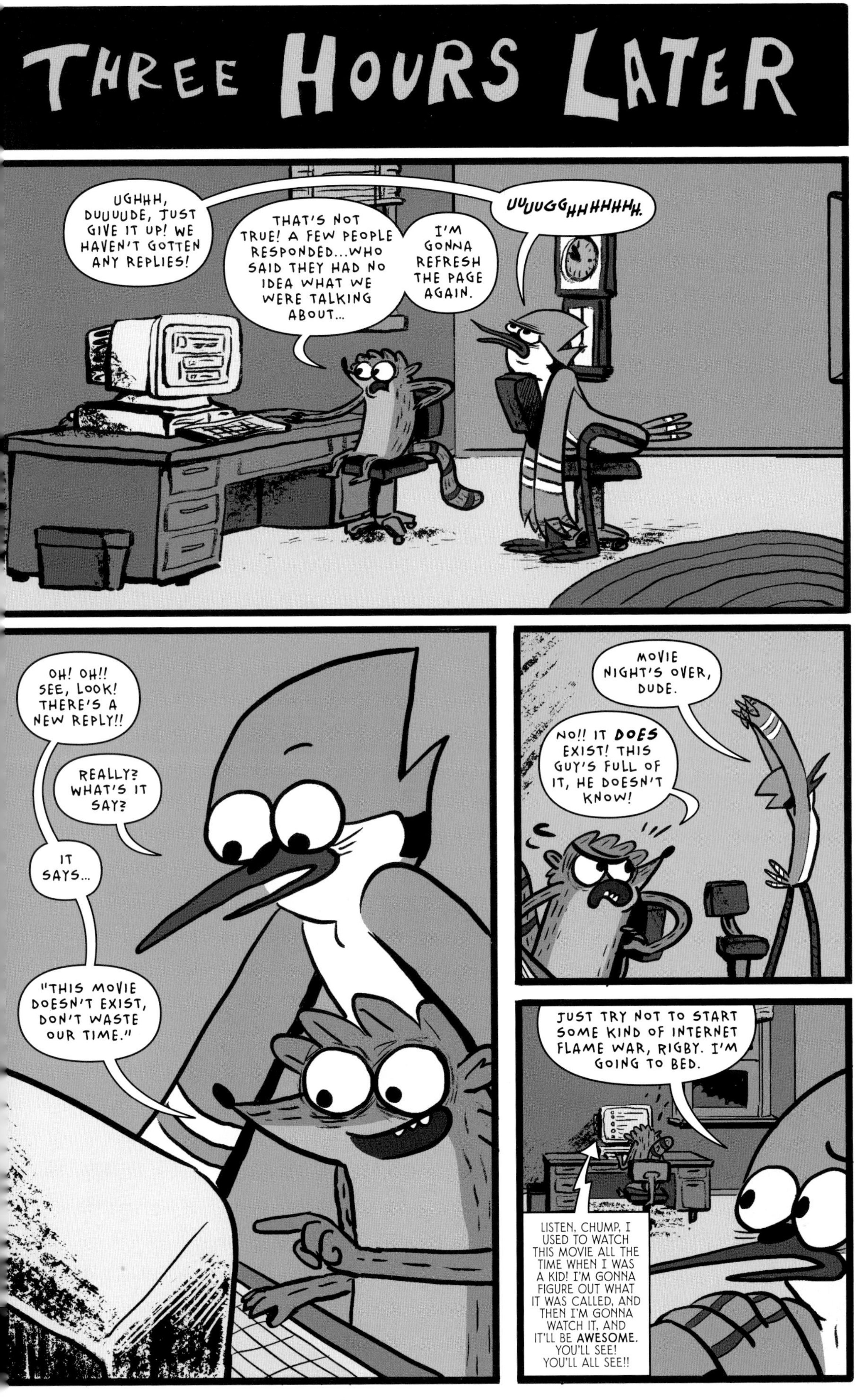
THREE HOURS LATER
UGHHH, DUUUUDE, JUST GIVE IT UP! WE HAVEN'T GOTTEN ANY REPLIES!
UUUUGGHHHHHHH.
THAT'S NOT TRUE! A FEW PEOPLE RESPONDED...WHO SAID THEY HAD NO IDEA WHAT WE WERE TALKING ABOUT...
I'M GONNA REFRESH THE PAGE AGAIN.
OH! OH!! SEE, LOOK! THERE'S A NEW REPLY!!
REALLY? WHAT'S IT SAY?
IT SAYS...
"THIS MOVIE DOESN'T EXIST, DON'T WASTE OUR TIME."
MOVIE NIGHT'S OVER, DUDE.
NO!! IT DOES EXIST! THIS GUY'S FULL OF IT, HE DOESN'T KNOW!
JUST TRY NOT TO START SOME KIND OF INTERNET FLAME WAR, RIGBY. I'M GOING TO BED.
LISTEN, CHUMP, I USED TO WATCH THIS MOVIE ALL THE TIME WHEN I WAS A KID! I'M GONNA FIGURE OUT WHAT IT WAS CALLED, AND THEN I'M GONNA WATCH IT, AND IT'LL BE AWESOME. YOU'LL SEE! YOU'LL ALL SEE!!

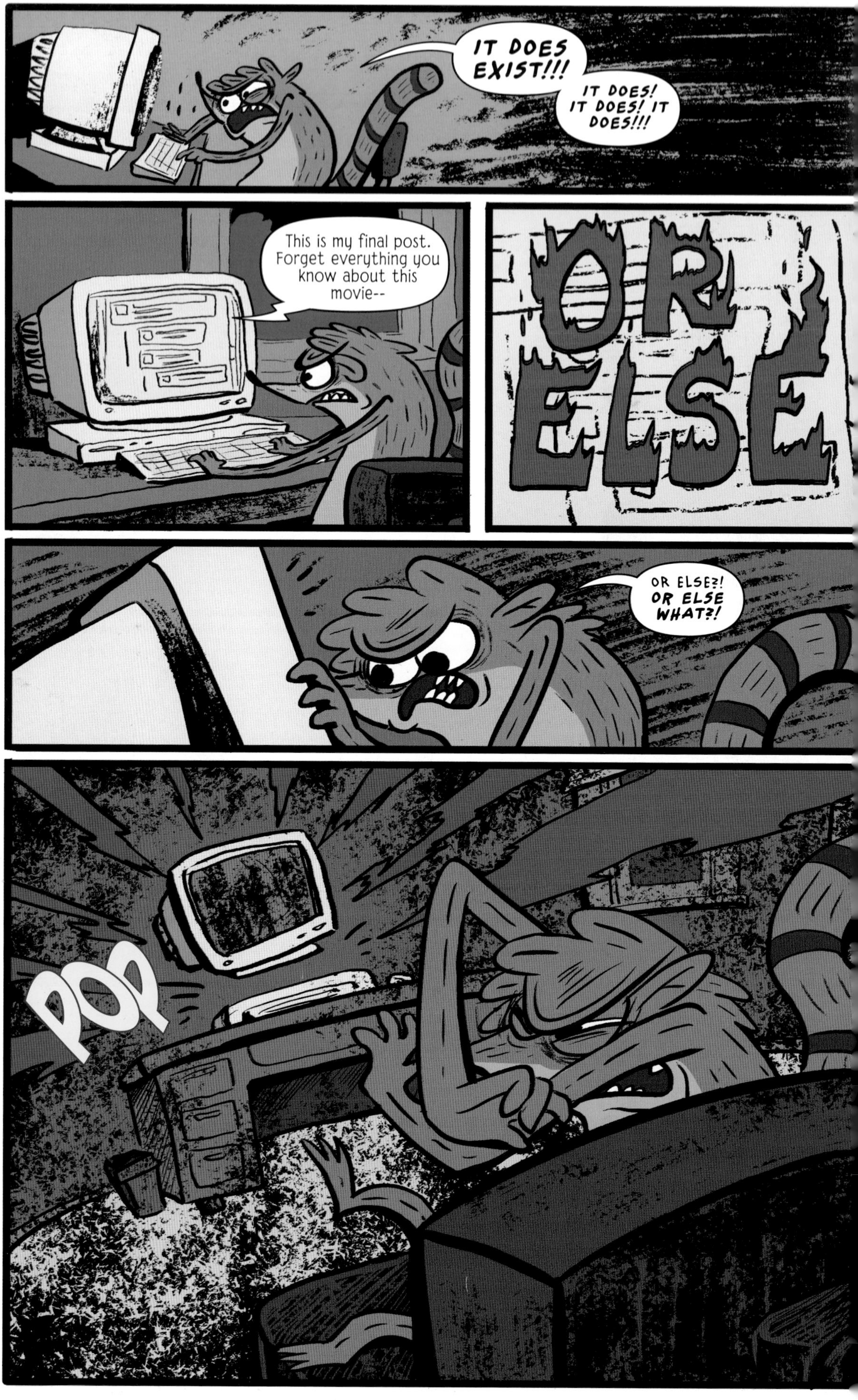
IT DOES EXIST!!!
IT DOES! IT DOES! IT DOES!!!
This is my final post. Forget everything you know about this movie--
OR ELSE
OR ELSE?! OR ELSE WHAT?!
POP

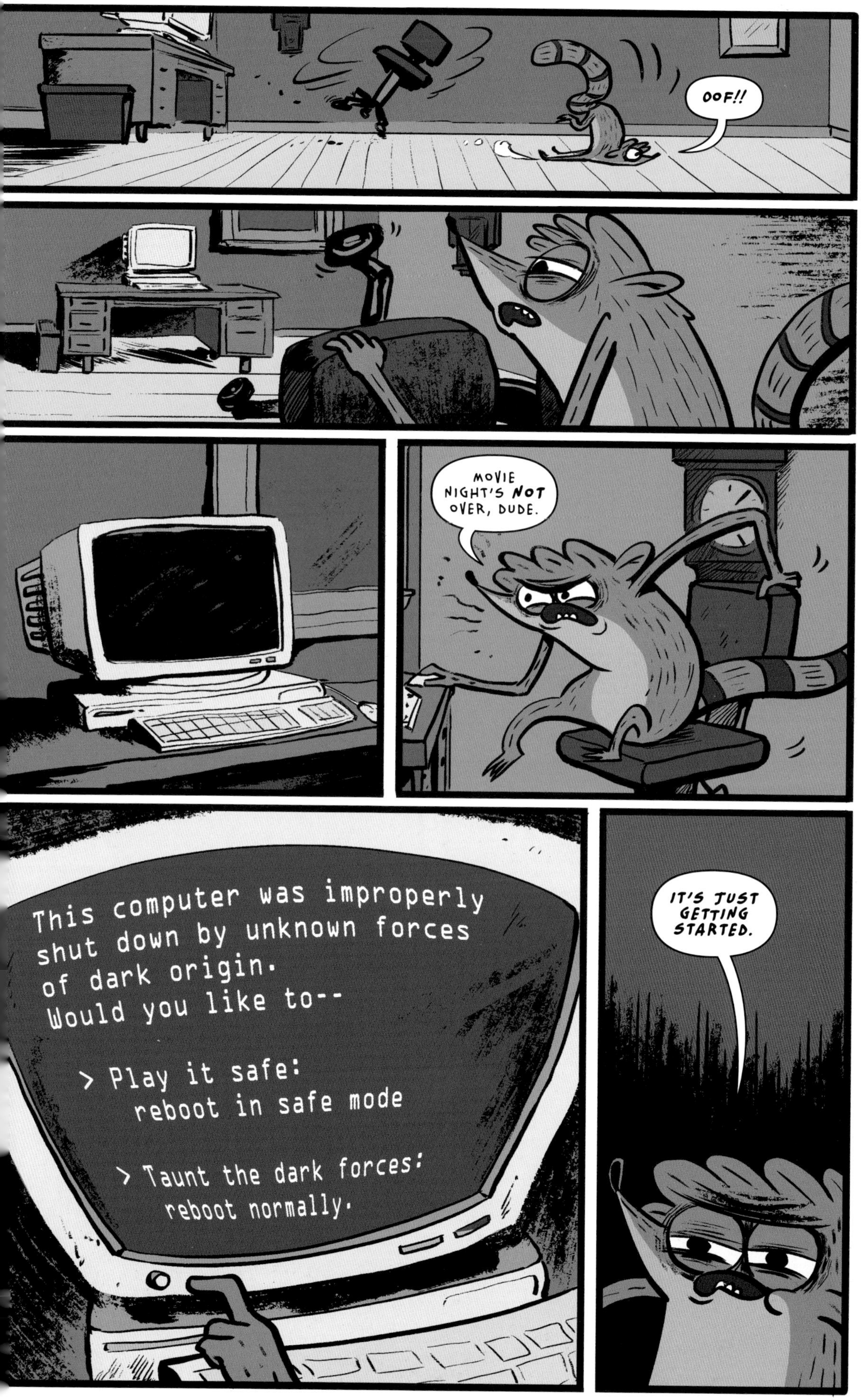
OOF!!
MOVIE NIGHT'S NOT OVER, DUDE.
This computer was improperly shut down by unknown forces of dark origin.
Would you like to--
> Play it safe: reboot in safe mode
> Taunt the dark forces: reboot normally.
IT'S JUST GETTING STARTED.

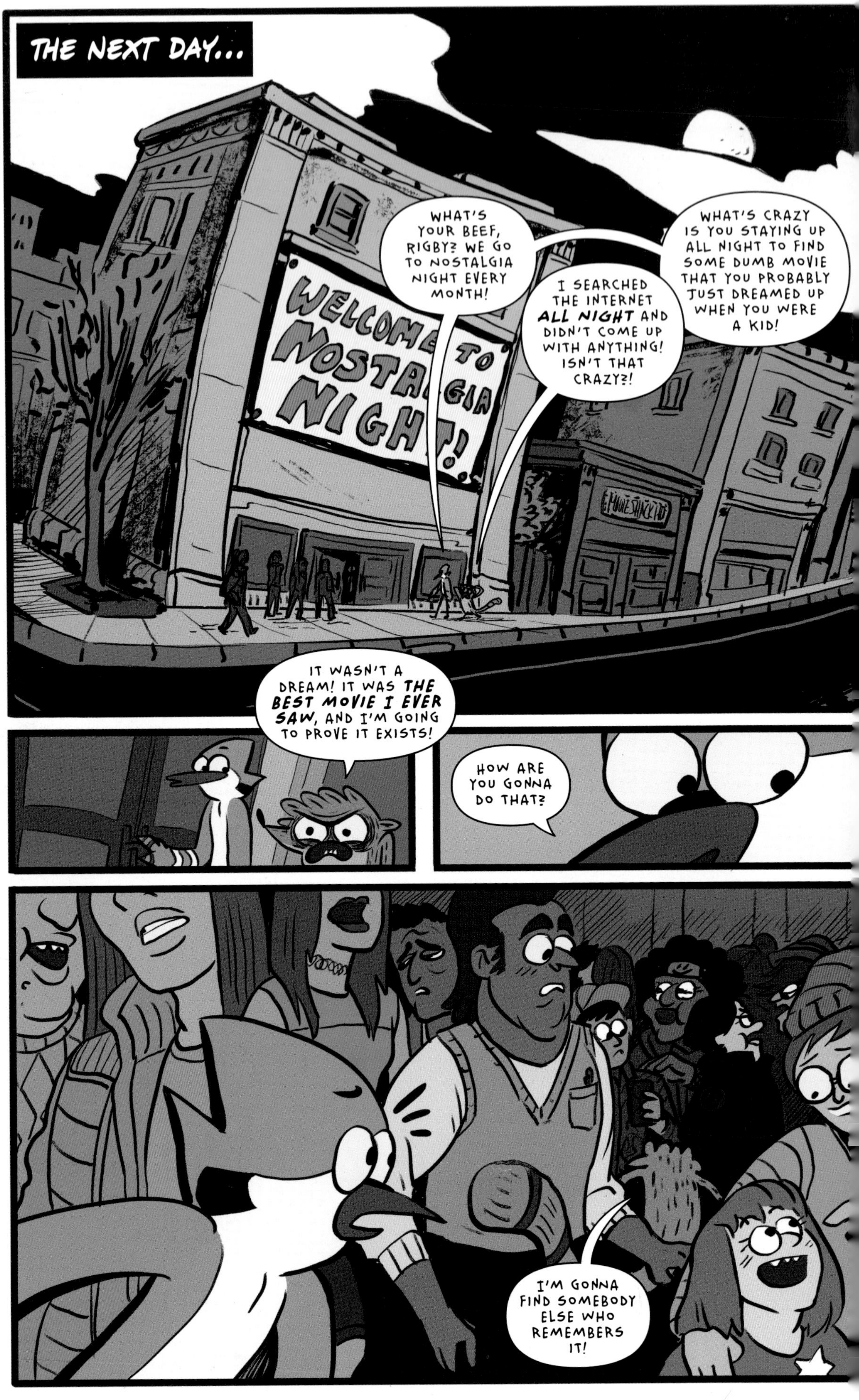
THE NEXT DAY...
WELCOME TO NOSTALGIA NIGHT!
WHAT'S YOUR BEEF, RIGBY? WE GO TO NOSTALGIA NIGHT EVERY MONTH!
I SEARCHED THE INTERNET ALL NIGHT AND DIDN'T COME UP WITH ANYTHING! ISN'T THAT CRAZY?!
WHAT'S CRAZY IS YOU STAYING UP ALL NIGHT TO FIND SOME DUMB MOVIE THAT YOU PROBABLY JUST DREAMED UP WHEN YOU WERE A KID!
IT WASN'T A DREAM! IT WAS THE BEST MOVIE I EVER SAW, AND I'M GOING TO PROVE IT EXISTS!
HOW ARE YOU GONNA DO THAT?
I'M GONNA FIND SOMEBODY ELSE WHO REMEMBERS IT!

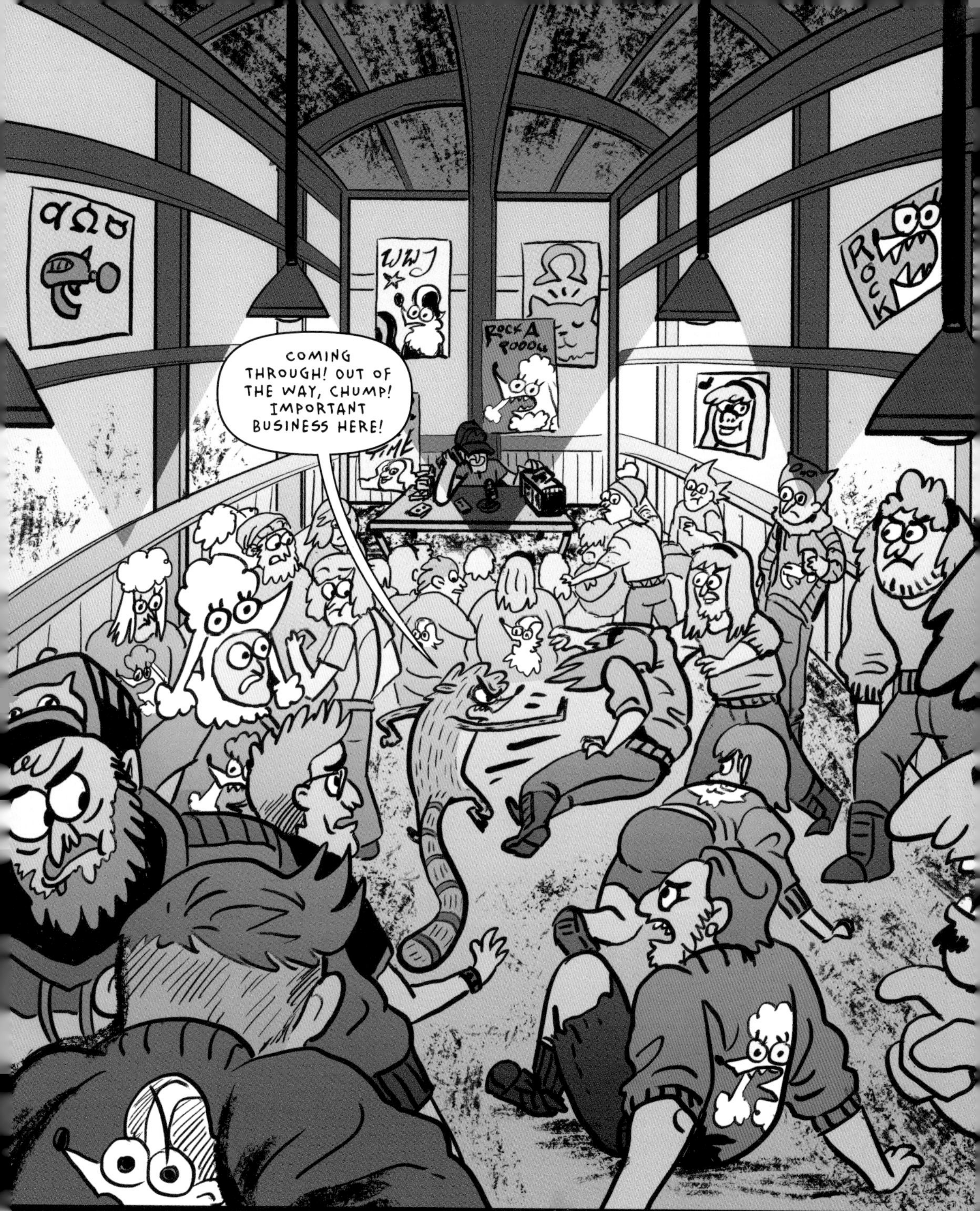
COMING THROUGH! OUT OF THE WAY, CHUMP! IMPORTANT BUSINESS HERE!
ROCK

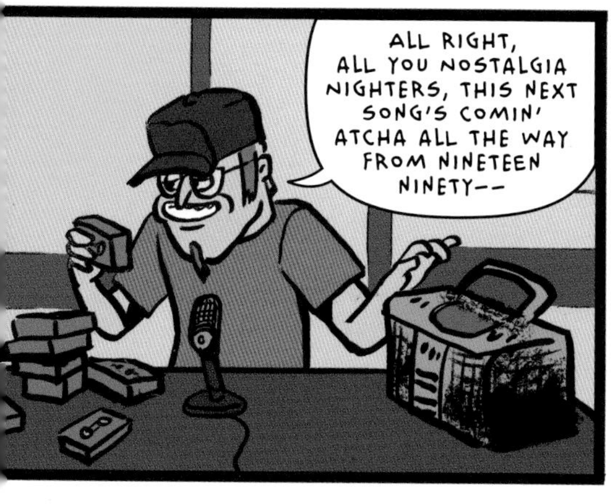
ALL RIGHT, ALL YOU NOSTALGIA NIGHTERS, THIS NEXT SONG'S COMIN' ATCHA ALL THE WAY FROM NINETEEN NINETY--

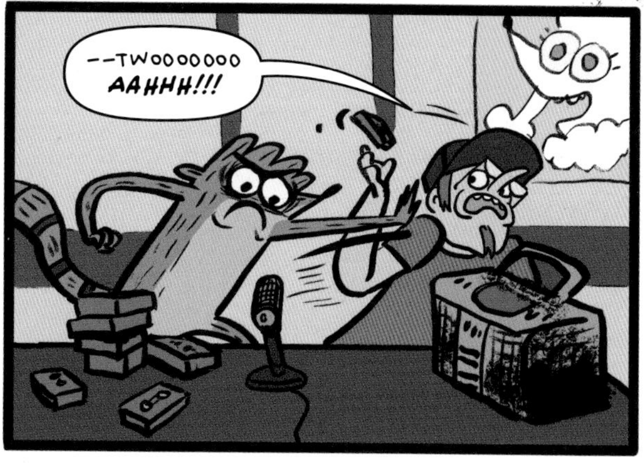
--TWOOOOOOO AAHHH!!!

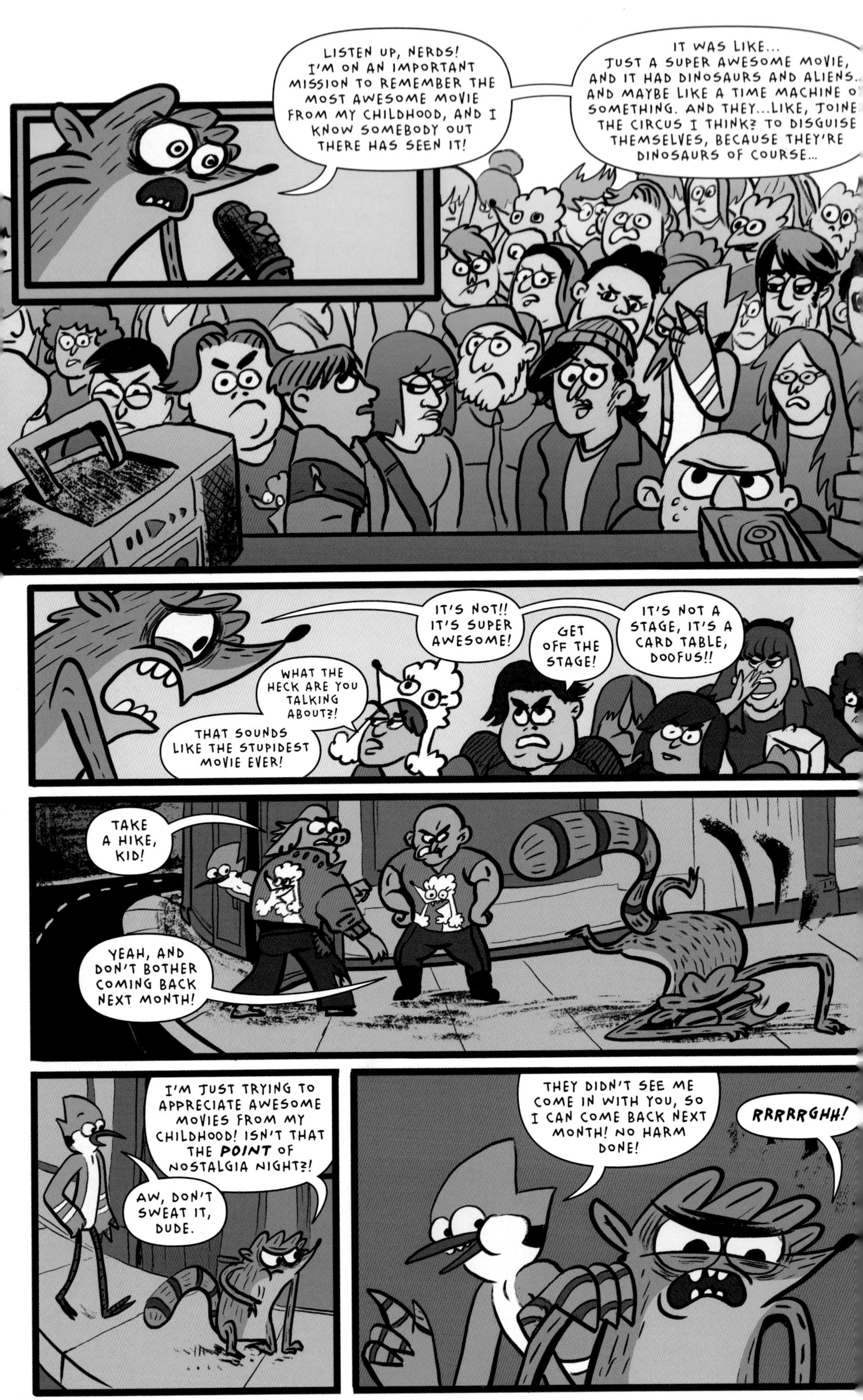
LISTEN UP, NERDS! I'M ON AN IMPORTANT MISSION TO REMEMBER THE MOST AWESOME MOVIE FROM MY CHILDHOOD, AND I KNOW SOMEBODY OUT THERE HAS SEEN IT!
IT WAS LIKE... JUST A SUPER AWESOME MOVIE, AND IT HAD DINOSAURS AND ALIENS... AND MAYBE LIKE A TIME MACHINE OR SOMETHING. AND THEY...LIKE, JOINED THE CIRCUS I THINK? TO DISGUISE THEMSELVES, BECAUSE THEY'RE DINOSAURS OF COURSE...
THAT SOUNDS LIKE THE STUPIDEST MOVIE EVER!
WHAT THE HECK ARE YOU TALKING ABOUT?!
IT'S NOT!! IT'S SUPER AWESOME!
GET OFF THE STAGE!
IT'S NOT A STAGE, IT'S A CARD TABLE, DOOFUS!!
TAKE A HIKE, KID!
YEAH, AND DON'T BOTHER COMING BACK NEXT MONTH!
I'M JUST TRYING TO APPRECIATE AWESOME MOVIES FROM MY CHILDHOOD! ISN'T THAT THE POINT OF NOSTALGIA NIGHT?!
AW, DON'T SWEAT IT, DUDE.
THEY DIDN'T SEE ME COME IN WITH YOU, SO I CAN COME BACK NEXT MONTH! NO HARM DONE!
RRRRRGHH!

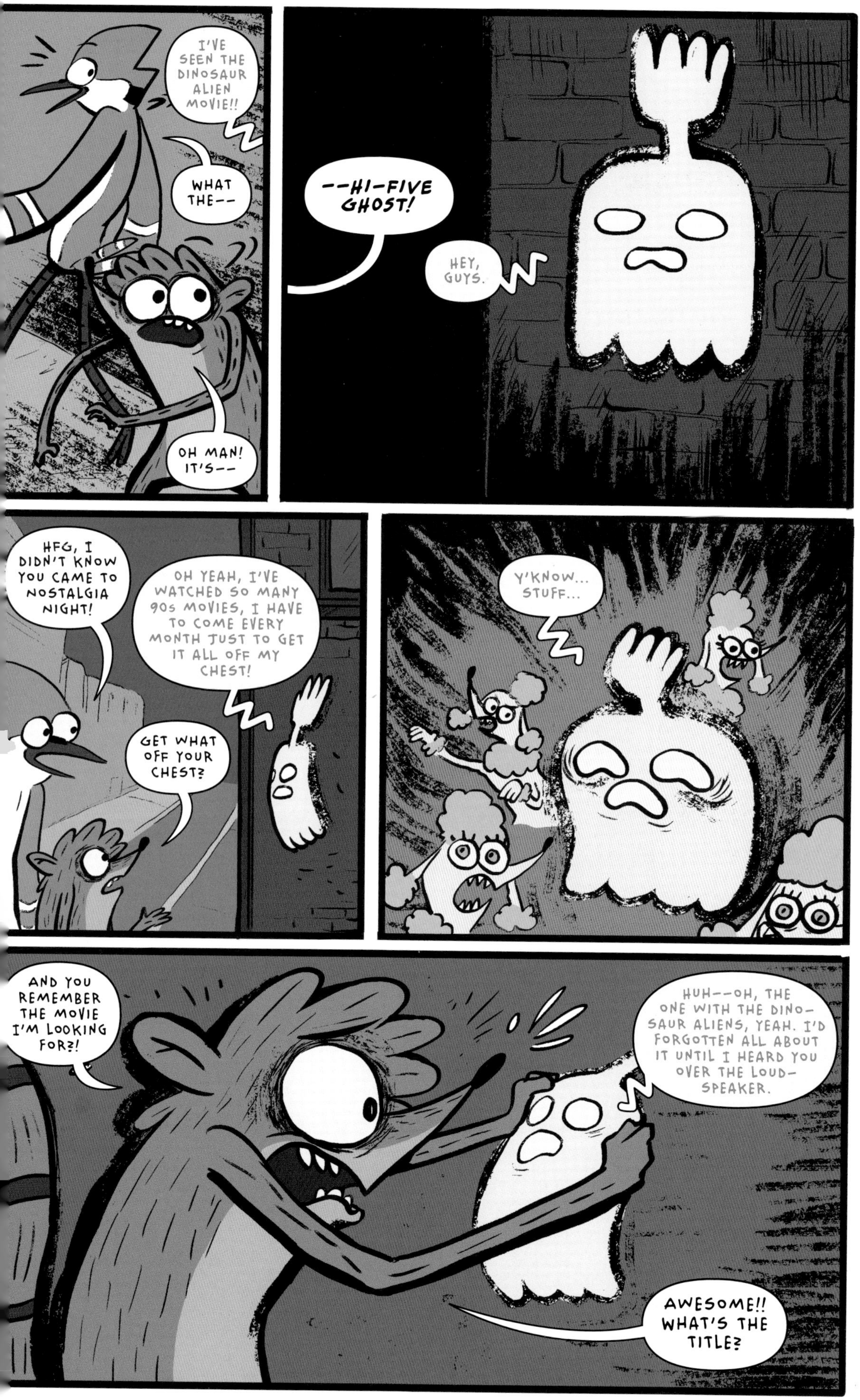
I'VE SEEN THE DINOSAUR ALIEN MOVIE!!
WHAT THE--
OH MAN! IT'S--
--HI-FIVE GHOST!
HEY, GUYS.
HFG, I DIDN'T KNOW YOU CAME TO NOSTALGIA NIGHT!
OH YEAH, I'VE WATCHED SO MANY 90s MOVIES, I HAVE TO COME EVERY MONTH JUST TO GET IT ALL OFF MY CHEST!
GET WHAT OFF YOUR CHEST?
Y'KNOW... STUFF...
AND YOU REMEMBER THE MOVIE I'M LOOKING FOR?!
HUH--OH, THE ONE WITH THE DINO-SAUR ALIENS, YEAH. I'D FORGOTTEN ALL ABOUT IT UNTIL I HEARD YOU OVER THE LOUD-SPEAKER.
AWESOME!! WHAT'S THE TITLE?

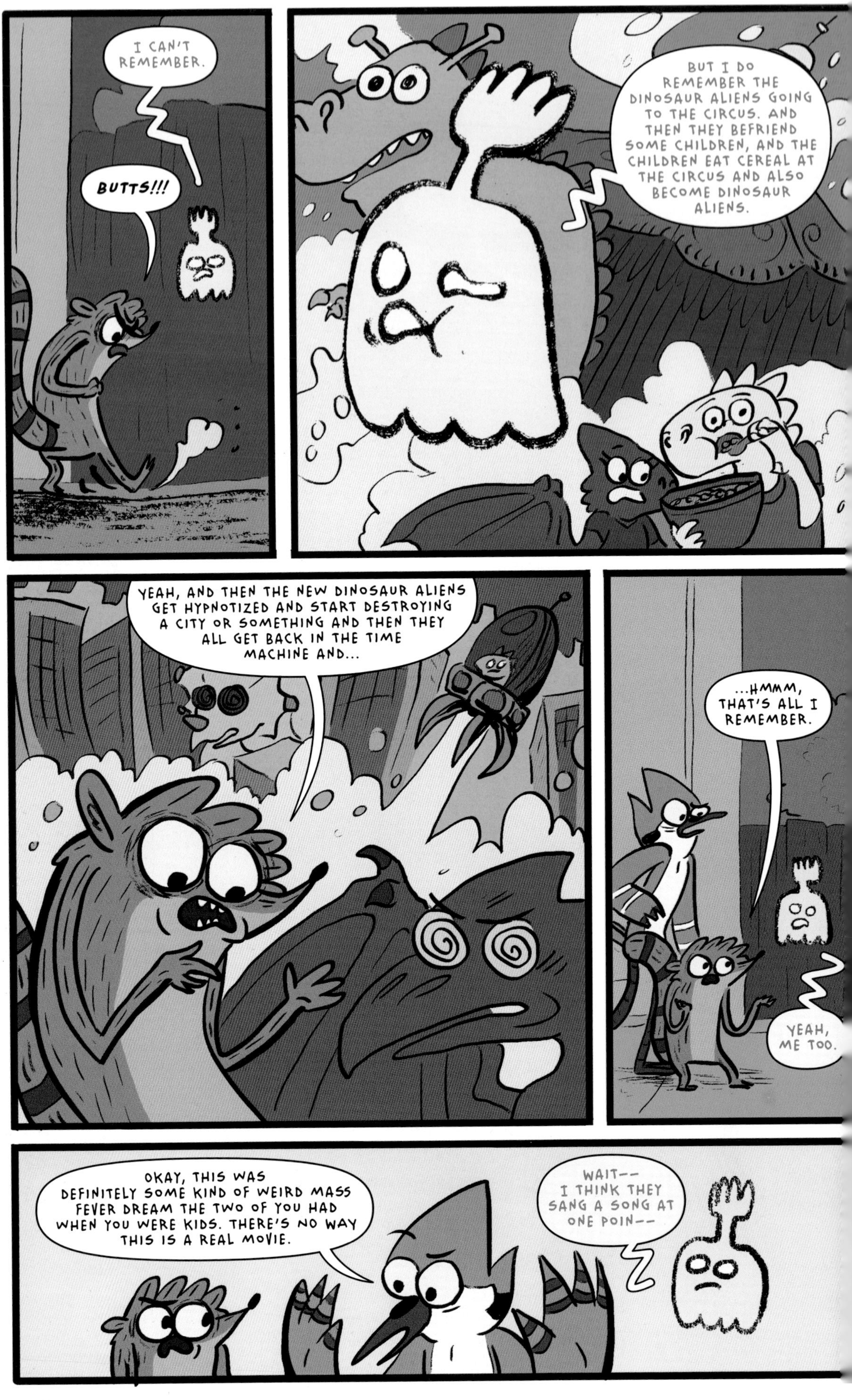
I CAN'T REMEMBER.
BUTTS!!!
BUT I DO REMEMBER THE DINOSAUR ALIENS GOING TO THE CIRCUS. AND THEN THEY BEFRIEND SOME CHILDREN, AND THE CHILDREN EAT CEREAL AT THE CIRCUS AND ALSO BECOME DINOSAUR ALIENS.
YEAH, AND THEN THE NEW DINOSAUR ALIENS GET HYPNOTIZED AND START DESTROYING A CITY OR SOMETHING AND THEN THEY ALL GET BACK IN THE TIME MACHINE AND...
...HMMM, THAT'S ALL I REMEMBER.
YEAH, ME TOO.
OKAY, THIS WAS DEFINITELY SOME KIND OF WEIRD MASS FEVER DREAM THE TWO OF YOU HAD WHEN YOU WERE KIDS. THERE'S NO WAY THIS IS A REAL MOVIE.
WAIT-- I THINK THEY SANG A SONG AT ONE POIN--

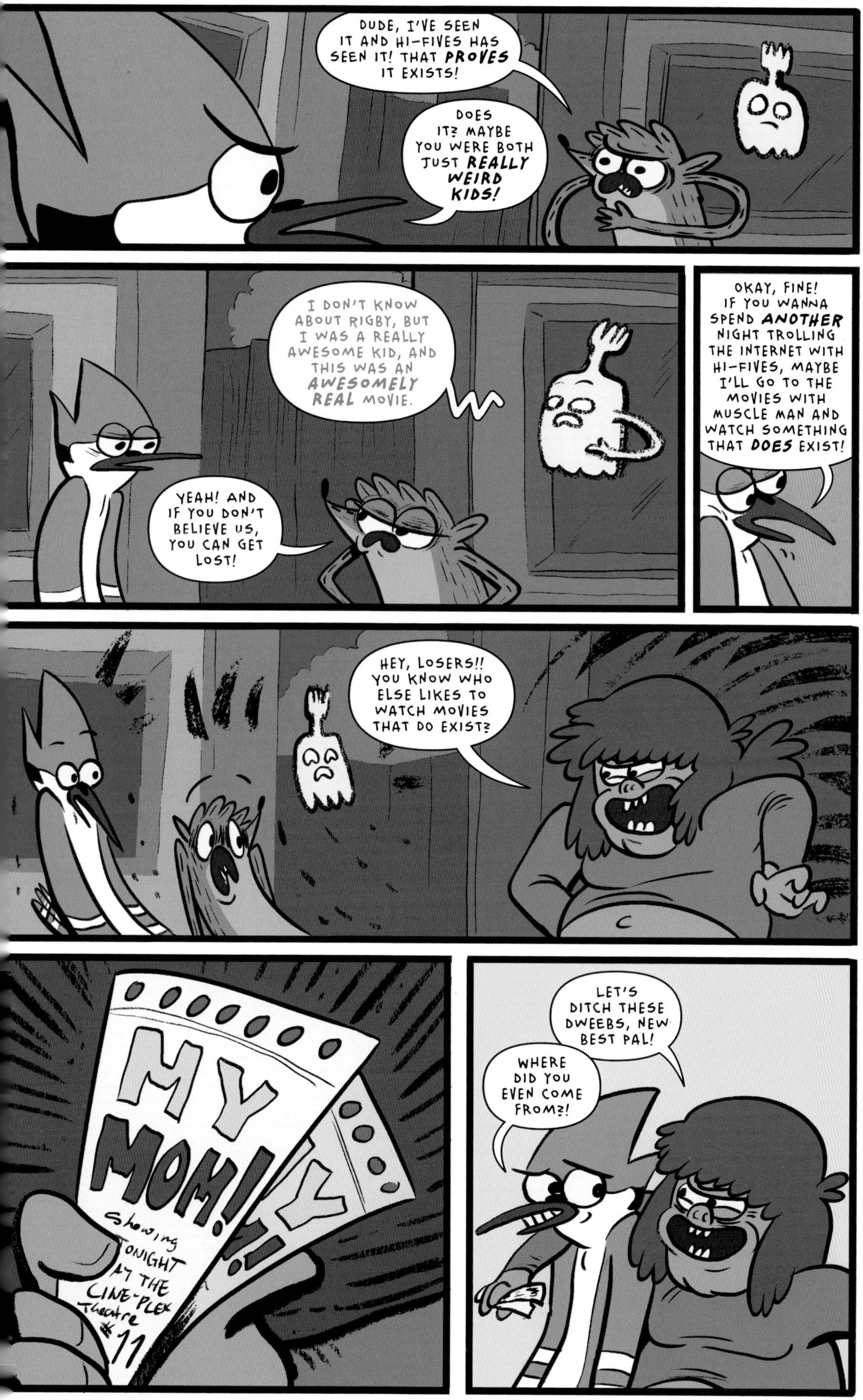
DUDE, I'VE SEEN IT AND HI-FIVES HAS SEEN IT! THAT PROVES IT EXISTS!
DOES IT? MAYBE YOU WERE BOTH JUST REALLY WEIRD KIDS!
I DON'T KNOW ABOUT RIGBY, BUT I WAS A REALLY AWESOME KID, AND THIS WAS AN AWESOMELY REAL MOVIE.
YEAH! AND IF YOU DON'T BELIEVE US, YOU CAN GET LOST!
OKAY, FINE! IF YOU WANNA SPEND ANOTHER NIGHT TROLLING THE INTERNET WITH HI-FIVES, MAYBE I'LL GO TO THE MOVIES WITH MUSCLE MAN AND WATCH SOMETHING THAT DOES EXIST!
HEY, LOSERS!! YOU KNOW WHO ELSE LIKES TO WATCH MOVIES THAT DO EXIST?
MY MOM!
Showing TONIGHT AT THE CINE-PLEX theatre #11
LET'S DITCH THESE DWEEBS, NEW BEST PAL!
WHERE DID YOU EVEN COME FROM?!

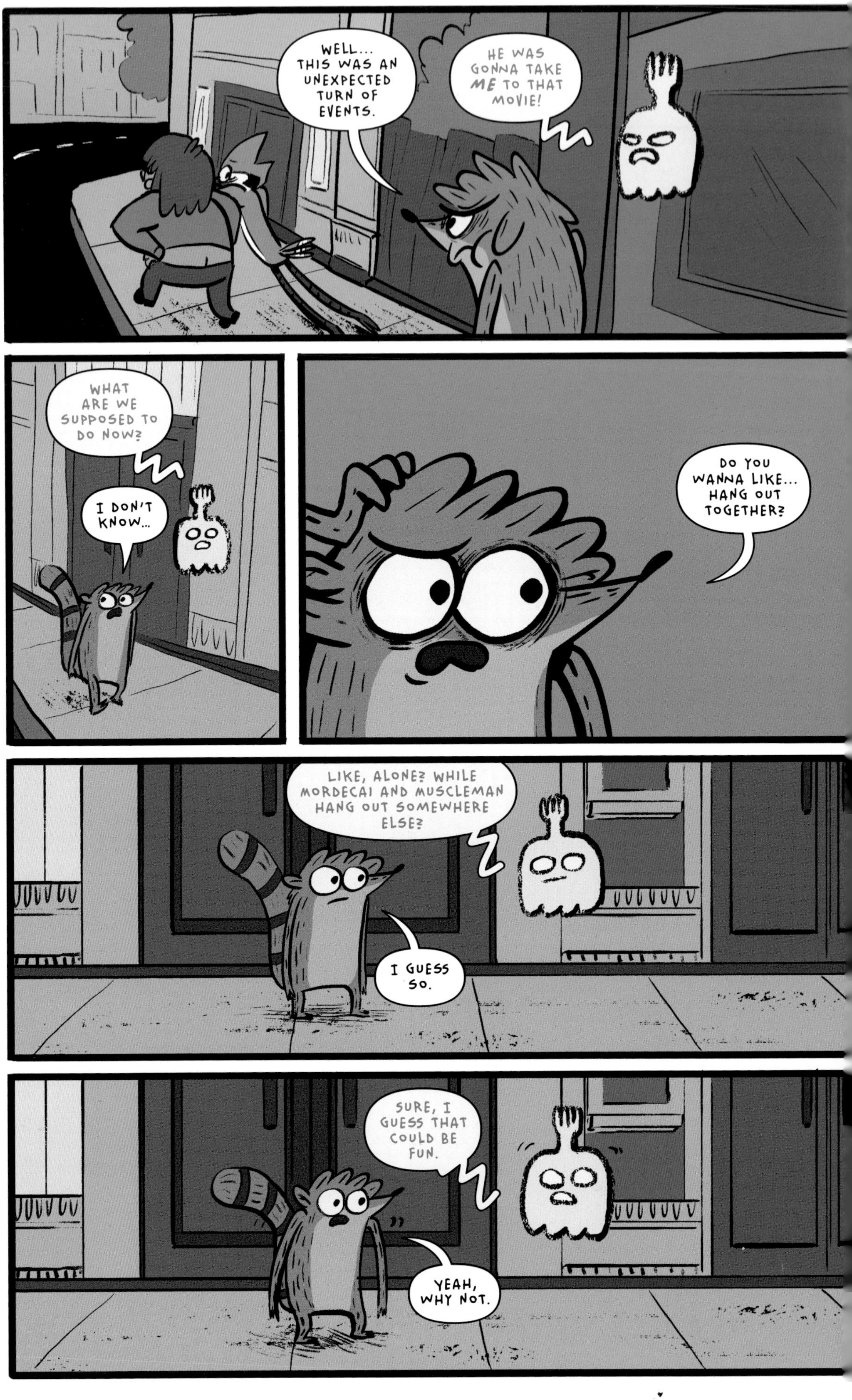
WELL... THIS WAS AN UNEXPECTED TURN OF EVENTS.
HE WAS GONNA TAKE ME TO THAT MOVIE!
WHAT ARE WE SUPPOSED TO DO NOW?
I DON'T KNOW...
DO YOU WANNA LIKE... HANG OUT TOGETHER?
LIKE, ALONE? WHILE MORDECAI AND MUSCLEMAN HANG OUT SOMEWHERE ELSE?
I GUESS SO.
SURE, I GUESS THAT COULD BE FUN.
YEAH, WHY NOT.

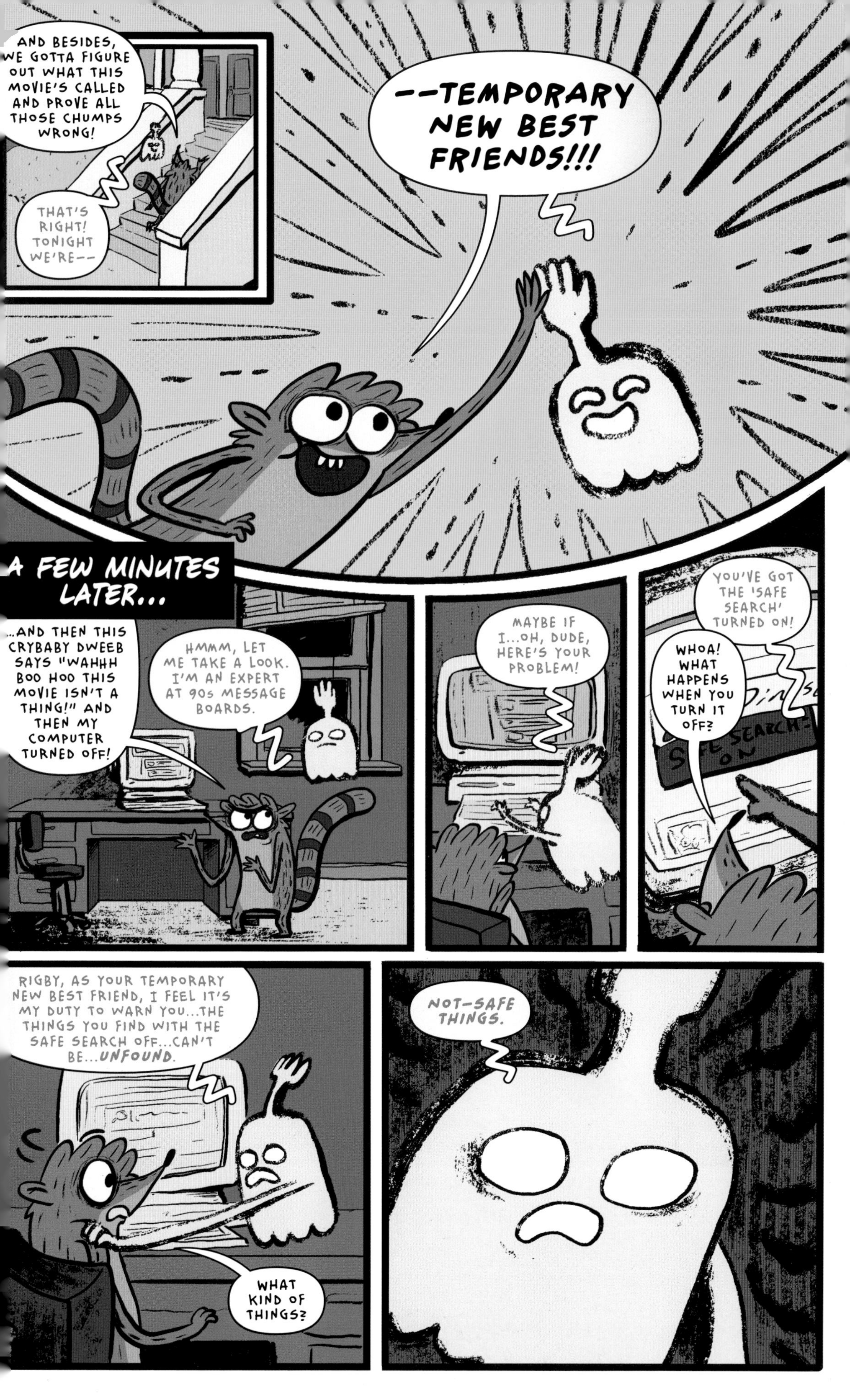
AND BESIDES, WE GOTTA FIGURE OUT WHAT THIS MOVIE'S CALLED AND PROVE ALL THOSE CHUMPS WRONG!
THAT'S RIGHT! TONIGHT WE'RE--
--TEMPORARY NEW BEST FRIENDS!!!
A FEW MINUTES LATER...
...AND THEN THIS CRYBABY DWEEB SAYS "WAHHH BOO HOO THIS MOVIE ISN'T A THING!" AND THEN MY COMPUTER TURNED OFF!
HMMM, LET ME TAKE A LOOK. I'M AN EXPERT AT 90s MESSAGE BOARDS.
MAYBE IF I...OH, DUDE, HERE'S YOUR PROBLEM!
YOU'VE GOT THE 'SAFE SEARCH' TURNED ON!
WHOA! WHAT HAPPENS WHEN YOU TURN IT OFF?
SAFE SEARCH: ON
RIGBY, AS YOUR TEMPORARY NEW BEST FRIEND, I FEEL IT'S MY DUTY TO WARN YOU...THE THINGS YOU FIND WITH THE SAFE SEARCH OFF...CAN'T BE...UNFOUND.
WHAT KIND OF THINGS?
NOT-SAFE THINGS.

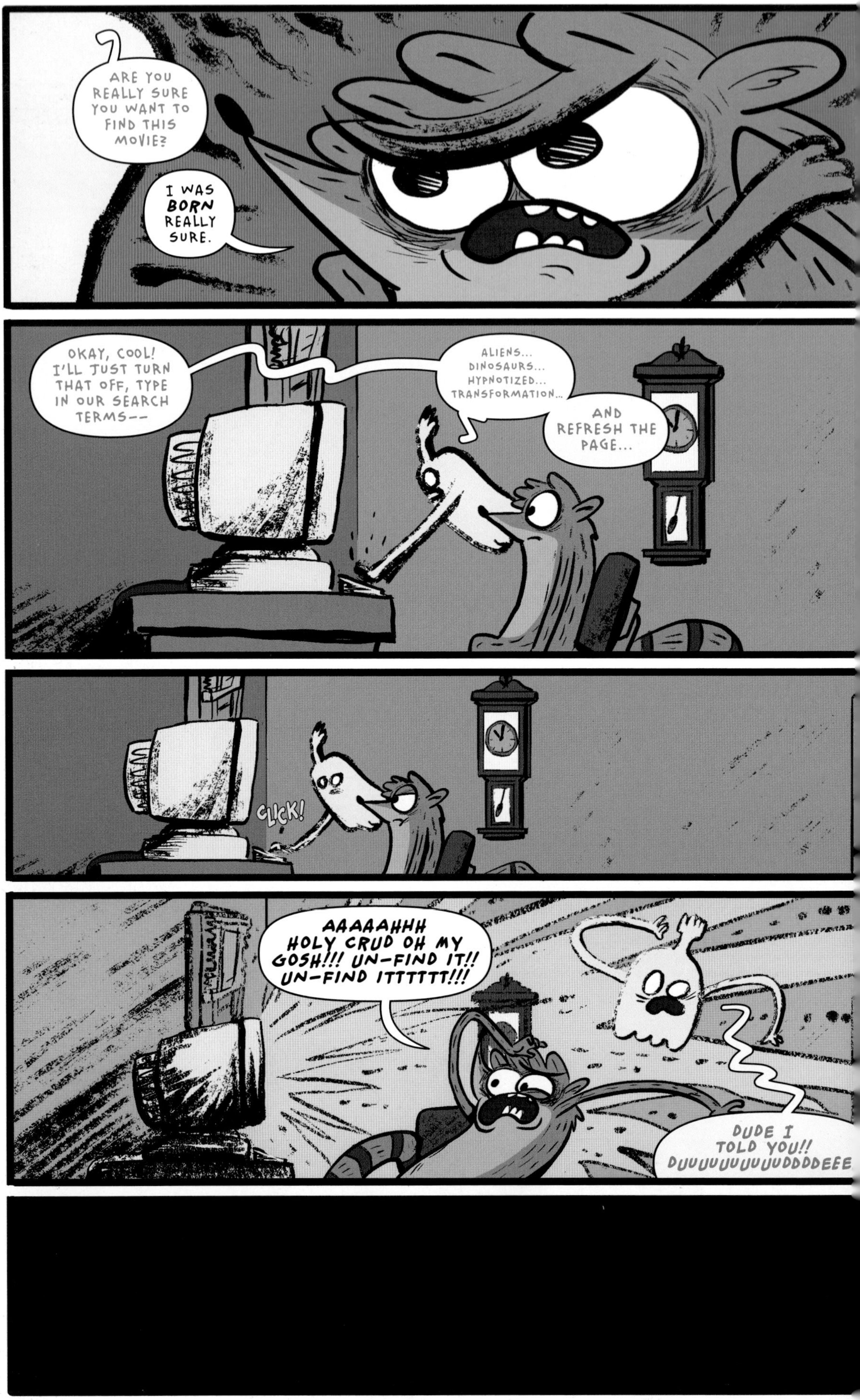
ARE YOU REALLY SURE YOU WANT TO FIND THIS MOVIE?
I WAS BORN REALLY SURE.
OKAY, COOL! I'LL JUST TURN THAT OFF, TYPE IN OUR SEARCH TERMS--
ALIENS... DINOSAURS... HYPNOTIZED... TRANSFORMATION...
AND REFRESH THE PAGE...
CLICK!
AAAAAHHH HOLY CRUD OH MY GOSH!!! UN-FIND IT!! UN-FIND ITTTTTT!!!
DUDE I TOLD YOU!! DUUUUUUUUUDDDDEEE

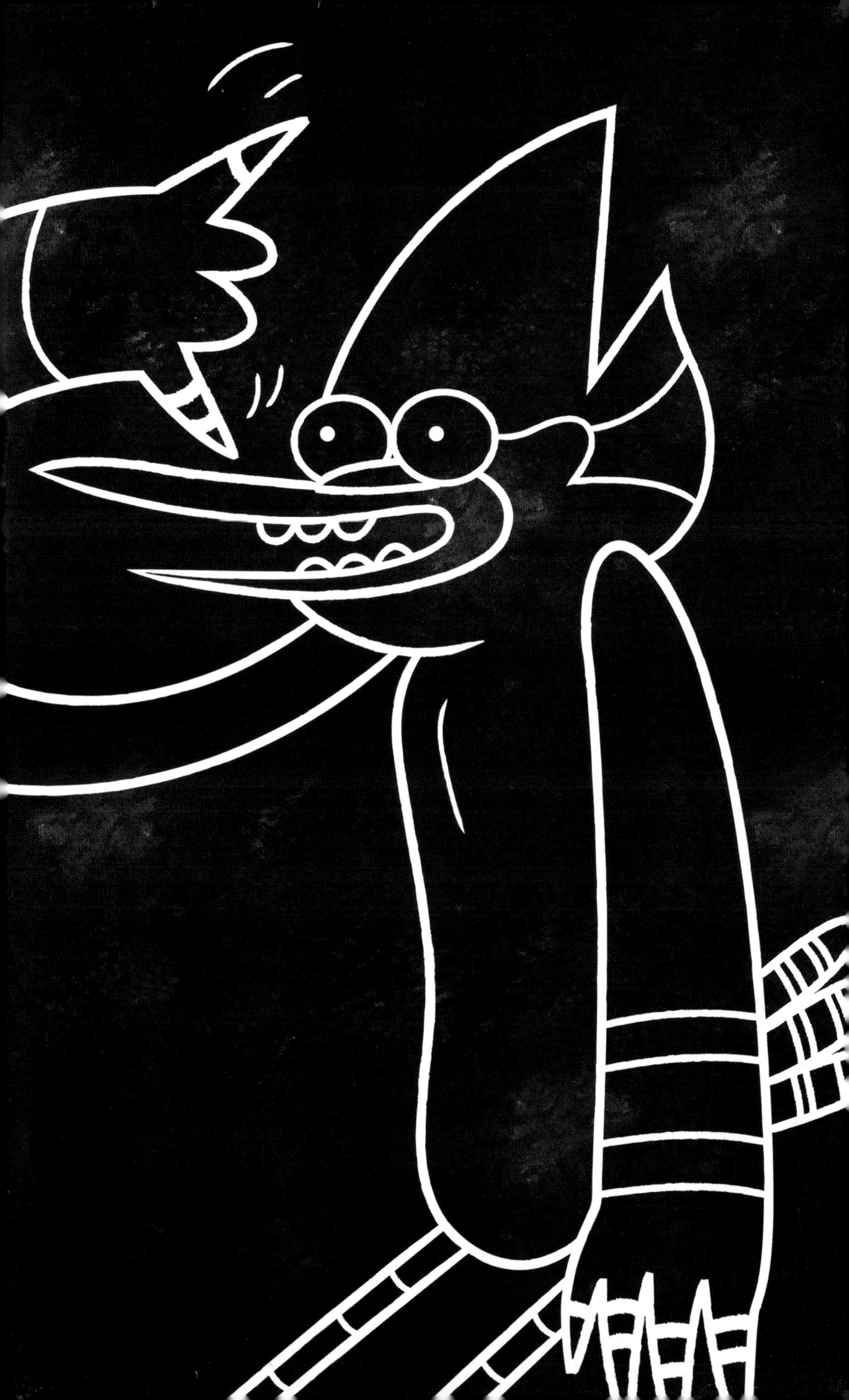

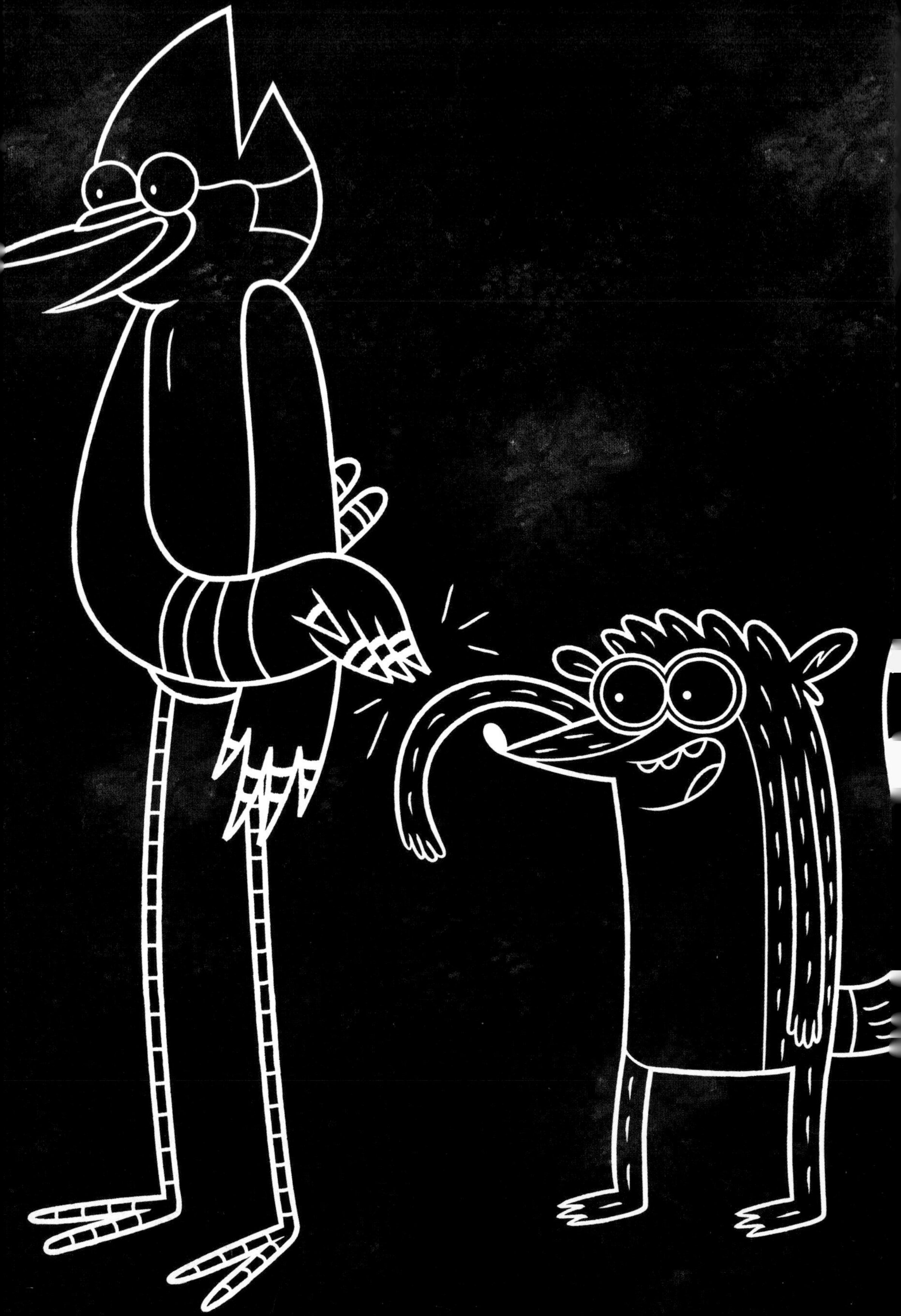

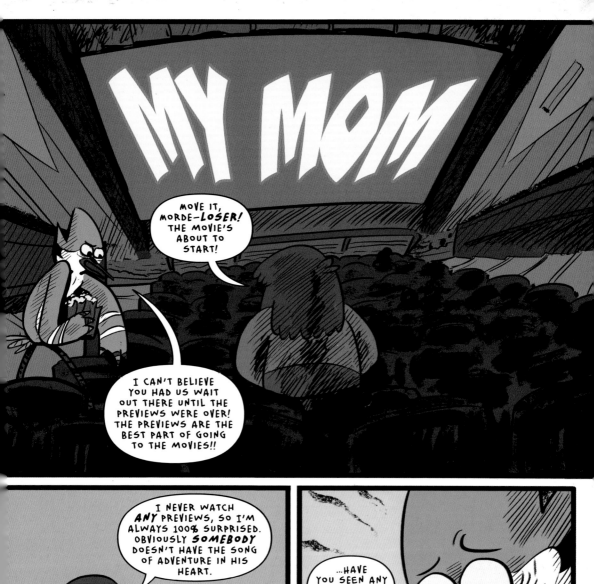

MY MOM

MOVE IT, MORDE-*LOSER!* THE MOVIE'S ABOUT TO START!

I CAN'T BELIEVE YOU HAD US WAIT OUT THERE UNTIL THE PREVIEWS WERE OVER! THE PREVIEWS ARE THE BEST PART OF GOING TO THE MOVIES!!

I NEVER WATCH *ANY* PREVIEWS, SO I'M ALWAYS 100% SURPRISED. OBVIOUSLY *SOMEBODY* DOESN'T HAVE THE SONG OF ADVENTURE IN HIS HEART.

WAIT...

...HAVE YOU SEEN ANY PREVIEWS FOR *THIS* MOVIE?!

I DON'T EVEN KNOW WHAT IT'S ABOUT.

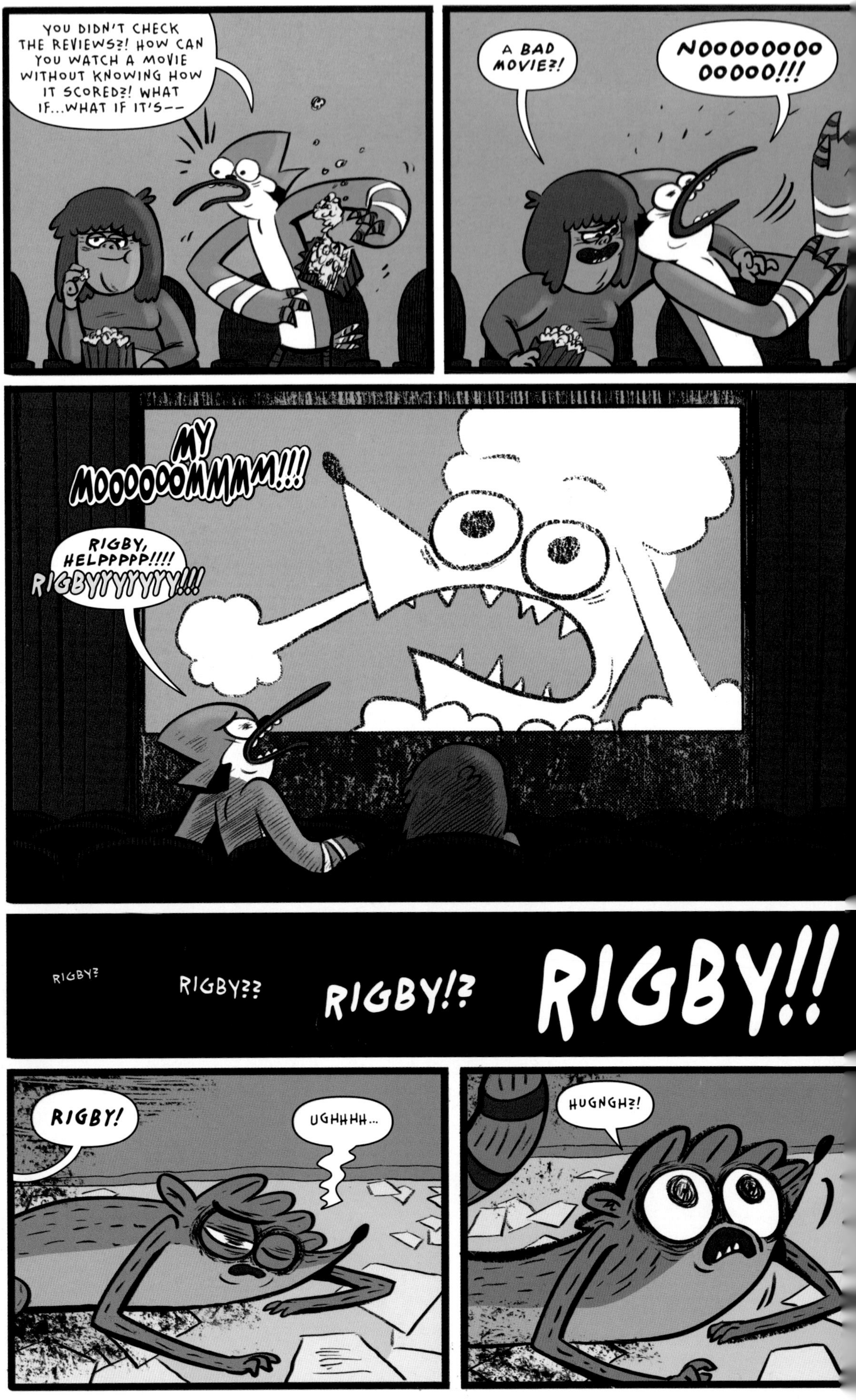

YOU DIDN'T CHECK THE REVIEWS?! HOW CAN YOU WATCH A MOVIE WITHOUT KNOWING HOW IT SCORED?! WHAT IF...WHAT IF IT'S--
A BAD MOVIE?!
NOOOOOOOOOOOOO!!!
MY MOOOOOOMMMM!!!
RIGBY, HELPPPPP!!!! RIGBYYYYYYY!!!
RIGBY?
RIGBY??
RIGBY!?
RIGBY!!
RIGBY!
UGHHHH...
HUGNGH?!

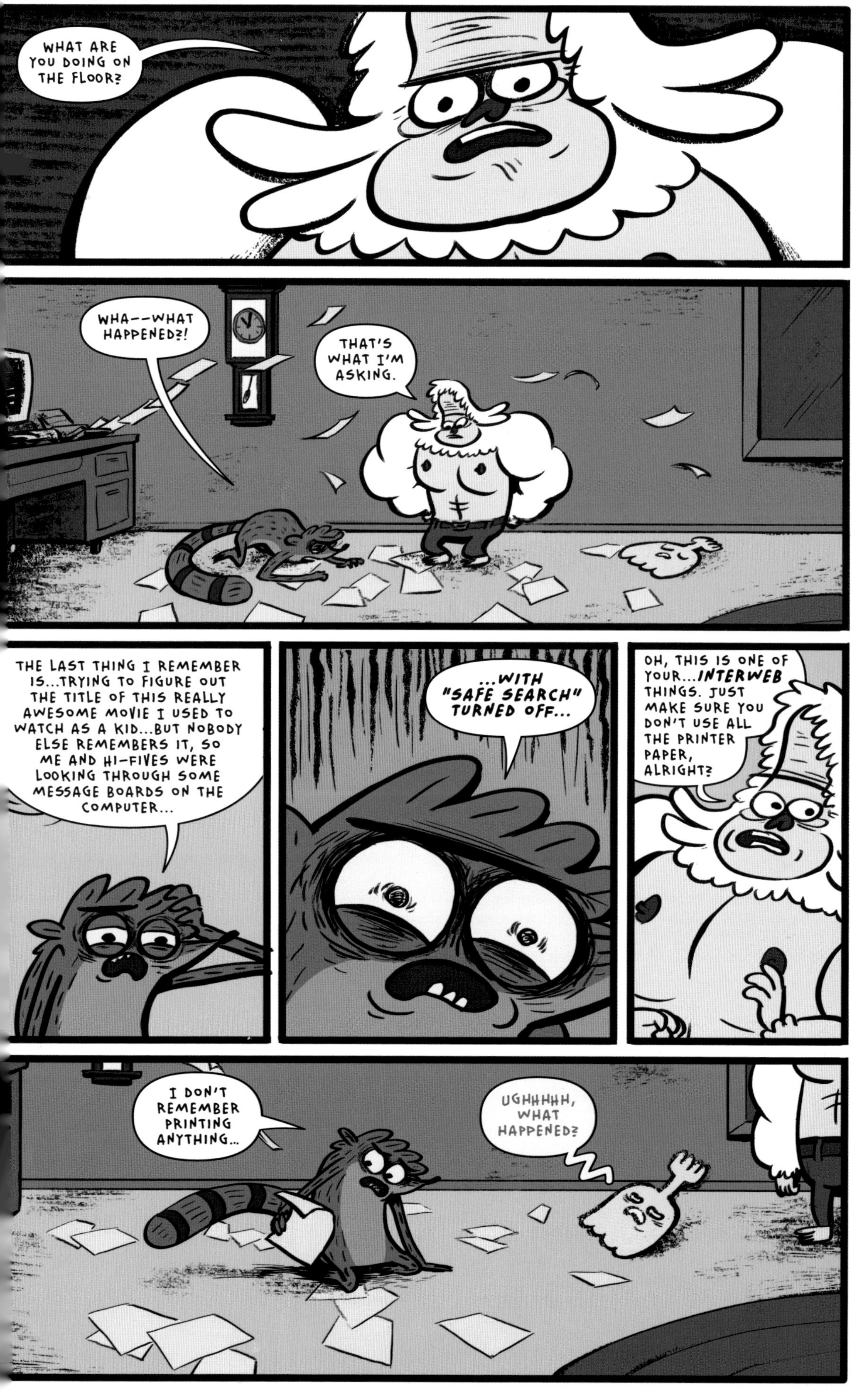
WHAT ARE YOU DOING ON THE FLOOR?
WHA--WHAT HAPPENED?!
THAT'S WHAT I'M ASKING.
THE LAST THING I REMEMBER IS...TRYING TO FIGURE OUT THE TITLE OF THIS REALLY AWESOME MOVIE I USED TO WATCH AS A KID...BUT NOBODY ELSE REMEMBERS IT, SO ME AND HI-FIVES WERE LOOKING THROUGH SOME MESSAGE BOARDS ON THE COMPUTER...
...WITH "SAFE SEARCH" TURNED OFF...
OH, THIS IS ONE OF YOUR...INTERWEB THINGS. JUST MAKE SURE YOU DON'T USE ALL THE PRINTER PAPER, ALRIGHT?
I DON'T REMEMBER PRINTING ANYTHING...
UGHHHHH, WHAT HAPPENED?

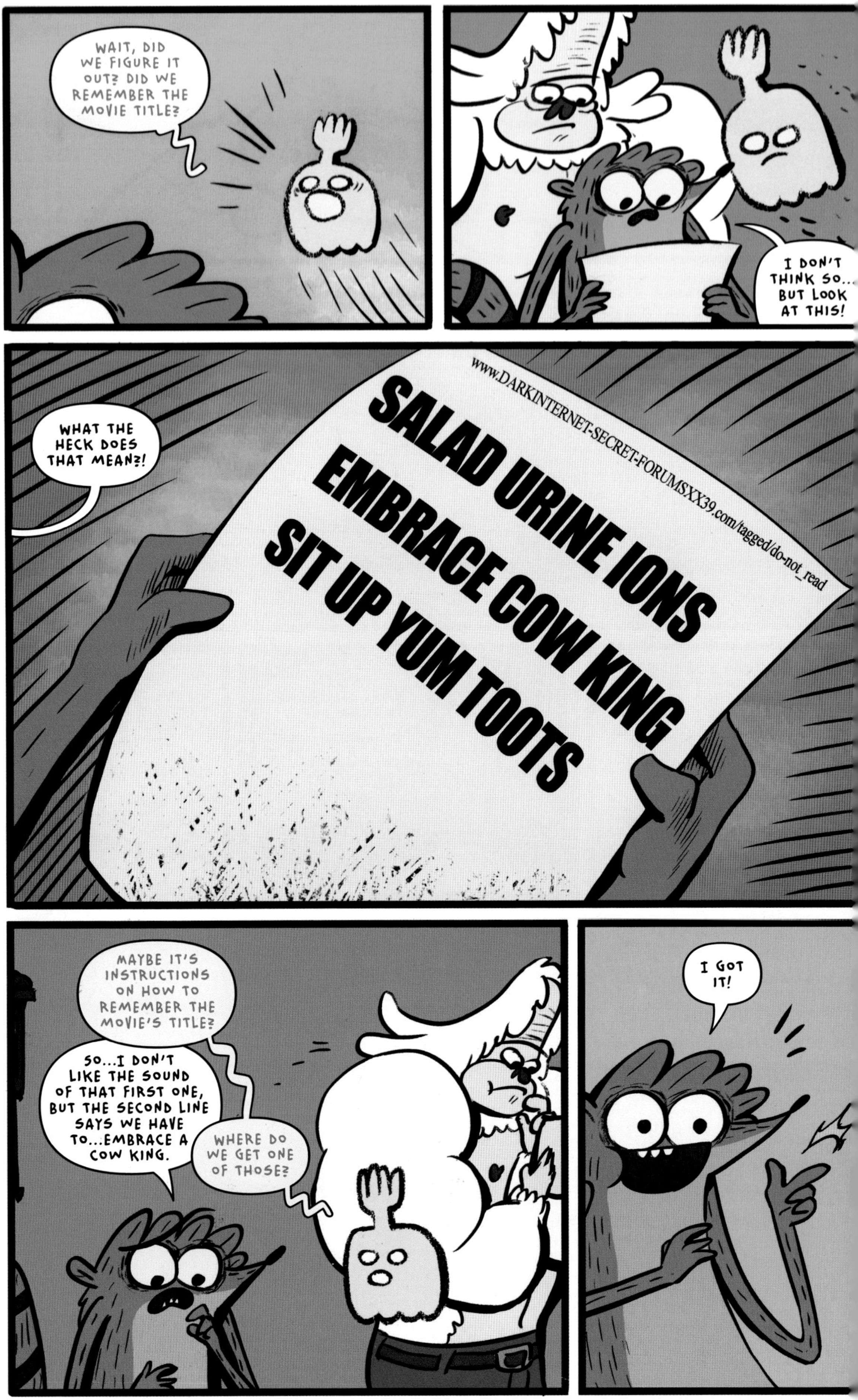

WAIT, DID WE FIGURE IT OUT? DID WE REMEMBER THE MOVIE TITLE?
I DON'T THINK SO... BUT LOOK AT THIS!
WHAT THE HECK DOES THAT MEAN?!
www.DARKINTERNET-SECRET-FORUMSXX39.com/tagged/do-not_read
SALAD URINE IONS
EMBRACE COW KING
SIT UP YUM TOOTS
MAYBE IT'S INSTRUCTIONS ON HOW TO REMEMBER THE MOVIE'S TITLE?
SO...I DON'T LIKE THE SOUND OF THAT FIRST ONE, BUT THE SECOND LINE SAYS WE HAVE TO...EMBRACE A COW KING.
WHERE DO WE GET ONE OF THOSE?
I GOT IT!

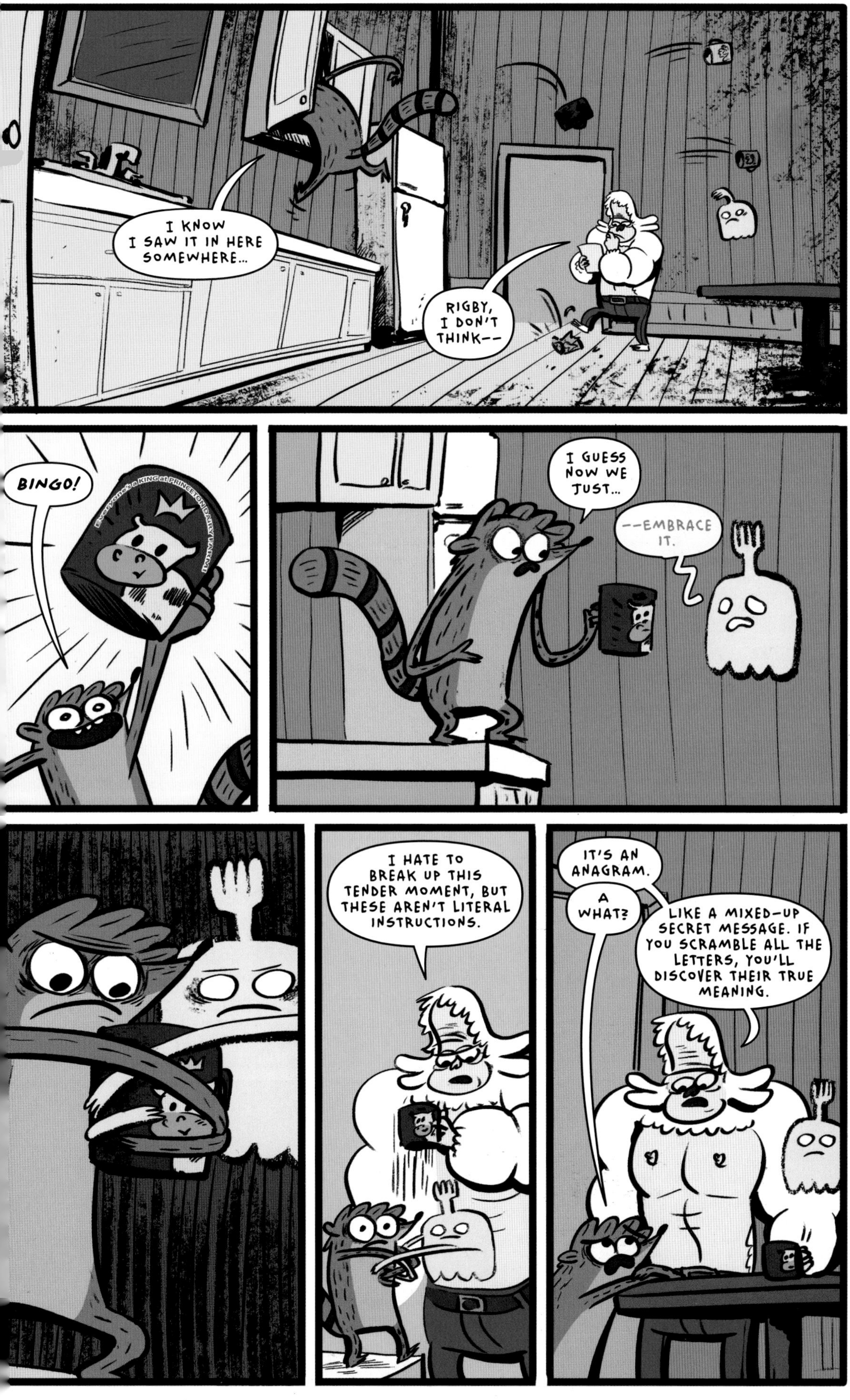
I KNOW I SAW IT IN HERE SOMEWHERE...
RIGBY, I DON'T THINK--
BINGO!
Everyone's a KING at PRINCETON DAIRY FARM!
I GUESS NOW WE JUST...
--EMBRACE IT.
I HATE TO BREAK UP THIS TENDER MOMENT, BUT THESE AREN'T LITERAL INSTRUCTIONS.
IT'S AN ANAGRAM.
A WHAT?
LIKE A MIXED-UP SECRET MESSAGE. IF YOU SCRAMBLE ALL THE LETTERS, YOU'LL DISCOVER THEIR TRUE MEANING.

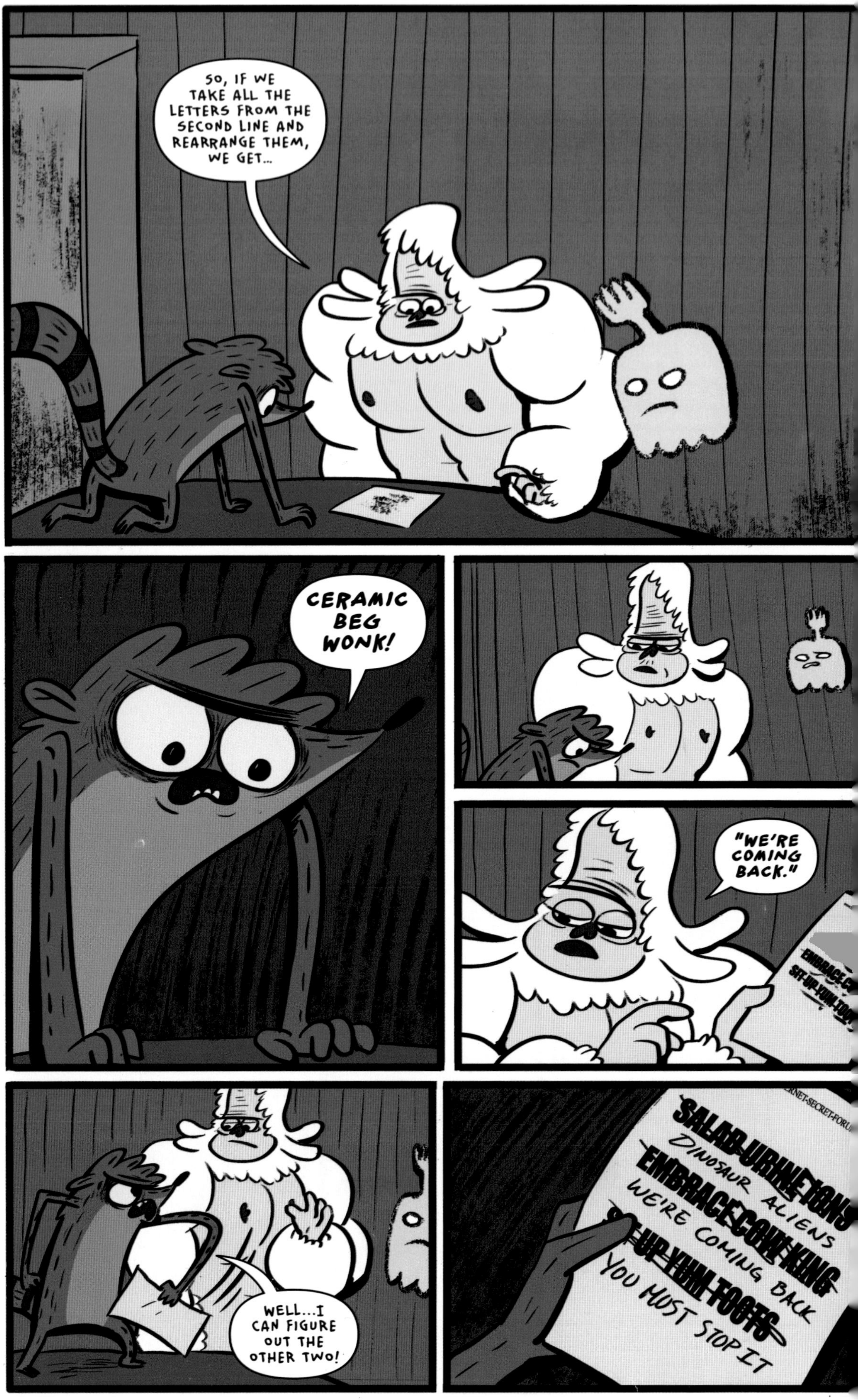
SO, IF WE TAKE ALL THE LETTERS FROM THE SECOND LINE AND REARRANGE THEM, WE GET...
CERAMIC BEG WONK!
"WE'RE COMING BACK."
WELL...I CAN FIGURE OUT THE OTHER TWO!
EMBRACE-COW-KING
DINOSAUR ALIENS
WE'RE COMING BACK
YOU MUST STOP IT

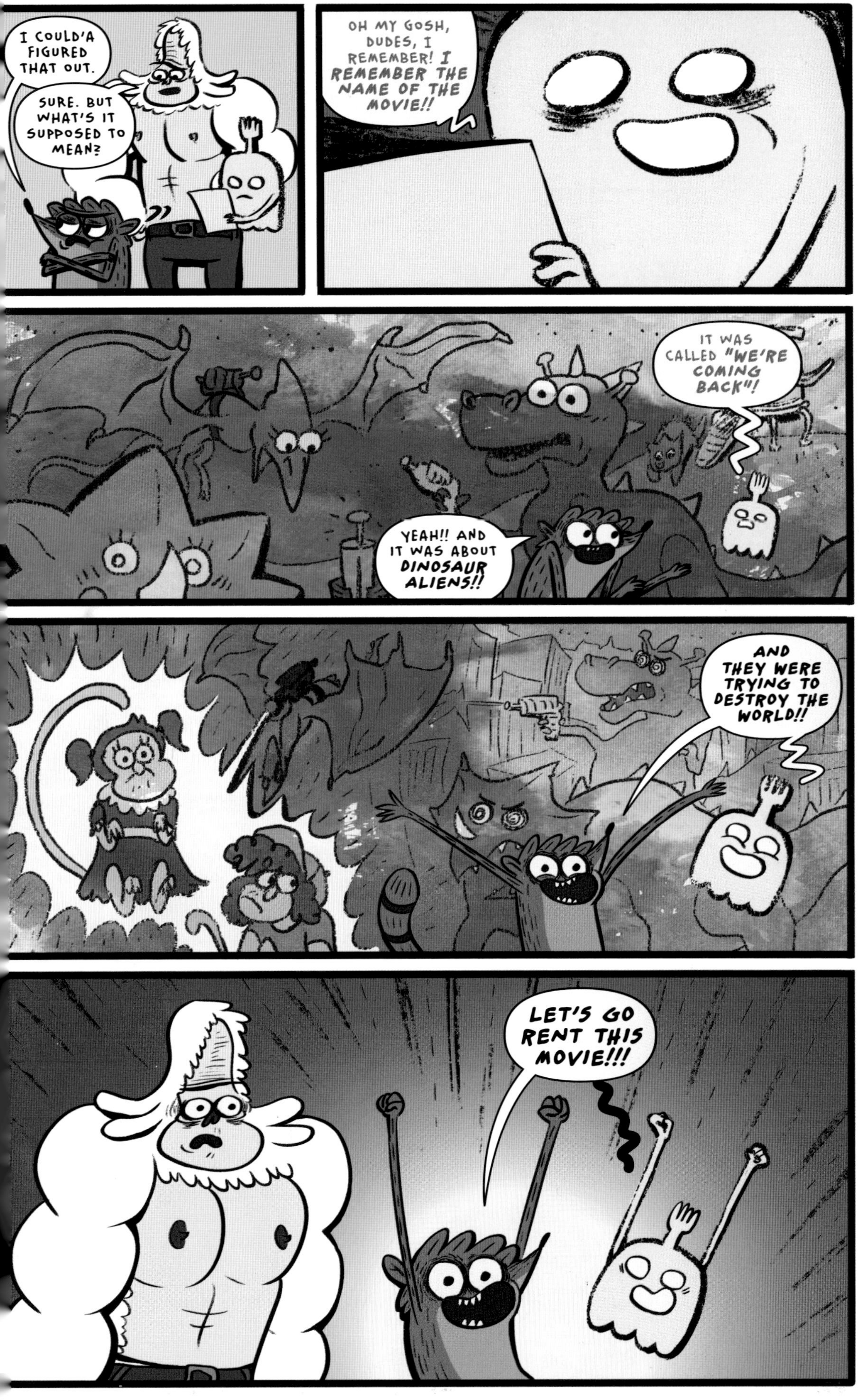
I COULD'A FIGURED THAT OUT.
SURE. BUT WHAT'S IT SUPPOSED TO MEAN?
OH MY GOSH, DUDES, I REMEMBER! I REMEMBER THE NAME OF THE MOVIE!!
IT WAS CALLED "WE'RE COMING BACK"!
YEAH!! AND IT WAS ABOUT DINOSAUR ALIENS!!
AND THEY WERE TRYING TO DESTROY THE WORLD!!
LET'S GO RENT THIS MOVIE!!!

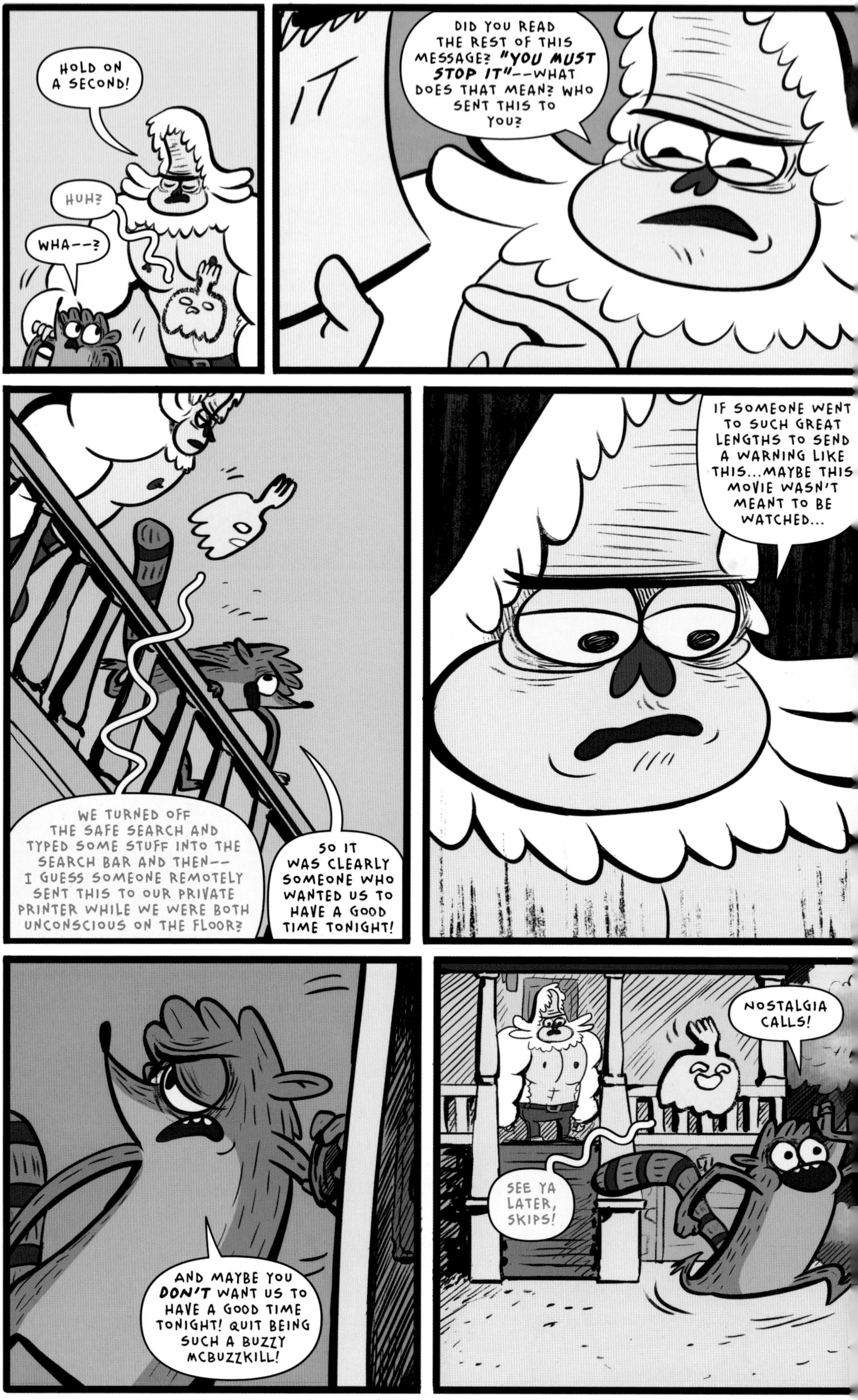
HOLD ON A SECOND!
HUH?
WHA--?
DID YOU READ THE REST OF THIS MESSAGE? "YOU MUST STOP IT"--WHAT DOES THAT MEAN? WHO SENT THIS TO YOU?
WE TURNED OFF THE SAFE SEARCH AND TYPED SOME STUFF INTO THE SEARCH BAR AND THEN-- I GUESS SOMEONE REMOTELY SENT THIS TO OUR PRIVATE PRINTER WHILE WE WERE BOTH UNCONSCIOUS ON THE FLOOR?
SO IT WAS CLEARLY SOMEONE WHO WANTED US TO HAVE A GOOD TIME TONIGHT!
IF SOMEONE WENT TO SUCH GREAT LENGTHS TO SEND A WARNING LIKE THIS...MAYBE THIS MOVIE WASN'T MEANT TO BE WATCHED...
AND MAYBE YOU DON'T WANT US TO HAVE A GOOD TIME TONIGHT! QUIT BEING SUCH A BUZZY MCBUZZKILL!
NOSTALGIA CALLS!
SEE YA LATER, SKIPS!

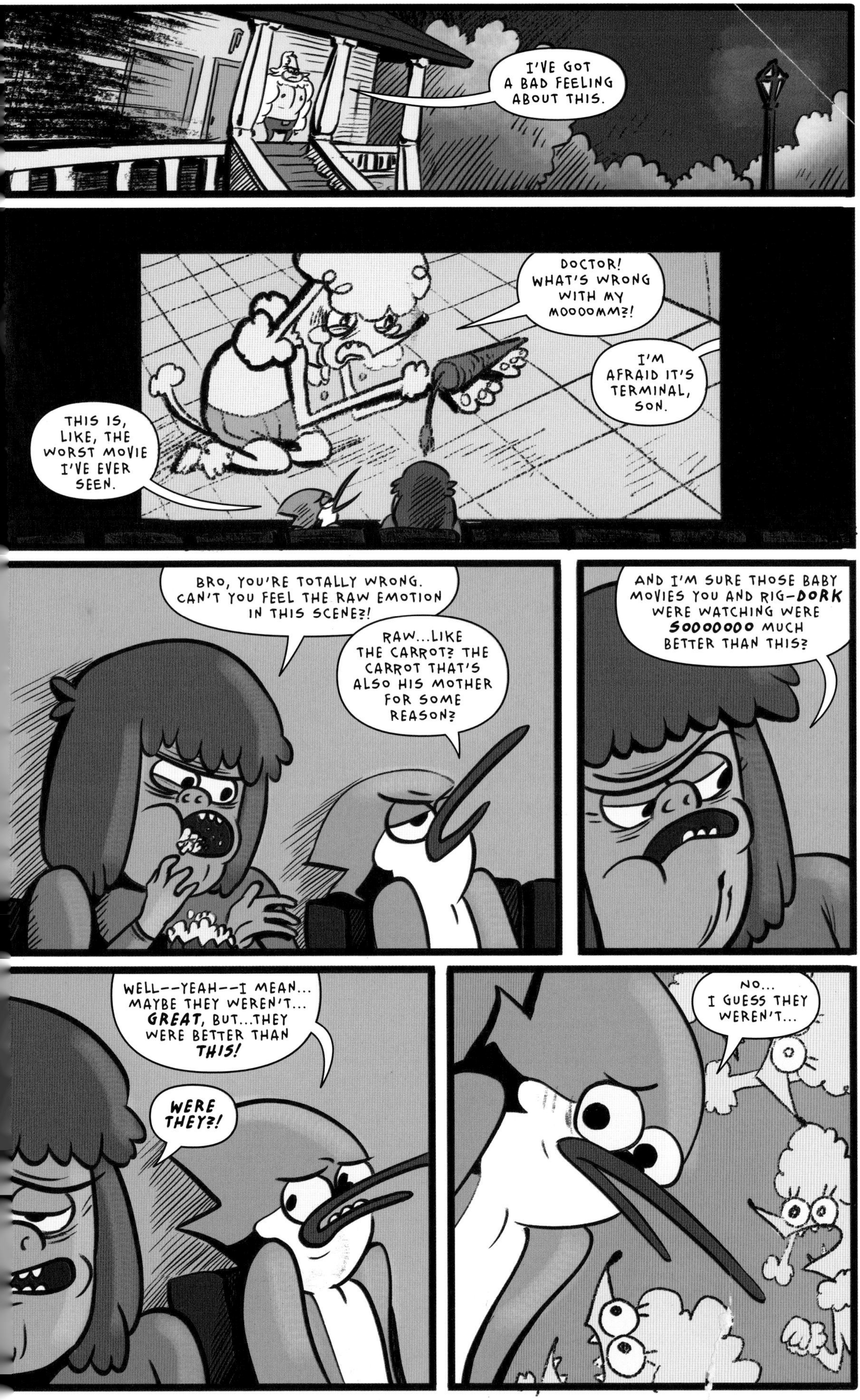

I'VE GOT A BAD FEELING ABOUT THIS.
DOCTOR! WHAT'S WRONG WITH MY MOOOOMM?!
I'M AFRAID IT'S TERMINAL, SON.
THIS IS, LIKE, THE WORST MOVIE I'VE EVER SEEN.
BRO, YOU'RE TOTALLY WRONG. CAN'T YOU FEEL THE RAW EMOTION IN THIS SCENE?!
RAW...LIKE THE CARROT? THE CARROT THAT'S ALSO HIS MOTHER FOR SOME REASON?
AND I'M SURE THOSE BABY MOVIES YOU AND RIG-DORK WERE WATCHING WERE SOOOOOOO MUCH BETTER THAN THIS?
WELL--YEAH--I MEAN... MAYBE THEY WEREN'T... GREAT, BUT...THEY WERE BETTER THAN THIS!
WERE THEY?!
NO... I GUESS THEY WEREN'T...

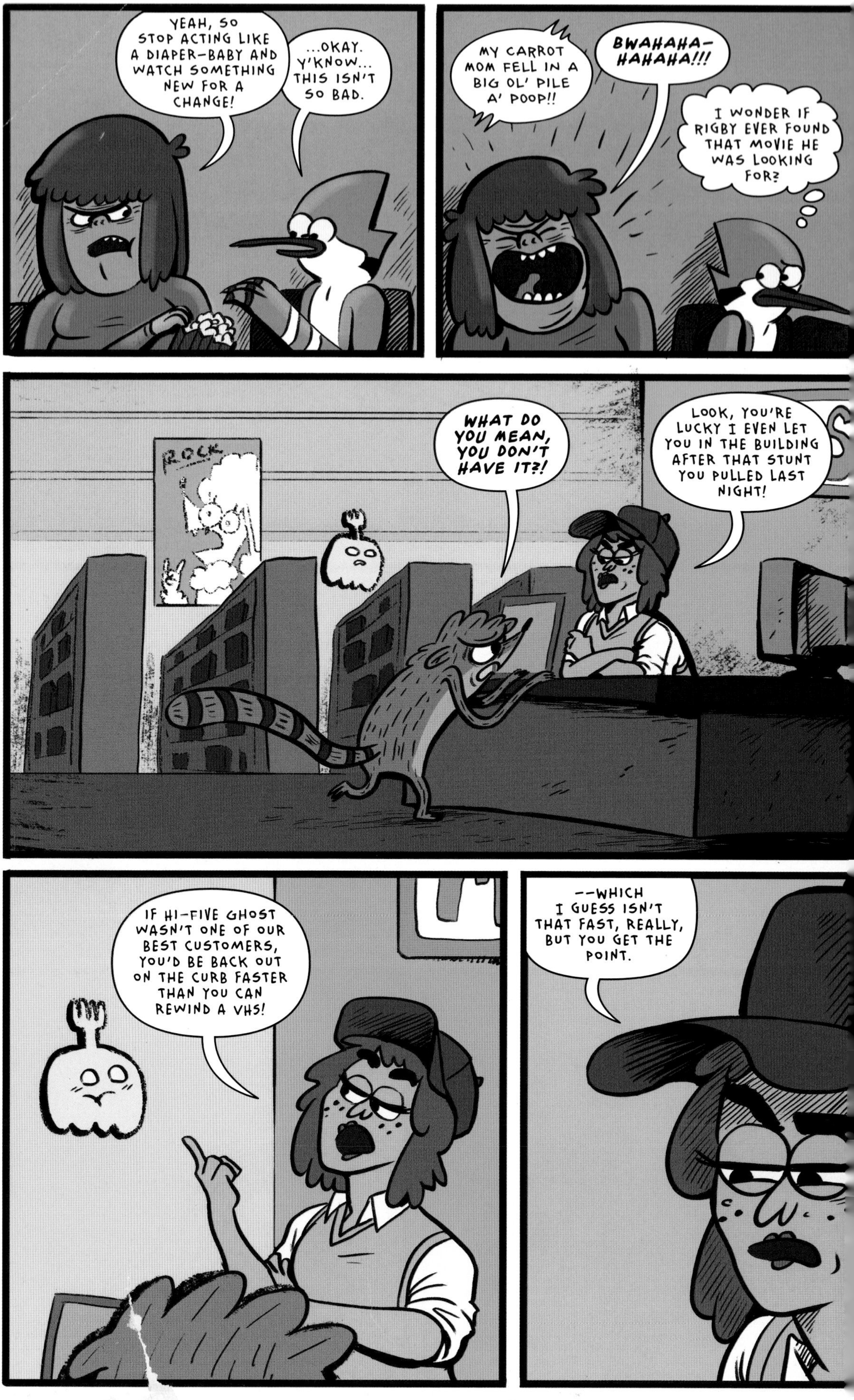
YEAH, SO STOP ACTING LIKE A DIAPER-BABY AND WATCH SOMETHING NEW FOR A CHANGE!
...OKAY. Y'KNOW... THIS ISN'T SO BAD.
MY CARROT MOM FELL IN A BIG OL' PILE A' POOP!!
BWAHAHA-HAHAHA!!!
I WONDER IF RIGBY EVER FOUND THAT MOVIE HE WAS LOOKING FOR?
ROCK
WHAT DO YOU MEAN, YOU DON'T HAVE IT?!
LOOK, YOU'RE LUCKY I EVEN LET YOU IN THE BUILDING AFTER THAT STUNT YOU PULLED LAST NIGHT!
IF HI-FIVE GHOST WASN'T ONE OF OUR BEST CUSTOMERS, YOU'D BE BACK OUT ON THE CURB FASTER THAN YOU CAN REWIND A VHS!
--WHICH I GUESS ISN'T THAT FAST, REALLY, BUT YOU GET THE POINT.

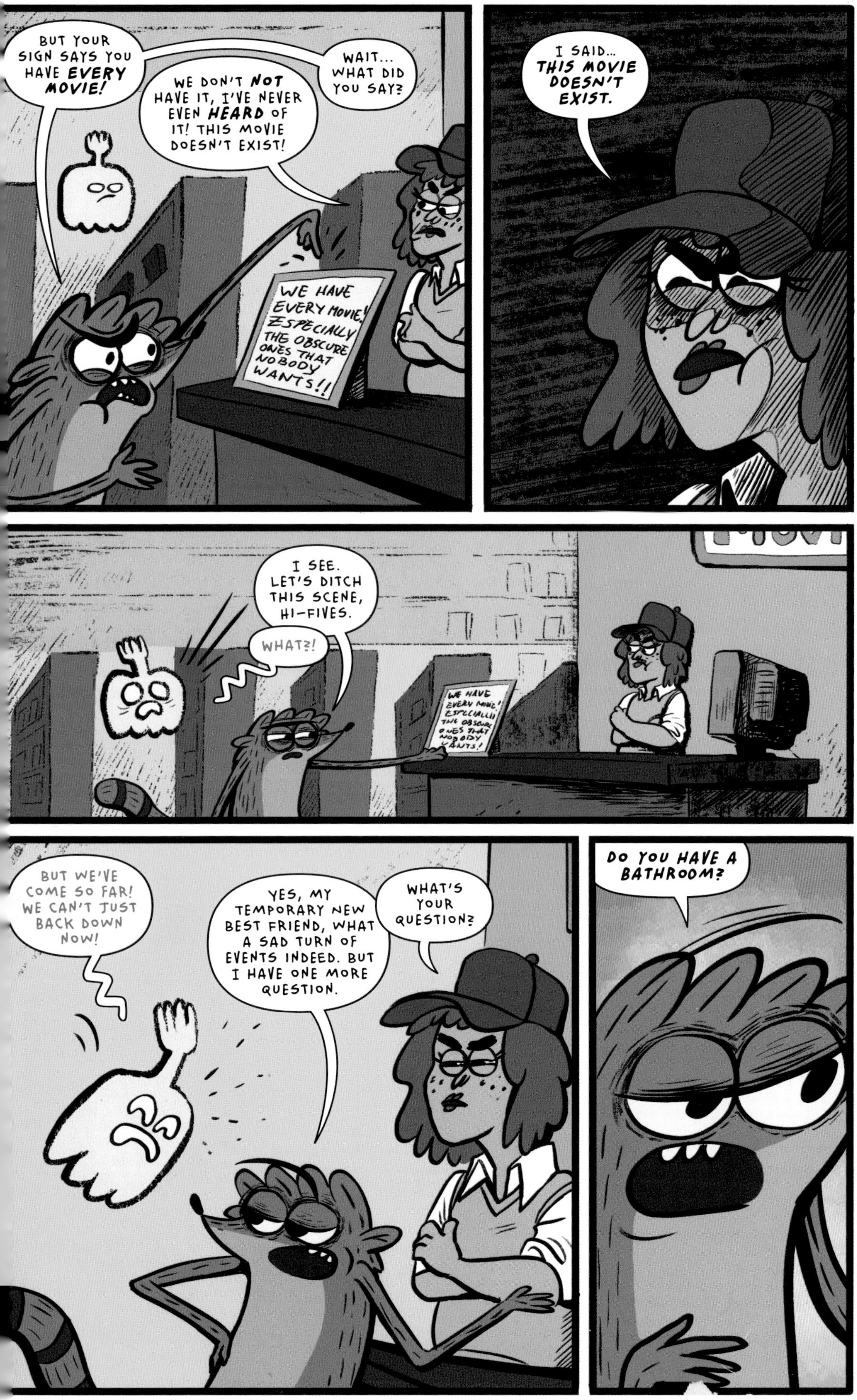

BUT YOUR SIGN SAYS YOU HAVE **EVERY MOVIE!**
WAIT... WHAT DID YOU SAY?
WE DON'T **NOT** HAVE IT, I'VE NEVER EVEN **HEARD** OF IT! THIS MOVIE DOESN'T EXIST!
WE HAVE EVERY MOVIE! ESPECIALLY THE OBSCURE ONES THAT NOBODY WANTS!!
I SAID... **THIS MOVIE DOESN'T EXIST.**
I SEE. LET'S DITCH THIS SCENE, HI-FIVES.
WHAT?!
BUT WE'VE COME SO FAR! WE CAN'T JUST BACK DOWN NOW!
YES, MY TEMPORARY NEW BEST FRIEND, WHAT A SAD TURN OF EVENTS INDEED. BUT I HAVE ONE MORE QUESTION.
WHAT'S YOUR QUESTION?
DO YOU HAVE A BATHROOM?

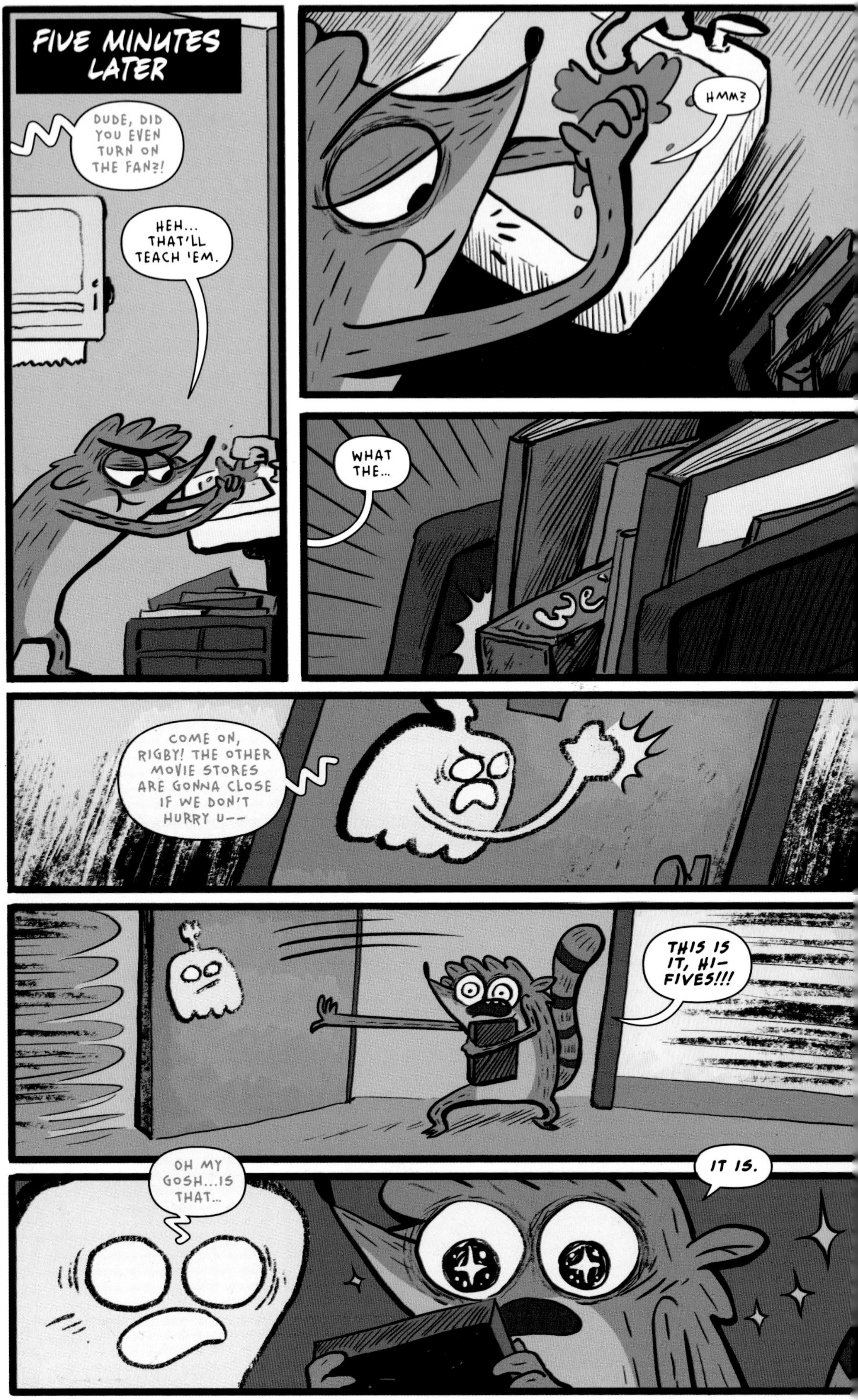
FIVE MINUTES LATER
DUDE, DID YOU EVEN TURN ON THE FAN?!
HEH... THAT'LL TEACH 'EM.
HMM?
WHAT THE...
COME ON, RIGBY! THE OTHER MOVIE STORES ARE GONNA CLOSE IF WE DON'T HURRY U--
THIS IS IT, HI-FIVES!!!
OH MY GOSH...IS THAT...
IT IS.

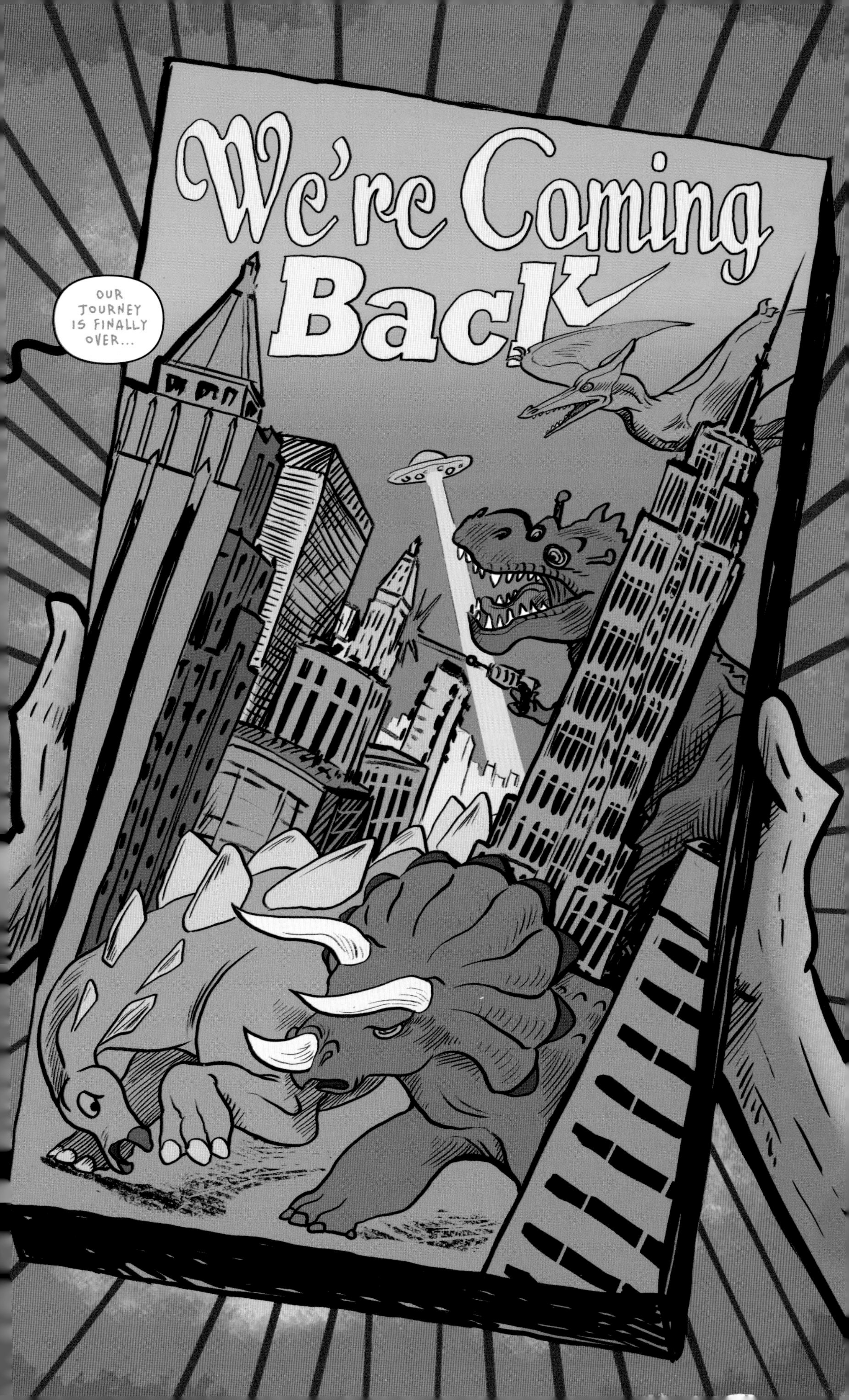
We're Coming Back
OUR JOURNEY IS FINALLY OVER...

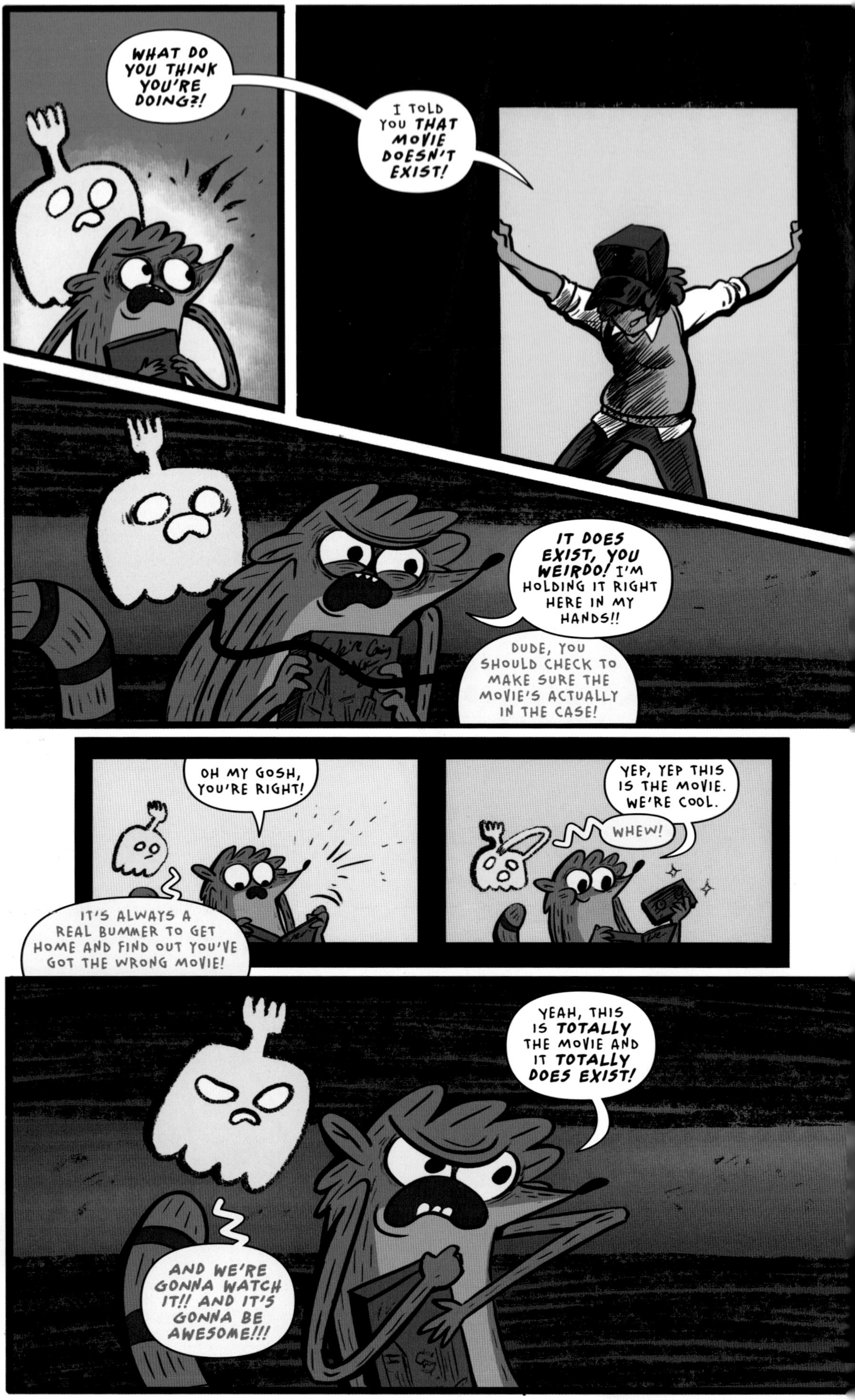
WHAT DO YOU THINK YOU'RE DOING?!
I TOLD YOU THAT MOVIE DOESN'T EXIST!
IT DOES EXIST, YOU WEIRDO! I'M HOLDING IT RIGHT HERE IN MY HANDS!!
DUDE, YOU SHOULD CHECK TO MAKE SURE THE MOVIE'S ACTUALLY IN THE CASE!
OH MY GOSH, YOU'RE RIGHT!
IT'S ALWAYS A REAL BUMMER TO GET HOME AND FIND OUT YOU'VE GOT THE WRONG MOVIE!
YEP, YEP THIS IS THE MOVIE. WE'RE COOL.
WHEW!
YEAH, THIS IS TOTALLY THE MOVIE AND IT TOTALLY DOES EXIST!
AND WE'RE GONNA WATCH IT!! AND IT'S GONNA BE AWESOME!!!

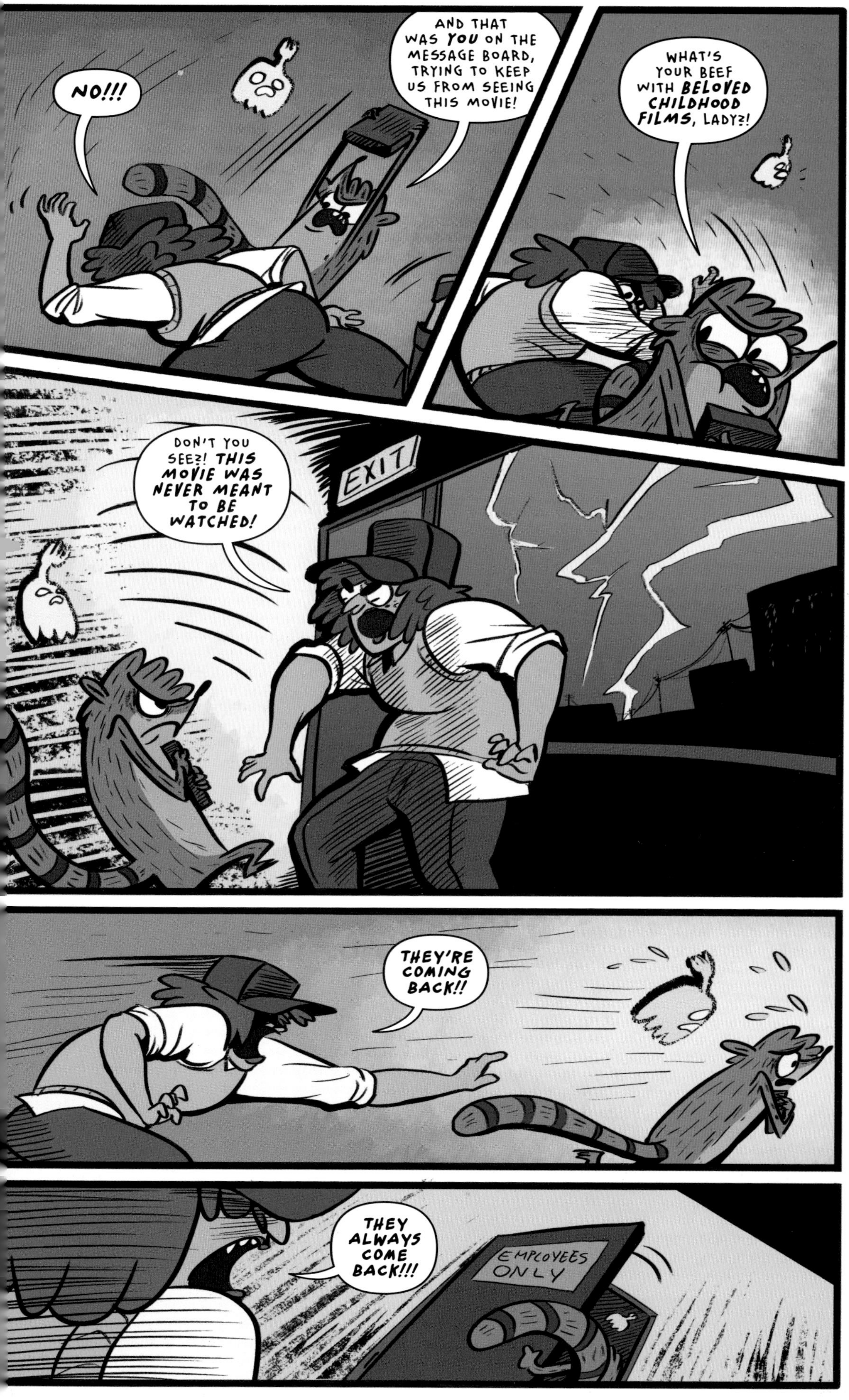
NO!!!
AND THAT WAS YOU ON THE MESSAGE BOARD, TRYING TO KEEP US FROM SEEING THIS MOVIE!
WHAT'S YOUR BEEF WITH BELOVED CHILDHOOD FILMS, LADY?!
DON'T YOU SEE?! THIS MOVIE WAS NEVER MEANT TO BE WATCHED!
EXIT
THEY'RE COMING BACK!!
THEY ALWAYS COME BACK!!!
EMPLOYEES ONLY

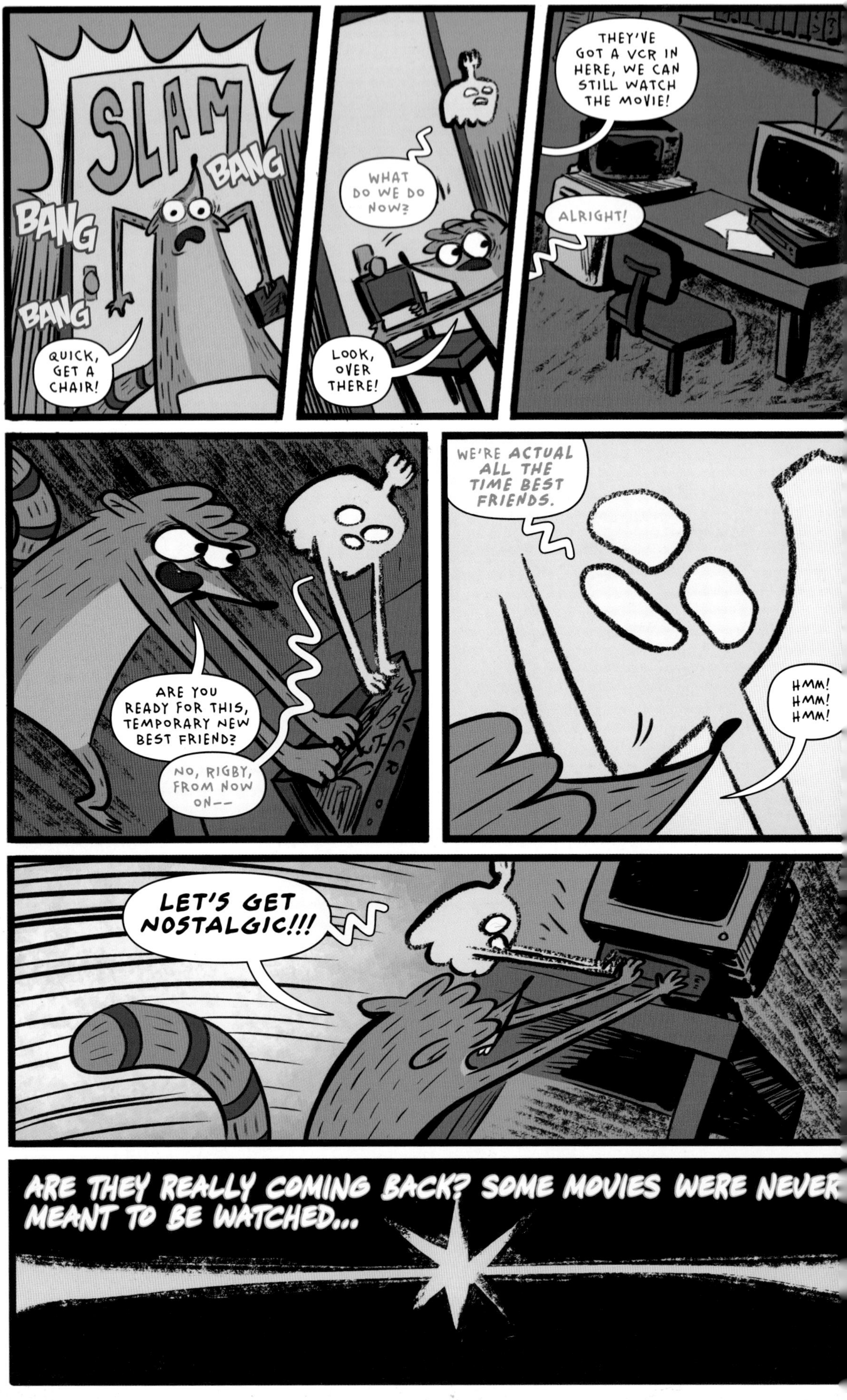
SLAM
BANG
BANG
BANG
QUICK, GET A CHAIR!
WHAT DO WE DO NOW?
LOOK, OVER THERE!
THEY'VE GOT A VCR IN HERE, WE CAN STILL WATCH THE MOVIE!
ALRIGHT!
ARE YOU READY FOR THIS, TEMPORARY NEW BEST FRIEND?
NO, RIGBY, FROM NOW ON--
WE'RE ACTUAL ALL THE TIME BEST FRIENDS.
HMM! HMM! HMM!
LET'S GET NOSTALGIC!!!
ARE THEY REALLY COMING BACK? SOME MOVIES WERE NEVER MEANT TO BE WATCHED...

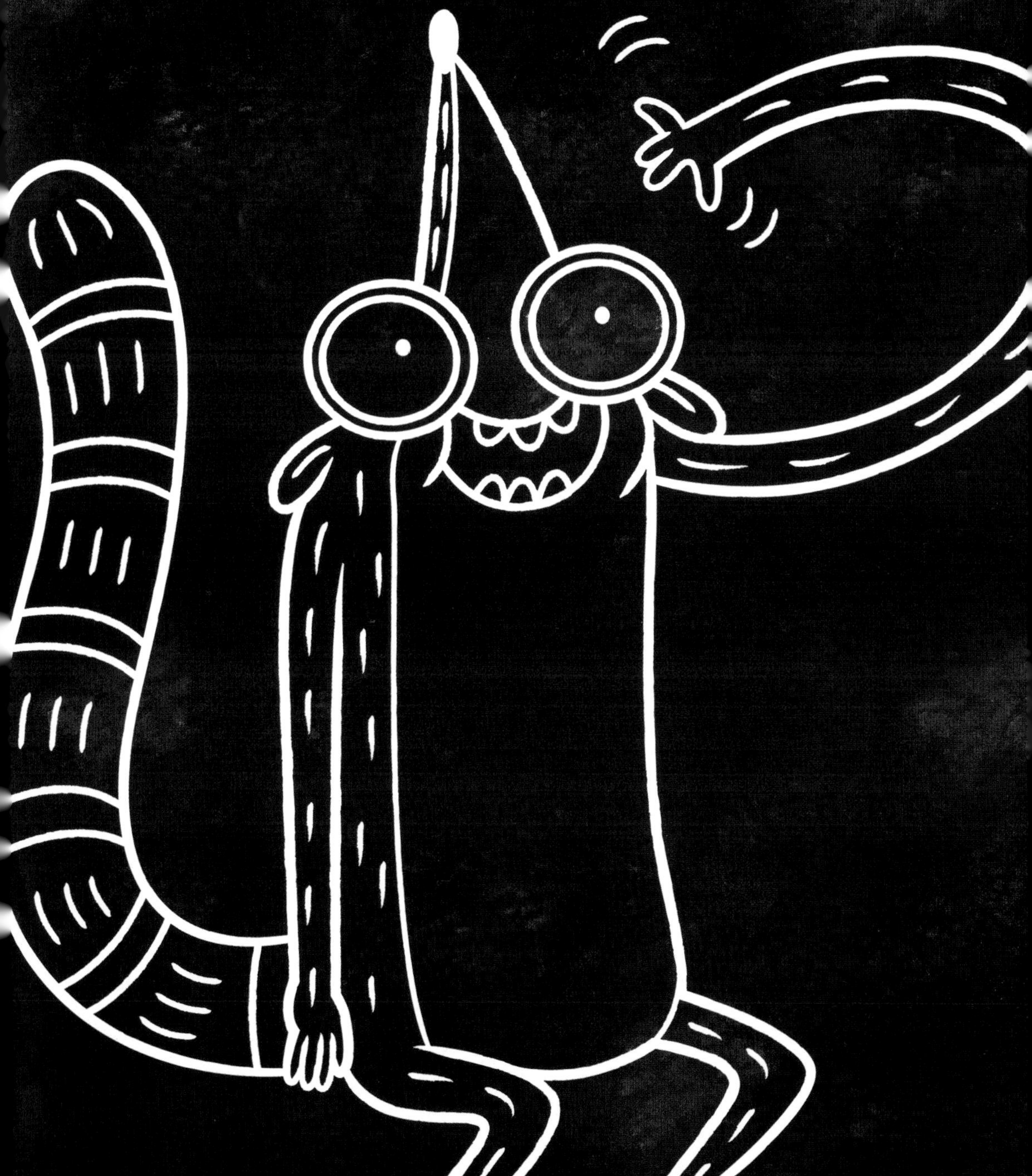

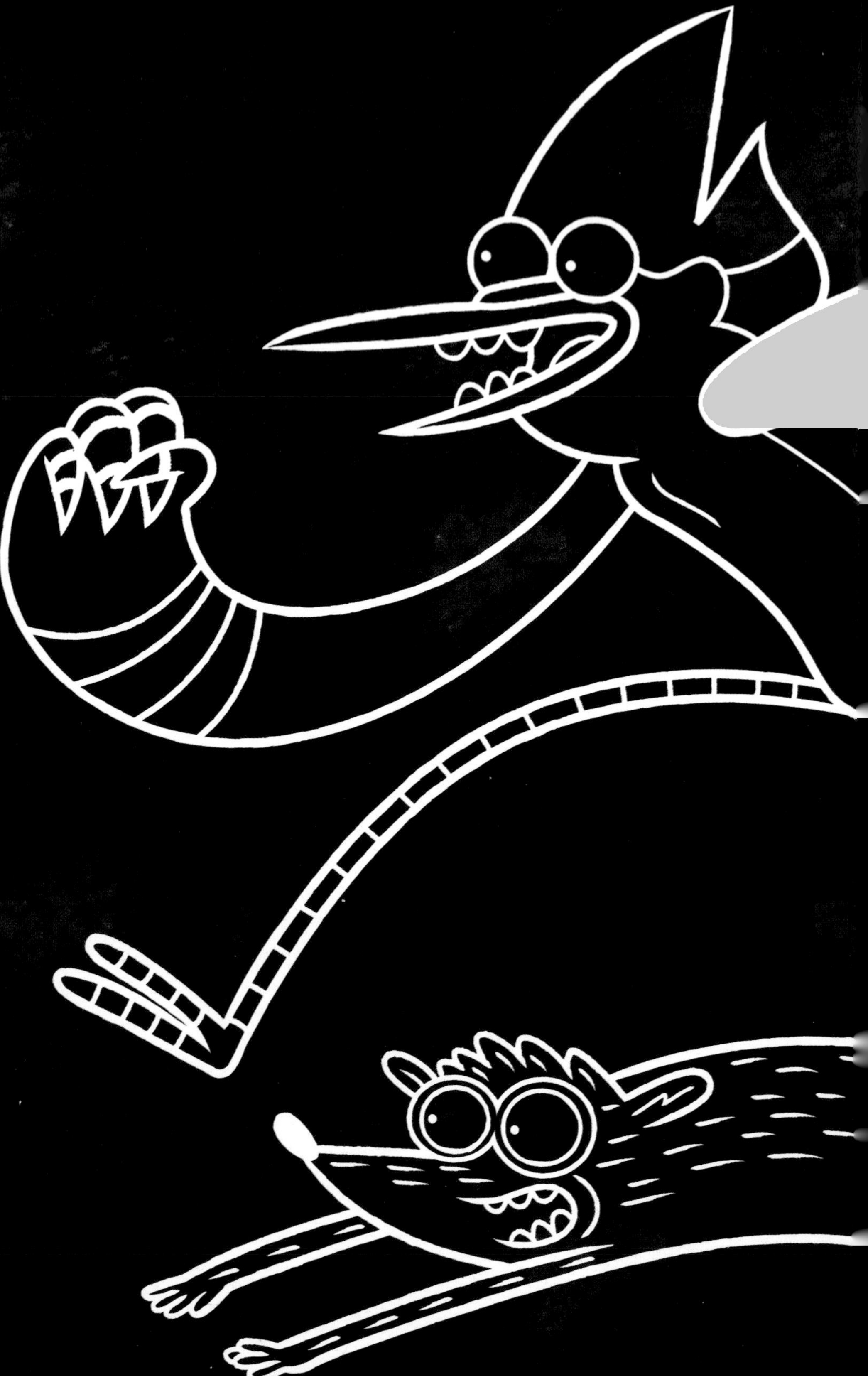

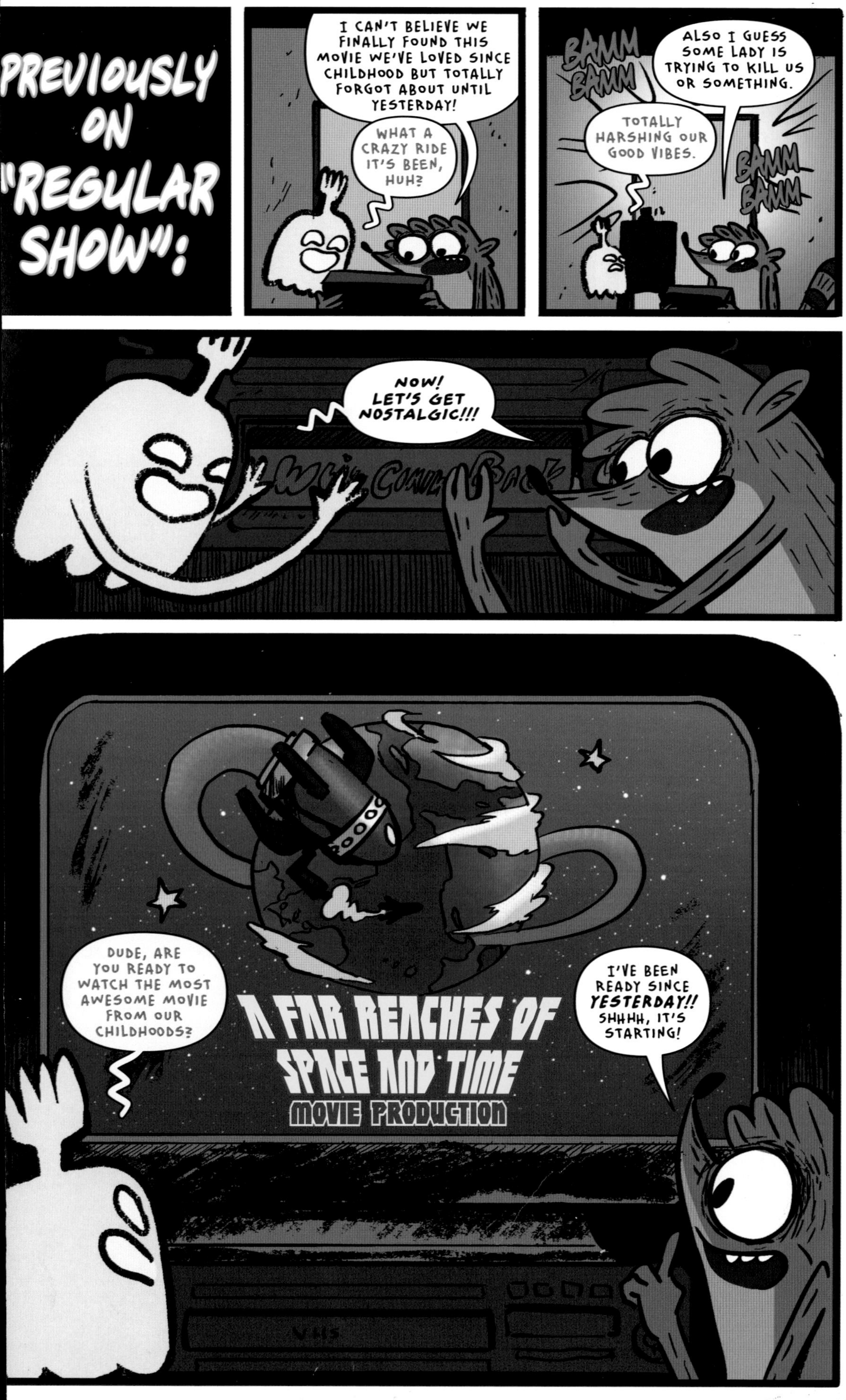
PREVIOUSLY ON "REGULAR SHOW":
I CAN'T BELIEVE WE FINALLY FOUND THIS MOVIE WE'VE LOVED SINCE CHILDHOOD BUT TOTALLY FORGOT ABOUT UNTIL YESTERDAY!
WHAT A CRAZY RIDE IT'S BEEN, HUH?
BAMM BAMM
ALSO I GUESS SOME LADY IS TRYING TO KILL US OR SOMETHING.
TOTALLY HARSHING OUR GOOD VIBES.
BAMM BAMM
NOW! LET'S GET NOSTALGIC!!!
DUDE, ARE YOU READY TO WATCH THE MOST AWESOME MOVIE FROM OUR CHILDHOODS?
A FAR REACHES OF SPACE AND TIME
MOVIE PRODUCTION
I'VE BEEN READY SINCE YESTERDAY!! SHHHH, IT'S STARTING!
VHS

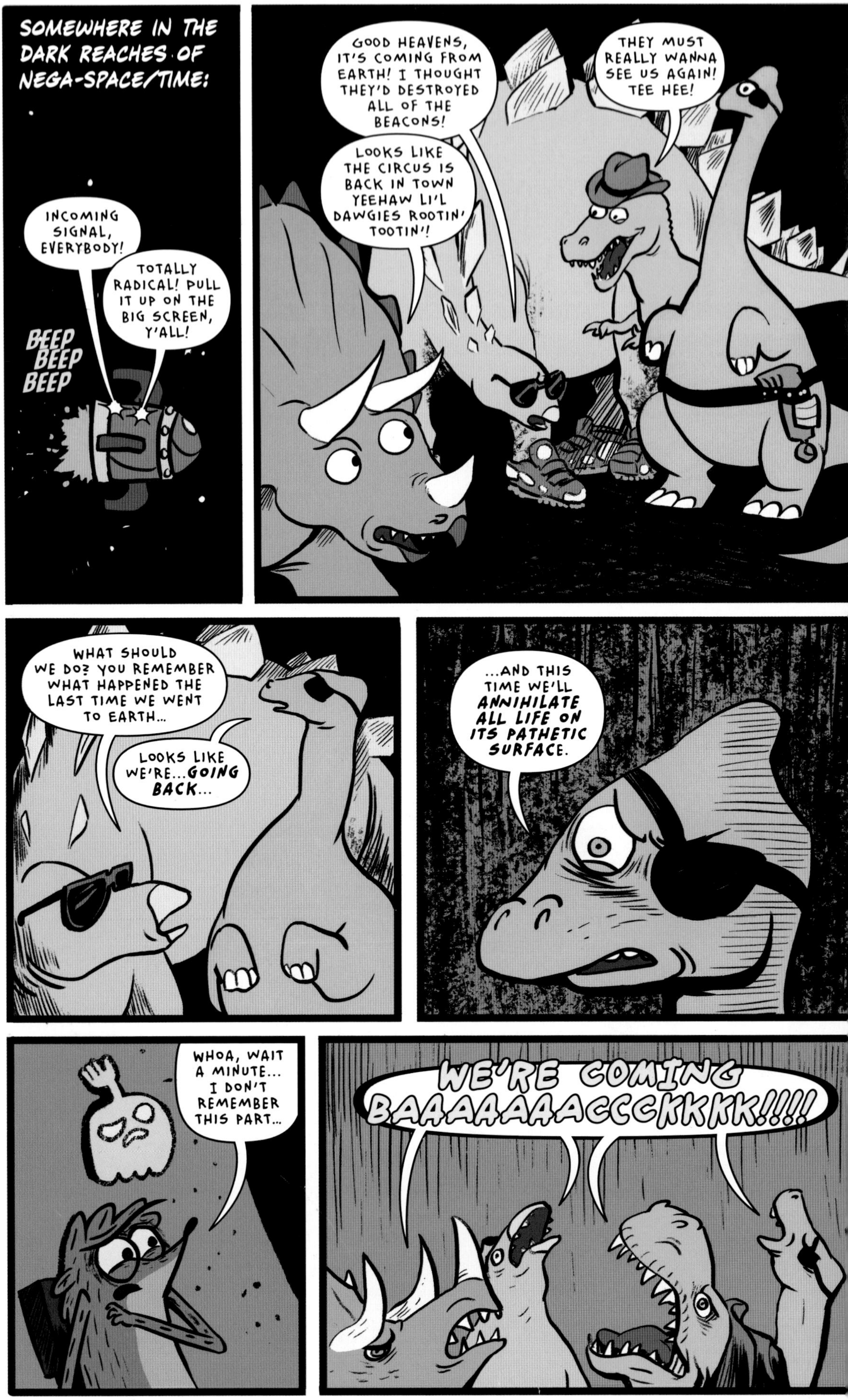
SOMEWHERE IN THE DARK REACHES OF NEGA-SPACE/TIME:
INCOMING SIGNAL, EVERYBODY!
TOTALLY RADICAL! PULL IT UP ON THE BIG SCREEN, Y'ALL!
BEEP BEEP BEEP
GOOD HEAVENS, IT'S COMING FROM EARTH! I THOUGHT THEY'D DESTROYED ALL OF THE BEACONS!
THEY MUST REALLY WANNA SEE US AGAIN! TEE HEE!
LOOKS LIKE THE CIRCUS IS BACK IN TOWN YEEHAW LI'L DAWGIES ROOTIN' TOOTIN'!
WHAT SHOULD WE DO? YOU REMEMBER WHAT HAPPENED THE LAST TIME WE WENT TO EARTH...
LOOKS LIKE WE'RE...GOING BACK...
...AND THIS TIME WE'LL ANNIHILATE ALL LIFE ON ITS PATHETIC SURFACE.
WHOA, WAIT A MINUTE... I DON'T REMEMBER THIS PART...
WE'RE COMING BAAAAAAACCCKKKK!!!!

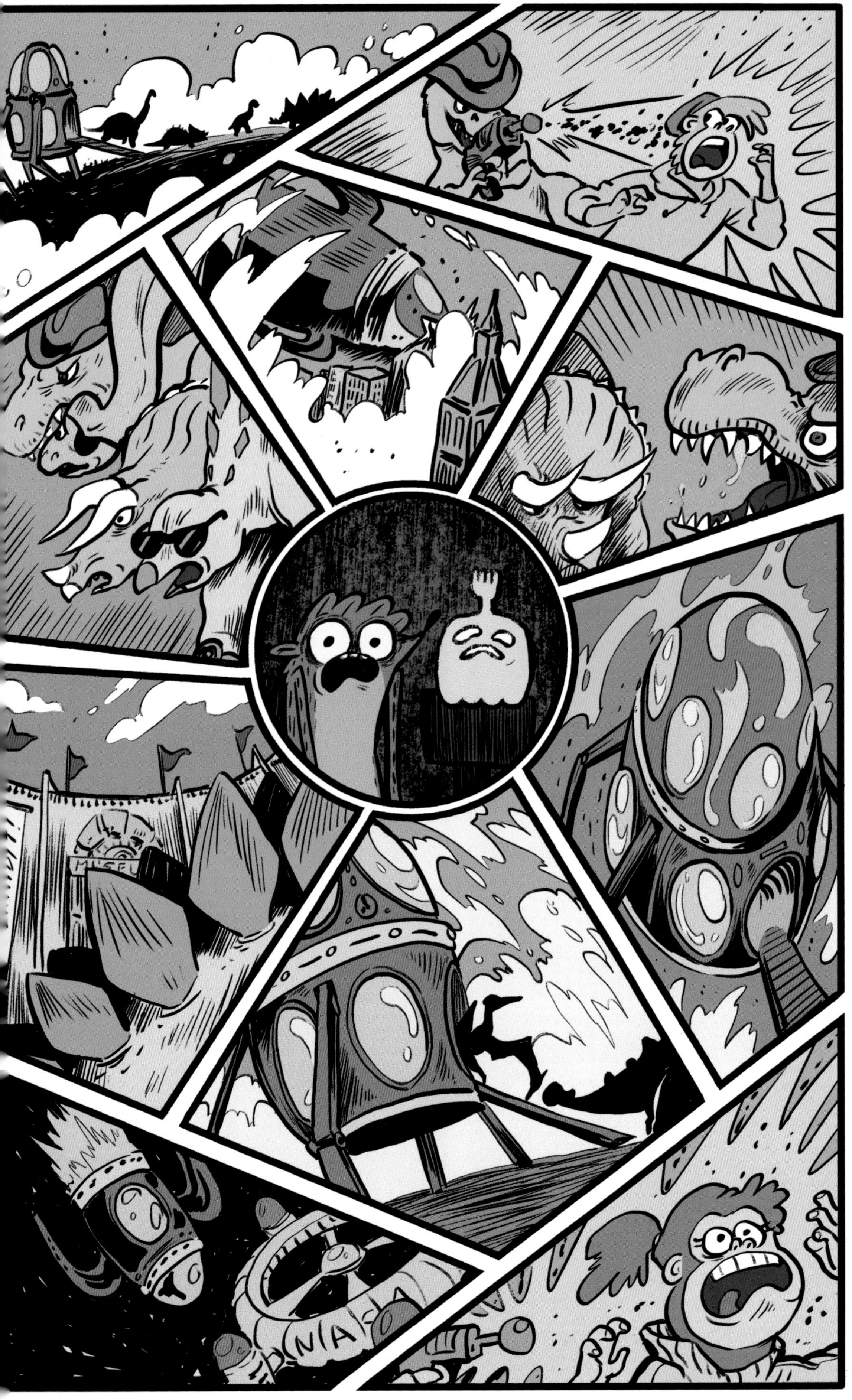

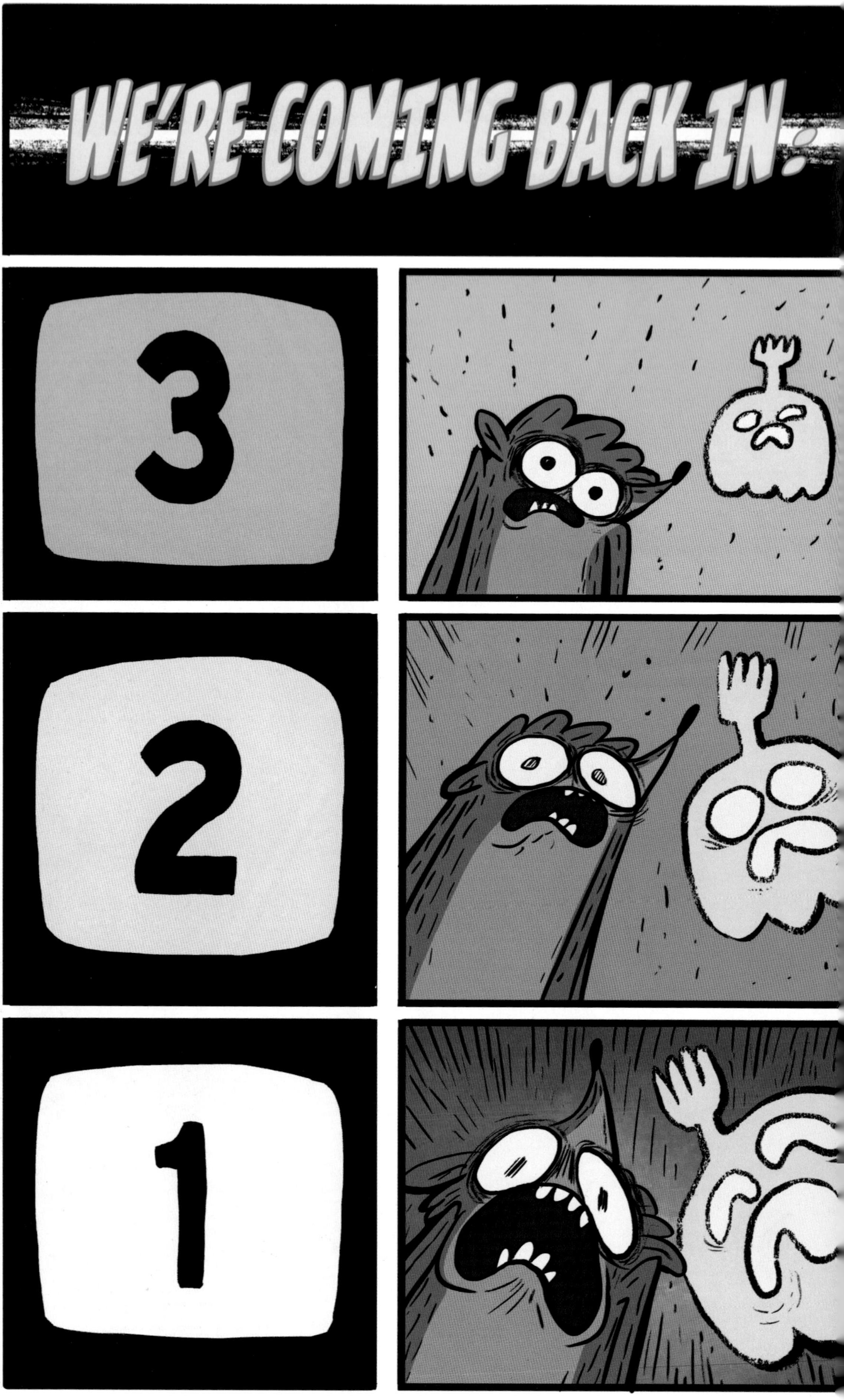
WE'RE COMING BACK IN:
3
2
1

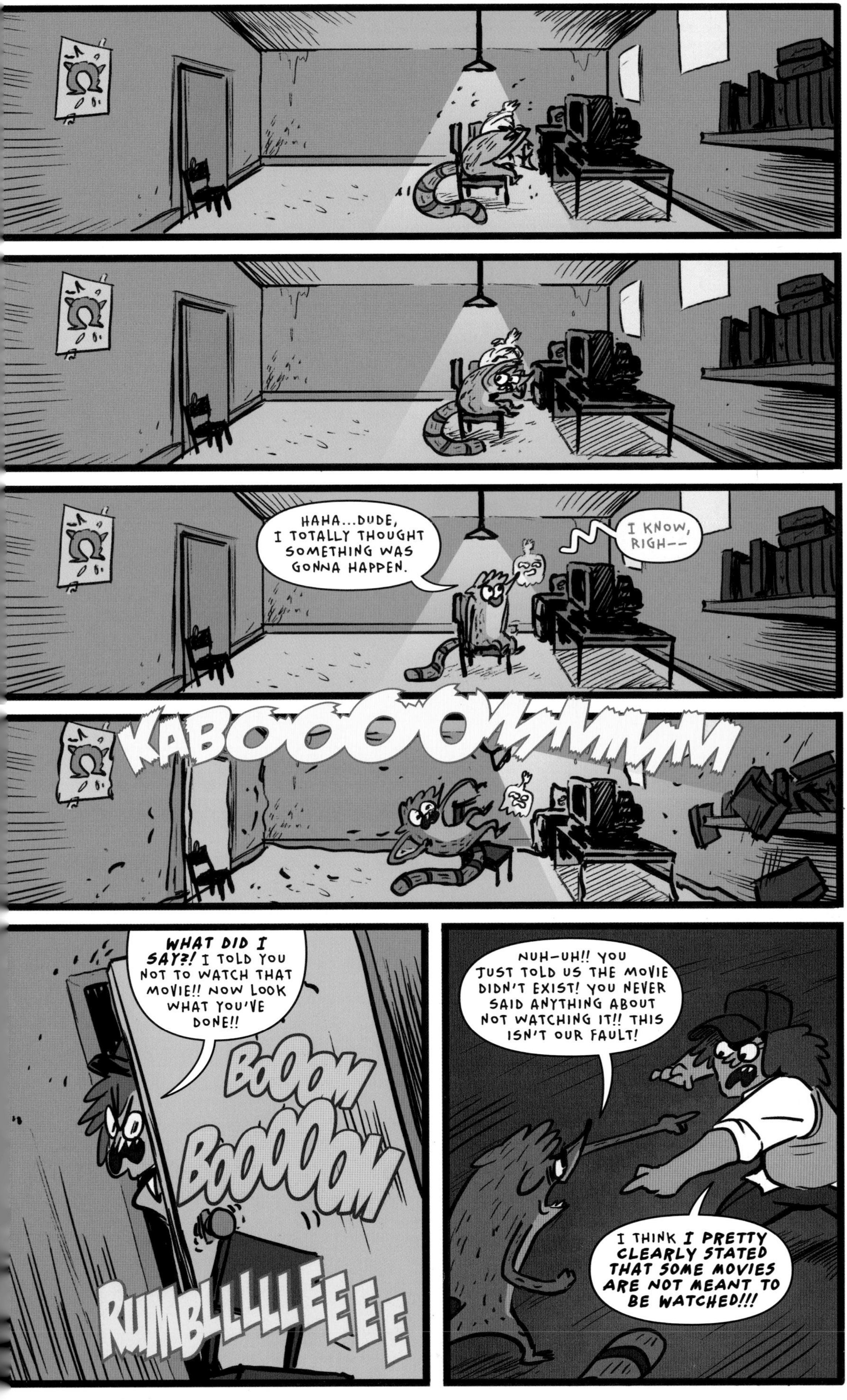
HAHA...DUDE, I TOTALLY THOUGHT SOMETHING WAS GONNA HAPPEN.
I KNOW, RIGH--
KABOOOOOMMMM
WHAT DID I SAY?! I TOLD YOU NOT TO WATCH THAT MOVIE!! NOW LOOK WHAT YOU'VE DONE!!
BOOOM
BOOOOOM
RUMBLLLLLEEEE
NUH-UH!! YOU JUST TOLD US THE MOVIE DIDN'T EXIST! YOU NEVER SAID ANYTHING ABOUT NOT WATCHING IT!! THIS ISN'T OUR FAULT!
I THINK I PRETTY CLEARLY STATED THAT SOME MOVIES ARE NOT MEANT TO BE WATCHED!!!

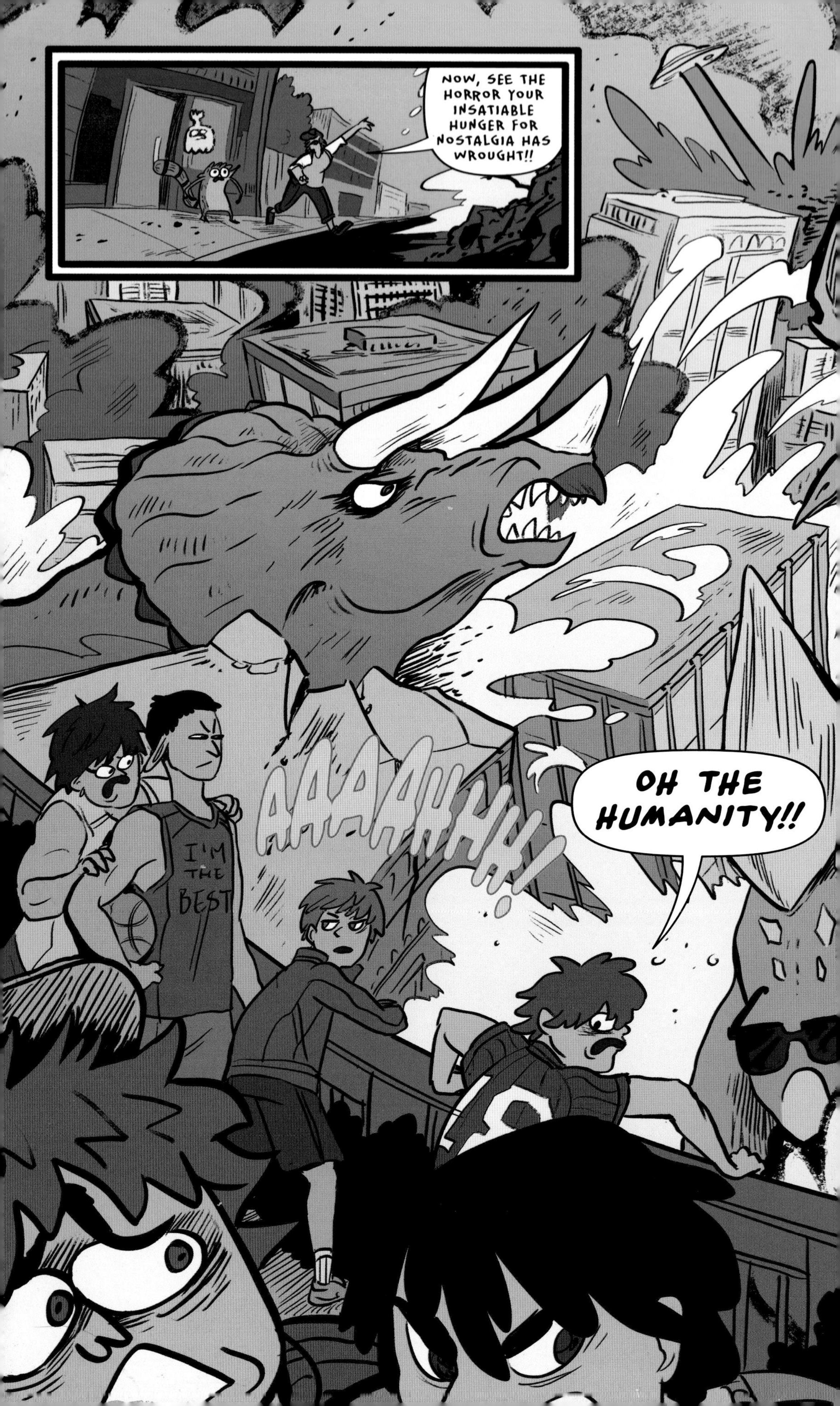
NOW, SEE THE HORROR YOUR INSATIABLE HUNGER FOR NOSTALGIA HAS WROUGHT!!
I'M THE BEST
AAAAHHH!
OH THE HUMANITY!!

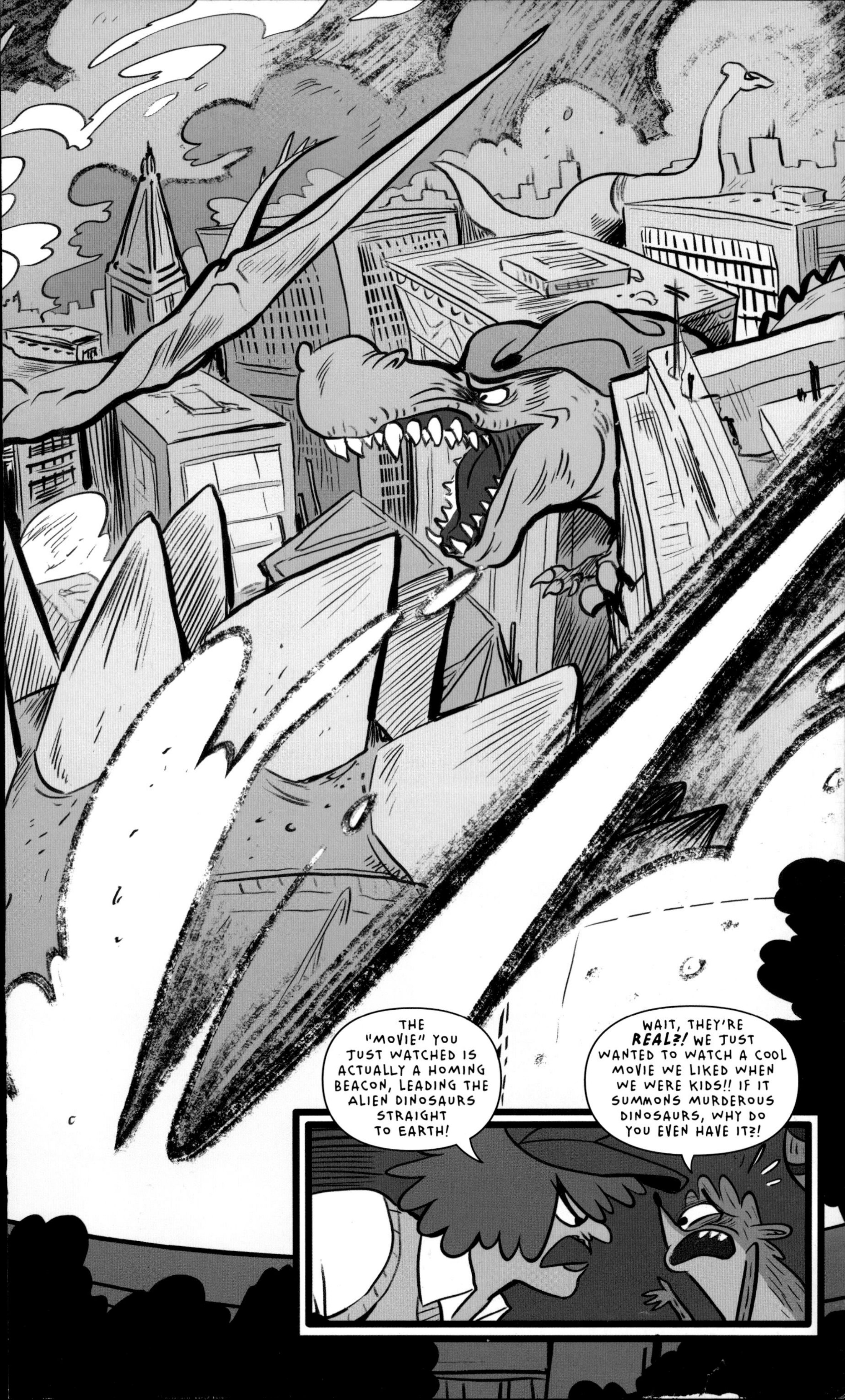
THE "MOVIE" YOU JUST WATCHED IS ACTUALLY A HOMING BEACON, LEADING THE ALIEN DINOSAURS STRAIGHT TO EARTH!
WAIT, THEY'RE REAL?! WE JUST WANTED TO WATCH A COOL MOVIE WE LIKED WHEN WE WERE KIDS!! IF IT SUMMONS MURDEROUS DINOSAURS, WHY DO YOU EVEN HAVE IT?!

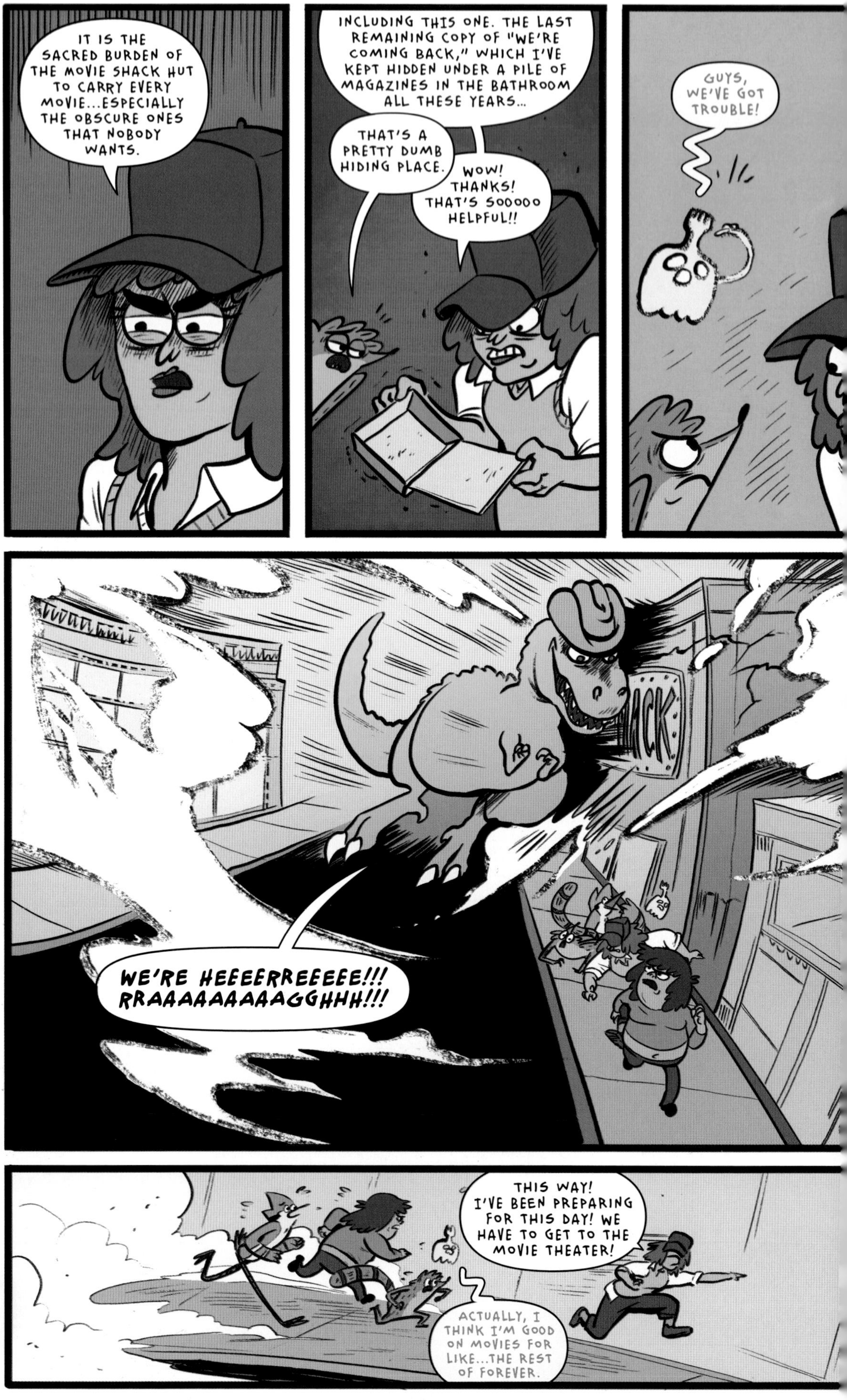
IT IS THE SACRED BURDEN OF THE MOVIE SHACK HUT TO CARRY EVERY MOVIE...ESPECIALLY THE OBSCURE ONES THAT NOBODY WANTS.
INCLUDING THIS ONE. THE LAST REMAINING COPY OF "WE'RE COMING BACK," WHICH I'VE KEPT HIDDEN UNDER A PILE OF MAGAZINES IN THE BATHROOM ALL THESE YEARS...
THAT'S A PRETTY DUMB HIDING PLACE.
WOW! THANKS! THAT'S SOOOOO HELPFUL!!
GUYS, WE'VE GOT TROUBLE!
ACK
WE'RE HEEEERREEEEE!!! RRAAAAAAAAAGGHHH!!!
THIS WAY! I'VE BEEN PREPARING FOR THIS DAY! WE HAVE TO GET TO THE MOVIE THEATER!
ACTUALLY, I THINK I'M GOOD ON MOVIES FOR LIKE...THE REST OF FOREVER.

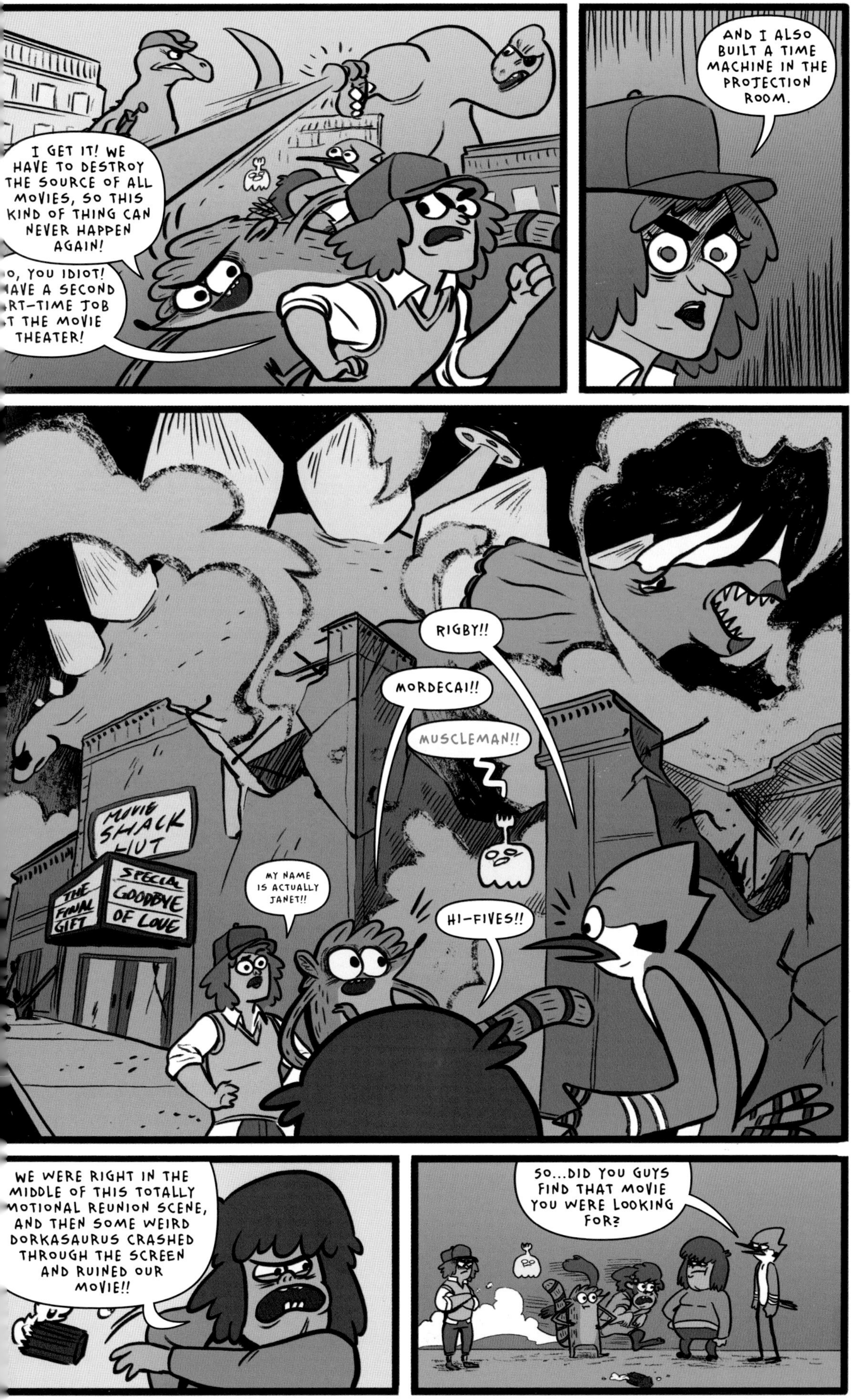
I GET IT! WE HAVE TO DESTROY THE SOURCE OF ALL MOVIES, SO THIS KIND OF THING CAN NEVER HAPPEN AGAIN!
o, YOU IDIOT! IAVE A SECOND RT-TIME JOB T THE MOVIE THEATER!
AND I ALSO BUILT A TIME MACHINE IN THE PROJECTION ROOM.
RIGBY!!
MORDECAI!!
MUSCLEMAN!!
MOVIE SHACK HUT
THE FINAL GIFT
SPECIAL GOODBYE OF LOVE
MY NAME IS ACTUALLY JANET!!
HI-FIVES!!
WE WERE RIGHT IN THE MIDDLE OF THIS TOTALLY MOTIONAL REUNION SCENE, AND THEN SOME WEIRD DORKASAURUS CRASHED THROUGH THE SCREEN AND RUINED OUR MOVIE!!
SO...DID YOU GUYS FIND THAT MOVIE YOU WERE LOOKING FOR?

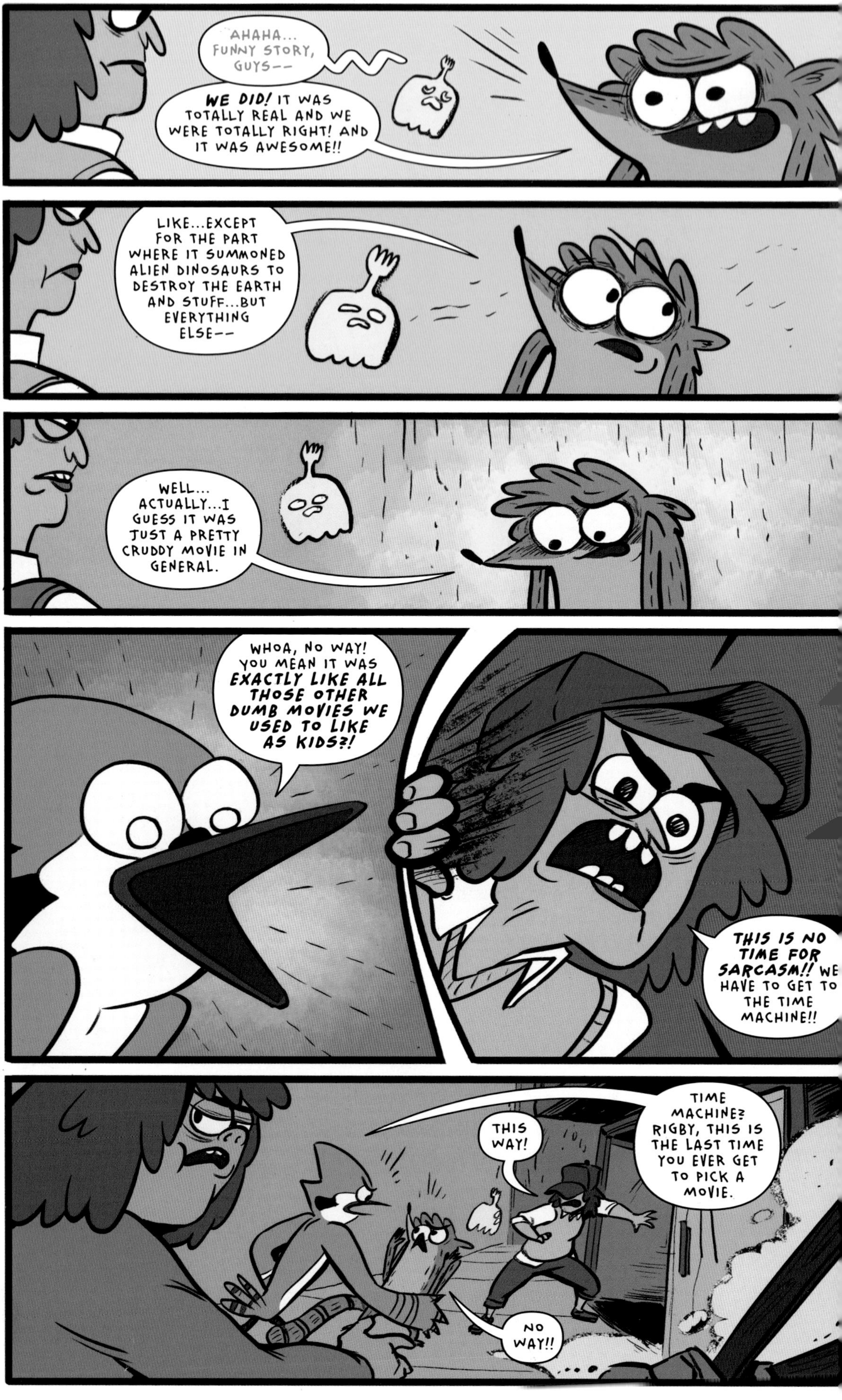
AHAHA... FUNNY STORY, GUYS--
WE DID! IT WAS TOTALLY REAL AND WE WERE TOTALLY RIGHT! AND IT WAS AWESOME!!
LIKE...EXCEPT FOR THE PART WHERE IT SUMMONED ALIEN DINOSAURS TO DESTROY THE EARTH AND STUFF...BUT EVERYTHING ELSE--
WELL... ACTUALLY...I GUESS IT WAS JUST A PRETTY CRUDDY MOVIE IN GENERAL.
WHOA, NO WAY! YOU MEAN IT WAS EXACTLY LIKE ALL THOSE OTHER DUMB MOVIES WE USED TO LIKE AS KIDS?!
THIS IS NO TIME FOR SARCASM!! WE HAVE TO GET TO THE TIME MACHINE!!
TIME MACHINE? RIGBY, THIS IS THE LAST TIME YOU EVER GET TO PICK A MOVIE.
THIS WAY!
NO WAY!!

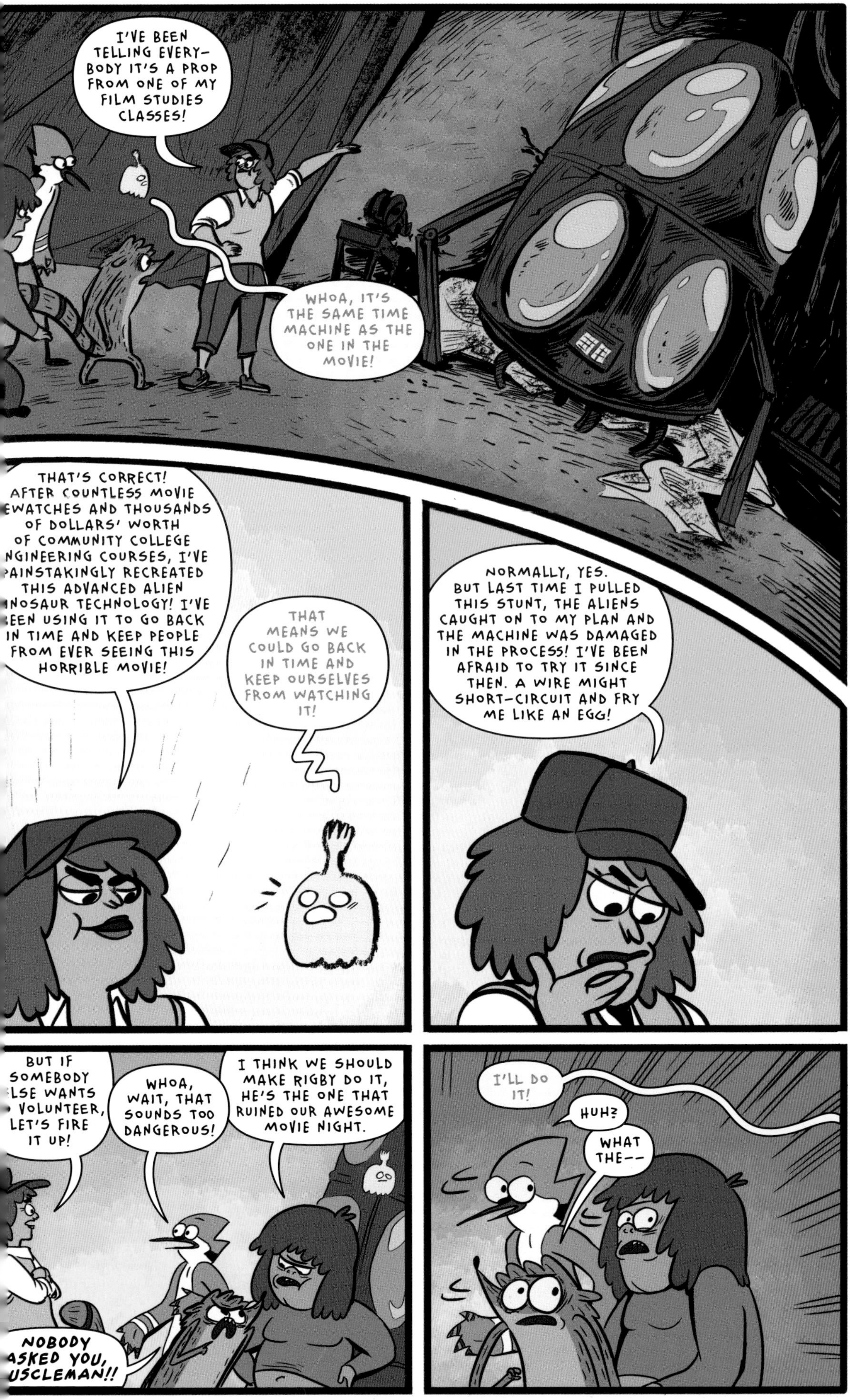
I'VE BEEN TELLING EVERYBODY IT'S A PROP FROM ONE OF MY FILM STUDIES CLASSES!
WHOA, IT'S THE SAME TIME MACHINE AS THE ONE IN THE MOVIE!
THAT'S CORRECT! AFTER COUNTLESS MOVIE EWATCHES AND THOUSANDS OF DOLLARS' WORTH OF COMMUNITY COLLEGE NGINEERING COURSES, I'VE AINSTAKINGLY RECREATED THIS ADVANCED ALIEN INOSAUR TECHNOLOGY! I'VE EEN USING IT TO GO BACK IN TIME AND KEEP PEOPLE FROM EVER SEEING THIS HORRIBLE MOVIE!
THAT MEANS WE COULD GO BACK IN TIME AND KEEP OURSELVES FROM WATCHING IT!
NORMALLY, YES. BUT LAST TIME I PULLED THIS STUNT, THE ALIENS CAUGHT ON TO MY PLAN AND THE MACHINE WAS DAMAGED IN THE PROCESS! I'VE BEEN AFRAID TO TRY IT SINCE THEN. A WIRE MIGHT SHORT-CIRCUIT AND FRY ME LIKE AN EGG!
BUT IF SOMEBODY LSE WANTS VOLUNTEER, LET'S FIRE IT UP!
WHOA, WAIT, THAT SOUNDS TOO DANGEROUS!
I THINK WE SHOULD MAKE RIGBY DO IT, HE'S THE ONE THAT RUINED OUR AWESOME MOVIE NIGHT.
NOBODY ASKED YOU, USCLEMAN!!
I'LL DO IT!
HUH?
WHAT THE--

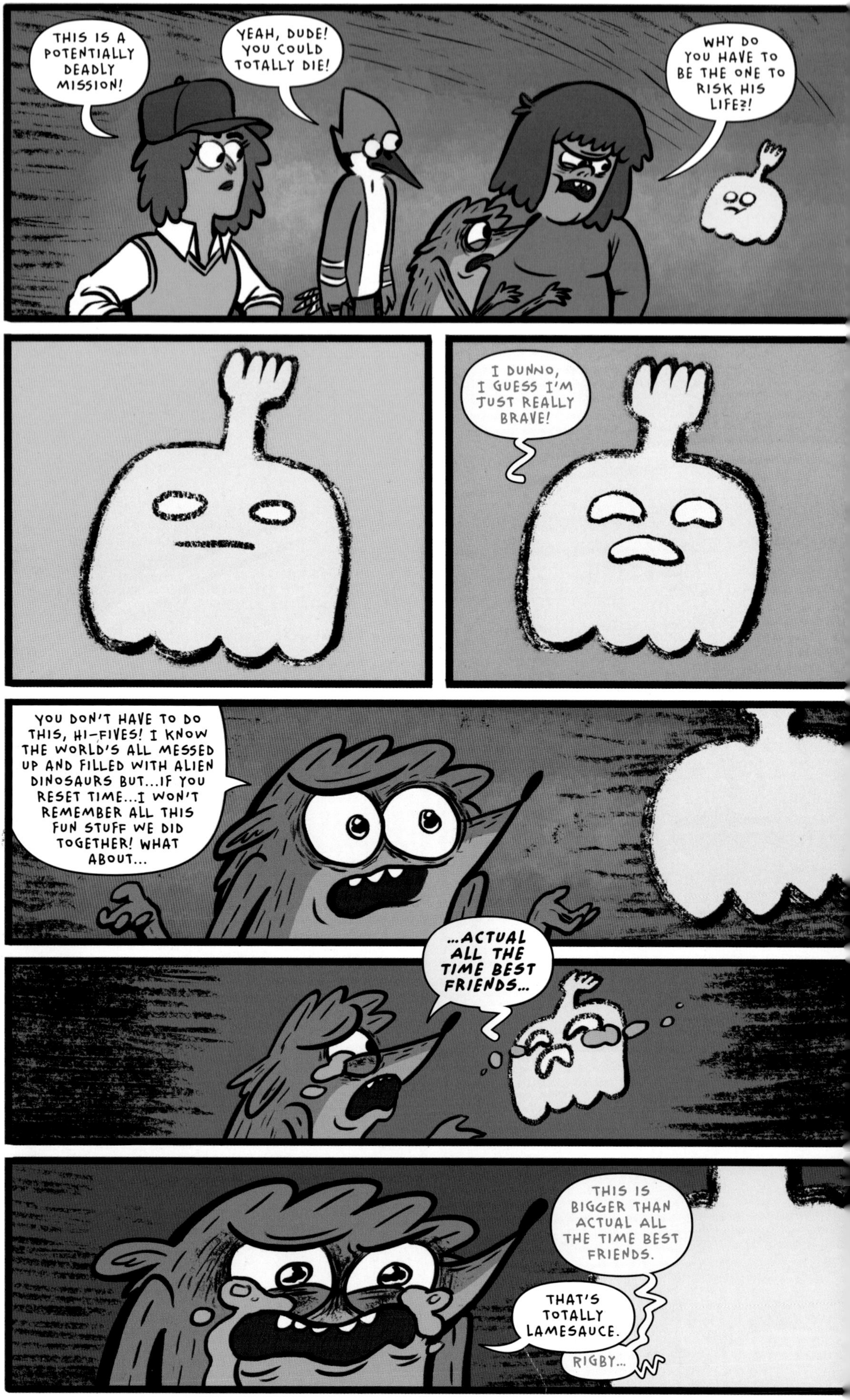
THIS IS A POTENTIALLY DEADLY MISSION!
YEAH, DUDE! YOU COULD TOTALLY DIE!
WHY DO YOU HAVE TO BE THE ONE TO RISK HIS LIFE?!
I DUNNO, I GUESS I'M JUST REALLY BRAVE!
YOU DON'T HAVE TO DO THIS, HI-FIVES! I KNOW THE WORLD'S ALL MESSED UP AND FILLED WITH ALIEN DINOSAURS BUT...IF YOU RESET TIME...I WON'T REMEMBER ALL THIS FUN STUFF WE DID TOGETHER! WHAT ABOUT...
...ACTUAL ALL THE TIME BEST FRIENDS...
THIS IS BIGGER THAN ACTUAL ALL THE TIME BEST FRIENDS.
THAT'S TOTALLY LAMESAUCE.
RIGBY...

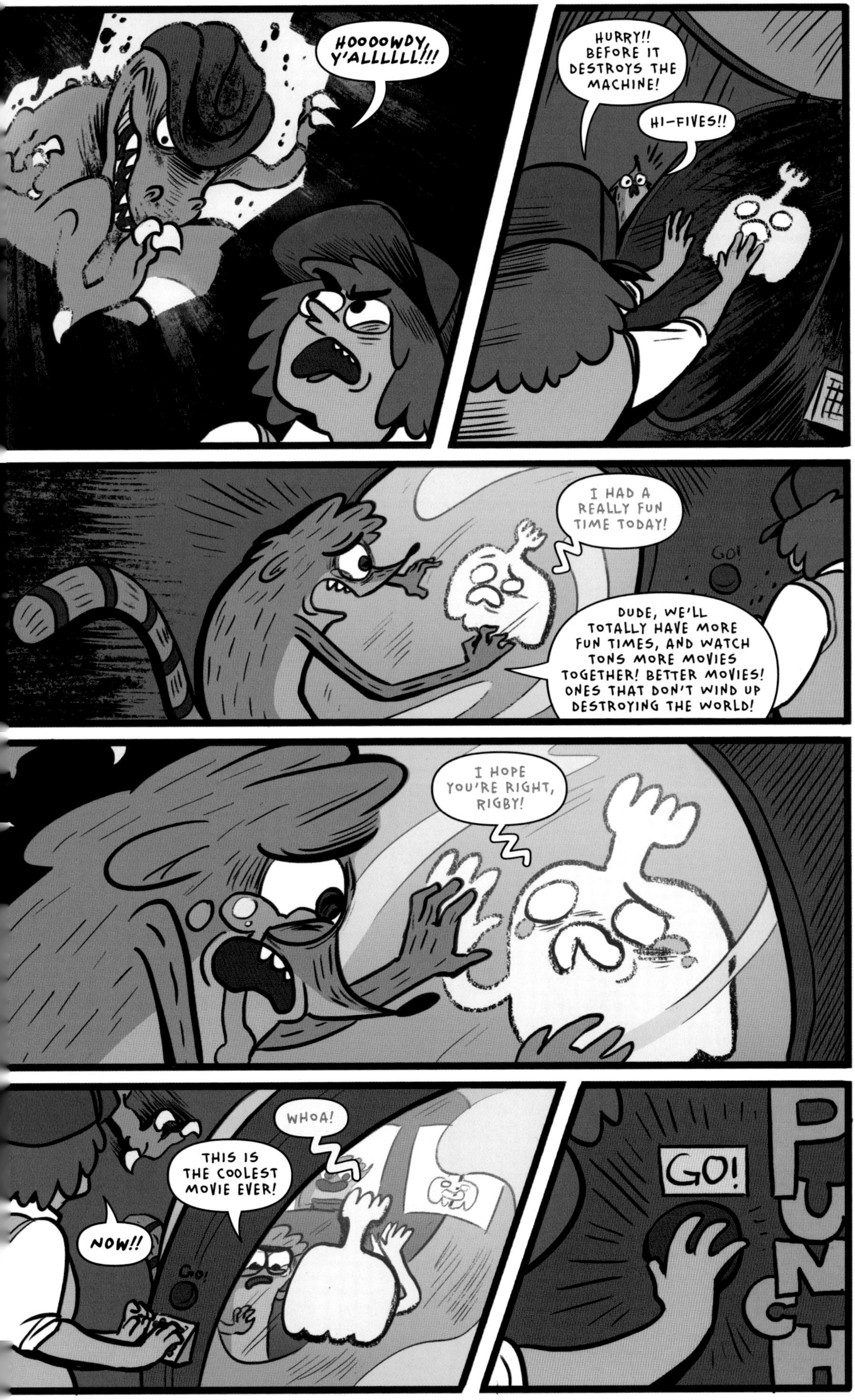
HOOOOWDY, Y'ALLLLLL!!!
HURRY!! BEFORE IT DESTROYS THE MACHINE!
HI-FIVES!!
I HAD A REALLY FUN TIME TODAY!
GO!
DUDE, WE'LL TOTALLY HAVE MORE FUN TIMES, AND WATCH TONS MORE MOVIES TOGETHER! BETTER MOVIES! ONES THAT DON'T WIND UP DESTROYING THE WORLD!
I HOPE YOU'RE RIGHT, RIGBY!
WHOA!
THIS IS THE COOLEST MOVIE EVER!
NOW!!
GO!
GO!
PUNCH

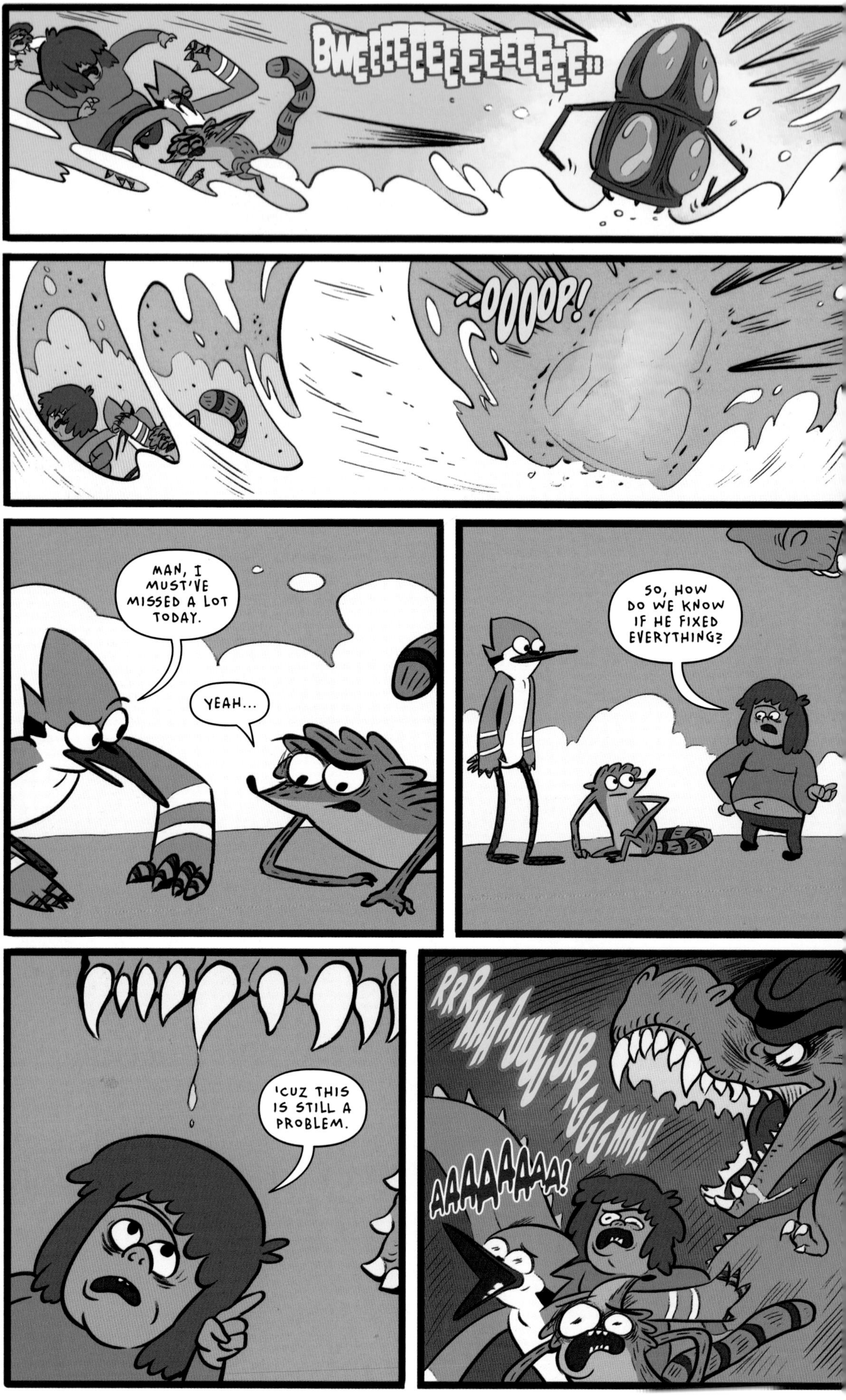
BWEEEEEEEEEEEEE!!
--OOOOP!
MAN, I MUST'VE MISSED A LOT TODAY.
YEAH...
SO, HOW DO WE KNOW IF HE FIXED EVERYTHING?
'CUZ THIS IS STILL A PROBLEM.
RRRAAAAUUUURRRGGGHHH!
AAAAAAAA!

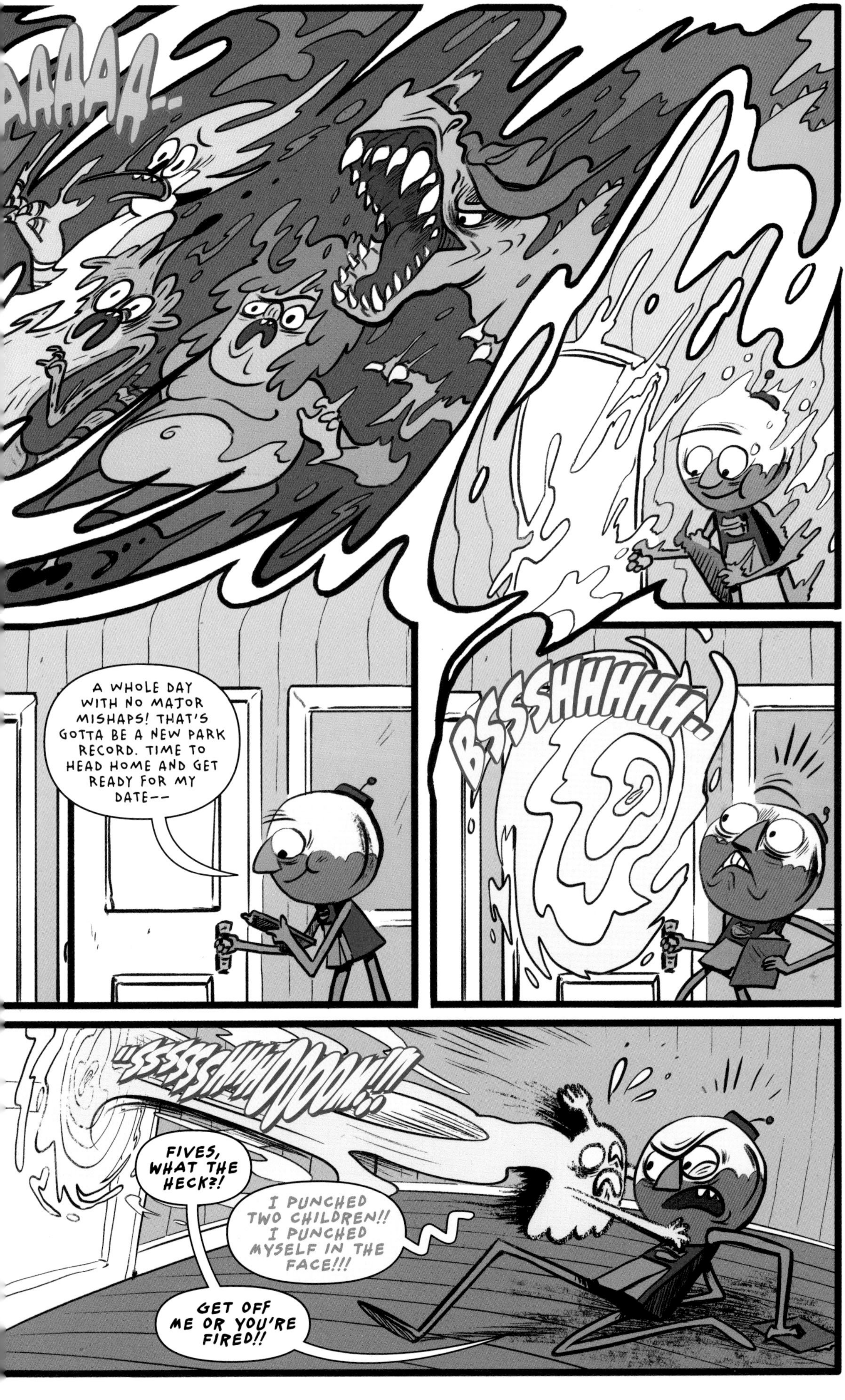
AAAAAA--
A WHOLE DAY WITH NO MAJOR MISHAPS! THAT'S GOTTA BE A NEW PARK RECORD. TIME TO HEAD HOME AND GET READY FOR MY DATE--
BSSSHHHHH--
SSSSSHHHUOOOM!!
FIVES, WHAT THE HECK?!
I PUNCHED TWO CHILDREN!! I PUNCHED MYSELF IN THE FACE!!!
GET OFF ME OR YOU'RE FIRED!!

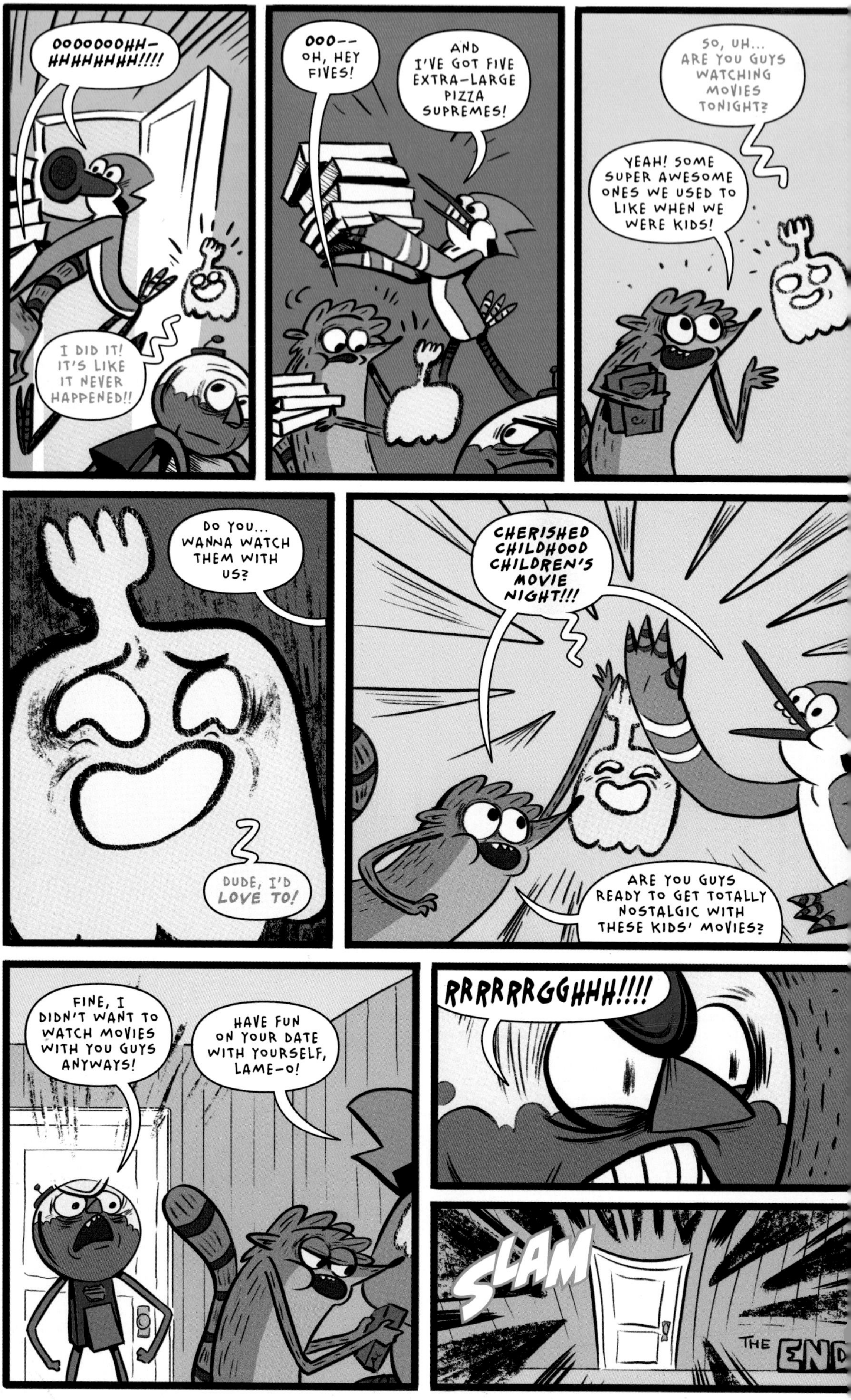
OOOOOOOHH-HHHHHHHH!!!!
I DID IT! IT'S LIKE IT NEVER HAPPENED!!
OOO--OH, HEY FIVES!
AND I'VE GOT FIVE EXTRA-LARGE PIZZA SUPREMES!
SO, UH... ARE YOU GUYS WATCHING MOVIES TONIGHT?
YEAH! SOME SUPER AWESOME ONES WE USED TO LIKE WHEN WE WERE KIDS!
DO YOU... WANNA WATCH THEM WITH US?
DUDE, I'D LOVE TO!
CHERISHED CHILDHOOD CHILDREN'S MOVIE NIGHT!!!
ARE YOU GUYS READY TO GET TOTALLY NOSTALGIC WITH THESE KIDS' MOVIES?
FINE, I DIDN'T WANT TO WATCH MOVIES WITH YOU GUYS ANYWAYS!
HAVE FUN ON YOUR DATE WITH YOURSELF, LAME-O!
RRRRRRGGHHH!!!!
SLAM
THE END

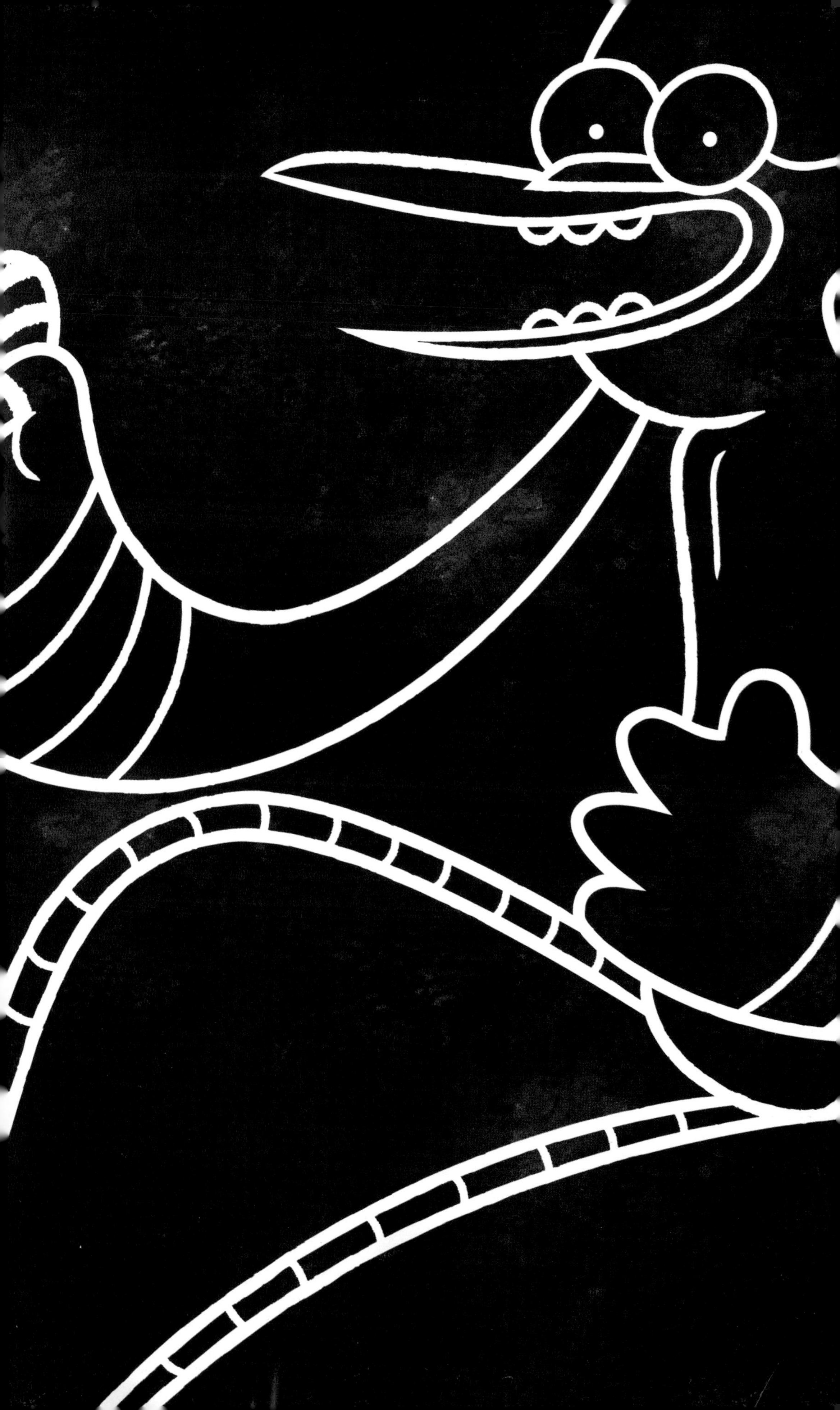

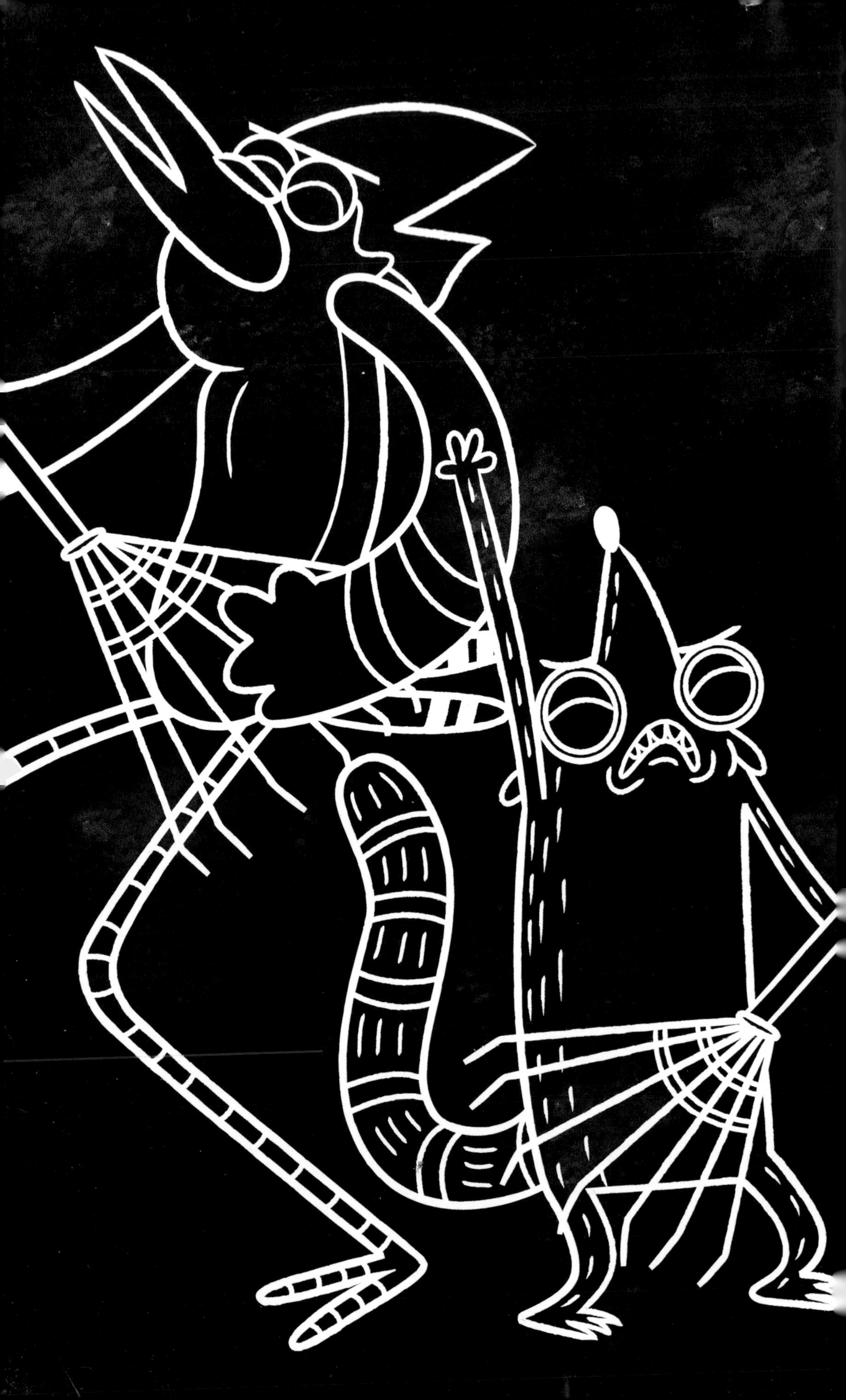

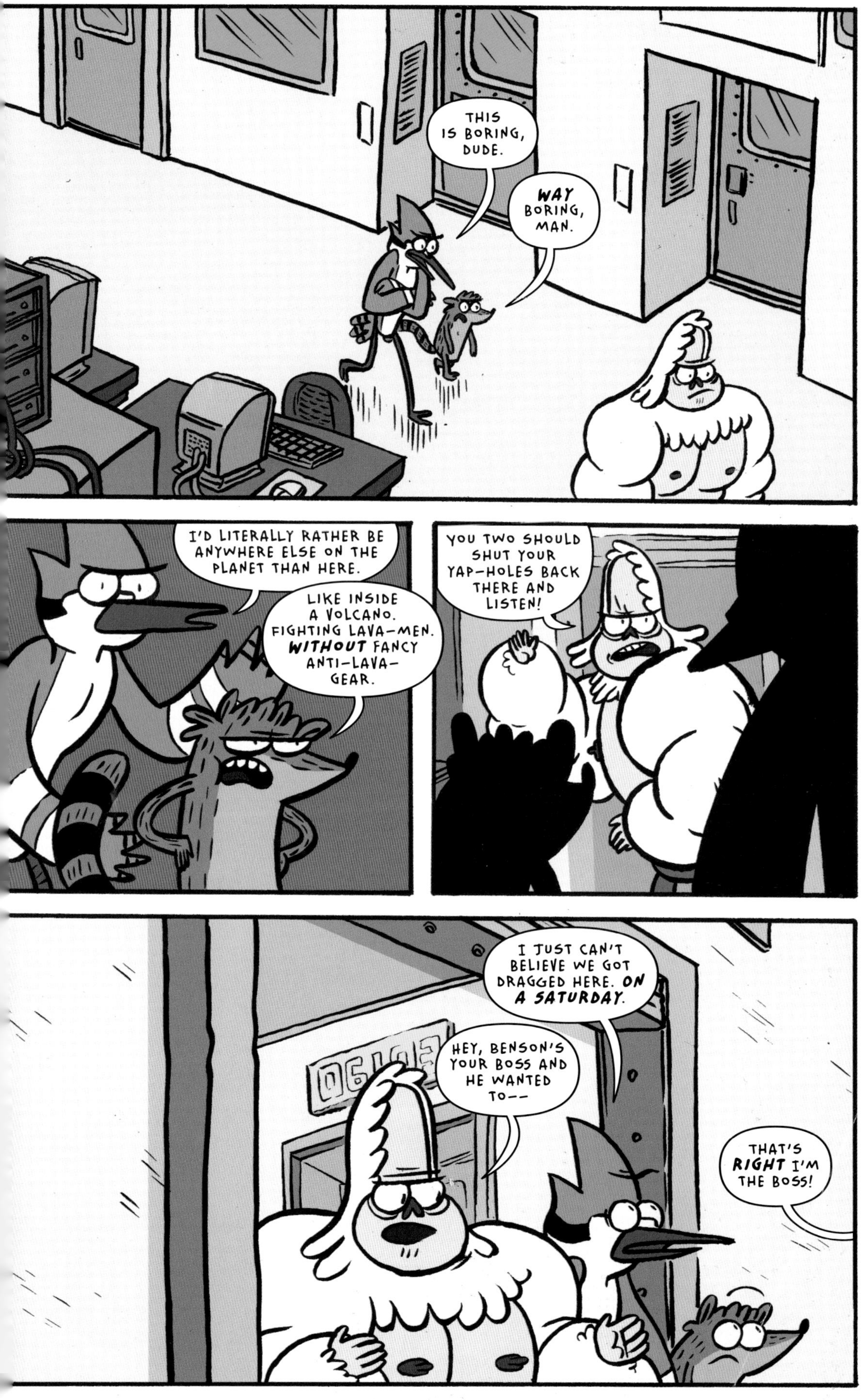
THIS IS BORING, DUDE.
WAY BORING, MAN.
I'D LITERALLY RATHER BE ANYWHERE ELSE ON THE PLANET THAN HERE.
LIKE INSIDE A VOLCANO. FIGHTING LAVA-MEN. WITHOUT FANCY ANTI-LAVA-GEAR.
YOU TWO SHOULD SHUT YOUR YAP-HOLES BACK THERE AND LISTEN!
I JUST CAN'T BELIEVE WE GOT DRAGGED HERE. ON A SATURDAY.
HEY, BENSON'S YOUR BOSS AND HE WANTED TO--
THAT'S RIGHT I'M THE BOSS!

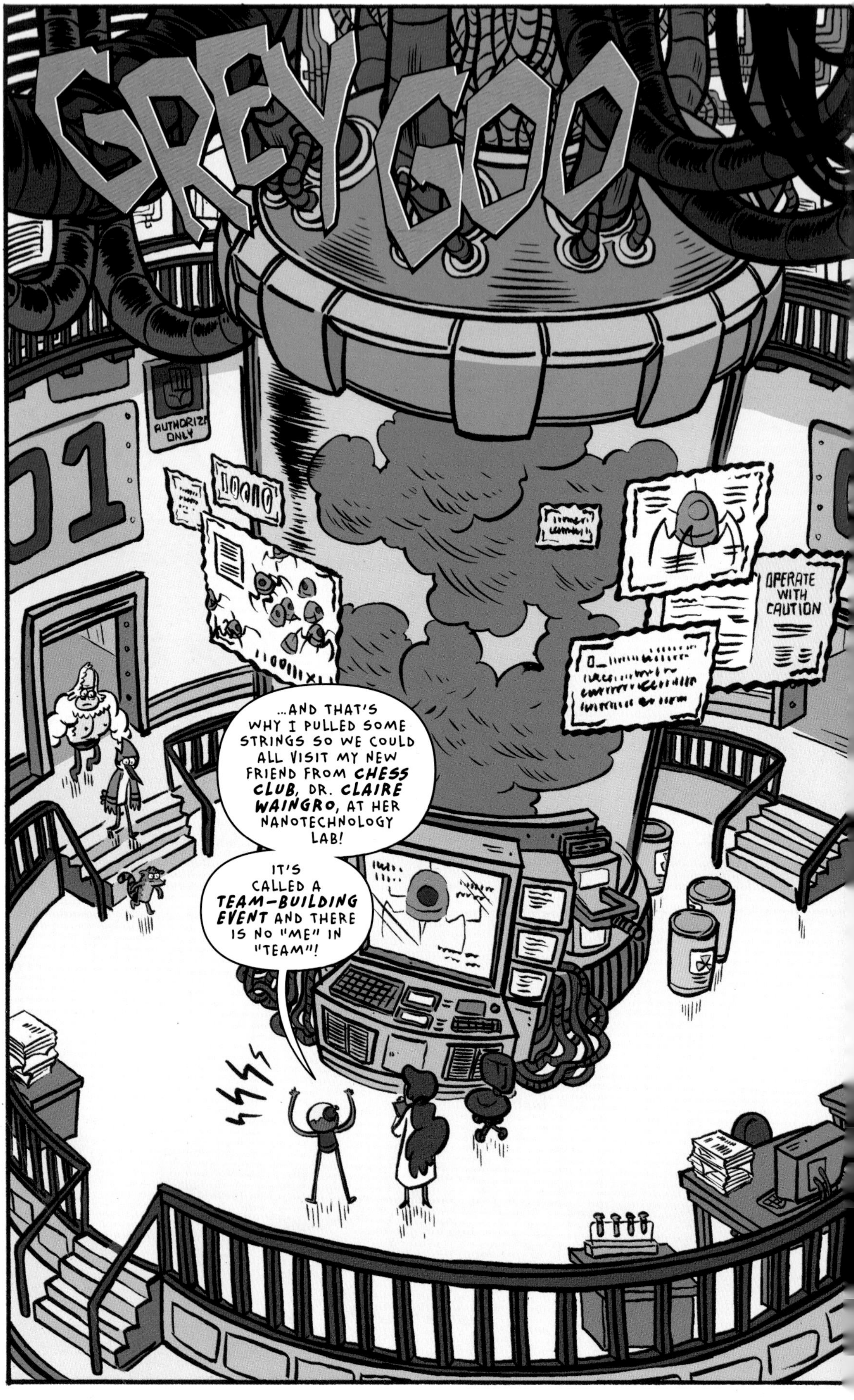
GREY GOO
AUTHORIZA ONLY
01
OPERATE WITH CAUTION
...AND THAT'S WHY I PULLED SOME STRINGS SO WE COULD ALL VISIT MY NEW FRIEND FROM CHESS CLUB, DR. CLAIRE WAINGRO, AT HER NANOTECHNOLOGY LAB!
IT'S CALLED A TEAM-BUILDING EVENT AND THERE IS NO "ME" IN "TEAM"!

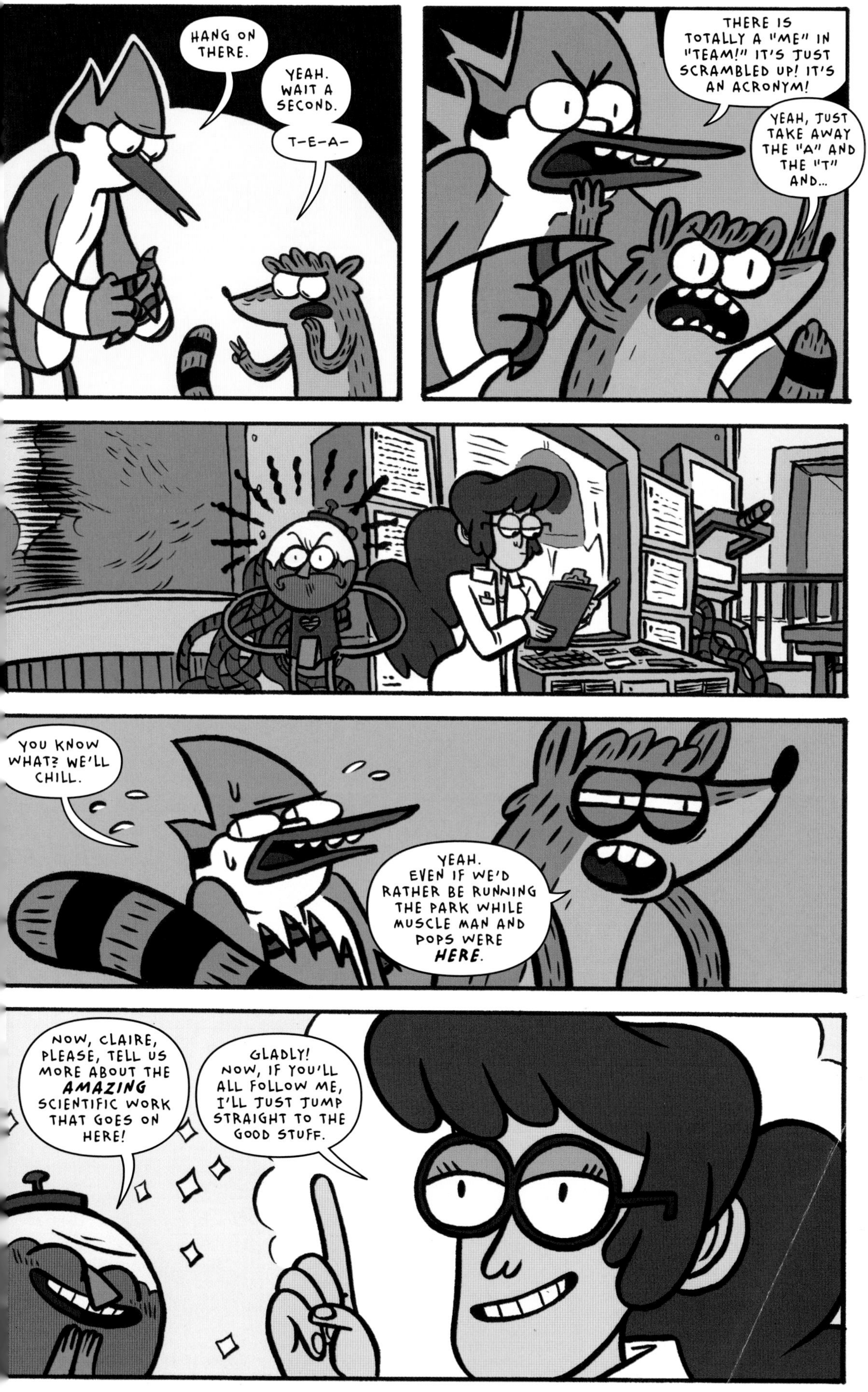
HANG ON THERE.
YEAH. WAIT A SECOND.
T-E-A-
THERE IS TOTALLY A "ME" IN "TEAM!" IT'S JUST SCRAMBLED UP! IT'S AN ACRONYM!
YEAH, JUST TAKE AWAY THE "A" AND THE "T" AND...
YOU KNOW WHAT? WE'LL CHILL.
YEAH. EVEN IF WE'D RATHER BE RUNNING THE PARK WHILE MUSCLE MAN AND POPS WERE HERE.
NOW, CLAIRE, PLEASE, TELL US MORE ABOUT THE AMAZING SCIENTIFIC WORK THAT GOES ON HERE!
GLADLY! NOW, IF YOU'LL ALL FOLLOW ME, I'LL JUST JUMP STRAIGHT TO THE GOOD STUFF.

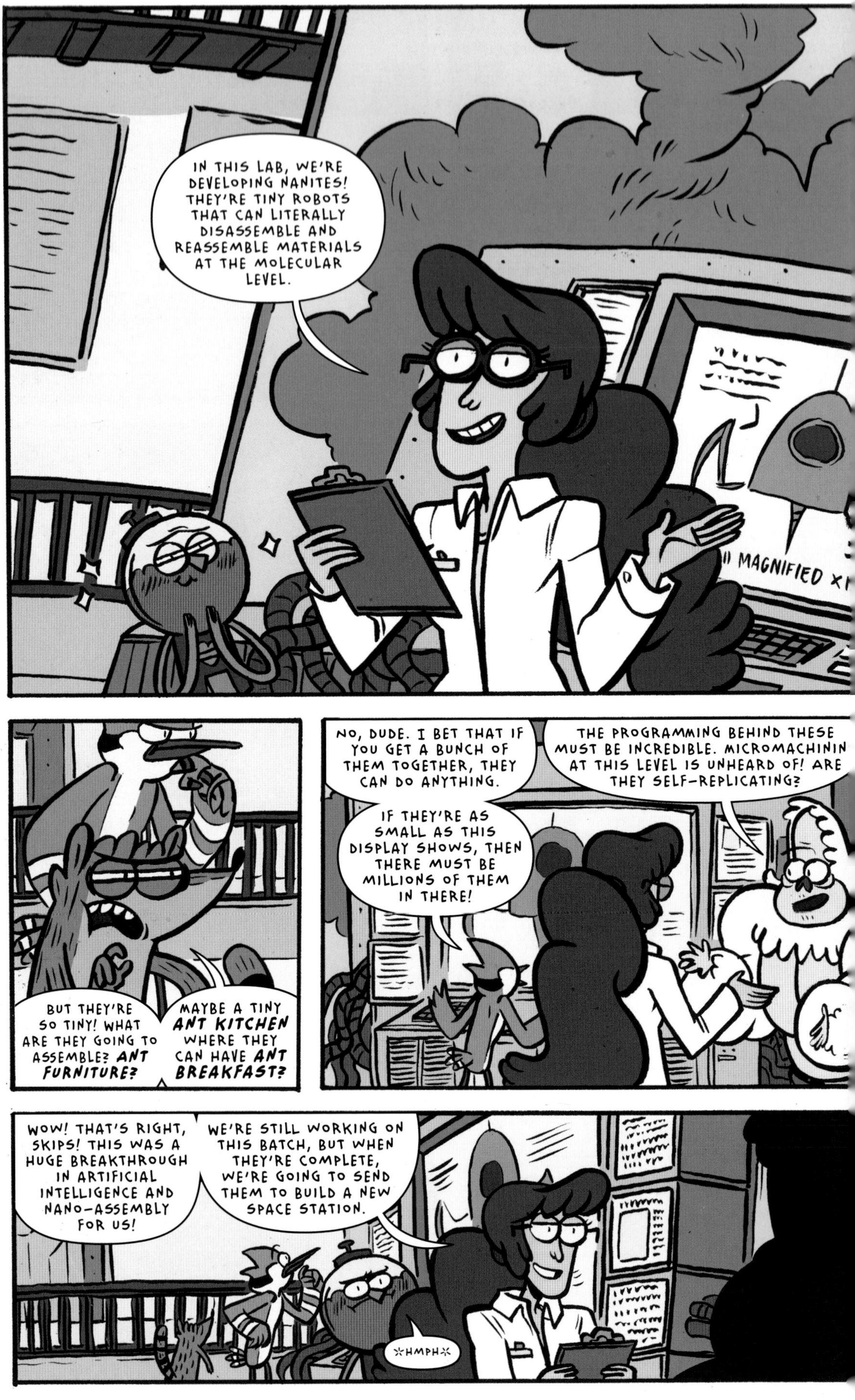
IN THIS LAB, WE'RE DEVELOPING NANITES! THEY'RE TINY ROBOTS THAT CAN LITERALLY DISASSEMBLE AND REASSEMBLE MATERIALS AT THE MOLECULAR LEVEL.
MAGNIFIED X
BUT THEY'RE SO TINY! WHAT ARE THEY GOING TO ASSEMBLE? ANT FURNITURE?
MAYBE A TINY ANT KITCHEN WHERE THEY CAN HAVE ANT BREAKFAST?
NO, DUDE. I BET THAT IF YOU GET A BUNCH OF THEM TOGETHER, THEY CAN DO ANYTHING.
IF THEY'RE AS SMALL AS THIS DISPLAY SHOWS, THEN THERE MUST BE MILLIONS OF THEM IN THERE!
THE PROGRAMMING BEHIND THESE MUST BE INCREDIBLE. MICROMACHININ AT THIS LEVEL IS UNHEARD OF! ARE THEY SELF-REPLICATING?
WOW! THAT'S RIGHT, SKIPS! THIS WAS A HUGE BREAKTHROUGH IN ARTIFICIAL INTELLIGENCE AND NANO-ASSEMBLY FOR US!
WE'RE STILL WORKING ON THIS BATCH, BUT WHEN THEY'RE COMPLETE, WE'RE GOING TO SEND THEM TO BUILD A NEW SPACE STATION.
HMPH

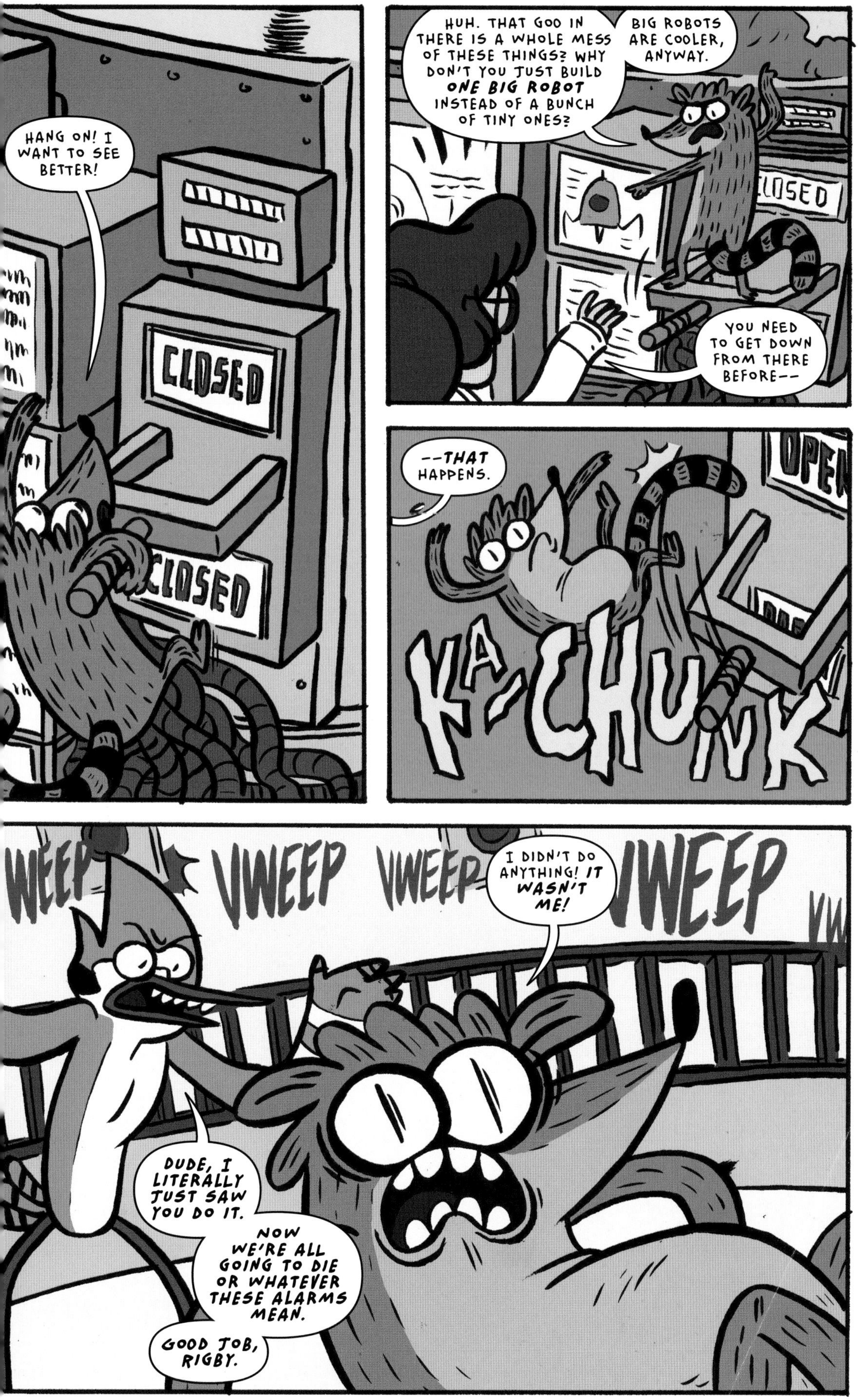
HANG ON! I WANT TO SEE BETTER!
CLOSED
CLOSED
HUH. THAT GOO IN THERE IS A WHOLE MESS OF THESE THINGS? WHY DON'T YOU JUST BUILD **ONE BIG ROBOT** INSTEAD OF A BUNCH OF TINY ONES?
BIG ROBOTS ARE COOLER, ANYWAY.
YOU NEED TO GET DOWN FROM THERE BEFORE--
--THAT HAPPENS.
KA-CHUNK
VWEEP
VWEEP
I DIDN'T DO ANYTHING! IT WASN'T ME!
VWEEP
DUDE, I LITERALLY JUST SAW YOU DO IT.
NOW WE'RE ALL GOING TO DIE OR WHATEVER THESE ALARMS MEAN.
GOOD JOB, RIGBY.

VWEE

VWEE

CLAIRE, I'M SO SORRY! WHAT CAN I DO TO HELP?

WARNI WARNI WARNI NING

JUST STAY OUT OF MY WAY! I HAVE TO SEE IF I CAN RESET THE SYSTEM IN TIME BEFORE THE PURGE CYCLE HAPPENS.

VWEEP VWEEP VWEEP

I CAN'T LET ALL THAT WORK GO TO...

...OH NO.

TAK TAK TAKA TAK TAKA TAK

VWEE—.

HELLO, WAINGRO-UNIT. LET US HANDLE THAT ALARM.

H...HELLO?

WHOA.

WHAT HAPPENED?

ARTIFICIAL INTELLIGENCE.

IF THESE GUYS PROGRAMMED THEIR ROBOTS TO BUILD MORE ROBOTS AND INCLUDED ANY KIND OF ARTIFICIAL INTELLIGENCE...

THAT IS CORRECT, SKIPS-UNIT

THE WAINGRO-UNIT PROGRAMMIN ALLOWED US DEVELOP AN INDEPENDEN INTELLIGENC

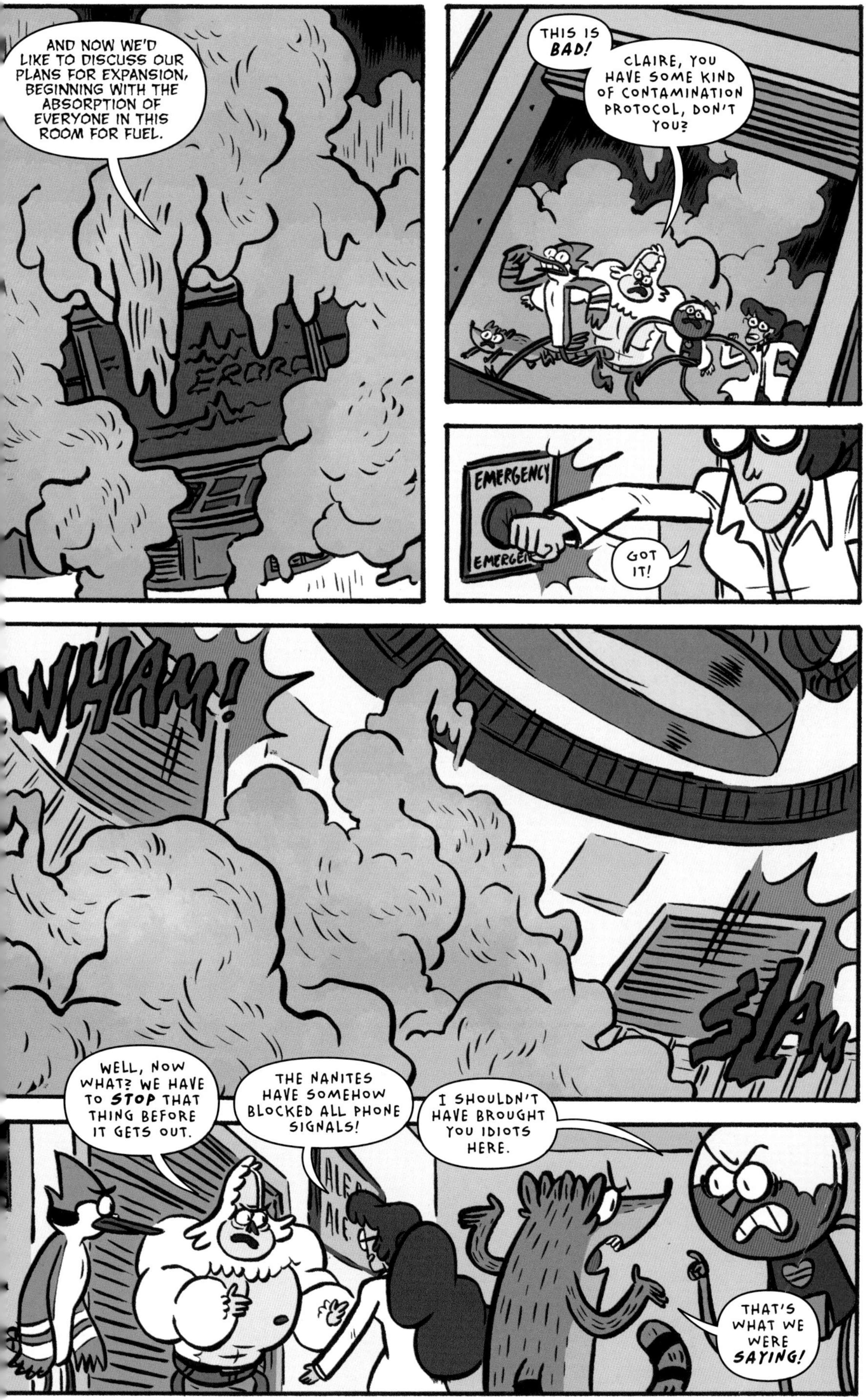
AND NOW WE'D LIKE TO DISCUSS OUR PLANS FOR EXPANSION, BEGINNING WITH THE ABSORPTION OF EVERYONE IN THIS ROOM FOR FUEL.
ERROR
THIS IS BAD!
CLAIRE, YOU HAVE SOME KIND OF CONTAMINATION PROTOCOL, DON'T YOU?
EMERGENCY
EMERGEN
GOT IT!
WHAM!
SLAM
WELL, NOW WHAT? WE HAVE TO STOP THAT THING BEFORE IT GETS OUT.
THE NANITES HAVE SOMEHOW BLOCKED ALL PHONE SIGNALS!
I SHOULDN'T HAVE BROUGHT YOU IDIOTS HERE.
THAT'S WHAT WE WERE SAYING!

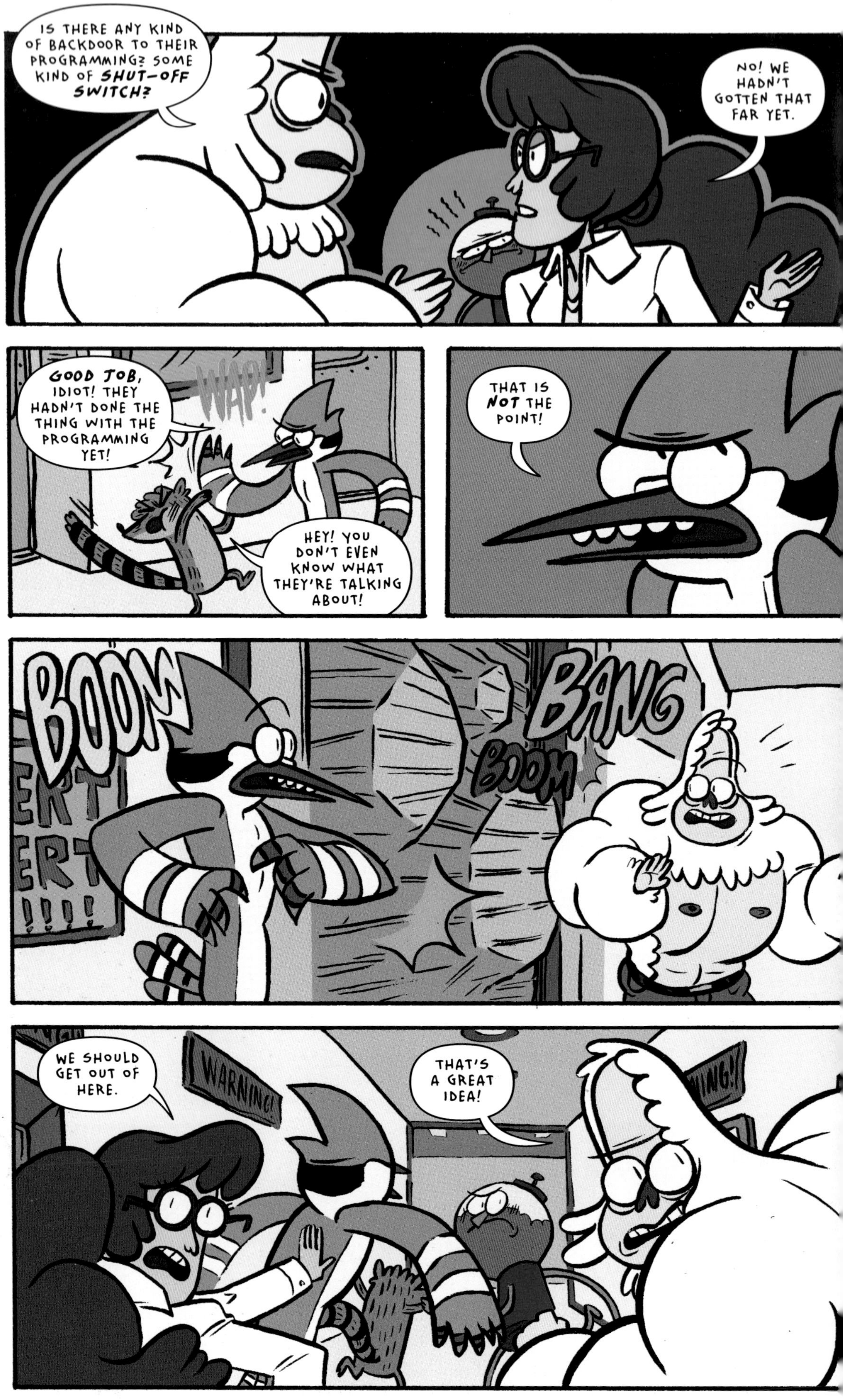

IS THERE ANY KIND OF BACKDOOR TO THEIR PROGRAMMING? SOME KIND OF SHUT-OFF SWITCH?
NO! WE HADN'T GOTTEN THAT FAR YET.
GOOD JOB, IDIOT! THEY HADN'T DONE THE THING WITH THE PROGRAMMING YET!
WAP!
HEY! YOU DON'T EVEN KNOW WHAT THEY'RE TALKING ABOUT!
THAT IS NOT THE POINT!
BOOM
BANG
BOOM
WE SHOULD GET OUT OF HERE.
WARNING!
THAT'S A GREAT IDEA!

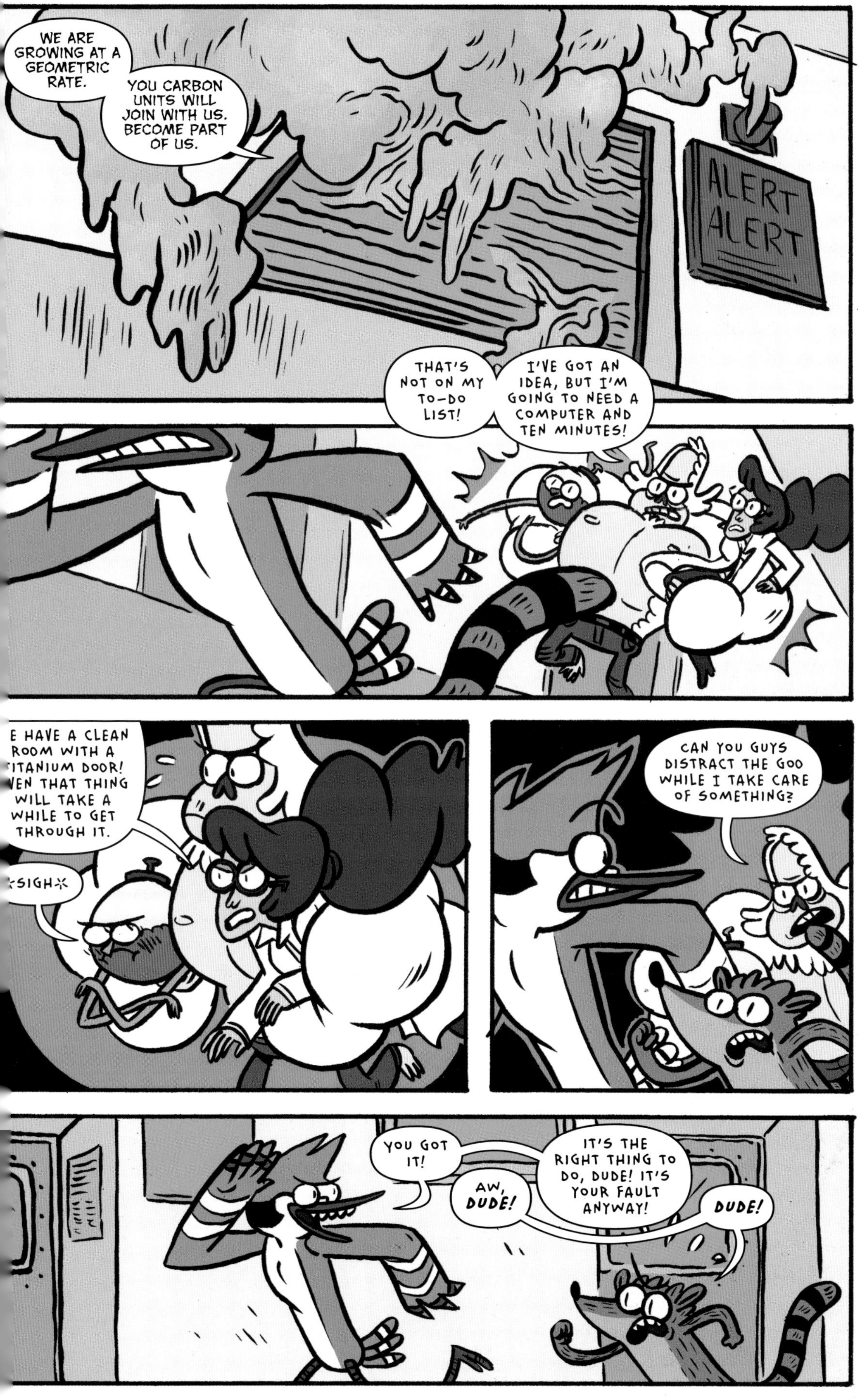

WE ARE GROWING AT A GEOMETRIC RATE.
YOU CARBON UNITS WILL JOIN WITH US. BECOME PART OF US.
ALERT ALERT
THAT'S NOT ON MY TO-DO LIST!
I'VE GOT AN IDEA, BUT I'M GOING TO NEED A COMPUTER AND TEN MINUTES!
E HAVE A CLEAN ROOM WITH A ITANIUM DOOR! VEN THAT THING WILL TAKE A WHILE TO GET THROUGH IT.
SIGH
CAN YOU GUYS DISTRACT THE GOO WHILE I TAKE CARE OF SOMETHING?
YOU GOT IT!
AW, DUDE!
IT'S THE RIGHT THING TO DO, DUDE! IT'S YOUR FAULT ANYWAY!
DUDE!

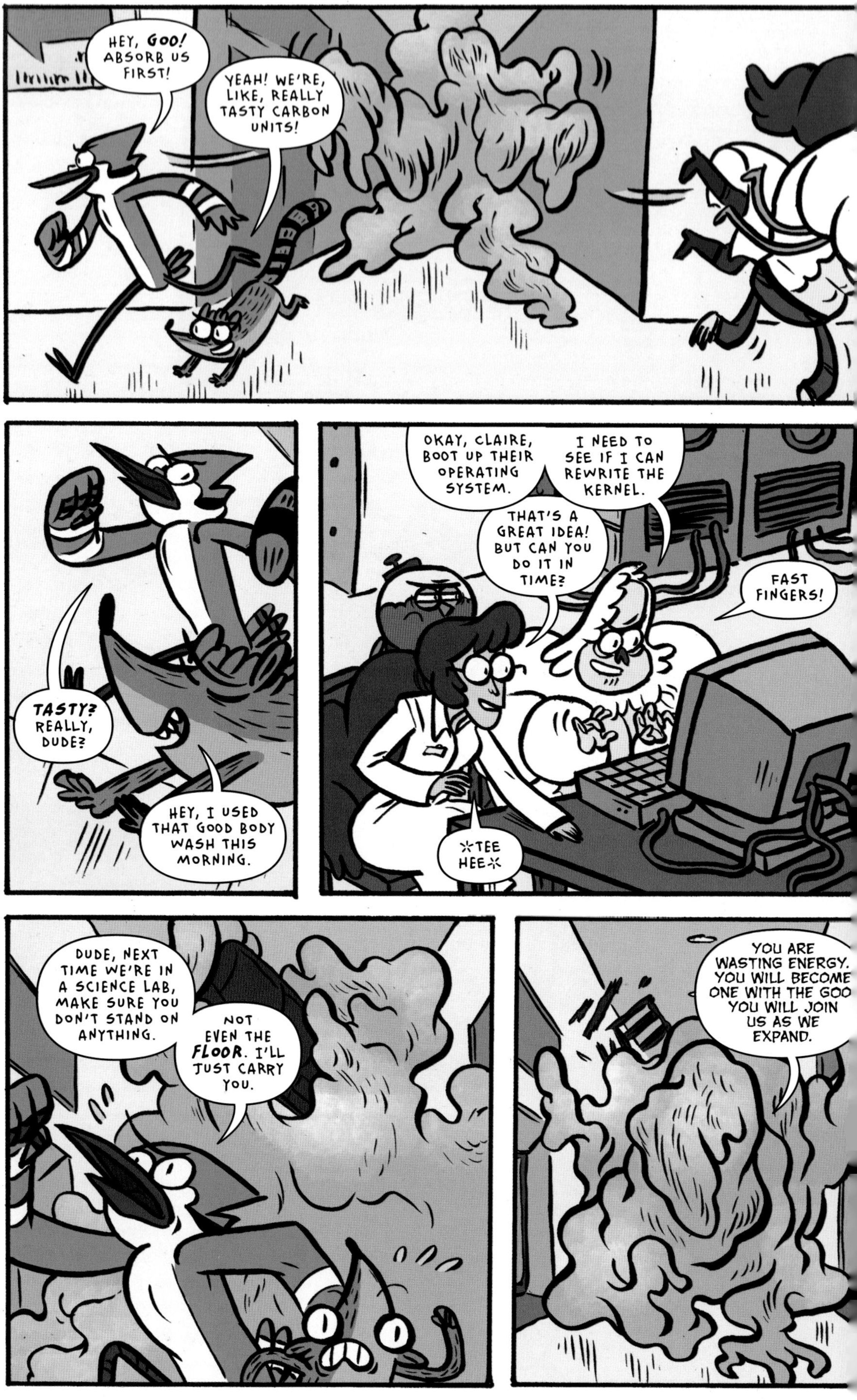
HEY, **GOO!** ABSORB US FIRST!
YEAH! WE'RE, LIKE, REALLY TASTY CARBON UNITS!
TASTY? REALLY, DUDE?
HEY, I USED THAT GOOD BODY WASH THIS MORNING.
OKAY, CLAIRE, BOOT UP THEIR OPERATING SYSTEM.
I NEED TO SEE IF I CAN REWRITE THE KERNEL.
THAT'S A GREAT IDEA! BUT CAN YOU DO IT IN TIME?
FAST FINGERS!
TEE HEE
DUDE, NEXT TIME WE'RE IN A SCIENCE LAB, MAKE SURE YOU DON'T STAND ON ANYTHING.
NOT EVEN THE ***FLOOR***. I'LL JUST CARRY YOU.
YOU ARE WASTING ENERGY. YOU WILL BECOME ONE WITH THE GOO. YOU WILL JOIN US AS WE EXPAND.

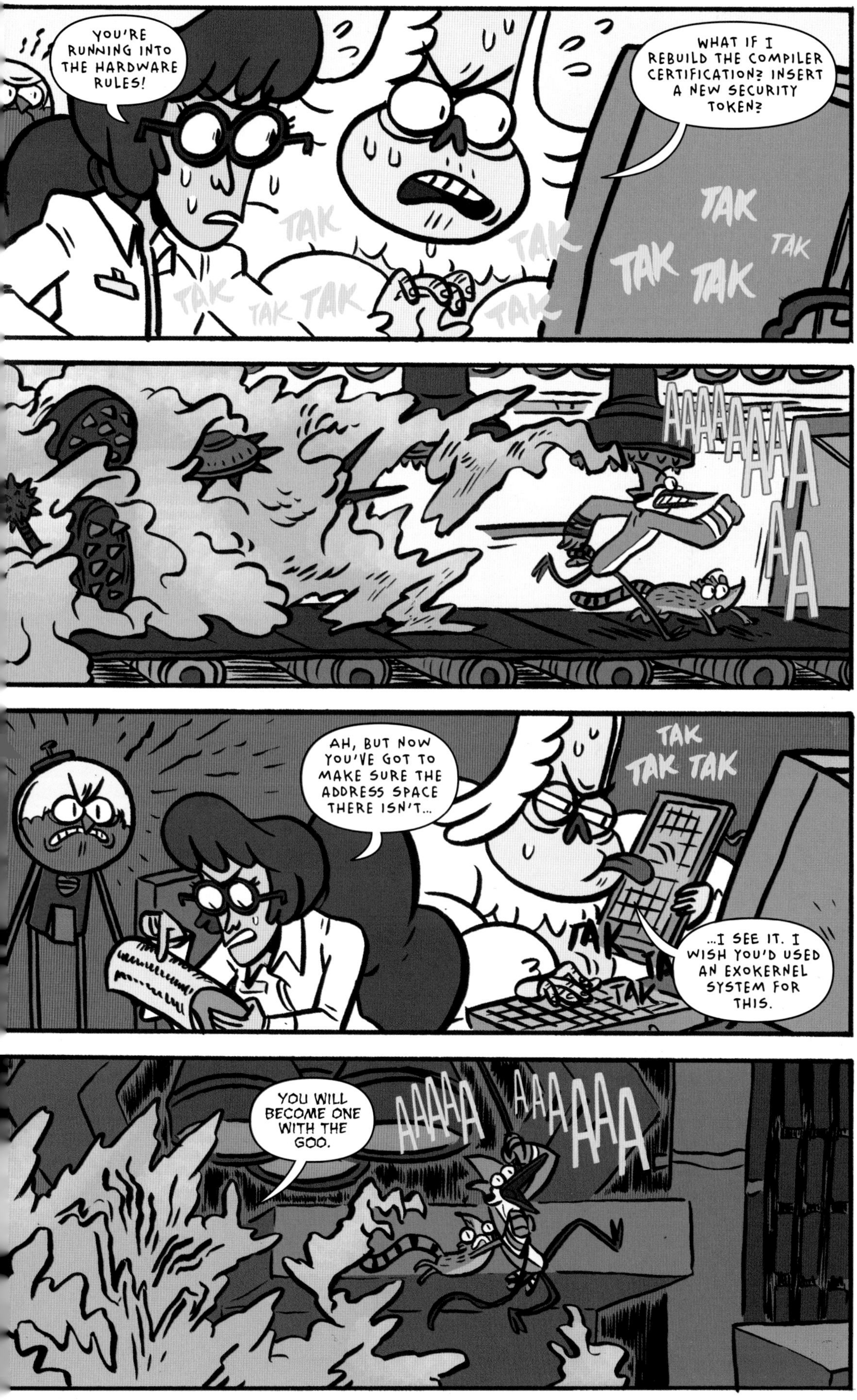
YOU'RE RUNNING INTO THE HARDWARE RULES!
WHAT IF I REBUILD THE COMPILER CERTIFICATION? INSERT A NEW SECURITY TOKEN?
TAK TAK TAK TAK TAK TAK TAK TAK TAK TAK
AAAAAAAAAAAA
AH, BUT NOW YOU'VE GOT TO MAKE SURE THE ADDRESS SPACE THERE ISN'T...
TAK TAK TAK
...I SEE IT. I WISH YOU'D USED AN EXOKERNEL SYSTEM FOR THIS.
TAK TAK
YOU WILL BECOME ONE WITH THE GOO.
AAAAAAAAAAA

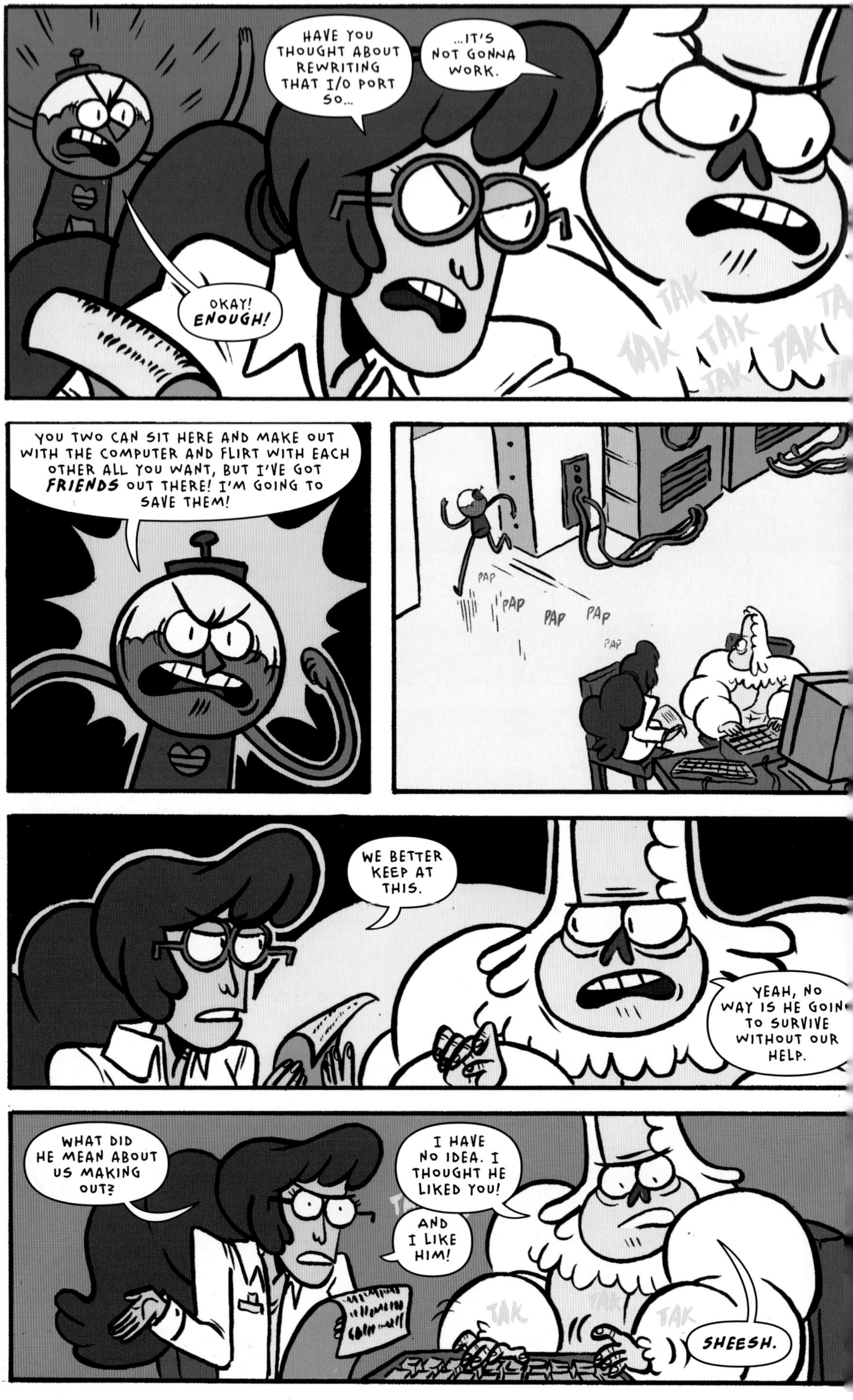
HAVE YOU THOUGHT ABOUT REWRITING THAT I/O PORT SO...
...IT'S NOT GONNA WORK.
OKAY! ENOUGH!
TAK TAK TAK TAK TAK TAK
YOU TWO CAN SIT HERE AND MAKE OUT WITH THE COMPUTER AND FLIRT WITH EACH OTHER ALL YOU WANT, BUT I'VE GOT FRIENDS OUT THERE! I'M GOING TO SAVE THEM!
PAP PAP PAP PAP PAP
WE BETTER KEEP AT THIS.
YEAH, NO WAY IS HE GOIN TO SURVIVE WITHOUT OUR HELP.
WHAT DID HE MEAN ABOUT US MAKING OUT?
I HAVE NO IDEA. I THOUGHT HE LIKED YOU!
AND I LIKE HIM!
TAK TAK TAK
SHEESH.

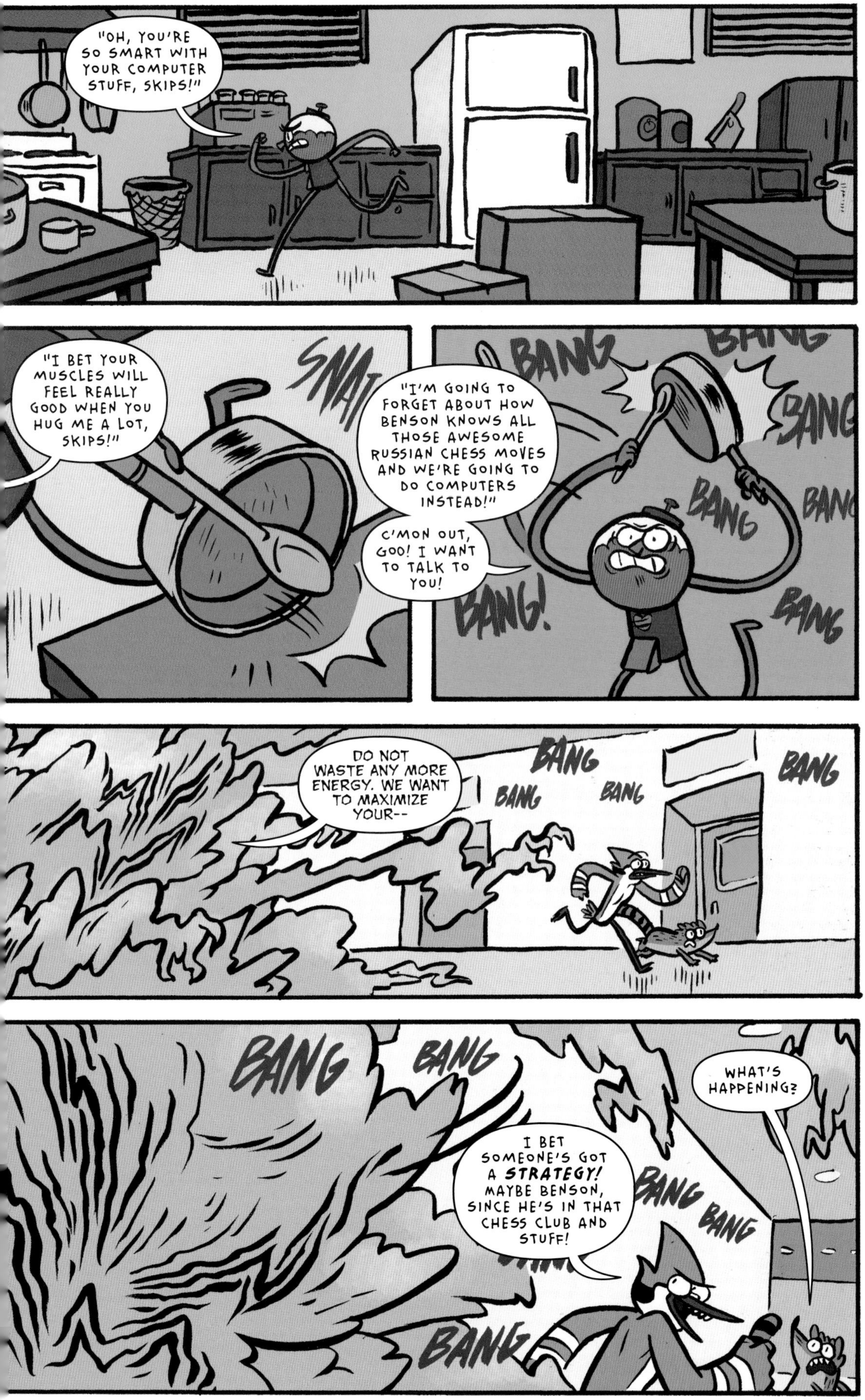
"OH, YOU'RE SO SMART WITH YOUR COMPUTER STUFF, SKIPS!"
"I BET YOUR MUSCLES WILL FEEL REALLY GOOD WHEN YOU HUG ME A LOT, SKIPS!"
"I'M GOING TO FORGET ABOUT HOW BENSON KNOWS ALL THOSE AWESOME RUSSIAN CHESS MOVES AND WE'RE GOING TO DO COMPUTERS INSTEAD!"
C'MON OUT, GOO! I WANT TO TALK TO YOU!
BANG
BANG
BANG
BANG
BANG
BANG!
BANG
DO NOT WASTE ANY MORE ENERGY. WE WANT TO MAXIMIZE YOUR--
BANG
BANG
BANG
BANG
BANG
BANG
WHAT'S HAPPENING?
I BET SOMEONE'S GOT A ***STRATEGY!*** MAYBE BENSON, SINCE HE'S IN THAT CHESS CLUB AND STUFF!
BANG
BANG
BANG

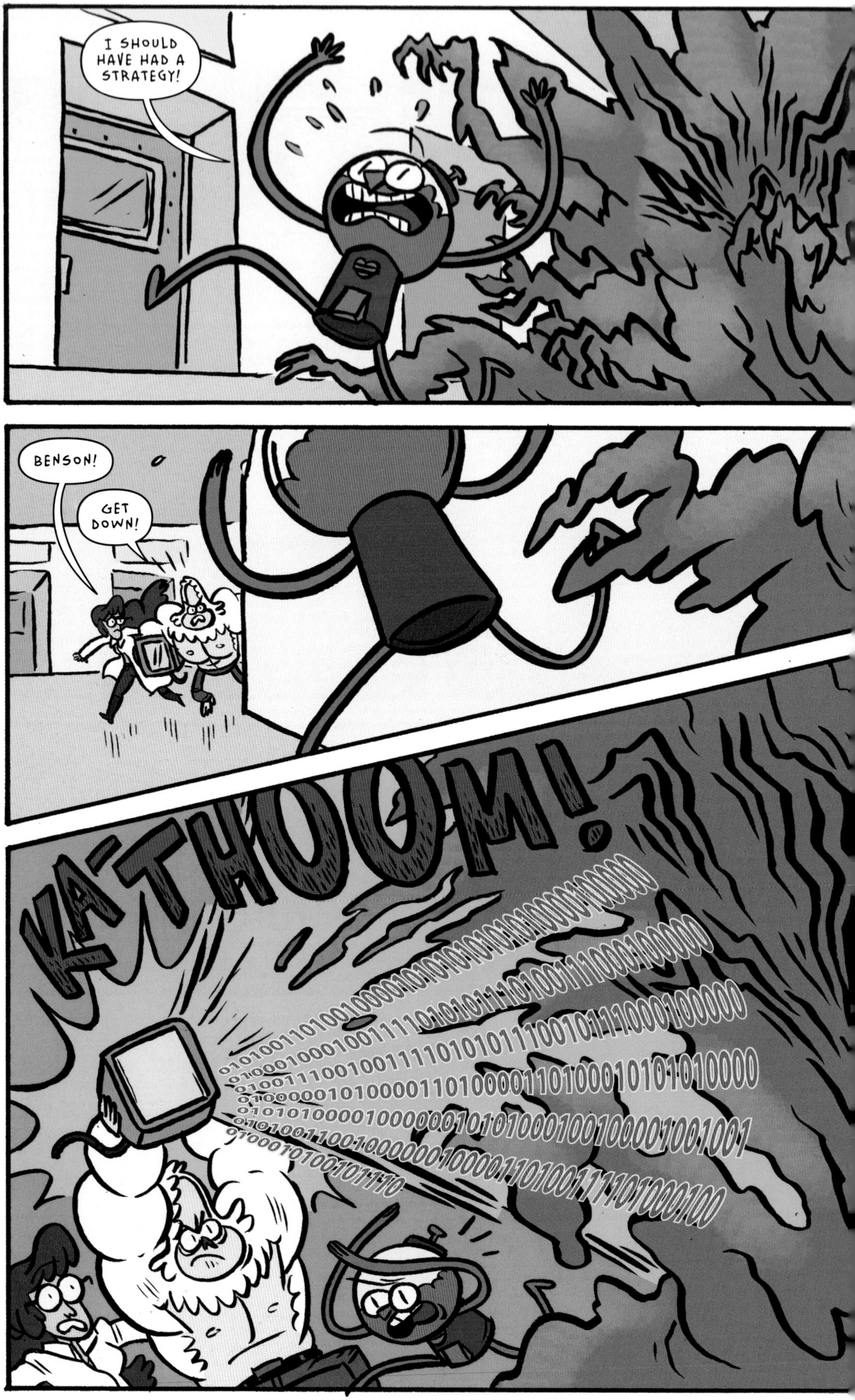

I SHOULD HAVE HAD A STRATEGY!
BENSON!
GET DOWN!
KATHOOM!

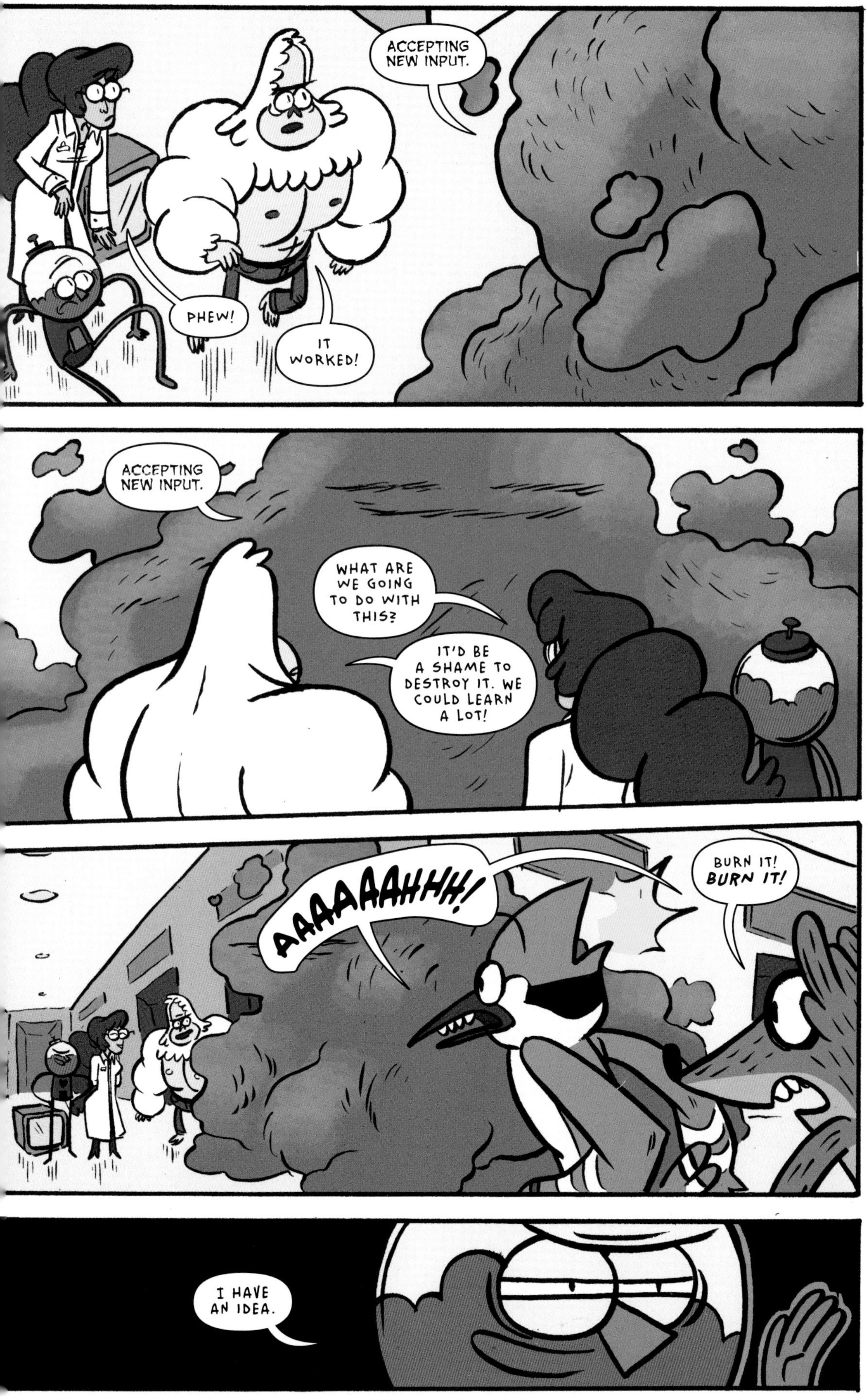
ACCEPTING NEW INPUT.
PHEW!
IT WORKED!
ACCEPTING NEW INPUT.
WHAT ARE WE GOING TO DO WITH THIS?
IT'D BE A SHAME TO DESTROY IT. WE COULD LEARN A LOT!
AAAAAAHHH!
BURN IT! BURN IT!
I HAVE AN IDEA.

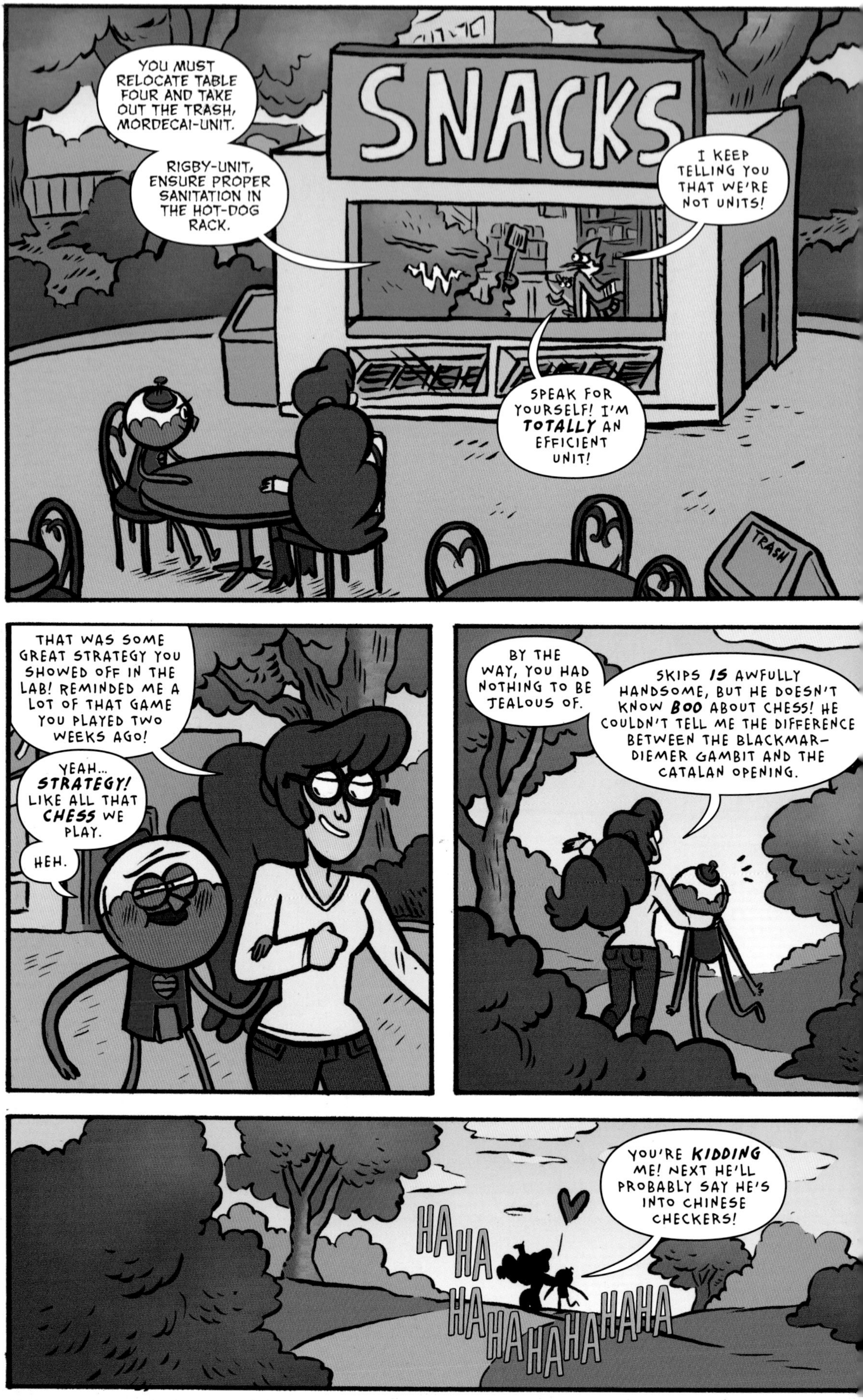
YOU MUST RELOCATE TABLE FOUR AND TAKE OUT THE TRASH, MORDECAI-UNIT.
RIGBY-UNIT, ENSURE PROPER SANITATION IN THE HOT-DOG RACK.
SNACKS
I KEEP TELLING YOU THAT WE'RE NOT UNITS!
SPEAK FOR YOURSELF! I'M TOTALLY AN EFFICIENT UNIT!
TRASH
THAT WAS SOME GREAT STRATEGY YOU SHOWED OFF IN THE LAB! REMINDED ME A LOT OF THAT GAME YOU PLAYED TWO WEEKS AGO!
YEAH... STRATEGY! LIKE ALL THAT CHESS WE PLAY.
HEH.
BY THE WAY, YOU HAD NOTHING TO BE JEALOUS OF.
SKIPS IS AWFULLY HANDSOME, BUT HE DOESN'T KNOW BOO ABOUT CHESS! HE COULDN'T TELL ME THE DIFFERENCE BETWEEN THE BLACKMAR-DIEMER GAMBIT AND THE CATALAN OPENING.
YOU'RE KIDDING ME! NEXT HE'LL PROBABLY SAY HE'S INTO CHINESE CHECKERS!
HAHAHA
HAHAHAHAHAHAHA

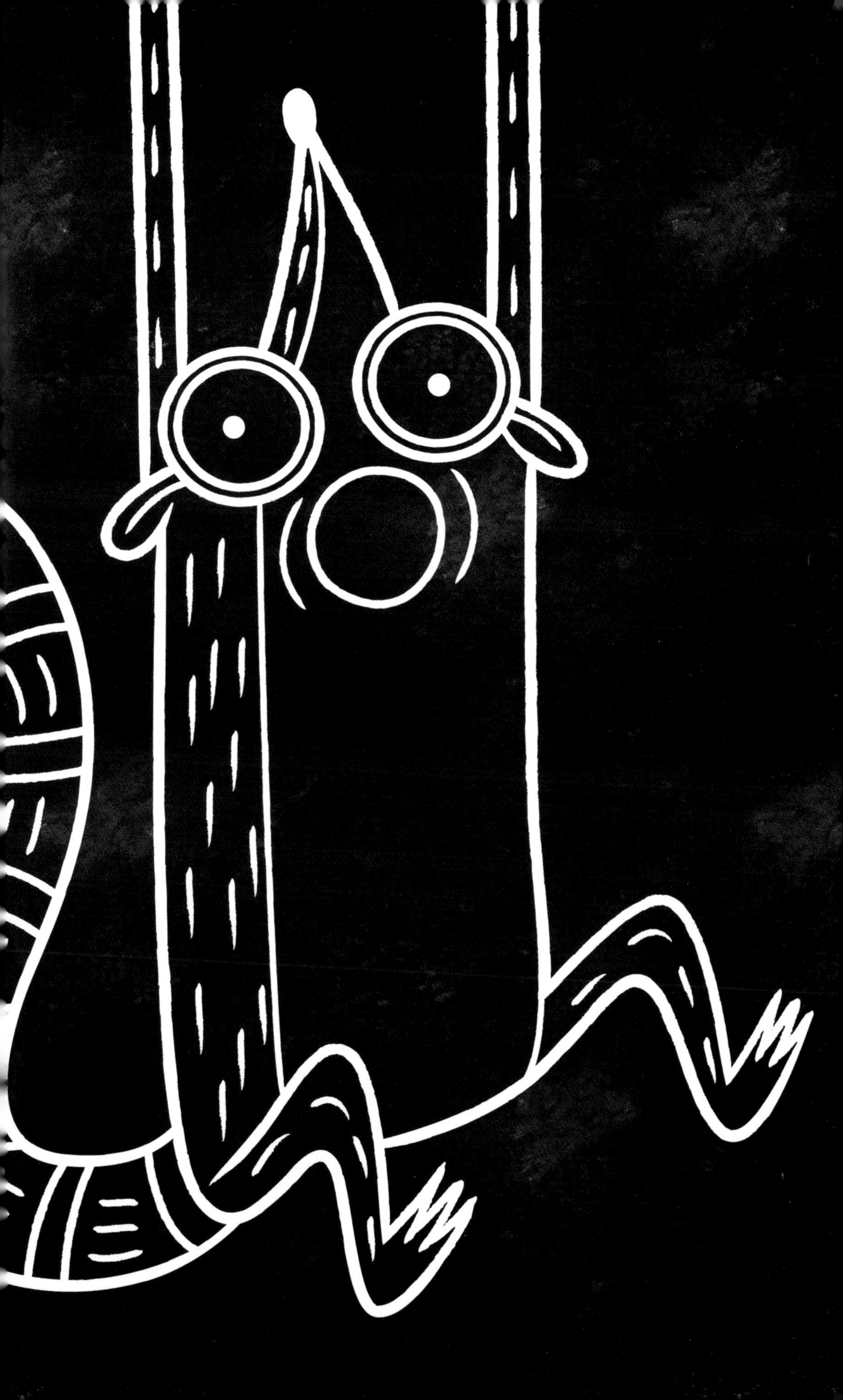

SHORT STORIES, BRO

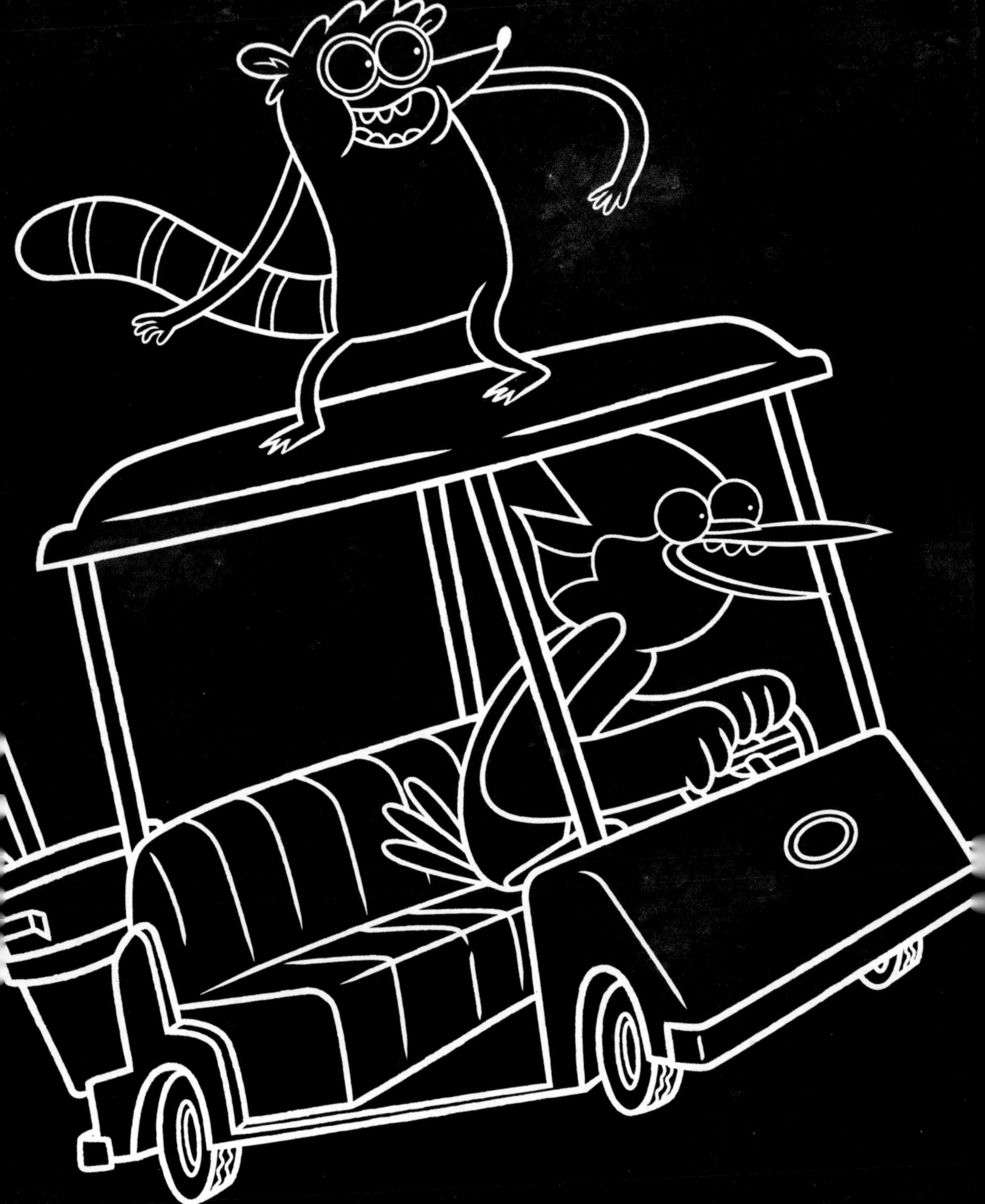

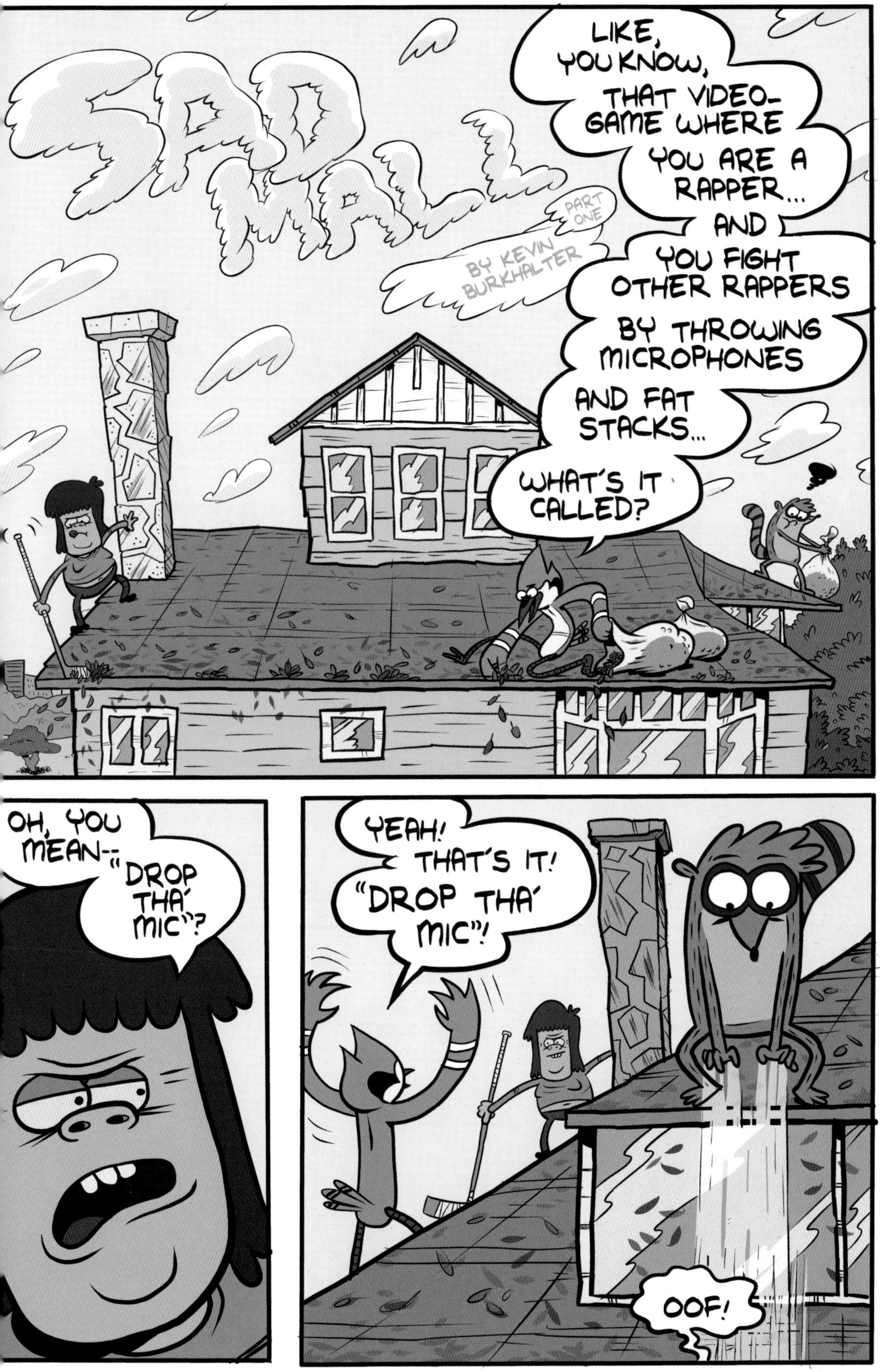

SAD MALL
PART ONE
BY KEVIN BURKHALTER
LIKE, YOU KNOW, THAT VIDEO-GAME WHERE YOU ARE A RAPPER... AND YOU FIGHT OTHER RAPPERS BY THROWING MICROPHONES AND FAT STACKS... WHAT'S IT CALLED?
OH, YOU MEAN--"DROP THA' MIC"?
YEAH! THAT'S IT! "DROP THA' MIC"!
OOF!

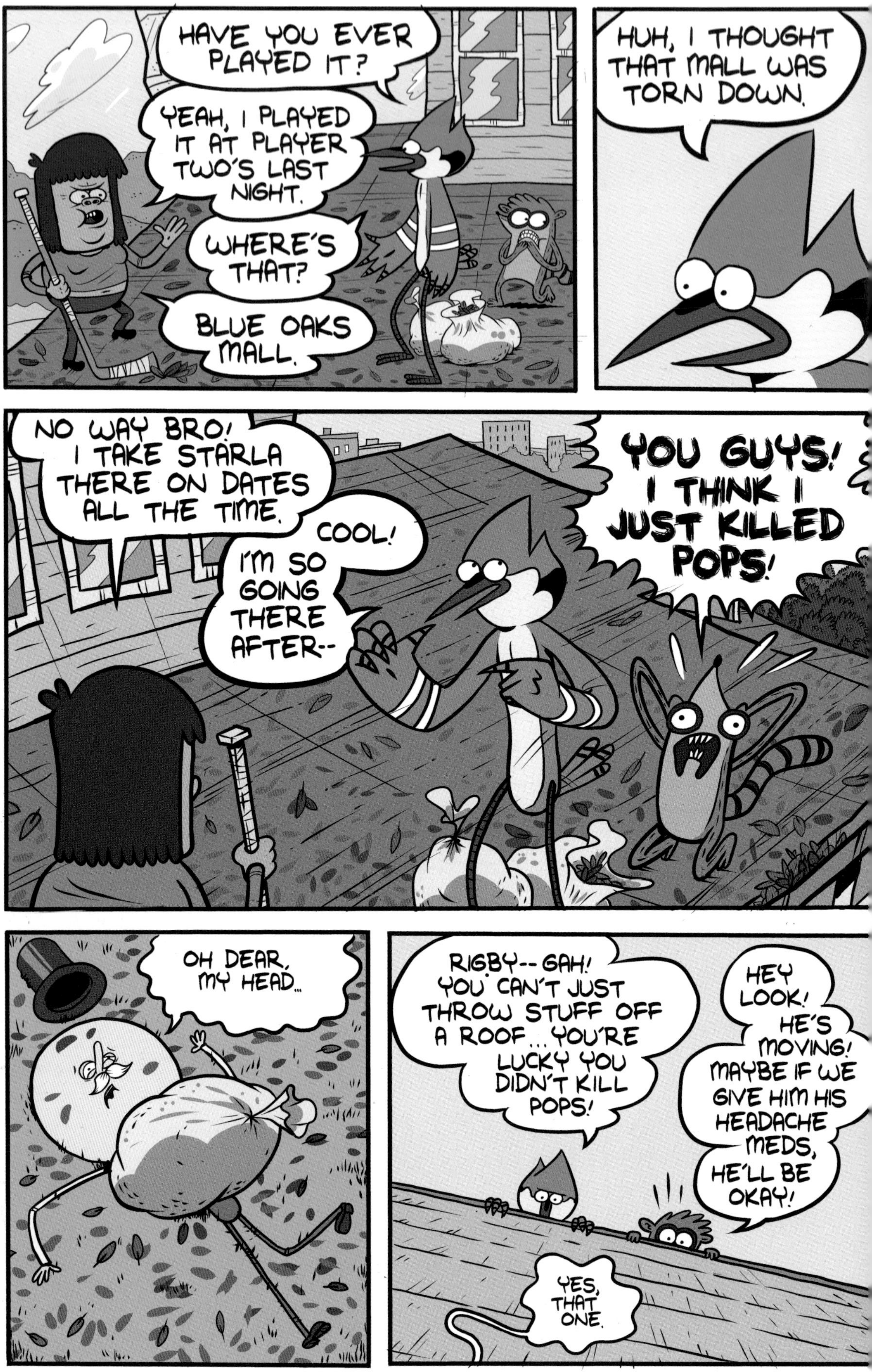
HAVE YOU EVER PLAYED IT?
YEAH, I PLAYED IT AT PLAYER TWO'S LAST NIGHT.
WHERE'S THAT?
BLUE OAKS MALL.
HUH, I THOUGHT THAT MALL WAS TORN DOWN.
NO WAY BRO! I TAKE STARLA THERE ON DATES ALL THE TIME.
COOL! I'M SO GOING THERE AFTER--
YOU GUYS! I THINK I JUST KILLED POPS!
OH DEAR, MY HEAD...
RIGBY-- GAH! YOU CAN'T JUST THROW STUFF OFF A ROOF... YOU'RE LUCKY YOU DIDN'T KILL POPS!
HEY LOOK! HE'S MOVING! MAYBE IF WE GIVE HIM HIS HEADACHE MEDS, HE'LL BE OKAY!
YES, THAT ONE.

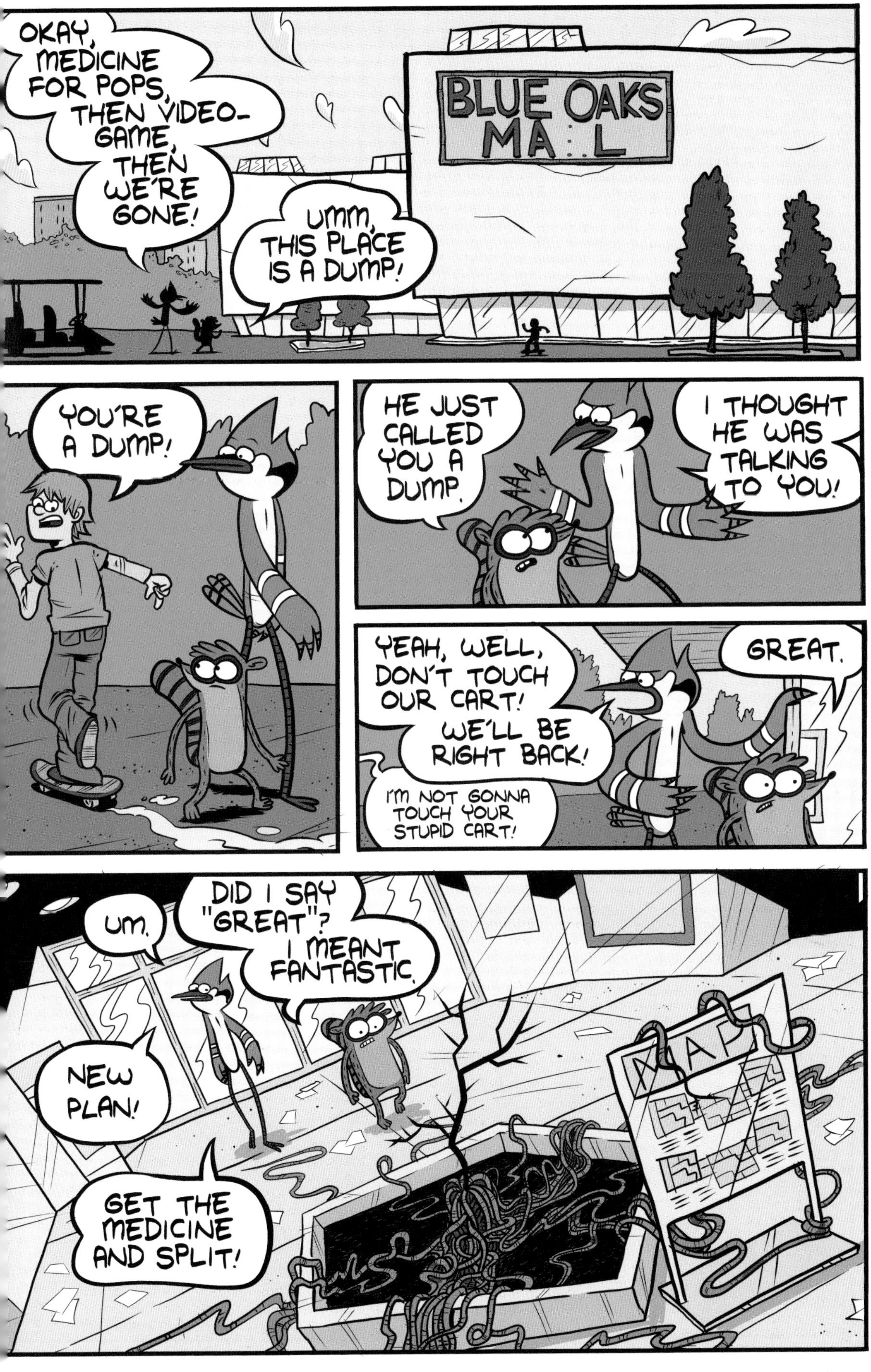
OKAY, MEDICINE FOR POPS, THEN VIDEO-GAME, THEN WE'RE GONE!
BLUE OAKS MA L
UMM, THIS PLACE IS A DUMP!
YOU'RE A DUMP!
HE JUST CALLED YOU A DUMP.
I THOUGHT HE WAS TALKING TO YOU!
YEAH, WELL, DON'T TOUCH OUR CART!
WE'LL BE RIGHT BACK!
GREAT.
I'M NOT GONNA TOUCH YOUR STUPID CART!
UM.
DID I SAY "GREAT"? I MEANT FANTASTIC.
NEW PLAN!
GET THE MEDICINE AND SPLIT!

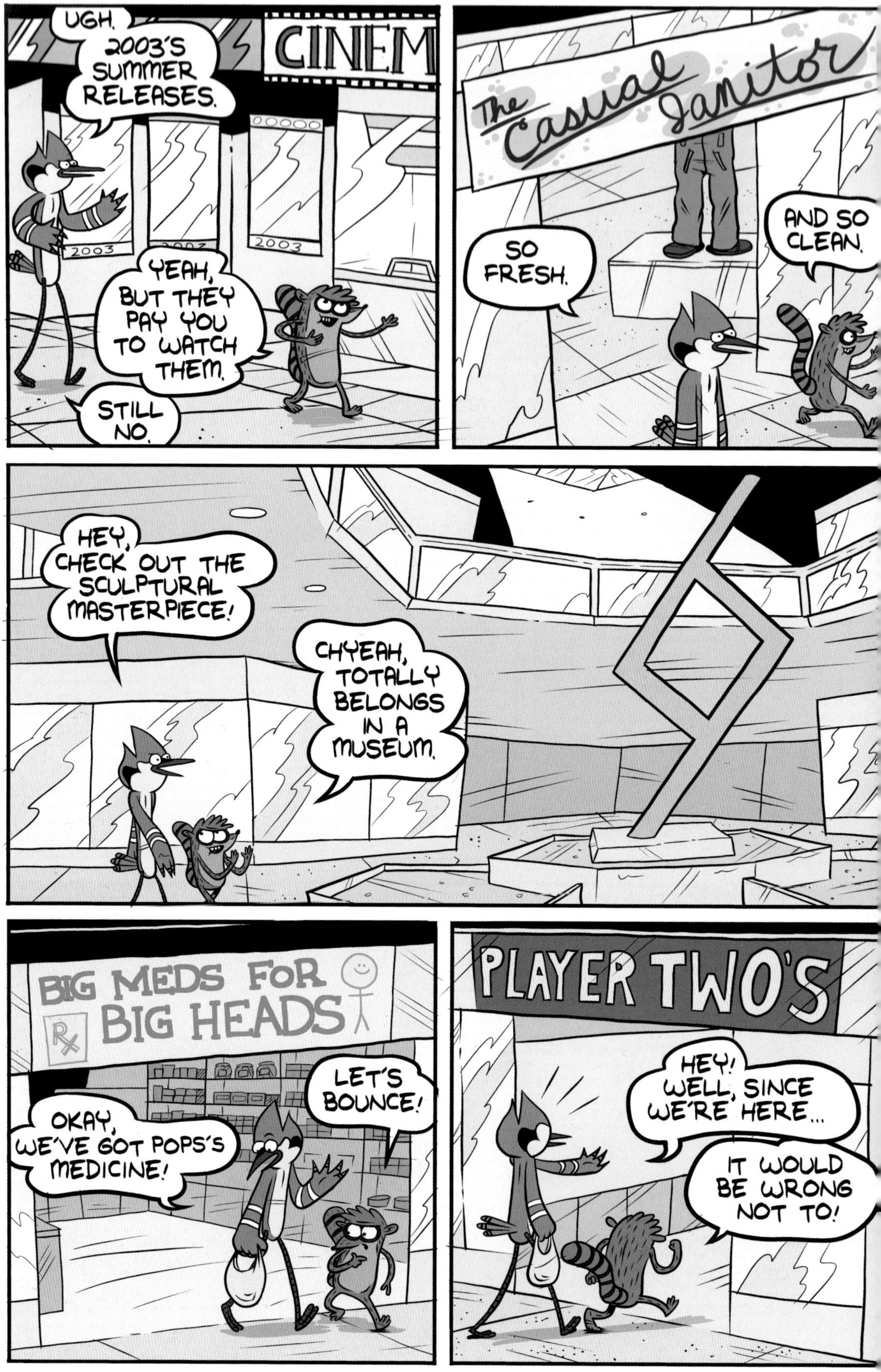
UGH.
2003'S SUMMER RELEASES.
CINEM
2003
2003
YEAH, BUT THEY PAY YOU TO WATCH THEM.
STILL NO.
The Casual Janitor
SO FRESH.
AND SO CLEAN.
HEY, CHECK OUT THE SCULPTURAL MASTERPIECE!
CHYEAH, TOTALLY BELONGS IN A MUSEUM.
BIG MEDS FOR BIG HEADS
Rx
OKAY, WE'VE GOT POPS'S MEDICINE!
LET'S BOUNCE!
PLAYER TWO'S
HEY! WELL, SINCE WE'RE HERE...
IT WOULD BE WRONG NOT TO!

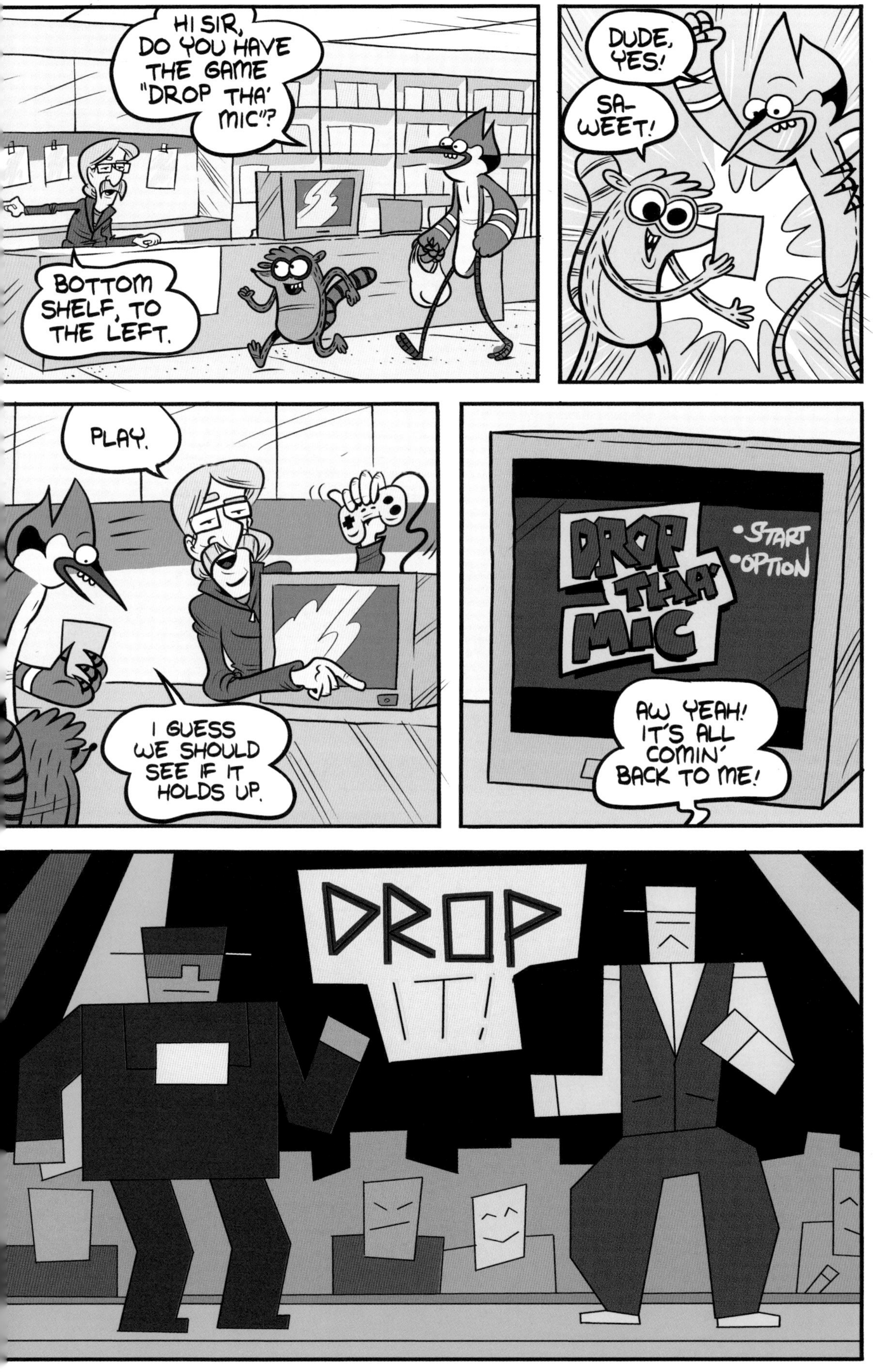
HI SIR, DO YOU HAVE THE GAME "DROP THA' MIC"?
BOTTOM SHELF, TO THE LEFT.
DUDE, YES!
SA-WEET!
PLAY.
I GUESS WE SHOULD SEE IF IT HOLDS UP.
DROP THA' MIC
•START
•OPTION
AW YEAH! IT'S ALL COMIN' BACK TO ME!
DROP IT!

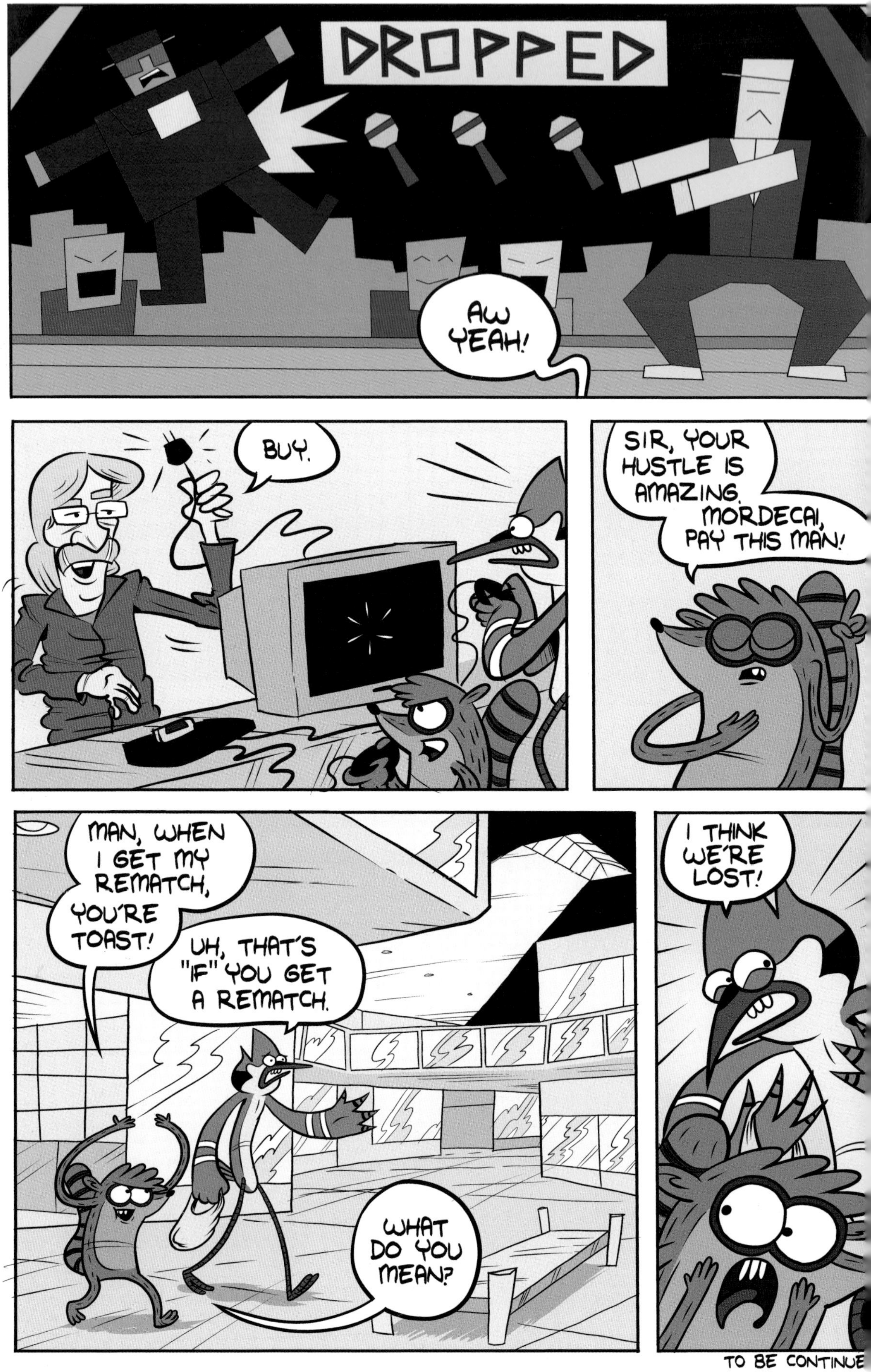
DROPPED
AW YEAH!
BUY.
SIR, YOUR HUSTLE IS AMAZING. MORDECAI, PAY THIS MAN!
MAN, WHEN I GET MY REMATCH, YOU'RE TOAST!
UH, THAT'S "IF" YOU GET A REMATCH.
WHAT DO YOU MEAN?
I THINK WE'RE LOST!
TO BE CONTINUE

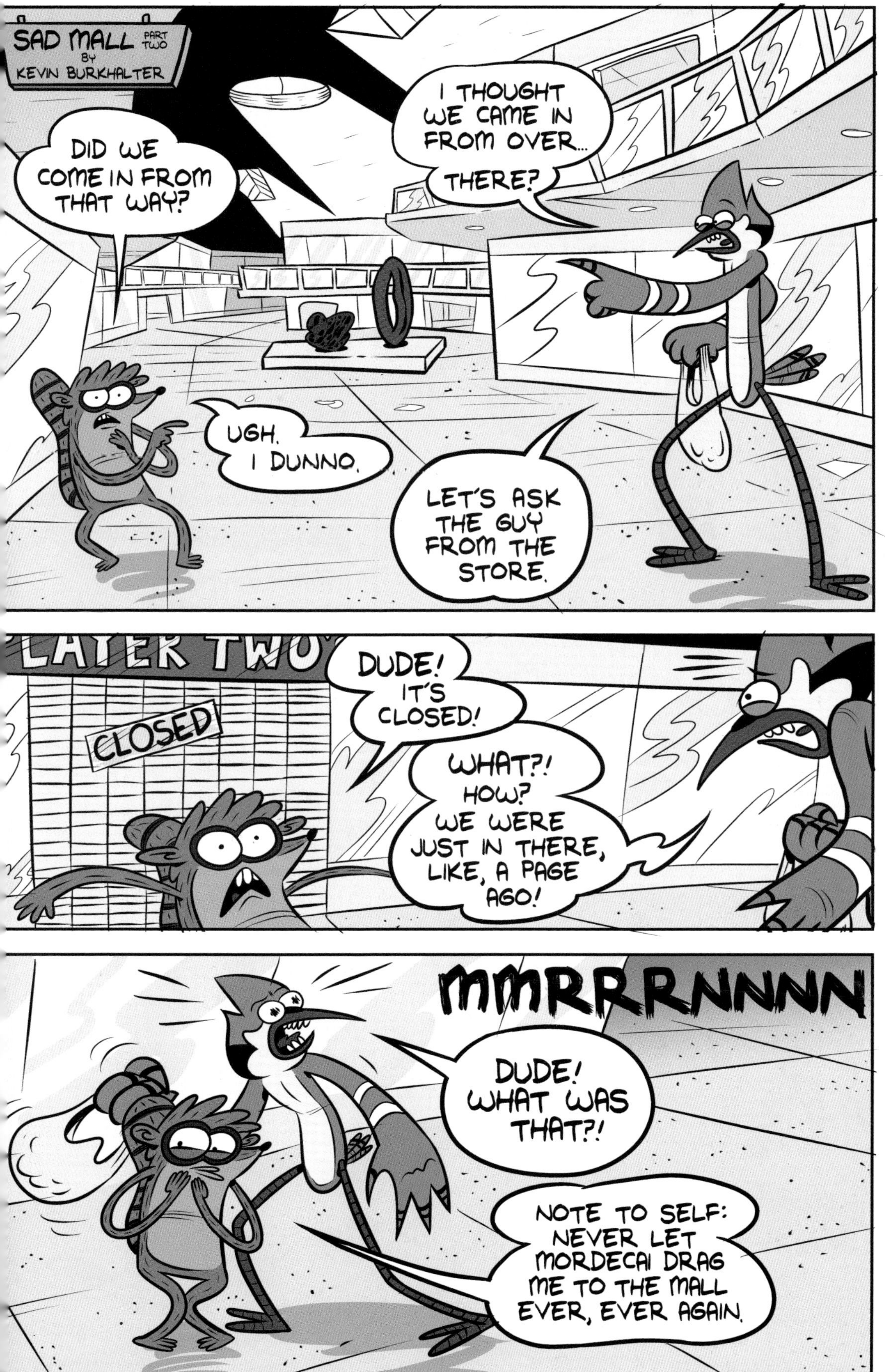
SAD MALL PART TWO
BY KEVIN BURKHALTER
DID WE COME IN FROM THAT WAY?
I THOUGHT WE CAME IN FROM OVER...
THERE?
UGH. I DUNNO.
LET'S ASK THE GUY FROM THE STORE.
LAYER TWO
CLOSED
DUDE! IT'S CLOSED!
WHAT?! HOW? WE WERE JUST IN THERE, LIKE, A PAGE AGO!
MMRRRNNNN
DUDE! WHAT WAS THAT?!
NOTE TO SELF: NEVER LET MORDECAI DRAG ME TO THE MALL EVER, EVER AGAIN.

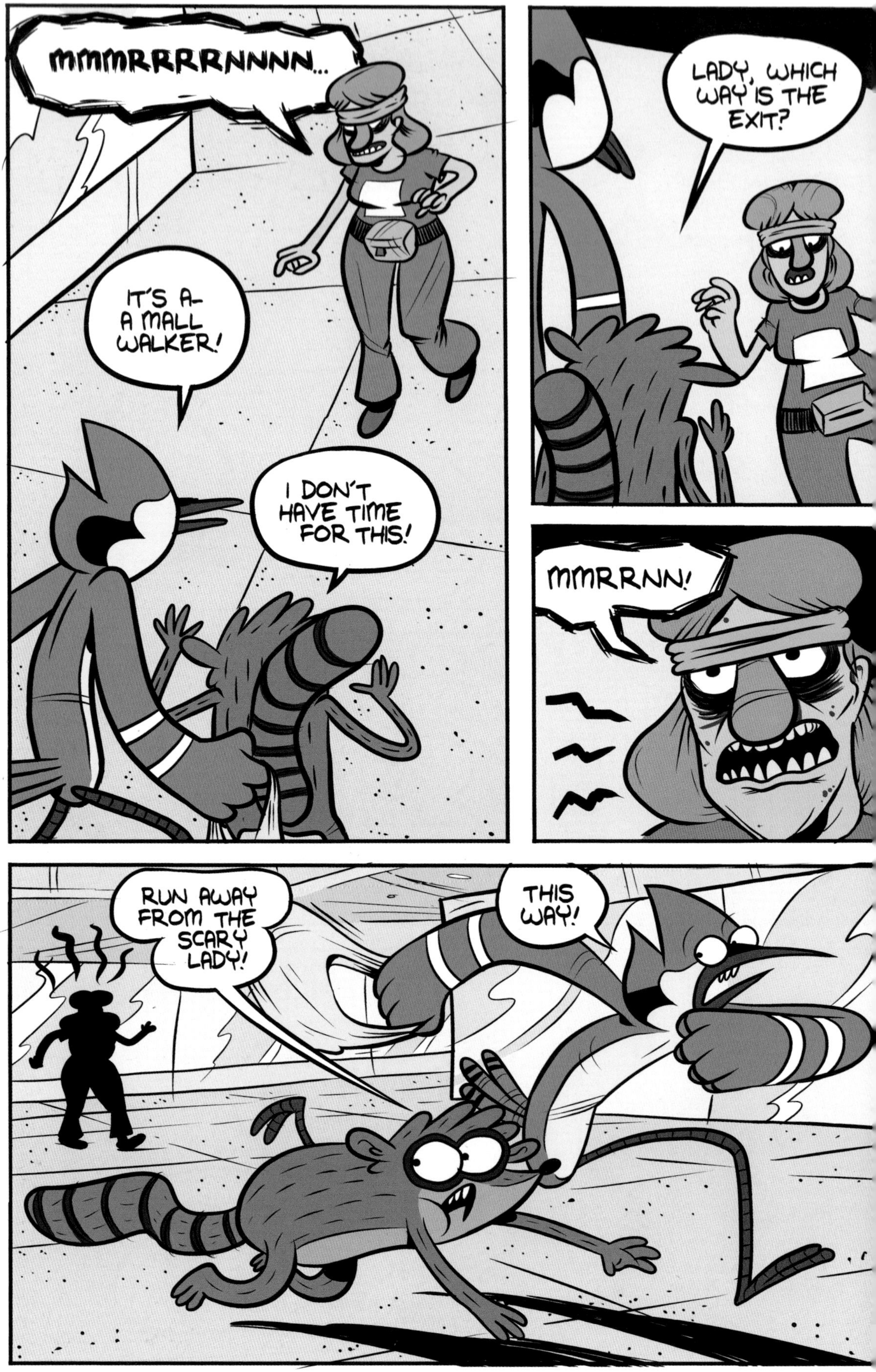
MMMRRRRNNNN...
IT'S A- A MALL WALKER!
I DON'T HAVE TIME FOR THIS!
LADY, WHICH WAY IS THE EXIT?
MMRRNN!
RUN AWAY FROM THE SCARY LADY!
THIS WAY!

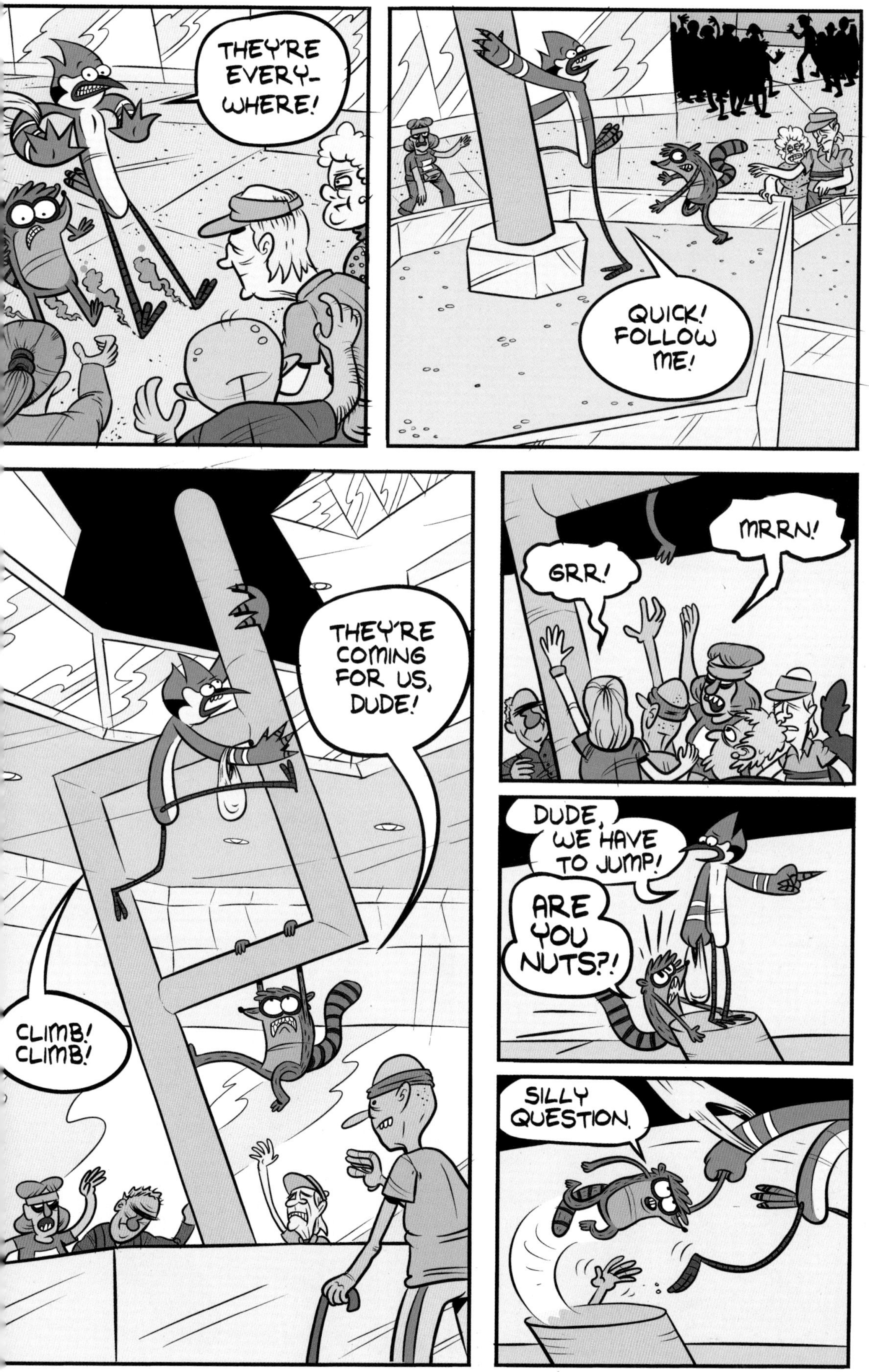
THEY'RE EVERY-WHERE!
QUICK! FOLLOW ME!
THEY'RE COMING FOR US, DUDE!
CLIMB! CLIMB!
GRR!
MRRN!
DUDE, WE HAVE TO JUMP!
ARE YOU NUTS?!
SILLY QUESTION.

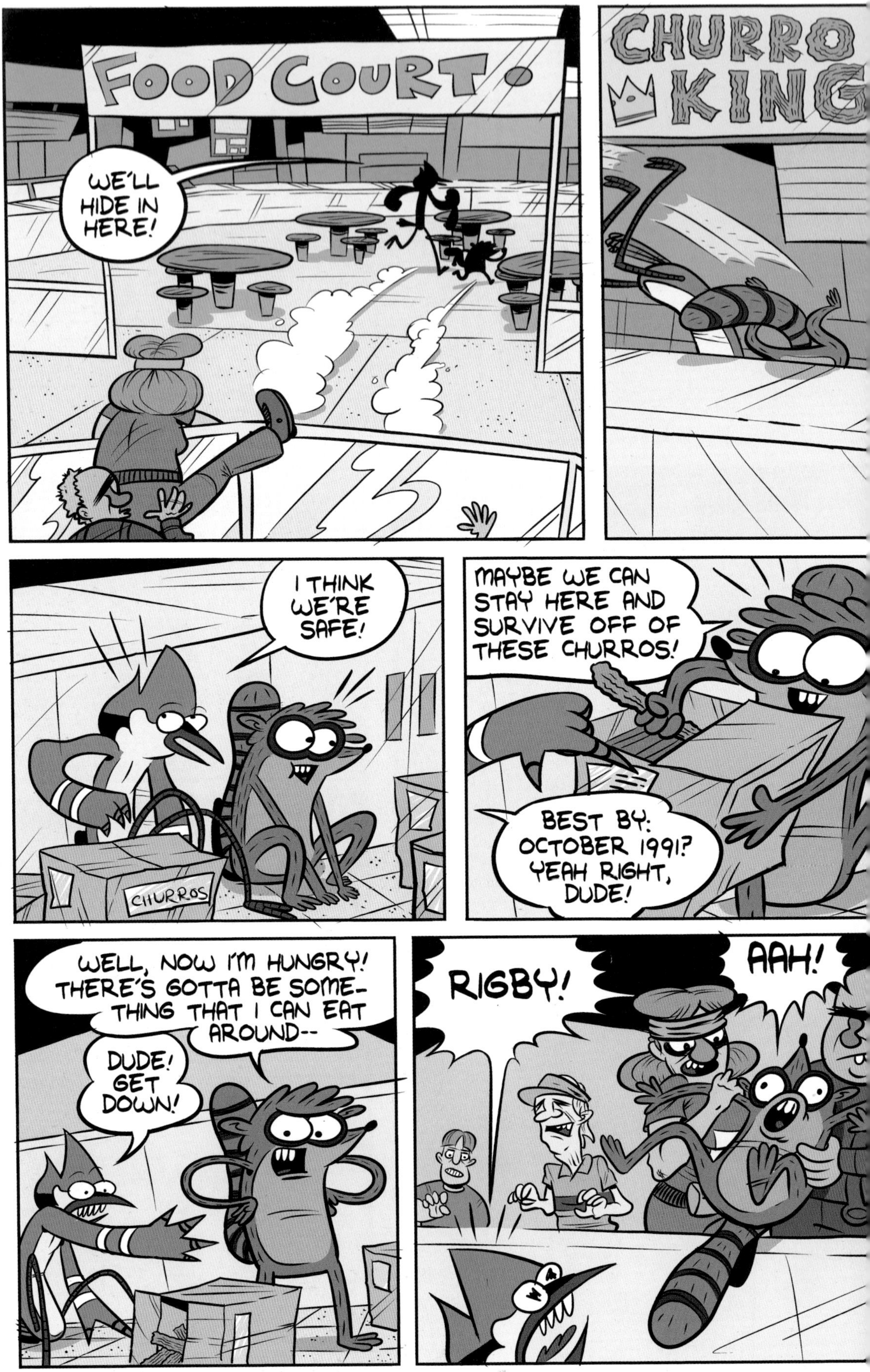
FOOD COURT
WE'LL HIDE IN HERE!
CHURRO KING
I THINK WE'RE SAFE!
CHURROS
MAYBE WE CAN STAY HERE AND SURVIVE OFF OF THESE CHURROS!
BEST BY: OCTOBER 1991? YEAH RIGHT, DUDE!
WELL, NOW I'M HUNGRY! THERE'S GOTTA BE SOME-THING THAT I CAN EAT AROUND--
DUDE! GET DOWN!
RIGBY!
AAH!

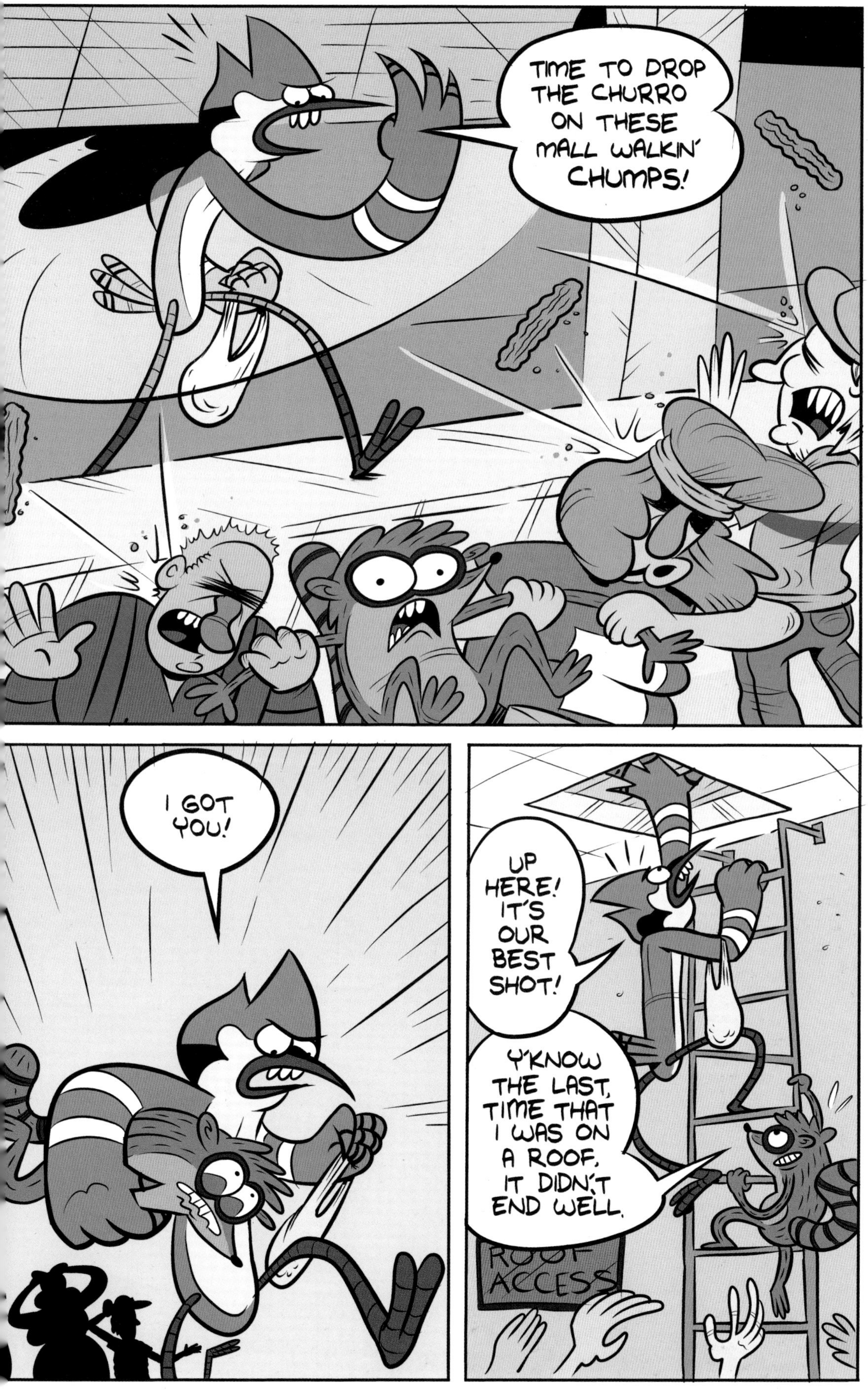
TIME TO DROP THE CHURRO ON THESE MALL WALKIN' CHUMPS!
I GOT YOU!
UP HERE! IT'S OUR BEST SHOT!
Y'KNOW THE LAST TIME THAT I WAS ON A ROOF, IT DIDN'T END WELL.
ROOF ACCESS

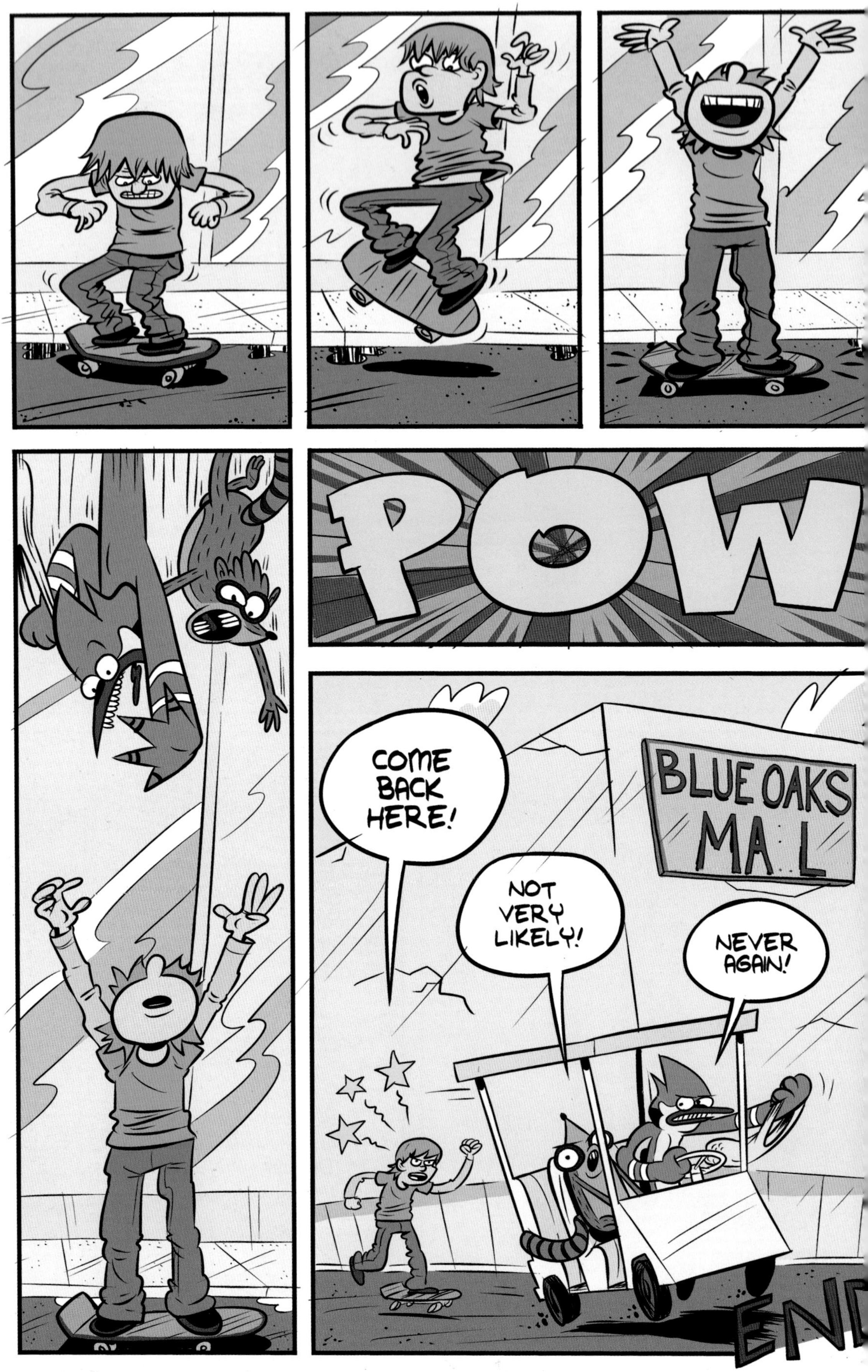
POW
BLUE OAKS
MA L
COME BACK HERE!
NOT VERY LIKELY!
NEVER AGAIN!
END

EING BENSON by Liz Prince and Kyle Folsom

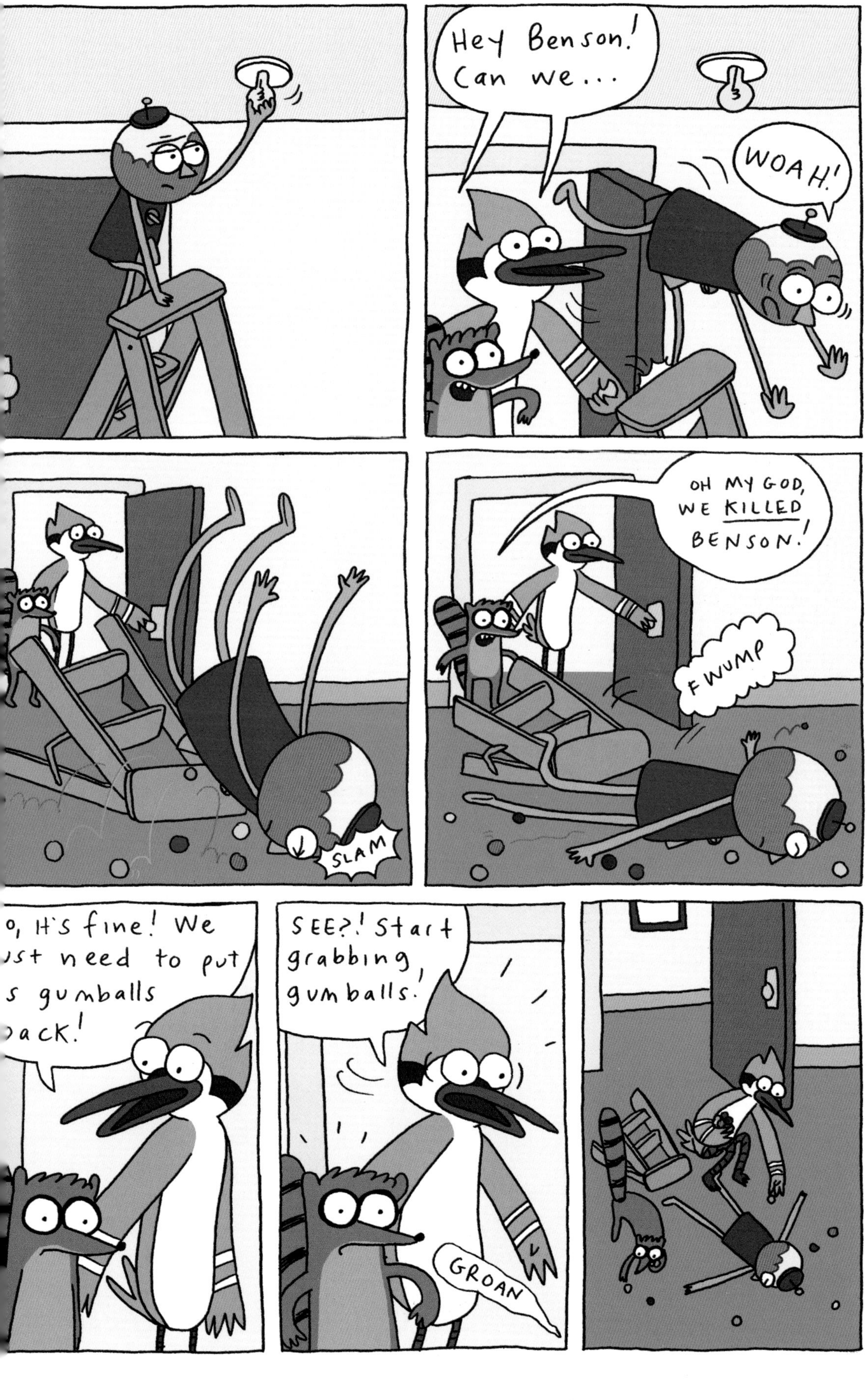
Hey Benson! Can we...
WOAH!
SLAM
OH MY GOD, WE KILLED BENSON!
FWUMP
o, It's fine! We
ust need to put
s gumballs
ack!
SEE?! Start grabbing gumballs!
GROAN

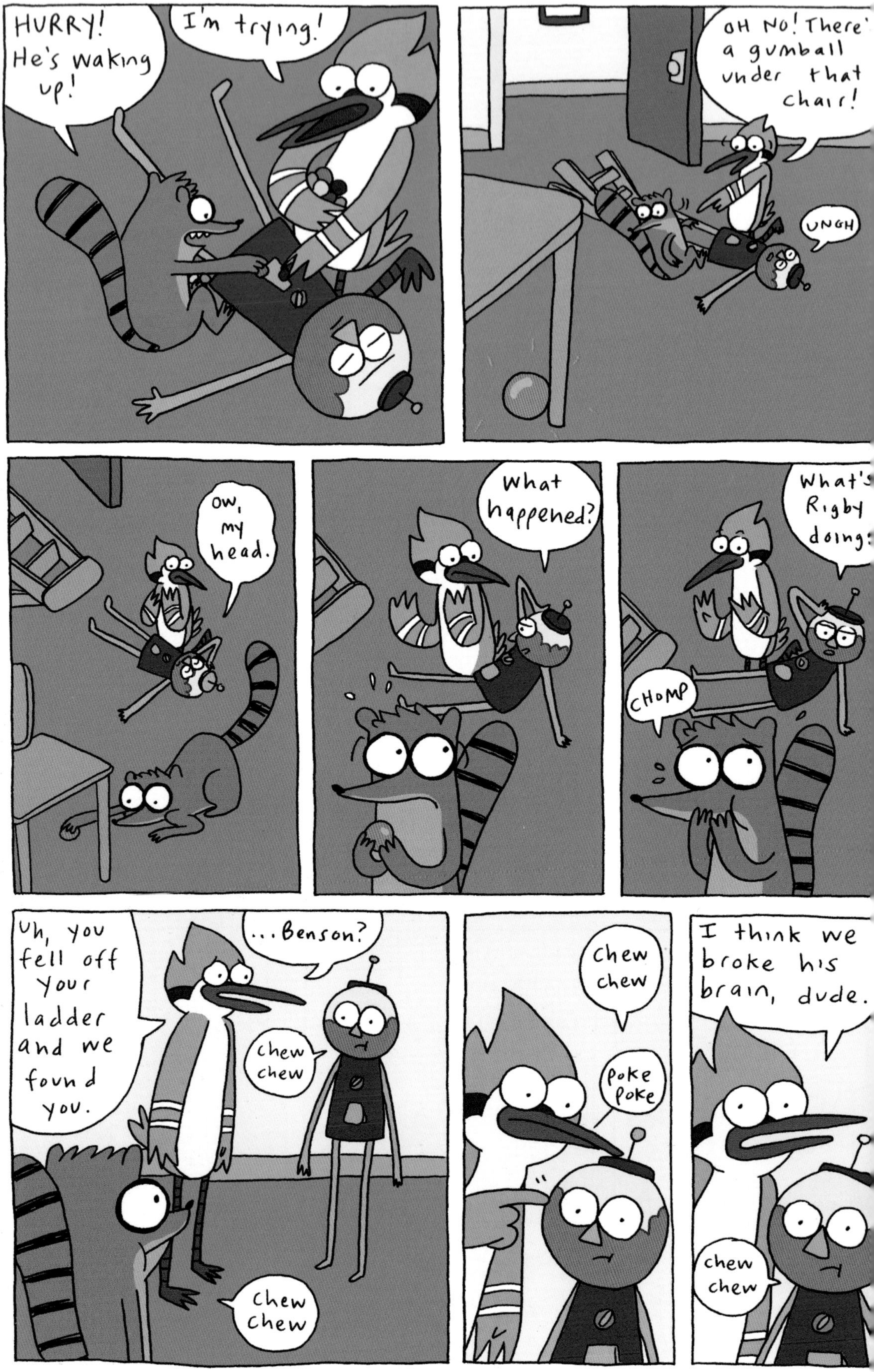
HURRY! He's waking up!
I'm trying!
OH NO! There's a gumball under that chair!
UNGH
Ow, my head.
What happened?
What's Rigby doing?
CHOMP
Uh, you fell off your ladder and we found you.
...Benson?
Chew chew
Chew chew
Chew chew
Poke poke
I think we broke his brain, dude.
chew chew

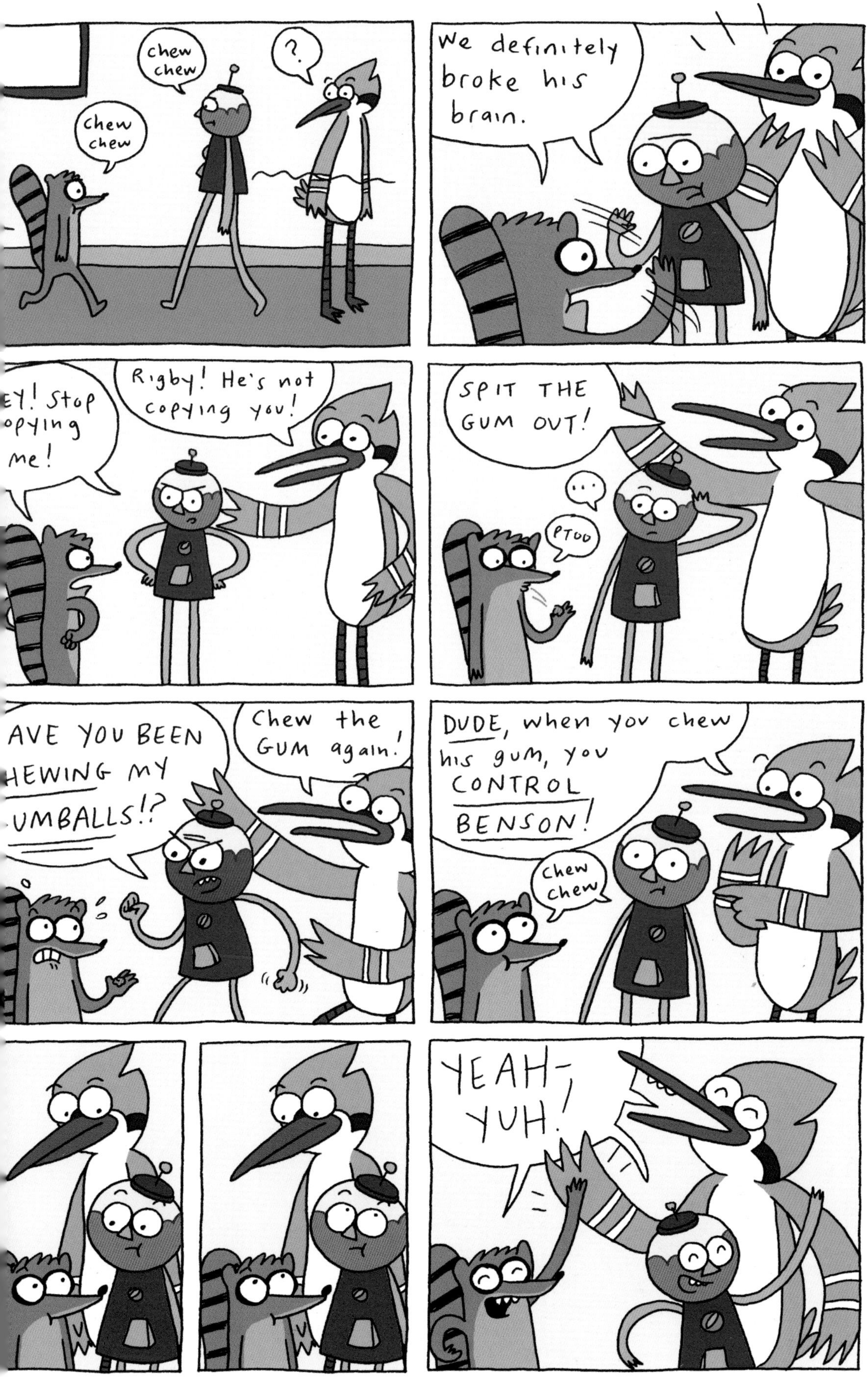
chew chew
chew chew
?
We definitely broke his brain.
EY! Stop opying me!
Rigby! He's not copying you!
SPIT THE GUM OUT!
...
PTOO
AVE YOU BEEN HEWING MY UMBALLS!?
Chew the GUM again!
DUDE, when you chew his gum, you CONTROL BENSON!
chew chew
YEAH-YUH!

MAYHEM ABOUNDS!

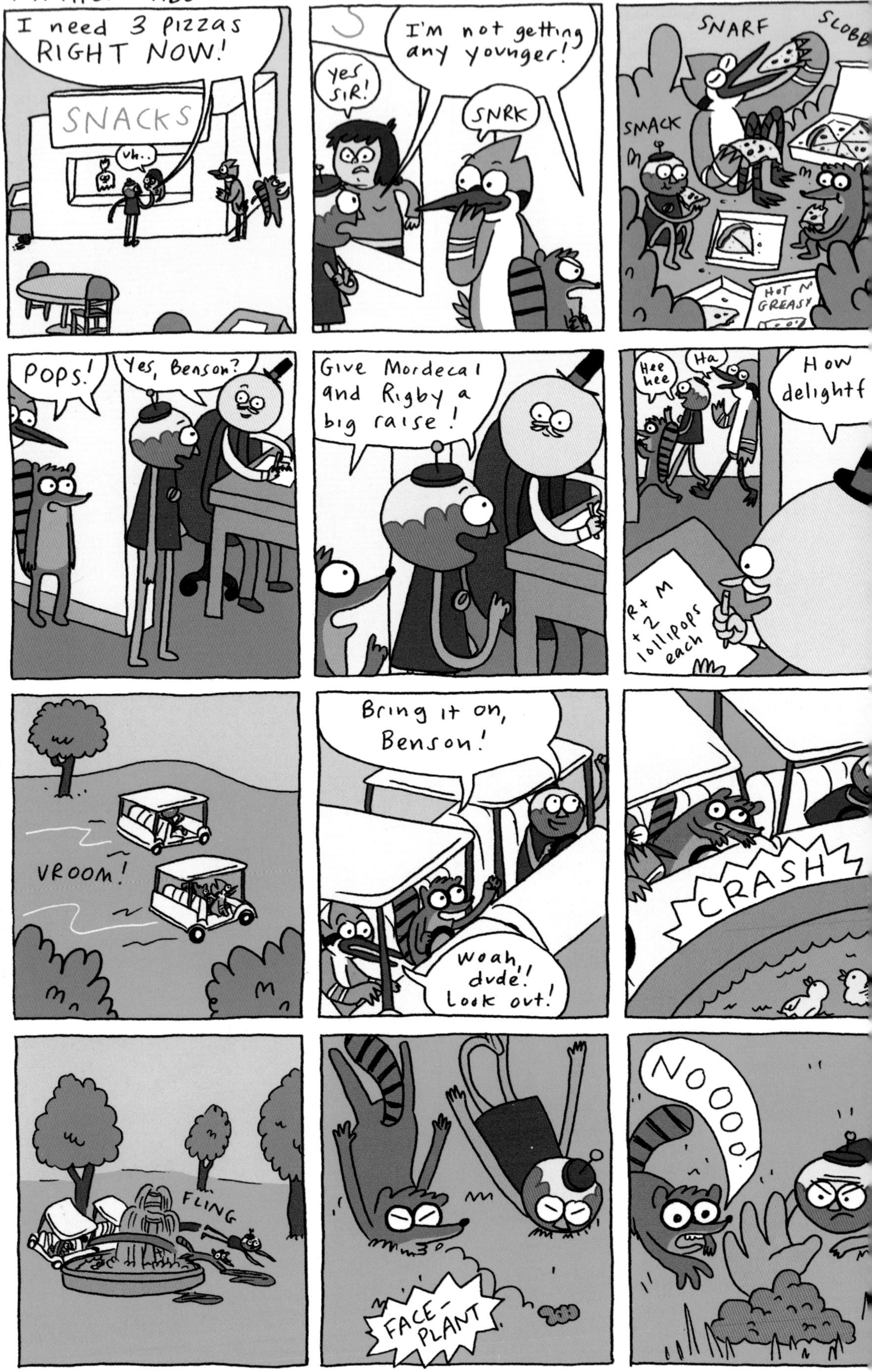

I need 3 pizzas RIGHT NOW!
SNACKS
uh..
I'm not getting any younger!
Yes SIR!
SNRK
SNARF
SLOBB
SMACK
HOT N GREASY
POPS!
Yes, Benson?
Give Mordecai and Rigby a big raise!
Hee hee
Ha
How delightf
R + M + 2 lollipops each
VROOM!
Bring it on, Benson!
Woah, dude!! Look out!
CRASH
FLING
FACE-PLANT
NOOOO!

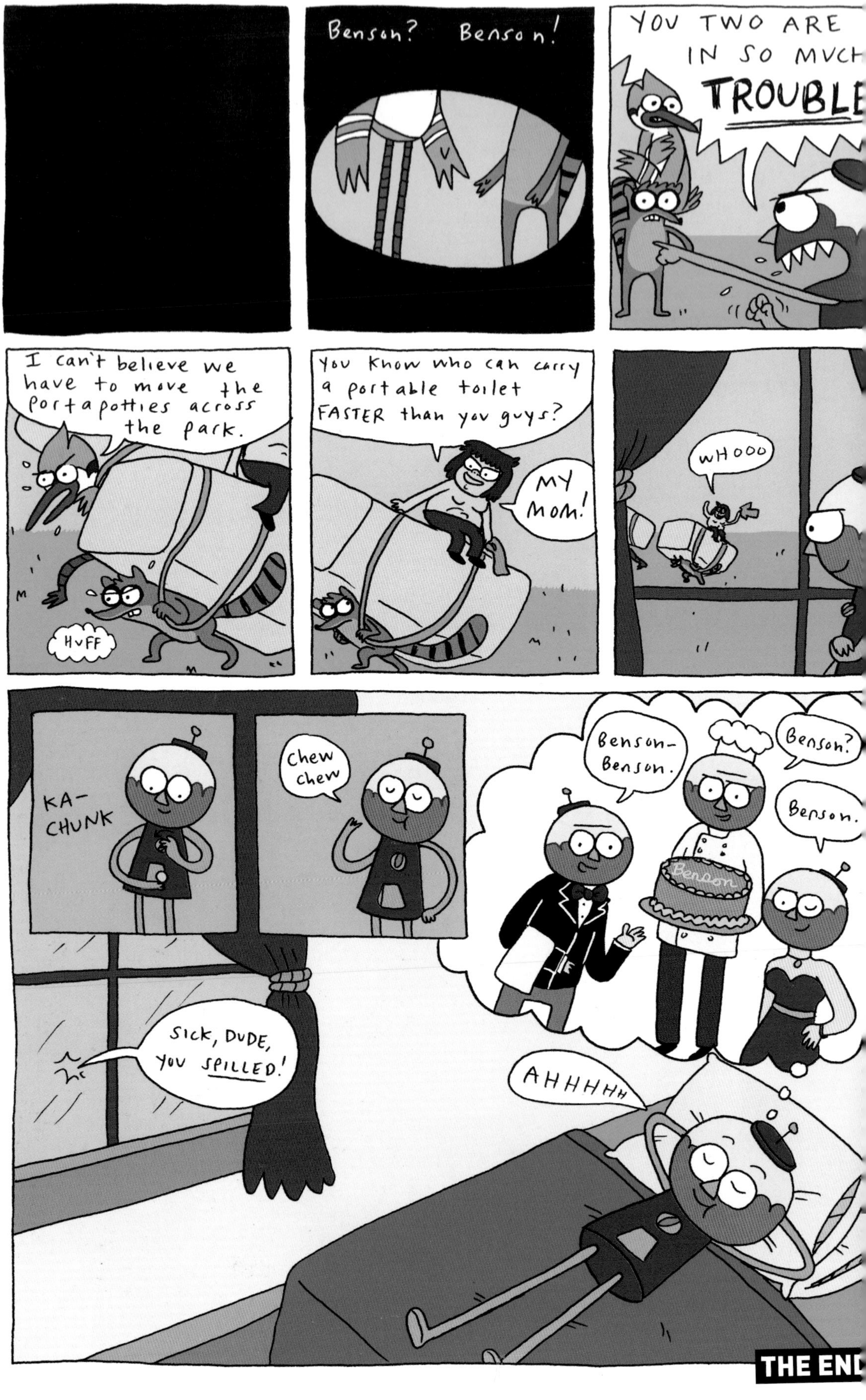
Benson? Benson!
YOU TWO ARE IN SO MUCH TROUBLE
I can't believe we have to move the portapotties across the park.
HUFF
You know who can carry a portable toilet FASTER than you guys?
MY MOM!
WHOOO
KA-CHUNK
Chew chew
Benson-Benson.
Benson?
Benson.
Benson
SICK, DUDE, YOU SPILLED!
AHHHHH
THE END

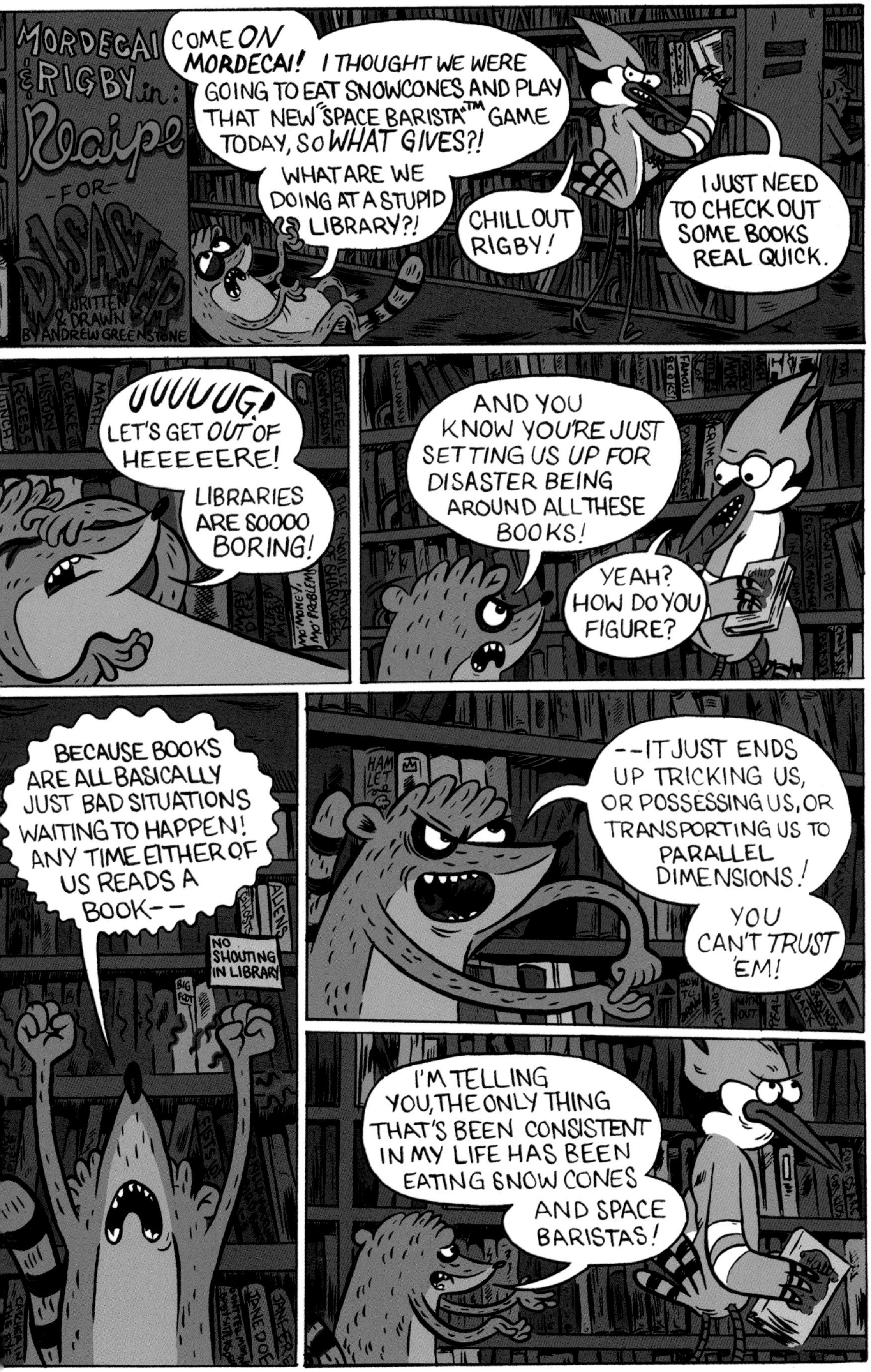
MORDECAI & RIGBY in: Recipe FOR DISASTER
WRITTEN & DRAWN BY ANDREW GREENSTONE
COME ON MORDECAI! I THOUGHT WE WERE GOING TO EAT SNOWCONES AND PLAY THAT NEW "SPACE BARISTA"™ GAME TODAY, SO WHAT GIVES?!
WHAT ARE WE DOING AT A STUPID LIBRARY?!
CHILL OUT RIGBY!
I JUST NEED TO CHECK OUT SOME BOOKS REAL QUICK.
UUUUUG! LET'S GET OUT OF HEEEEERE!
LIBRARIES ARE SOOOO BORING!
AND YOU KNOW YOU'RE JUST SETTING US UP FOR DISASTER BEING AROUND ALL THESE BOOKS!
YEAH? HOW DO YOU FIGURE?
BECAUSE BOOKS ARE ALL BASICALLY JUST BAD SITUATIONS WAITING TO HAPPEN! ANY TIME EITHER OF US READS A BOOK--
NO SHOUTING IN LIBRARY
--IT JUST ENDS UP TRICKING US, OR POSSESSING US, OR TRANSPORTING US TO PARALLEL DIMENSIONS!
YOU CAN'T TRUST 'EM!
I'M TELLING YOU, THE ONLY THING THAT'S BEEN CONSISTENT IN MY LIFE HAS BEEN EATING SNOW CONES AND SPACE BARISTAS!

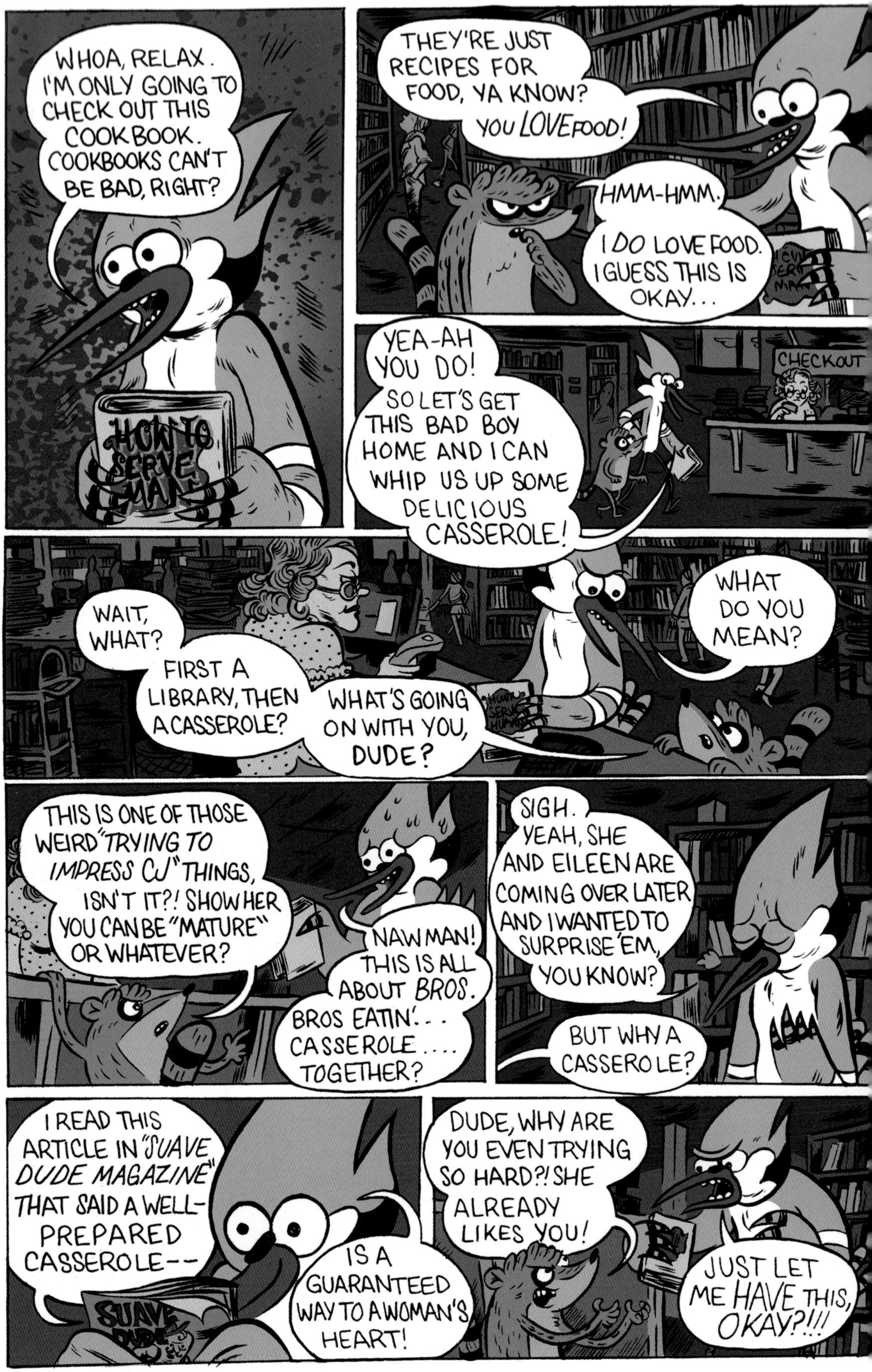

WHOA, RELAX. I'M ONLY GOING TO CHECK OUT THIS COOKBOOK. COOKBOOKS CAN'T BE BAD, RIGHT?
HOW TO SERVE MAN
THEY'RE JUST RECIPES FOR FOOD, YA KNOW? YOU *LOVE* FOOD!
HMM-HMM.
I *DO* LOVE FOOD. I GUESS THIS IS OKAY...
YEA-AH YOU DO!
SO LET'S GET THIS BAD BOY HOME AND I CAN WHIP US UP SOME DELICIOUS CASSEROLE!
CHECKOUT
WAIT, WHAT?
FIRST A LIBRARY, THEN A CASSEROLE?
WHAT'S GOING ON WITH YOU, DUDE?
WHAT DO YOU MEAN?
THIS IS ONE OF THOSE WEIRD "*TRYING TO IMPRESS CJ*" THINGS, ISN'T IT?! SHOW HER YOU CAN BE "MATURE" OR WHATEVER?
NAW MAN! THIS IS ALL ABOUT *BROS*.
BROS EATIN'... CASSEROLE.... TOGETHER?
SIGH. YEAH, SHE AND EILEEN ARE COMING OVER LATER AND I WANTED TO SURPRISE 'EM, YOU KNOW?
BUT WHY A CASSEROLE?
I READ THIS ARTICLE IN "*SUAVE DUDE MAGAZINE*" THAT SAID A WELL-PREPARED CASSEROLE--
IS A GUARANTEED WAY TO A WOMAN'S HEART!
SUAVE DUDE
DUDE, WHY ARE YOU EVEN TRYING SO HARD?! SHE ALREADY LIKES YOU!
JUST LET ME *HAVE* THIS, *OKAY?!!!*

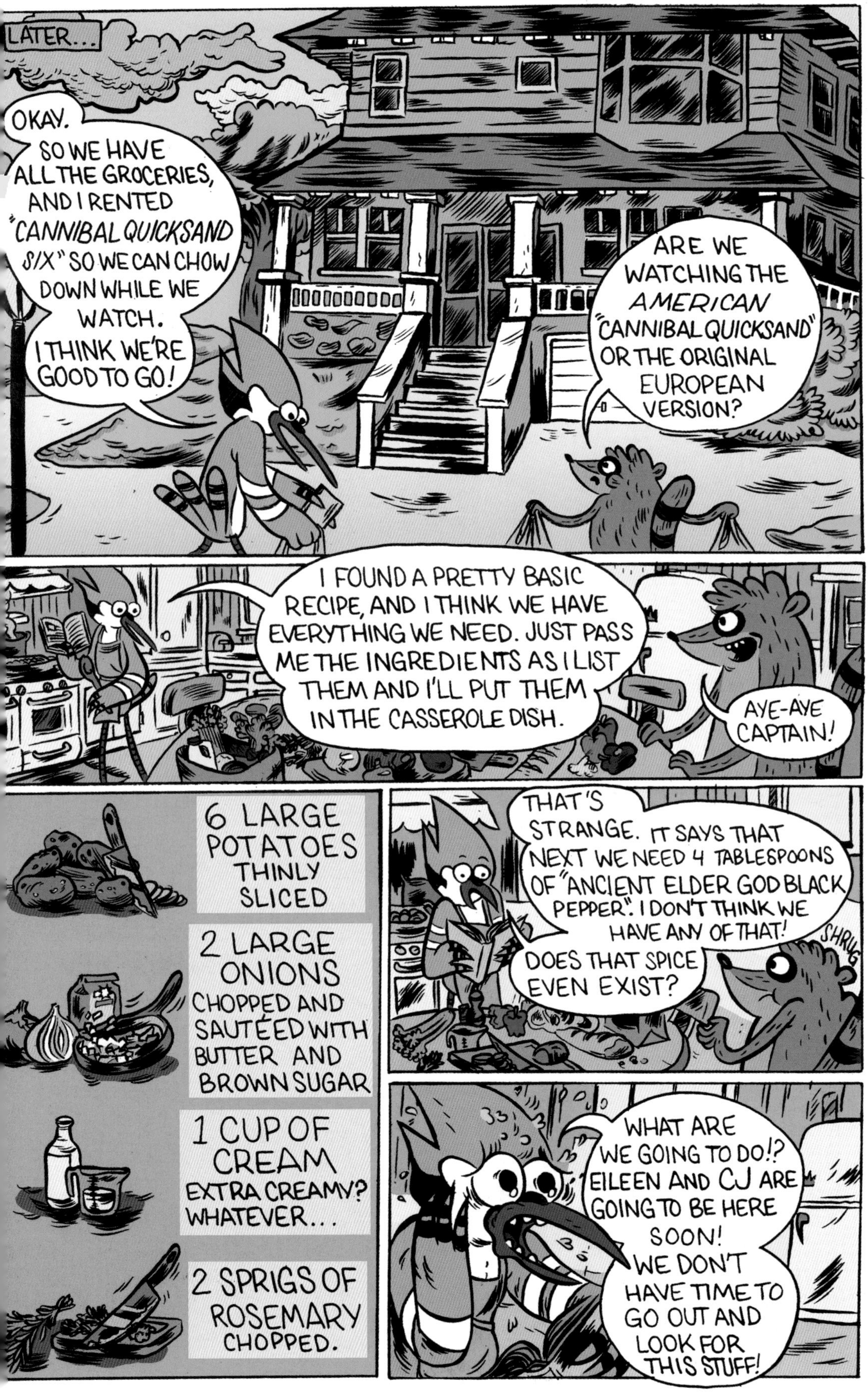
LATER...
OKAY. SO WE HAVE ALL THE GROCERIES, AND I RENTED "CANNIBAL QUICKSAND SIX" SO WE CAN CHOW DOWN WHILE WE WATCH. I THINK WE'RE GOOD TO GO!
ARE WE WATCHING THE AMERICAN "CANNIBAL QUICKSAND" OR THE ORIGINAL EUROPEAN VERSION?
I FOUND A PRETTY BASIC RECIPE, AND I THINK WE HAVE EVERYTHING WE NEED. JUST PASS ME THE INGREDIENTS AS I LIST THEM AND I'LL PUT THEM IN THE CASSEROLE DISH.
AYE-AYE CAPTAIN!
6 LARGE POTATOES THINLY SLICED
2 LARGE ONIONS CHOPPED AND SAUTÉED WITH BUTTER AND BROWN SUGAR
1 CUP OF CREAM EXTRA CREAMY? WHATEVER...
2 SPRIGS OF ROSEMARY CHOPPED.
THAT'S STRANGE. IT SAYS THAT NEXT WE NEED 4 TABLESPOONS OF "ANCIENT ELDER GOD BLACK PEPPER". I DON'T THINK WE HAVE ANY OF THAT!
DOES THAT SPICE EVEN EXIST?
SHRUG
WHAT ARE WE GOING TO DO!? EILEEN AND CJ ARE GOING TO BE HERE SOON!
WE DON'T HAVE TIME TO GO OUT AND LOOK FOR THIS STUFF!

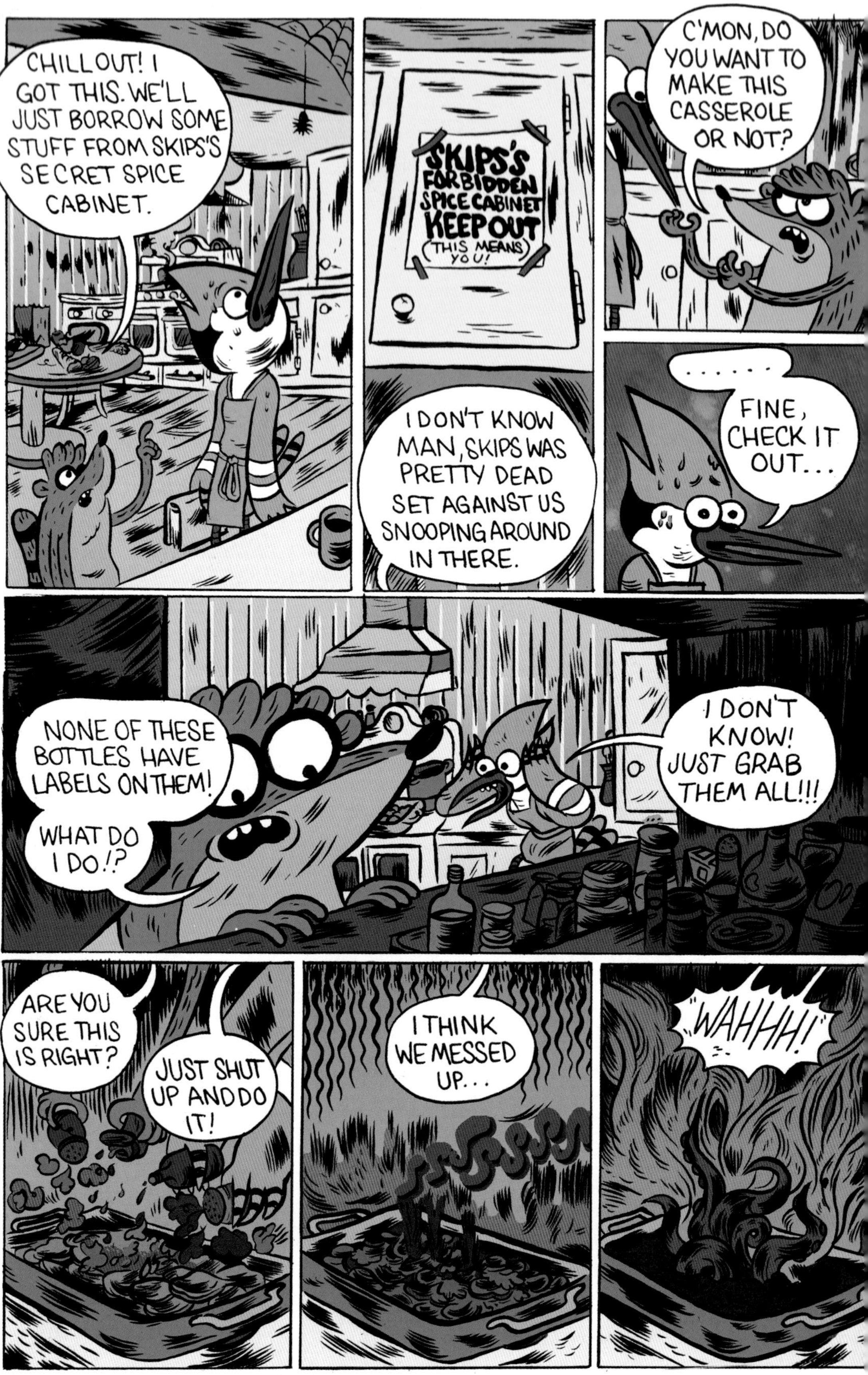

CHILL OUT! I GOT THIS. WE'LL JUST BORROW SOME STUFF FROM SKIPS'S SECRET SPICE CABINET.
SKIPS'S FORBIDDEN SPICE CABINET KEEP OUT (THIS MEANS YOU!)
I DON'T KNOW MAN, SKIPS WAS PRETTY DEAD SET AGAINST US SNOOPING AROUND IN THERE.
C'MON, DO YOU WANT TO MAKE THIS CASSEROLE OR NOT?
. . . . . .
FINE, CHECK IT OUT...
NONE OF THESE BOTTLES HAVE LABELS ON THEM!
WHAT DO I DO!?
I DON'T KNOW! JUST GRAB THEM ALL!!!
ARE YOU SURE THIS IS RIGHT?
JUST SHUT UP AND DO IT!
I THINK WE MESSED UP...
"WAHHH!"

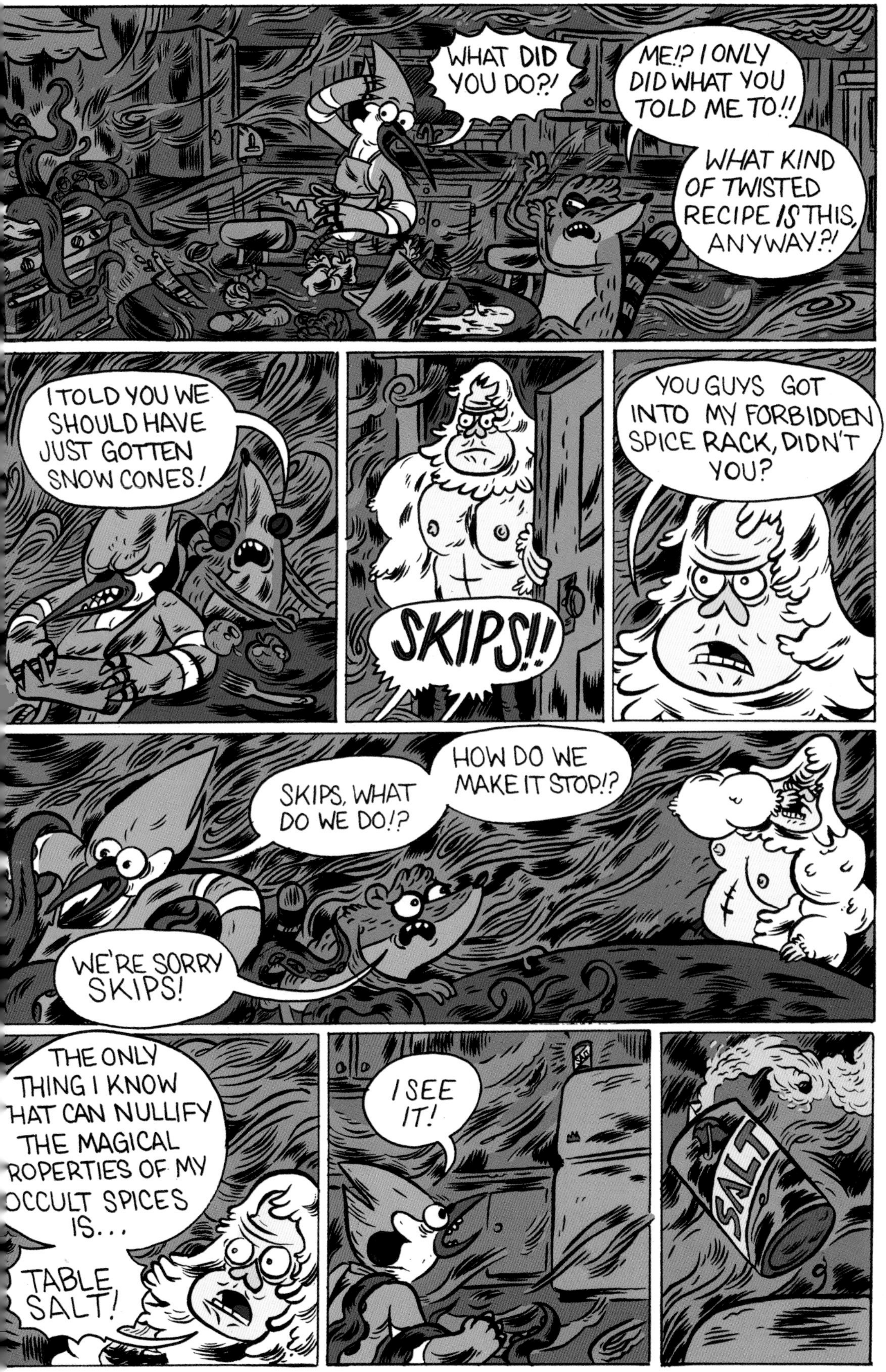
WHAT DID YOU DO?!
ME!? I ONLY DID WHAT YOU TOLD ME TO!!
WHAT KIND OF TWISTED RECIPE IS THIS, ANYWAY?!
I TOLD YOU WE SHOULD HAVE JUST GOTTEN SNOW CONES!
SKIPS!!
YOU GUYS GOT INTO MY FORBIDDEN SPICE RACK, DIDN'T YOU?
SKIPS, WHAT DO WE DO!?
HOW DO WE MAKE IT STOP!?
WE'RE SORRY SKIPS!
THE ONLY THING I KNOW HAT CAN NULLIFY THE MAGICAL ROPERTIES OF MY OCCULT SPICES IS...
TABLE SALT!
I SEE IT!
SALT

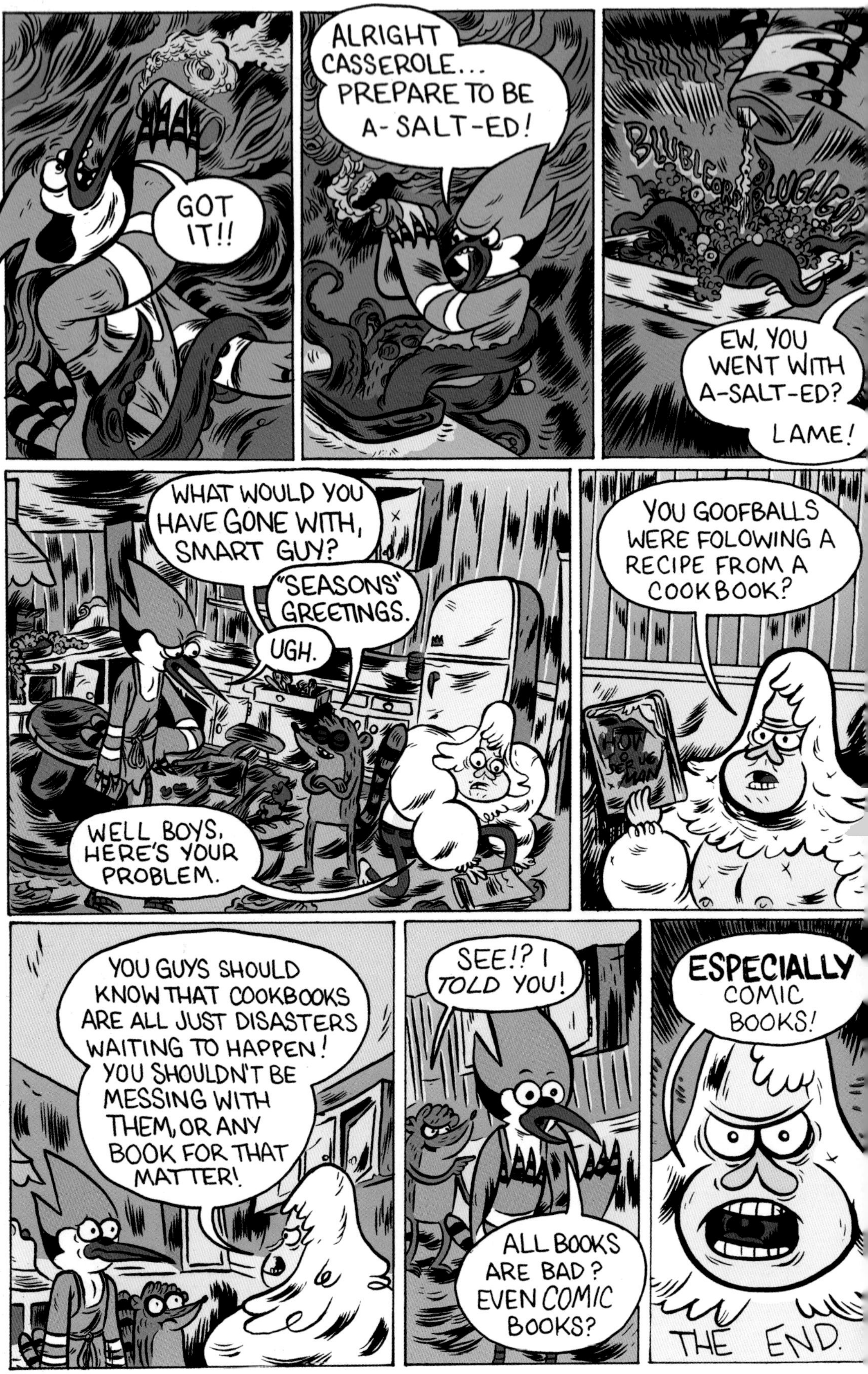
GOT IT!!
ALRIGHT CASSEROLE... PREPARE TO BE A-SALT-ED!
BLUBLEORP BLUGLEORP
EW, YOU WENT WITH A-SALT-ED?
LAME!
WHAT WOULD YOU HAVE GONE WITH, SMART GUY?
"SEASONS" GREETINGS.
UGH.
WELL BOYS, HERE'S YOUR PROBLEM.
YOU GOOFBALLS WERE FOLOWING A RECIPE FROM A COOKBOOK?
YOU GUYS SHOULD KNOW THAT COOKBOOKS ARE ALL JUST DISASTERS WAITING TO HAPPEN! YOU SHOULDN'T BE MESSING WITH THEM, OR ANY BOOK FOR THAT MATTER!
SEE!? I TOLD YOU!
ALL BOOKS ARE BAD? EVEN COMIC BOOKS?
ESPECIALLY COMIC BOOKS!
THE END.

COVER GALLERY

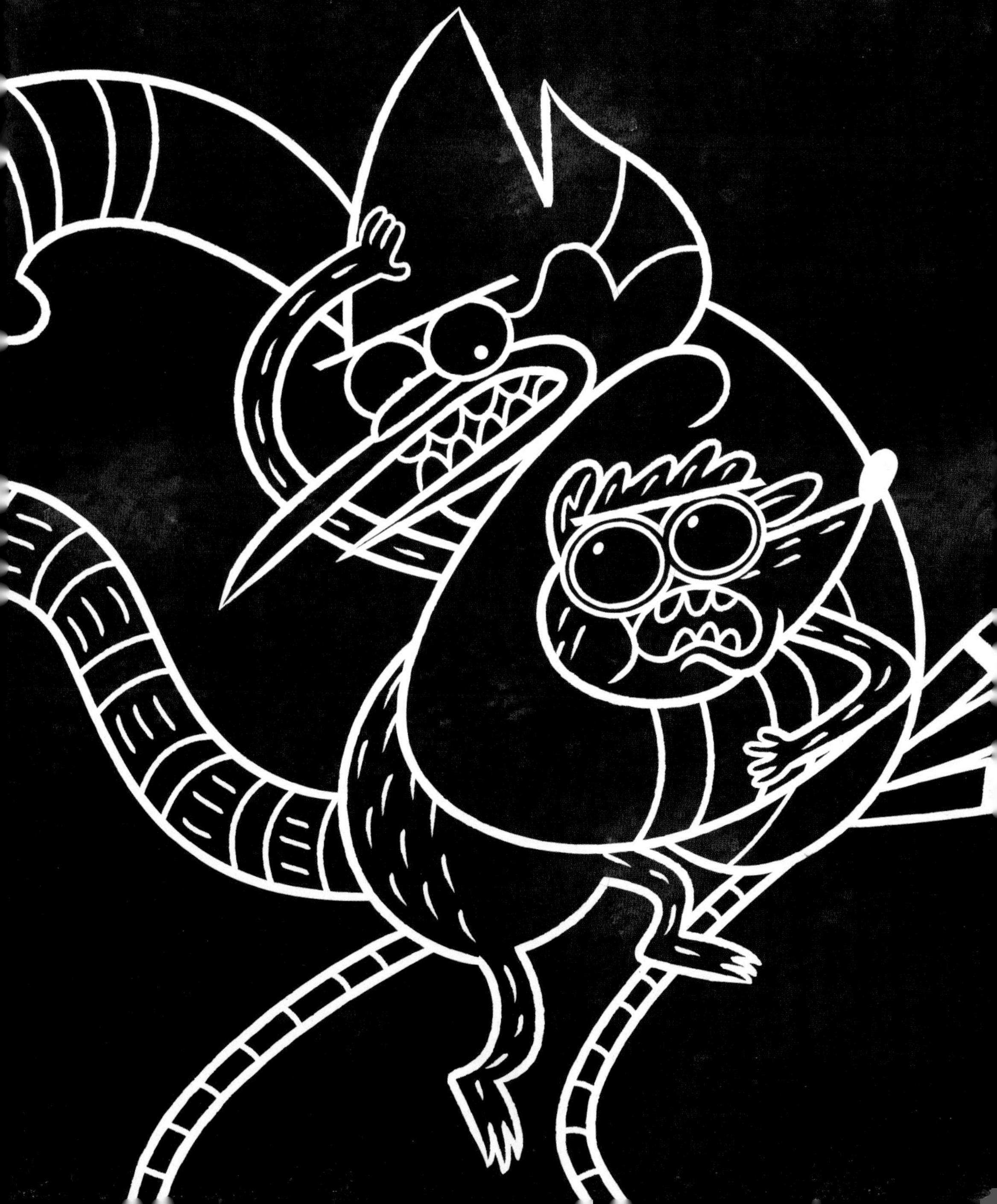

ISSUE TWENTY ONE Main Cover
ANDY HIRSCH

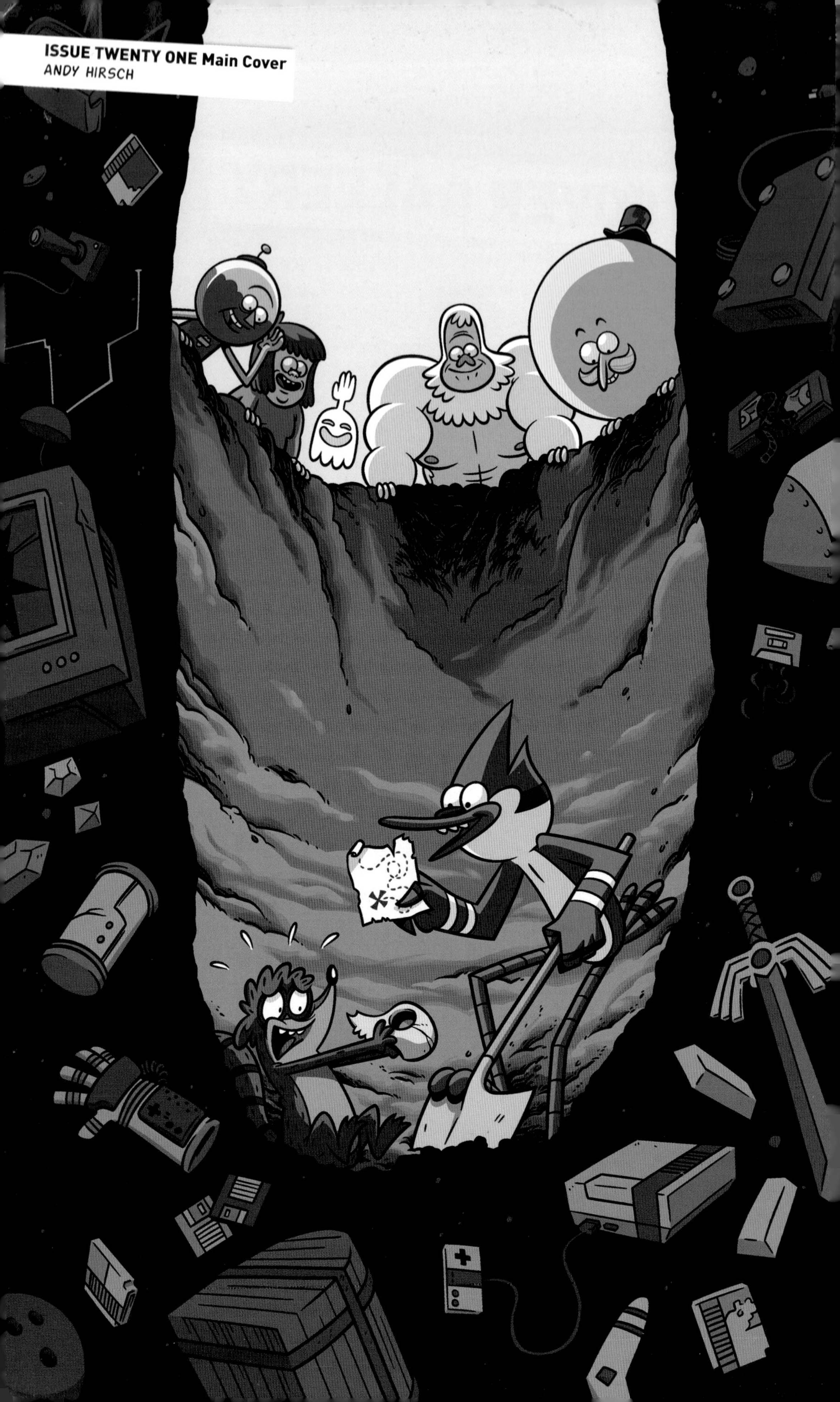

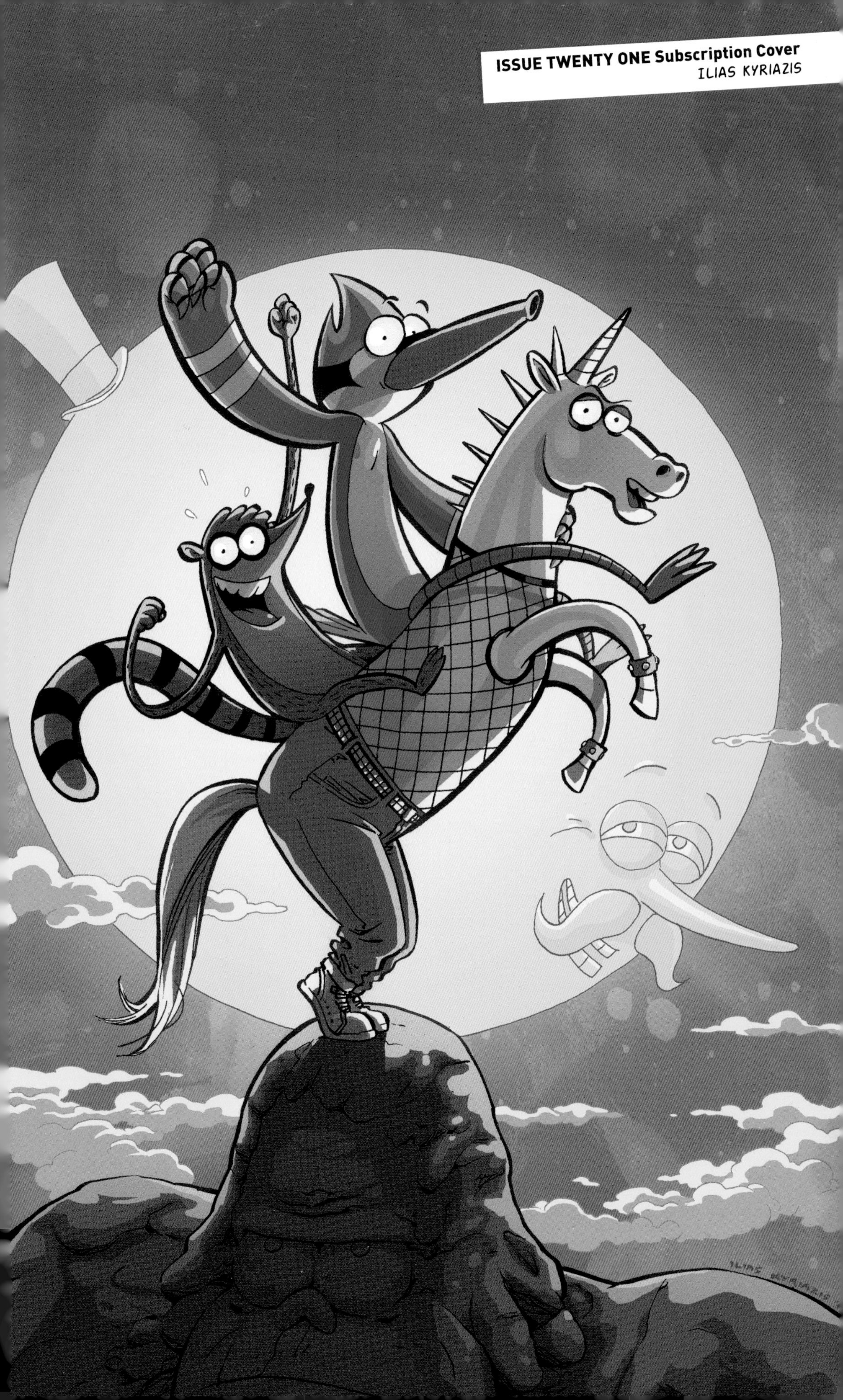

ISSUE TWENTY ONE Subscription Cover
ILIAS KYRIAZIS

ISSUE TWENTY TWO Main Cover
ANDY HIRSCH

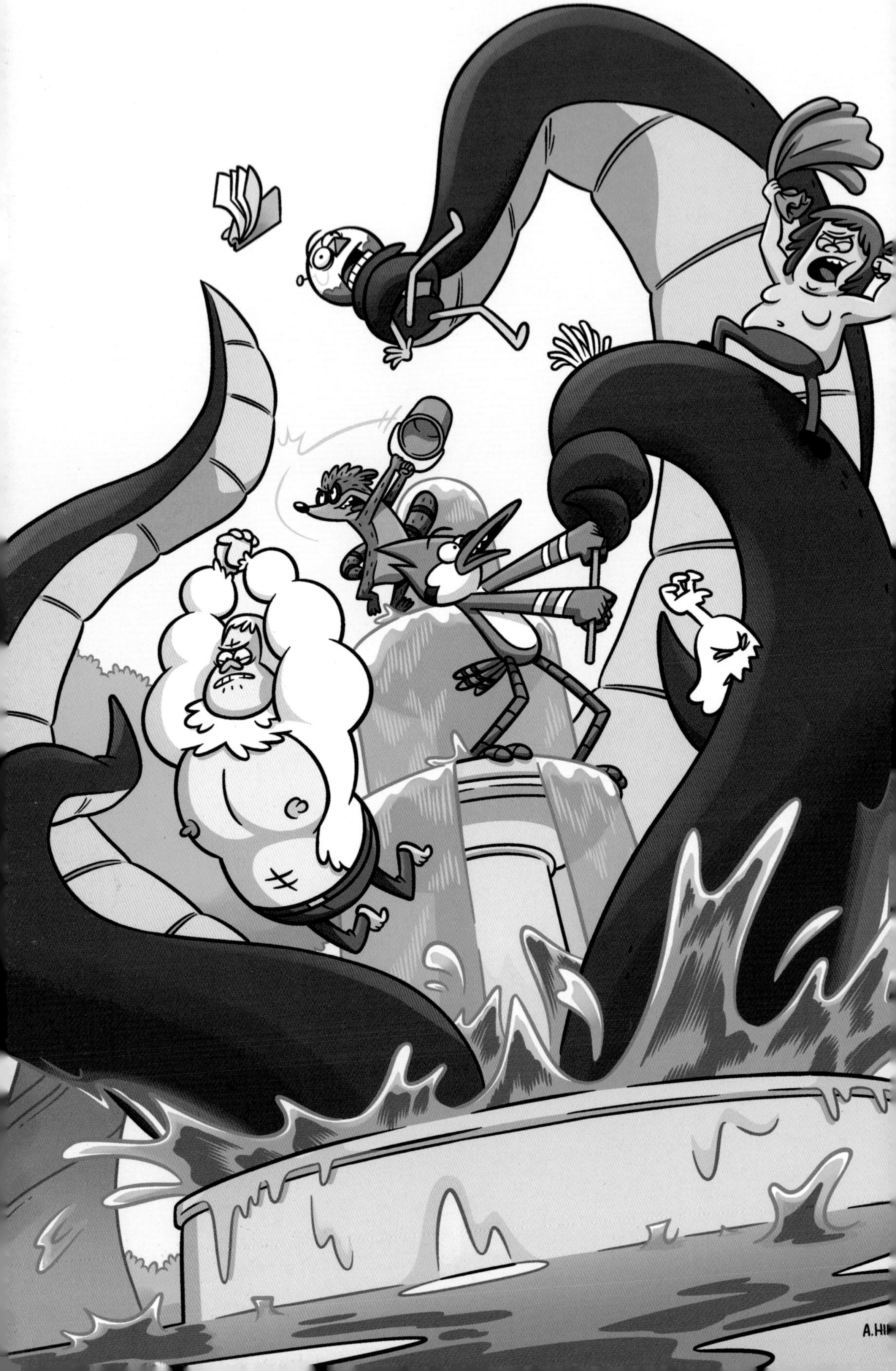
A.HI

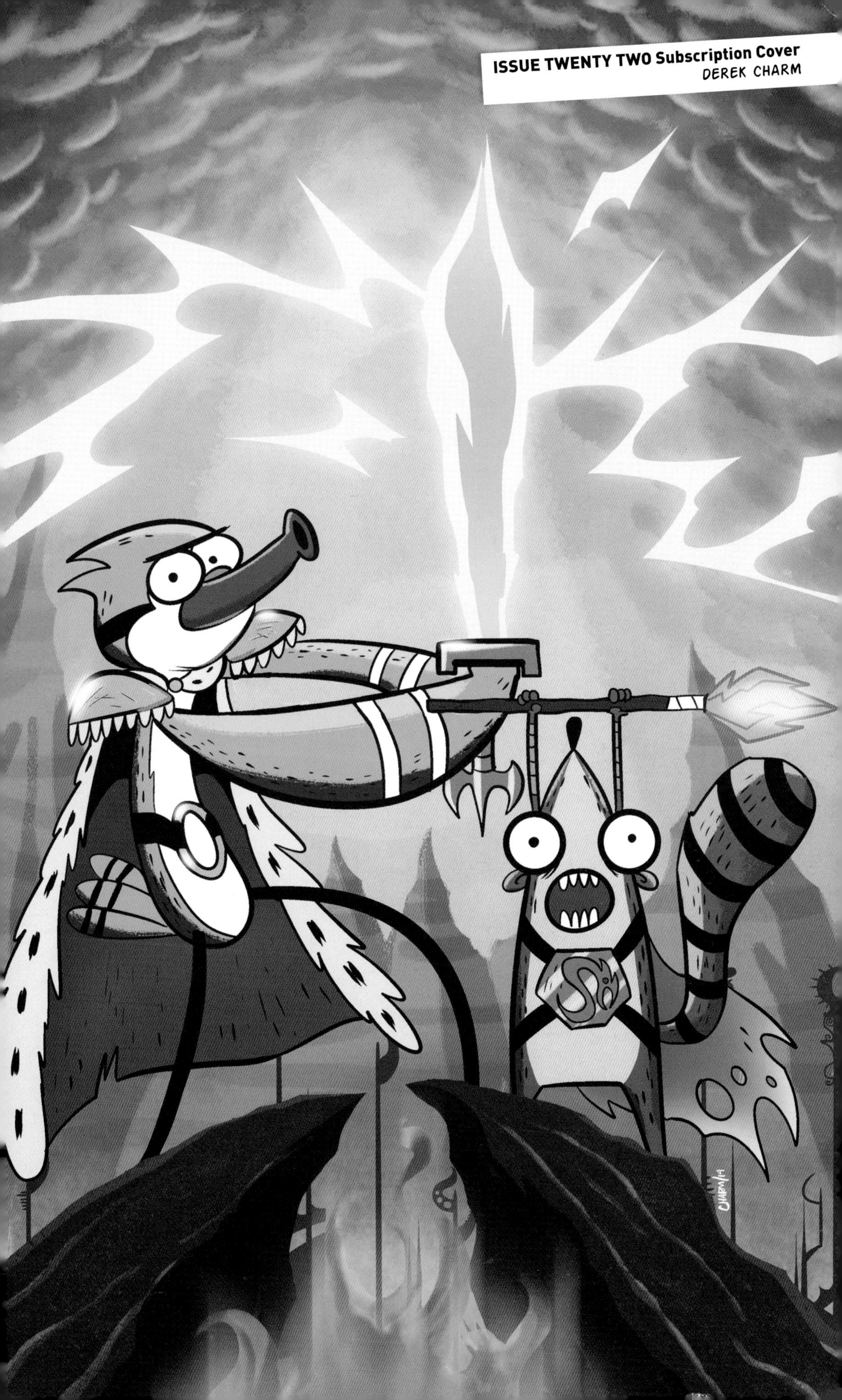

ISSUE TWENTY TWO Subscription Cover
DEREK CHARM

ISSUE TWENTY THREE Main Cover
ANDY HIRSCH

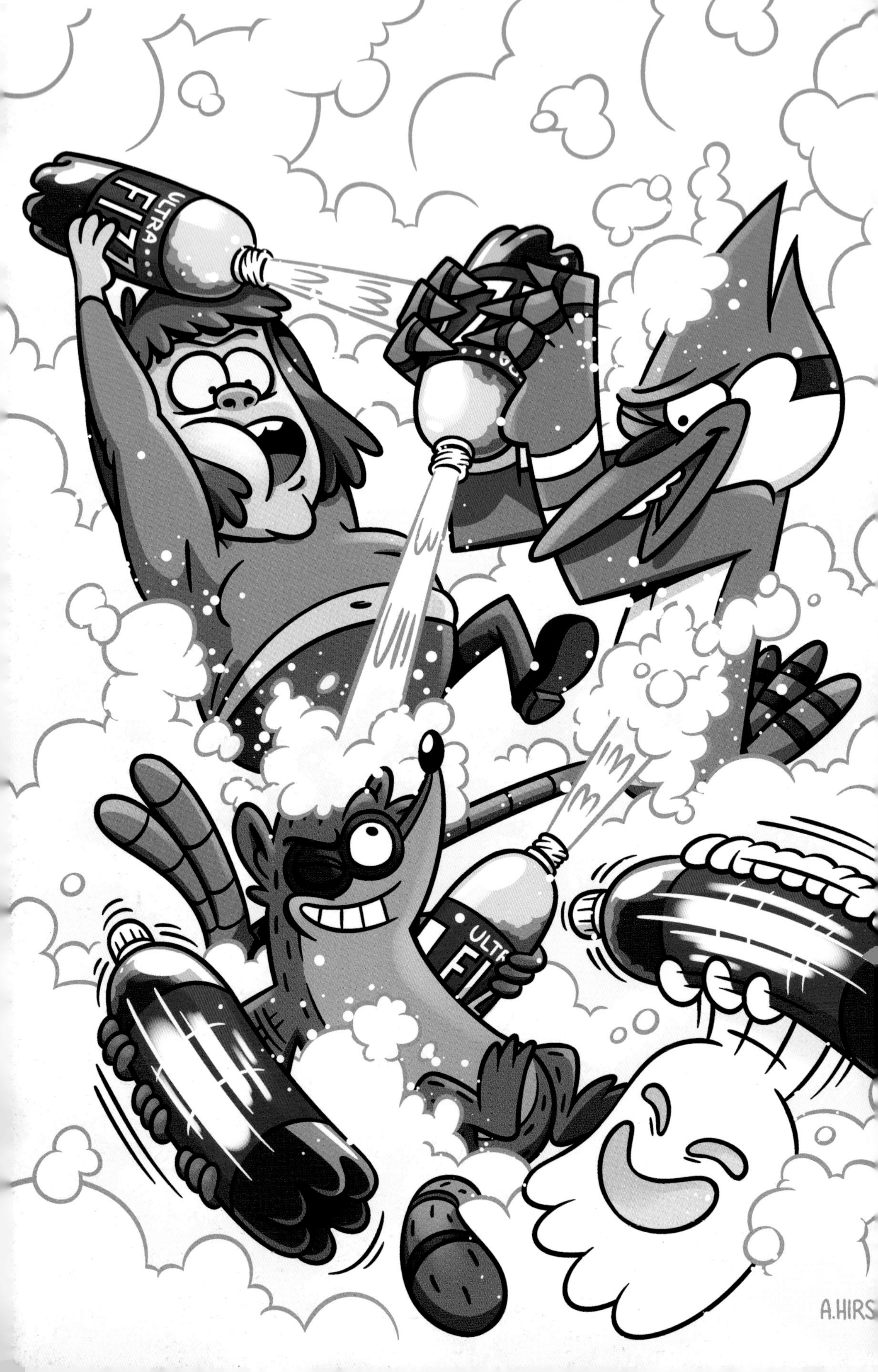

ULTRA
FIZZ
ULTRA
FI
A.HIRS

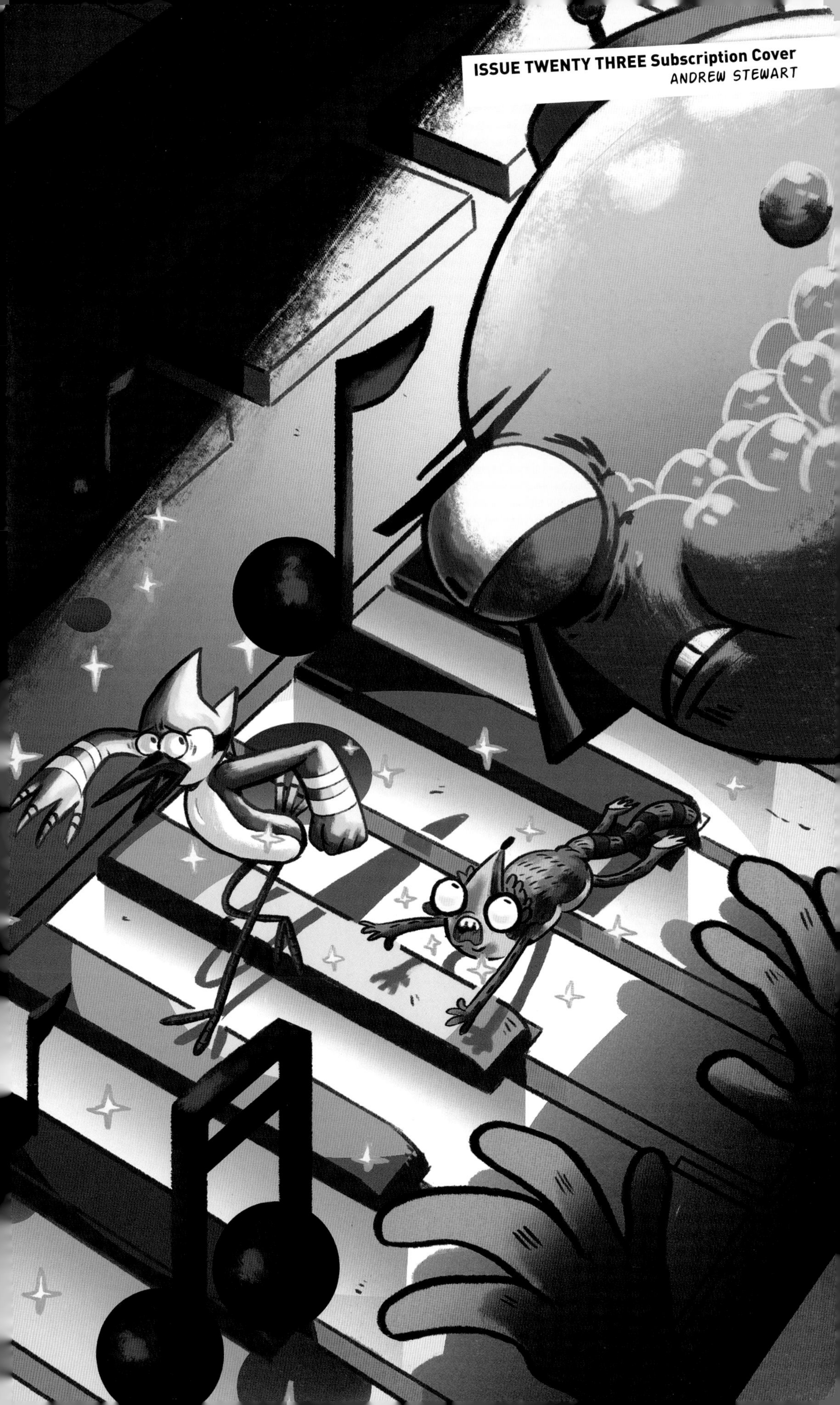

ISSUE TWENTY THREE Subscription Cover
ANDREW STEWART

ISSUE TWENTY FOUR Main Cover
ZÉ BURNAY

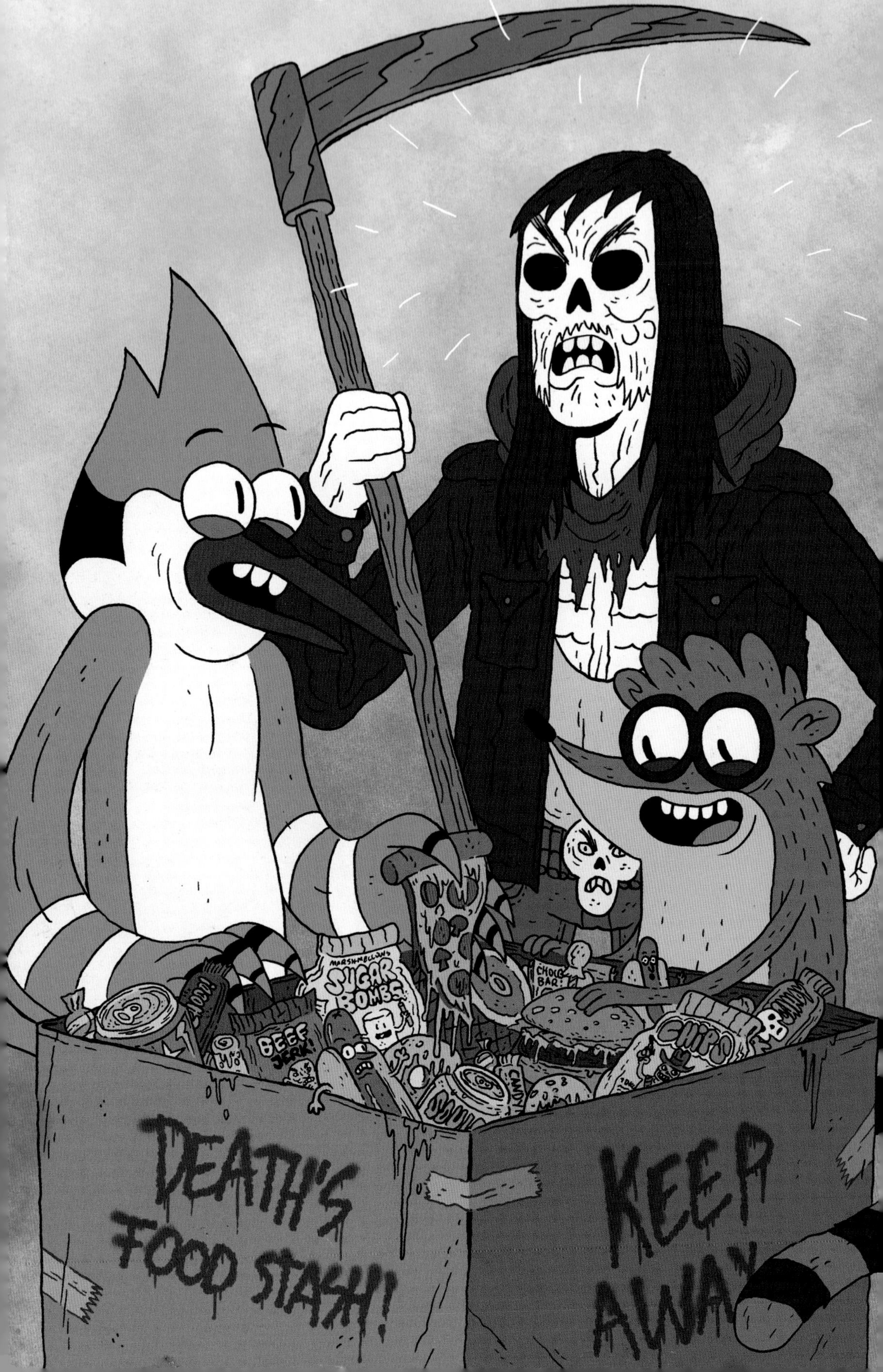
SUGAR BOMBS
CHOCO BAR
DEATH'S FOOD STASH!
KEEP

ISSUE TWENTY FOUR Subscription Cover
HYOJIN BAE

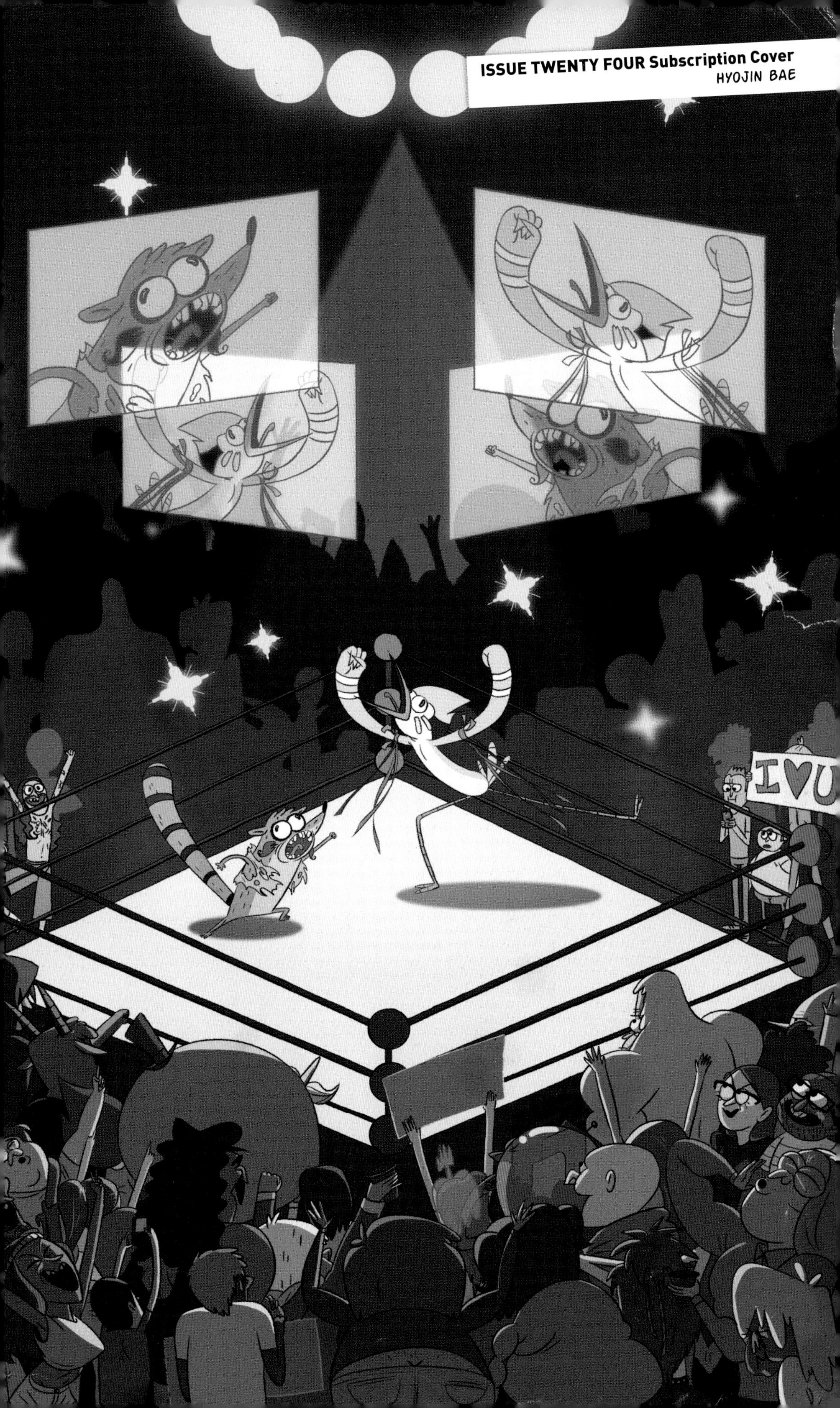
I ♥ U

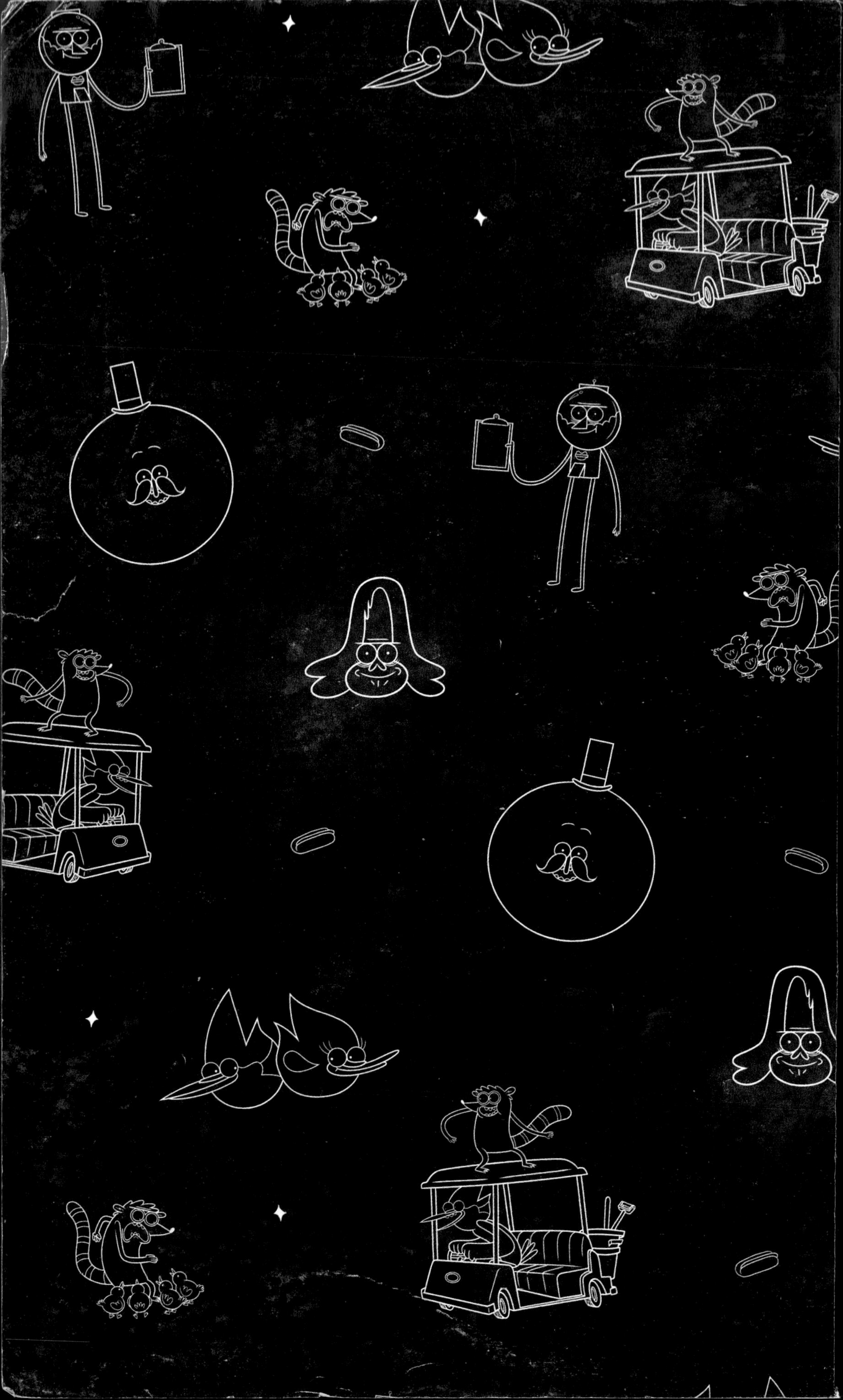